# ERIN JONES

Mendota Heights, Minnesota

First Edition
First Printing, 2019

Book design by Jake Slavik
Cover design by Jake Slavik
Cover and interior images by Irina Vaneeva/Shutterstock, xpixel/Shutterstock, Mara008/Shutterstock

Flux, an imprint of North Star Editions, Inc.

**Library of Congress Cataloging-in-Publication Data (pending)**
978-1-63583-032-3

Flux
North Star Editions, Inc.
2297 Waters Drive
Mendota Heights, MN 55120
www.fluxnow.com

Printed in the United States of America

FOR MOM, DAD, AND ABBEY

Fit held her phone up to the aquarium, camera on, thumb poised over the record button. It had been two weeks since the Twin Suns Casino posted a picture of the purple octopus on their Instagram with the caption **Meet Maggie! Our latest addition!** And despite having been to the casino four times since, Fit had yet to catch a glimpse of the animal. Her best friend Diamond had seen Maggie twice; her little brother, Frankie, once; and her grandpa, Dubs, who worked as a janitor at the casino, had seen the animal almost every day. "She's something," Dubs had told Fit after his first sighting.

The aquarium, which was the centerpiece of the casino's lobby, stood as tall as a movie theater screen and stretched twice as wide. More than three hundred species of sea life called the tank home. Fish as big as Fit's head floated in front of her, two eels slithered through the muck on the bottom, and a small shark circled high and to her right. The display was dazzling but Fit didn't care. She wanted Maggie.

Frankie walked up and knocked his knuckles on the glass, startling Fit and a few fish. "Any luck?" he asked before digging into a bag of caramel corn, his prize of choice from the arcade.

"Nah," Fit said. "It's like she knows I'm here." She gave up and instead filmed two yellow fish that swam by at eye level, flicking their tails in unison. She added a vintage-looking filter to the video and posted it for everyone to see. That would have to do for now.

They had twenty minutes to kill before Dubs got off work. It was summer, and if Fit wanted to use her grandfather's truck on the days he worked the early shift, she had to act as his chauffeur.

Disappointed about Maggie, Fit turned away from the aquarium and made her way deeper into the casino, Frankie by her side. At seventeen and fifteen, respectively, Fit and Frankie were too young to gamble, so they leaned on the railing encircling the gaming floor and watched as the visitors fed coins into the hungry, beeping machines. Fit was familiar with the sight—the casino well-trodden territory—but that didn't make the mindless repetition, the dark cloud of desperation, or the static feel of the smoke-filled air any easier to bear.

"Lots of Q-tips out today," she said, referring to the old women with poufy white hair who filled the casino during the week.

"They've got to do something with all their free time," Frankie said, upending the bag of caramel corn to his mouth, polishing off the crumbs. He'd always been slight, cutting a small, fragile figure, but over the past four months he'd grown three inches, eating everything he could get his hands on. He was almost as tall as Fit now.

Fit looked at her phone. Only two minutes had passed since they'd left the lobby, and she was already bored. But then she had an idea. Smirking at Frankie, she asked, "Wanna strike it rich?"

"Hell no," he said.

"C'mon. I haven't seen a single security guard today."

"Dubs is going to lose his mind if we get caught again."

Fit grabbed hold of his shoulders, shook them playfully, and yelled, "Stop being so lame!" Frankie was gentle, shy, and had always been a little on the anxious side. His timidity was often the butt of Fit's jokes, but secretly she loved how tender he was, envied it even. She nudged his shoulder and said, "Deep down, I know you wanna."

He ran a hand through his hair, dark and curly, just like hers, only shorter. "Fine," he said. "But if we get caught, I'm telling Dubs you hypnotized me."

"Fine by me," Fit said, clapping her hands.

The casino was busy and Fit took in the crowd of saggy-looking people making their way from the shops to the gambling area. She'd have quite the audience, she thought. Perfect.

She asked Frankie, "Wanna do the honors?"

"It's all you," he said.

Fit hopped the railing they'd been leaning on, sidled her way to the edge of the slot machines, and picked up a discarded receipt from the floor. She held it up high over her head and yelled, "I just won fifty thousand dollars!" Frankie, in step right behind her, yelled, "We're eating steak tonight!"

They took their time as they wove through the rows of slots, celebrating their big win, as they'd learned from experience that starting off at a run was a sure indication they were up to no good.

Each time Fit called out—thanking Lady Luck and the casino gods—she got a spark of energy, like she'd really hit the jackpot. She and Frankie worked the crowds and played it up when people congratulated them. It was easy to do. These were gamblers, after all, people willing to accept insurmountable odds.

Fit fed off the attention, her actions growing more exuberant with each step, her words more confident. And by the time they got to the blackjack tables at the far end of the casino, she felt invincible. After one particularly exhilarating shout, she fell to her knees, held the receipt up to the ceiling like a holy relic, and exclaimed, "Jesus up in heaven, I thank you!" She took Frankie by the hand. "My sick little son and I have been blessed! No more soup kitchens for us."

The epitome of a Q-tip walked by, pushing a walker, and said, "Good for you, dear. What are you going to do with the rest of your winnings?"

Fit knew exactly what she'd do. She'd get out. It didn't matter how she left or where she went, she just needed to leave the only town she'd ever known. She often imagined herself sneaking out in the middle of the night, leaving a note for Frankie and Dubs to find in the morning, and hopping on a plane or a bus. Or even a boat if that's what it took.

Fit stood up, put her hands on her hips, and stuck out her chest. She looked the old Q-tip right in the eye and said, "I'm going to get a boob job." The Q-tip clicked her tongue, and then shook her head as she walked away.

They'd almost crossed the entire gaming floor when Fit saw a security guard headed in their direction. "Shit," she said, grabbing Frankie by the arm and pointing ahead. "We've been spotted."

She turned around, ready to run back the way they'd come, but Marcus, the head of security, was walking right toward them. He had worked at the casino for as long as Fit could remember. He was tall and stern faced. When he got up close he gave them a *You're-not-going-anywhere* look and said, "Got 'em," into his radio.

"Dubs is going to flip," Frankie said, sounding nervous. "If we get grounded, I'm going to be so pissed."

Still flying high from her performance and unshaken by being caught, Fit ignored Frankie and flashed Marcus a big smile. "What's up, Marky Mark?" Marcus looked unamused by the question, but Fit pressed on, unable to stop herself. "You look taller," she said, pointing at his chest. "New vitamins or something?" She peered down at his shoes. "Or are you wearing lifts?"

Marcus nodded his head in the direction of the security office. "Let's go."

As he led them away, Fit noticed a small crowd had formed. Vultures looking for some action. She waved to the bystanders and called out, "Tell my husband it was worth it!"

The unadorned security office always felt too quiet and sterile in comparison to the rest of the casino. Marcus sat behind his desk and Fit and Frankie sat on the other side. Soon Dubs arrived, flustered, his uniform wrinkled and stained from a day's worth of mopping. A retired welder, he had gotten the job as a custodian when Fit and Frankie moved in with him.

"Again?!" he said, huffing down into the seat next to Fit. Red splotches had begun to creep up his neck—his anger manifested. "This is—what!—the third time this month?" His eyes darted from Fit to Frankie, then back again.

"Oh, yeah?" Fit said. "Guess we've had some pretty good luck. Huh, Frank?" Frankie dug a hole in the floor with his gaze, making it clear he wanted no part in her joking. Fit didn't care; she had no problem going into battle on her own. She looked to Marcus. "It's not *my* fault I've been on a winning streak."

Marcus leaned forward and rested his elbows on the desk. "Listen. I can't have you and your casino crew on the floor." He sighed and leaned back a little, his rolling chair releasing its own frustrated creak. *Casino crew.* Fit liked that name, made a mental note to text it to Diamond and Pistols when she got out of there. Pistols was Diamond's first cousin, and the two of them lived in the same apartment complex as Fit and Frankie. Diamond's mom worked in housekeeping for the casino's hotel, and Pistols's parents were both card dealers. Growing up, Fit and Frankie along with Diamond and Pistols had treated the casino like a giant smoke-filled second home, but over the past year their antics had grown wilder. They'd put bubbles in the fountain, raced through the shopping area in wheelchairs, and glitter-bombed the main elevators.

"You're kids," Marcus said. "It's illegal."

Fit crossed her arms. "I'm going to be eighteen in a few months. And Frankie's even got an armpit hair."

"Jessica!" Dubs hissed, the red spots on his neck now reaching his chin. He only used her real name when she was in serious trouble.

He stood from his chair and Fit got a whiff of bleach and cigarette smoke, his take from the casino. "It won't happen again," he assured Marcus. He turned and looked straight at Fit. "Right?" She contemplated storming out, flipping them all the bird. Dubs would forgive her eventually. He always did. But as she looked at him, she studied the sheen of sweat on his cheeks and the few white hairs that stuck straight up on the top of his head. He looked old. She had the urge to reach out and smooth his hair down.

Fit let her head fall back, like her neck had been deboned, and groaned, "Whatever, fiiine."

Marcus let them go with a final warning. Dubs remained silent as he marched in front of them on the way to the parking garage, not speaking until they got to the truck and demanded the keys. He got in the driver's seat and slammed the door behind him. Fit took her usual spot in the front passenger seat and Frankie climbed into the back, which was cramped and only meant for a child. Dubs asked them both, "So, the first few times weren't enough? Hmm?"

Fit buckled up, refusing to look his way. "If I had my own

car, maybe this wouldn't have happened." Fit had wanted a ride of her own ever since she'd gotten her license. She knew they didn't have the money, but she pushed anyway. "So, this isn't really my fault."

"You're something, you know that?" Dubs's voice was strained, tired. "What's your preference? A Ferrari? Jaguar? An understated yet still expensive Volvo?"

For a moment, Fit felt guilty for adding to Dubs's stress and thought about apologizing. Instead, she pulled out her phone and checked Twitter. "I don't see why you're mad," she said, scrolling through her feed without reading anything. "It's not like we hurt anyone."

"I could lose my job. You could lose yours too!"

Fit rolled her eyes. She picked up the occasional house-keeping shift at the casino hotel and had managed to save a whopping three hundred dollars over the past few months. "Oh no! Not our glamorous careers cleaning toilets."

"Jesus Christ!" Dubs yelled, gripping the steering wheel. The cab went quiet. Fit considered throwing another barb but figured she'd wreaked enough havoc for one day. After a few moments, Dubs reached up and touched the gold crucifix around his neck. He said, "Sorry, buddy," then started the truck. "Can the both of you just promise me you won't pull that nonsense again?"

"Got it, boss," Frankie said. He kicked the back of Fit's seat.

"Sure," she said reluctantly. "I guess it's time I got out of the gambling game."

Dubs put the car in drive, but before pulling away he said, "And fifty grand? With the way you text and Frankie eats, you'd blow through that in a year. Two, tops."

Fit fought the smile sneaking onto her face. "Noted," she

said. As they wound their way out of the garage, she rolled down her window and let the warm summer air wash over her.

Fit should have seen it coming, known something was up. Dubs hadn't taken her and Frankie out for ice cream since before she could drive. But when he came into the living room the next day asking, "Anyone up for DQ?" Fit chalked it up to the late June heat wave blasting the Northeast. She slipped on her flip-flops and said, "I'm down."

The three of them sat at a picnic table off to the side of the building. Fit was taking a selfie with her ice cream cone (**#summerdayz**) when Dubs cleared his throat, sounding kind of like a goose, and she could tell he was trying to get her attention. She ignored him for a few more shots, then looked up from her screen. He and Frankie were both looking at her, seriously, like they needed to say something. Her stomach dropped. Turning defensive, she barked, "What?"

"I know you don't want to talk about your mother—" Dubs started to say before Fit cut him off with, "So don't."

"We're down to two weeks," Dubs went on.

"If you know I don't want to talk about it," Fit said, her anger rising, "then why are we talking about it?" She took an angry bite of her ice cream. The dessert tasted like nothing, felt like paste in her mouth. She forced herself to swallow.

Dubs wiped his hands methodically with a napkin. "Because I need to know you're going to be okay," he said. "When she gets here."

Fit balked. "Okay?" Her mother, the woman she hated more than *anything* else in the world, was moving in with them in two weeks. And Dubs expected her to be okay? Fit had always been good at getting her way. She'd curse and cry and threaten to throw the TV off the roof until Dubs would eventually cave. And she'd sure as hell pulled out all the stops when Dubs had sat her and Frankie down a few weeks before to tell them the news about their mother. But even her largest tantrum to date had proved futile, so she did her best to pretend it wasn't happening, shot down anytime Dubs or Frankie (who was excited about the return of the she-devil) brought it up.

She went back to looking at her phone and mumbled, "Like you care."

"Yes, Jess. I care."

Fit hated when Dubs used her first name, and anger struck like a drop of lava at the back of her neck.

"The name," she said, trying to keep her voice as icy as soft serve, "is Fit."

"Fine," Dubs said, crumpling the napkin in his right hand. "Fit, I'm worried about what stunt you're going to pull."

She felt her reserve slipping. "This is a prank, right?" She turned over the napkin dispenser, inspected the bottom of it. "Where's the hidden camera?" She looked under her paper cup of water, then the table. "No, nothing." She was really hitting her stride, shielding her eyes from the sun and inspecting the parking lot like a ship's captain, when Frankie said, "Stop being an idiot. Where else is she going to go?"

She looked at him, betrayed, and asked, "Who cares?"

Frankie stabbed at his milkshake. "I do."

The heat in the back of Fit's neck bloomed, spreading over her shoulders and down her arms. It reached her hands and rendered her powerless for what she did next. She wound-up and chucked her ice cream cone as hard as she could into the side of the building. Her breathing was heavy, ragged. Frankie hung his head between his shoulders, obviously embarrassed. Dubs's unflinching gaze bared down on her and after a few quiet moments he asked, "Done now?"

"Whatever," Fit said, and she stalked off angrily toward the truck.

When they got home, Fit slammed the door to her room and locked herself in. **Anyone else out there DYING to move the f out?!?** she tweeted. Within ten minutes her tweet had been favorited 107 times, retweeted fourteen times, and eight people had responded to her with agreement and love and **lots and lots of hugs**. Even if her family sucked, at least she had her fans. They would never let her down.

Fit hadn't set out to become a YouTube star; it just sort of happened. Her first video sprang purely from boredom during the February break of her junior year. Frankie had won a scholarship to an art camp in Washington, DC, and Diamond had gotten a new boyfriend, Riley, and was spending all her time with him. And Dubs was pulling doubles at the casino all week. So, Fit spent three days alone, binge-watching *Law & Order SVU*. Toward the end of the third day she grew restless and decided to dye her hair. Dubs never allowed her to pierce anything other than her earlobes, but he let her have free reign with the color of her mass of curls. She'd had blue, pink, green, but that day she was feeling purple.

She walked the cold mile to the drugstore and picked out the most vibrant shade she could find, a color called "Precious Purple," that claimed on the package to be designed for brunettes. Back home, she watched a YouTube tutorial on how to give herself highlights, then got to work. As she slathered chunks of her hair with purple dye and wrapped them in tinfoil, she began to write rap lyrics about one of the characters from *Law & Order SVU* in her head. She loved writing lyrics, setting them to a beat, performing them for Frankie and Diamond. By the time Fit had put the last bit of dye in her hair, she had the lyrics planned out and decided to record the song during the fifteen to twenty minutes she had to wait for the color to set. Even if Frankie and Diamond were gone, she still wanted them to hear it. She found a beat she liked, opened the video camera on her computer, and got to work. The song only lasted forty-five seconds, but it took her three tries to record because she kept laughing at the line, "Elliot's wife will beg me not to do it, but I'll be the victim of Stabler's special unit."

She already had a YouTube account under the name "Fitted Sheet." It was an inside joke between her and Diamond from when she had broken up with her first boyfriend, Jackson. He'd been older than her—a senior when Fit was a sophomore—and they became official after a month of Facebook messaging. But things quickly turned sour. He always wanted to know where she was, got mad at her if she went to the casino without him. The constant checking in was suffocating. In the last few weeks of their relationship, when Fit knew it was over, she started posting an overload of pictures of herself doing fun things without him. The Instagram post that had finally pushed him over the edge was one of her and Pistols having snuck onto the casino floor, sitting side-by-side at the slot machines. He'd sent her a screenshot of her own post and said, Im done with this bullshit. You're a mess. Like a goddamn fitted sheet. You're only good on the bed. Fit didn't respond. She and Diamond laughed about the ludicrous yet inventive insult later that night. "Fitted sheet, huh?" Diamond had said. "You should take that as a compliment. Means no one can tell you what to do. No matter how hard they try." And the nickname stuck.

The *Law & Order* video was Fit's first upload. Before that, she'd only used her account to follow her favorite YouTubers. She sent the link to Frankie and Diamond and wrote, look at this dumb thing i made lol.

Fit rinsed the dye out of her hair, leaving a bluish circle around the shower drain, and while she was admiring the perfect purple ringlets scattered throughout her dark brown curls, her phone buzzed.

Lololol, Diamond had written, followed by

♡ ♡ ♡

Fit smiled. you don't think i look like a dumbass????

Well. Yeah. But a funny dumbass.

😃

In the first four days, the video only got fifteen views. But two weeks later, Fit's hair having faded to a mellow lavender, the song ended up on the homepage of Reddit. It was Frankie, back from DC, who told her the news. "You're blowing up!"

Fit checked the video. It had 20,078 views, 48 comments, and 564 people were following her channel. Thousands of people had seen her face, heard her voice; it was an odd yet powerful feeling. Like nothing she'd ever experienced before.

Frankie asked, "You gonna make another one?"

"Duh."

Fit stuck with the TV theme; her knowledge of shows was vast, the television like another parent to her and Frankie. They generally took care of themselves after school, Dubs either at the casino or sleeping if he was working the night shift. Fit would make a bag of popcorn and she and Frankie would park themselves in front of the TV for the afternoon. Dubs tried to get them to watch less, claiming they'd ruin their eyes, but he was usually too tired to enforce any rules.

For her second video, Fit decided on the original *Beverly Hills 90210*. Like her first song, the lyrics didn't take long. She was about to start recording when Frankie yelled, "Wait!" and ran to the kitchen to grab a roll of tinfoil. "People keep commenting about your hair." He tore off a piece and quickly fashioned a necklace. She put it on, ignoring a sharp edge poking into the side of her neck.

Fit started recording: "What up, freaks? This is Fitted Sheet, back by popular demand."

She started the beat and launched into her lyrics, calling out the characters for being rich and spoiled. Making fun of the show was easier than telling the truth, that watching reruns of *90210* made her envious. When she saw the characters' large houses with perfectly cut lawns she couldn't help but compare her own life to theirs. She ached for money, a normal life, but thanks to her mother, she'd never have any of those things.

The rap was longer than the first one, taking her eight tries to get it right. She uploaded it and within the first hour it had more than five hundred views. In a day it was at three thousand, and over the next week it bounced around the internet, taking only six days to surpass her first video.

**have i gone viral? #awesome**

Over the course of the next few months, Fit continued to make and post videos. She started off with one upload a week, but soon that wasn't enough for her fans. **We want more,** they'd write in the comments section. So, in addition to her weekly TV show song, she'd post a random video that had no rhyme or reason. In one she pretended to be a beauty guru giving a makeup tutorial that ended up with the result looking like horrifying clown makeup. Or sometimes she'd just talk to the camera in a stream of consciousness, unloading all her thoughts, unfiltered. No matter what type of video it was, Fit always wore something made out of tinfoil. People loved her. She gained more subscribers by the day, and each video she posted got more views than the previous one.

She also started to get a check from YouTube every couple of weeks. Most of her videos contained cursing, which lowered her ad value or demonetized her content altogether, so the payments were rarely over a hundred dollars. The money that she did end up making she put toward new equipment: a tripod, a few lights, a remote for her camera, and an external hard drive to store all her raw files. Sometimes, with any leftover money, she'd buy the casino crew coins at the arcade or treat Dubs and Frankie to take-out. Her first song that hit the two hundred thousand mark was her *Game of Thrones* rap where she wore a crown made of tinfoil. When she saw the number of hits it received, she ran into Frankie's room holding out her phone for him to look, asking, "Does this mean I'm famous?"

"Compared to everyone else in this town. You're like the Queen of Juniper Hills."

Fit laughed. "Like that's an accomplishment."

"Shut up," Frankie said.

Fit went back into her room, dug through the box where she kept all the tinfoil accessories Frankie made for her, and found the crown. She placed it on her head, took a selfie, and posted it with the caption, **queeeeen #bowdown**.

Back in the apartment feeling suffocated and still riled up after throwing the ice cream cone against the wall of the Dairy Queen, Fit went into the living room to ask Dubs if she could borrow the truck. She found him asleep in his reclining chair, the eleven o'clock news on the TV. The glow of the screen lit half his face, casting the other half in shadow. She wished she hadn't been so mean to him earlier. One of his shoes lay on the floor next to the chair and the other hung dangling off his toes, like he'd fallen asleep smack in middle of kicking it off. She tiptoed over to him and slipped the shoe off, placed it quietly on the carpet. She thought about reaching out, gently shaking his shoulder, and telling him to go to bed. Instead, she grabbed his keys from the hook by the door and headed out.

She drove slowly, the old truck grumbling down the back roads of Juniper Hills. Dubs had told her when the casino was built everyone in town was certain it was going to flush their area of rural Connecticut with money. They believed real estate prices would go up, downtown would fill with new blood, and the schools might even get a little better. There was a small economic boom, but after a year or so everything went back to normal: the houses and shops still run-down, the schools understaffed. Dubs always liked to say the town had character. But Fit knew that "character" was just another word for shithole.

The night was dark, no moon to speak of, and the houses became less and less frequent the farther she got away from the center of town. A headlight had gone out the day before, Dubs cursing under his breath as he ordered a replacement bulb because the local auto parts store didn't have the right kind, so she could only see a few yards ahead. She felt suspended in space, like the only objects in existence were her, the truck, and the small bit of pavement lit up in front of her.

She drove until she found herself on Windward Lane, the dead-end street where she spent the first three years of her life. She parked in front of her old house at the end of the cul-de-sac and turned off the engine. The one-story Cape Cod style house was well maintained. The freshly mowed lawn, the light blue exterior, the dogwood tree in the front yard: it all looked the same since the last time a nightly drive had brought her there.

Fit looked at the garage. Her hands tightened on the steering wheel, and she couldn't think about anything but being inside that house, that garage. She started the truck and ripped away from the curb.

"You're a queen," she said under her breath as she pushed

the pedal to the floor. "You're a queen. You're a queen. You're a queen."

The two gray buildings of the Meadow Lane Apartment Complex made the shape of an "L." From her window, Fit could see the parking lot, the small stretch of grass described as a "lawn" on the Meadow Lane promotional materials, and Route 12 where casino traffic rushed by at all hours of the day. On the nights when Fit couldn't sleep, she'd listen to the *whoosh* of the cars and pretend it was the ocean.

About a week after Fit's tantrum at the Dairy Queen, she woke up and saw a blue plastic kiddie pool upside down on the "lawn." She and Frankie tried to find the owner of the pool, knocking on all their neighbors' doors, but no one knew where it came from. "Mine now," Fit said after they'd finished canvassing. "Let's fill her up."

Only one person could fit in the pool at a time, and when it was Fit's turn, she stretched her arms and legs out, and it felt like she was lying in a bathtub. The heatwave was still in full force and the cool water had warmed up in a matter of minutes. She'd invited Diamond and Pistols to come swimming, and now Pistols was dealing a game of blackjack for Frankie and Diamond.

"We almost made it across the floor," Frankie said, bragging about their jackpot stunt that landed them in Marcus's office. Fit thought about calling him out, letting Diamond and Pistols in on the fact that Frankie was almost too chicken to go through with it. But he sounded so proud that she decided to keep her mouth shut and let him have this one.

"Not bad, not bad," Diamond said, holding a can of soda to her neck. She'd recently changed her hair, now wearing it in a short Afro. Fit loved the new look; it made Diamond look even more sophisticated. Diamond took a sip of her drink and said, "But talk to me when you make it to The Peaks." Diamond was referring to The Peaks Room, a gentleman's club located right off the gambling floor.

She'd once walked across the casino floor without being noticed, sat down at a table, and ordered a rum and coke. Not that the feat was *that* surprising. Diamond was tall, striking, and looked older than eighteen. She seemed to get away with everything. The mastermind behind most of their pranks, Diamond always escaped unscathed.

"You think you could handle The Peaks, little man?" Pistols asked Frankie. Pistols and Diamond looked like they could have been brother and sister, rather than just cousins, except he had his father's straight dark hair. Both of his parents were card dealers at the casino and it was his goal to follow in their footsteps. Never without a deck of cards, he used any opportunity he could find to practice his shuffling skills. "I have the quickest draw this side of Connecticut," he liked to brag, which is where the nickname "Pistols" came from.

"Oh, I could more than handle that," Frankie said, sounding boastful. "If you know what I mean." Pistols laughed.

Fit smacked Frankie on the shoulder and said, "Don't be gross." He and Pistols had been spending more time together recently and it was starting to show. Six months ago, Frankie would have never made that joke.

Fit tilted her head back, closed her eyes, and listened to the sounds of the game: the gentle *thwack thwack* of the cards,

Diamond's quick and confident "Hit me's," and Frankie's more measured, "Yeah. Hit."

During one turn Diamond shouted, "Ah ha!" after she'd gotten twenty-one. Even with her eyes closed, Fit knew the way Diamond's face looked at the moment: crinkled nose, lopsided smile, high cheeks. The face of joy.

After Fit's turn was up in the pool, she went inside for a popsicle run. Dubs was relaxing in his reclining chair in the living room, reading a fishing magazine. Over his hang-around clothes, he wore his fishing vest; he only made it out to the river once or twice a year, but he said it wasn't really summer if he wasn't sporting his vest.

"What do you think about this one?" he said, holding out the magazine toward her, pointing at something on the page. Fit walked over and took a closer look at what Dubs was tapping at: a picture of a man standing knee deep in the water, a fishing line out in front of him. Next to the picture it read, "Expert Casting Rod $299."

"I like it," Fit said. "Go for it." She knew he wouldn't. Every summer Dubs said he was going to get a new fishing rod, but he never made it beyond the pages of his favorite fishing magazine. *Enjoy your retirement,* she always wanted to tell him. *Stop working yourself so hard.* But she knew any bit of extra money went toward her and Frankie's college fund. It was why he never bought himself anything new and picked up extra shifts that made him too exhausted to fish.

"Yeah," Dubs said, taking a closer look at the picture. "Maybe I will."

Fit snagged the box of popsicles—enjoying the brief burst of cold air on her cheeks—and headed back outside. Diamond had taken up court in the kiddie pool, her long arms draped over the sides.

"Feels kinda luxurious if you close your eyes, right?" Fit asked Diamond as she doled out the popsicles. Diamond, taking a green one, said, "That's one way to describe it."

Her voice sounded drained, less enthusiastic than normal. The month before, Diamond, who was a year older than Fit, had had to defer at Tufts because she didn't get enough financial aid. At first Diamond was pissed. "Like I could afford that shit on my own!" she'd yelled after telling Fit the news. But over the past few weeks she'd become downtrodden, and it broke Fit's heart to see her best friend so defeated. Especially since Diamond had been the one who made Fit believe she could get out of Juniper Hills in the first place. During sleepovers, they'd talk about where they were going to move when they were older and all the buckets of money they would have. And when Diamond had gotten her acceptance letter, it had been proof that their middle school dreams could become a reality.

"Dubs is looking at fishing rods again," Fit said, sitting down on the grass next to Frankie. "Typical."

"Yeah," Diamond said, tearing the plastic wrapper off the top of the popsicle with her teeth. "Kinda how Frankie over here never wears sunscreen and complains when he's burnt to a crisp."

"Oh, shut up," Frankie said, laughing along with the rest of them. As the youngest, he'd grown up being the butt of many of their jokes and had learned to take them in stride. "I'm fine."

Fit poked his reddening shoulder. "Once you're done with your popsicle you should put some sunscreen on. You're looking a little pink."

Fit and Frankie looked a lot alike, except that he was much paler than her. Dubs liked to joke that Fit had taken all the Italian genes, leaving Frankie with the Irish, which resulted in his fair complexion. "Did you hear that?" Fit said. "If you blister again, you know Dubs is going to yell at *me*."

"Whatever," Frankie said. "It'll fade to a tan."

"Yeah, in like a week," Pistols added.

Diamond laughed, slapped her hand on the water. The action made Fit smile. Maybe Diamond was getting back to her old self.

Fit looked at the side of the apartment building. The angle of the sun hitting the windows made it look like a bunch of camera flashes were going off all at once. With the pool and her friends and the way she had to squint her eyes to look at the building, the place seemed not too terrible.

The popsicle melted quickly as she ate it, and when she was done she dunked her sticky sugar-covered hand in the pool. Her fingertips grazed Diamond's elbow. "Sorry," she said, ignoring the slight hitch in her pulse.

"Mhm," Diamond hummed, eyes closed. "Hey. I thought you were coming with me to Riley's tomorrow."

"I am," Fit said. "Why?"

"Frankie said you have to stay in and clean."

Fit glared at her brother, but he kept his eyes down while ripping out a few blades of grass. Their mother was arriving in two days, and Dubs and Frankie had been buzzing around the apartment in excitement all week. Dubs had been fixing something new every day. He'd spent an entire evening on his knees in front of the oven. When Fit had asked him what he was doing, Dubs said, "The door sticks." And when Fit reminded him that they never cooked he'd responded, "Well maybe if the damn thing worked right."

Frankie had been a bit subtler in his excitement, but it was there nonetheless. He'd been making art. There were a few spots on the living room wall reserved for Frankie's creations.

Normally, he put new ones up every month, but he'd switched the piece of art hanging over the TV three times in the past week. First there was a peacock mosaic made of small chunks of teal, yellow, and purple tissue paper. He'd then switched it with a collage of newspaper clippings, receipts, and wadded-up balls of unused floss. And third, the one still hanging, was a tinfoil heart the size of a dinner plate. With each new piece Fit couldn't help but feel betrayed, like no one was on her side.

"Screw that noise," Fit said to Diamond. "Dubs has been cleaning all week. There's nothing left to do."

Dubs worked the graveyard shift that night. After he left for the casino, Fit hung out in Frankie's room. She worked on the lyrics for her next song as Frankie fashioned her glasses out of tinfoil. Holding the frames up to his face, Frankie asked, "Want to film tomorrow?"

"Hanging out with Diamond, remember?" Fit snapped.

"Does Dubs know? He mentioned a movie night."

"Do you think he's really going to be able to sit still for a whole movie?"

Frankie looked hurt but Fit knew how to make him laugh. She sprung up from the bed, pulled her sweatpants up over her belly button, and did an exaggerated impression of Dubs's hunched gait as she waddled over to the bookshelf. She ran her hand across the top shelf, a move she'd seen Dubs do countless times when he was inspecting something, then knocked on the side. Deepening her voice, she said, "Sounds a little loose, huh?" She dropped to one knee and inspected the base. "Yep. I see the problem. Get me some WD-40. Stat!"

Frankie rolled his eyes and smiled. "Give him a break," he said. "He's excited."

Fit sighed and leaned against the bookshelf. She asked him, "Are you?"

"What?"

"Excited."

Frankie looked back down at the tinfoil in his hands. "I guess."

"Do you think this is going to fix everything?"

Frankie shrugged and mumbled, "I don't know. Maybe."

They sat for a few moments in silence before he got up and pulled out a deck of cards from his desk. "Want to see what Pistols taught me?"

"Sure."

He sat down on the floor next to her. He cut the deck of cards in two, then shuffled. The execution was much messier than Pistols's, but the attempt wasn't half bad. "I'm still working on it," he said. He shuffled a few more times, and as the cards bent and bridged, he chewed at the inside of his cheek. Fit knew he wanted to say something.

"Dude," she said. "Spit it out."

Frankie held the cards tight and said, "I don't think having Mom here is going to be as bad as you think."

Fit wanted to reach out and shake him, tell him not to get his hopes up. He didn't remember what their mother was capable of. He'd only been a baby.

"We'll see," she said. "Let's play war."

Frankie dealt the cards into two stacks. When he was done, they each picked up their pile, and, on the count of three, flipped over the top card. Frankie had a ten, Fit an eight. Frankie swept his cards away, claiming his small victory. They played the game until late that night. The air outside cooled, and a small breeze occasionally came in through the screen. The lights from the parking lot filled the room with a deep glow. Fit didn't want the game or the night to end. She wanted to press pause, freeze everything.

River Underwood was standing at the kitchen sink, washing dishes and looking out at the snow falling over her backyard, when she got the urge to go upstairs, wake her eight-month-old, Frankie, from his nap and hold him under the soapy water. At first, River imagined he'd flail his arms and legs, splashing warm suds on the counter and down the front of her sweatshirt. But, after a minute or so, he'd go limp. There'd be silence.

The vision froze River's body, stopping her mid-scrub and holding her hostage for a few terrifying, yet satisfactory, seconds. Once the image passed, releasing River from its clutches, she let out a small, guttural cry and dropped the plate in the water. The thought of Frankie's motionless body submerged in the sink turned her stomach. Bile filled her mouth. She wiped her sudsy hands on the oversized navy-issued sweatpants she'd been wearing for three days straight and hurried to the bathroom and threw up. When she was done, she went to her bedroom and lay down with a pillow over her head. Her brain hadn't been her own for some time now, but up until that day she'd been able to snuff out the irrational thoughts before they became anything bigger than a spark. River rolled over, pressed the pillow into the side of her head. Her thoughts ran out of control, yet her mind kept finding its way back to one main question: Did she want to kill her son?

The trouble started about four months after Frankie was born. Every time he cried, it felt like metal in her shoulders. She missed a string of Frankie's check-ups at the doctor because she never knew what day it was. At night she remained wide awake, her brain running wild, but getting out of bed in the morning seemed impossible. Sometimes the piles of dirty clothes seemed so insurmountable she'd throw them out instead of cleaning them. Her body ached in random places, like her earlobes or in between her toes. And along her jawline her skin had erupted with hard bumps that felt like they were sprouting from her bones. She'd poke and prod at the blemishes, irritating them further. When she finally got the date right and took Frankie in for a check-up she asked the pediatrician to take a look. "Cystic pimples," the doctor said. "Those are common when your hormones have been thrown out of whack. Things will settle."

*Things will settle*, River tried to tell herself when brushing her teeth felt like she was scraping her gums with a Brillo pad. *Things better settle.*

A soft cry came over the baby monitor. River took the pillow off her head and looked at the clock: 3:02. Naptime was over. Her kids needed to eat, they needed to be bathed. But after the intensity with which her latest vision had struck her, the idea of being alone with Frankie terrified her. She wished her husband were home, but he was out on deployment, gliding through some far-off ocean in a submarine. He'd be gone for another three months.

River walked down the hallway and slowly pushed open the door to the nursery. Frankie, swaddled in a green blanket in the middle of the crib, let out a quiet murmur. A small pinch formed between River's shoulder blades, and her hands felt dangerous. She crossed her arms, shoved her hands in her armpits, and went to Jessica's room.

Jessica, who had recently turned three, was sprawled out on her bed, one arm hanging over the side and her comforter crumpled on the floor. No matter how tightly River tucked her in, Jessica always managed to kick off her blanket and sheets while she slept. River looked at her daughter and wondered what had happened. When Jessica was a baby, getting up in the middle of the night hadn't been so hard, doing simple chores hadn't felt like climbing a mountain.

River turned on the overhead light, but Jessica didn't stir. She opened the window shade. The pale winter sun fell on Jessica's face, yet she remained sound asleep. River walked over to the side of the bed, pulled the sleeve of her sweatshirt down over her hand, and shook Jessica's shoulder, recoiling quickly, fearing the contact.

Jessica opened her eyes. River bent down beside her and whispered, "Want to play a game?"

Jessica nodded, rubbing her face.

"We're going to play 'mommy,'" River said. "How does that sound?"

"You're Mommy."

River's mind clouded with a desperate irritation. She needed Jessica to understand. "But today it's *your* turn. I promise you'll have lots of fun." She forced the side of her mouth up into a smile. "But to play, we have to go see your brother. How about it?"

"Okay," Jessica said. She crawled out of bed, reaching for River's hand. "I'm feeling a little crummy today," River said, pulling away. "I don't want to get you sick."

As they walked to the nursery, Frankie began to cry. His wails enveloped the whole house, and the pinch in River's back grew tighter, like her muscles were being twisted with a pair of pliers.

A mobile with sheep and stars hung above Frankie's crib. River pulled the string and "Twinkle Twinkle Little Star" began to play. The song normally soothed Frankie, but today River swore it made him angrier.

She looked down at Jessica and asked, "You know what mommies do?"

"Braid my hair."

"We do that. But we also get our babies up from their nap. Sound fun?"

Jessica shrugged her shoulders. "I guess."

River grabbed Frankie's bouncer seat, which was navy blue and covered in yellow moons, from the corner of the room and set it nearby. She removed one of the crib's detachable sides and placed it against the wall. "First," she said to Jessica, "you have to get him out of his little sleepsack." Jessica climbed up onto the crib and crawled over to Frankie. She began to unzip the front of Frankie's green wearable blanket that he slept in on cold days, then looked back at River, as if she knew something was wrong.

"You're doing great," River said, the words catching in her throat.

Jessica finished unzipping the sleepsack, gently, doing her best not to disturb Frankie. The scene was so sweet, and River felt pathetic.

Once Jessica had freed Frankie's arms from the green quilted fabric, River said, "Great. Now let's move him to his seat. I'm going to take him under the arms, you grab his feet." River knew it was ridiculous, but she felt that if someone else were touching Frankie, even if it were only Jessica, he'd somehow be safer.

River winced as she picked up Frankie, his body soft and warm, his chest moving in and out with his cries. Jessica looked confused but did exactly as she was told and held onto his toes.

They got Frankie in his seat. River released her grip and

sighed. The pinch in her back loosened, gave way to a melting sensation—a flood of fatigue. She slid to the floor, laid her head on the ground.

"It's a little cold in here," she said, the carpet rough on her cheek. "Why don't you cover him with his blanket?"

Jessica grabbed the blanket from the crib and spread it over her baby brother, irritating him further.

"He's crying," Jessica said.

River pulled her knees to her chest, covered her ears. She thought about who she could reach out to for help. She'd withdrawn from her friends over the past few months, coming up with excuse after excuse until people finally stopped calling. And she couldn't bring herself to call her father. He'd always been so proud of her, constantly telling her what a "bang up" job she was doing with the kids, especially with Seth gone so much. If he saw what a mess she really was, knew the horrible images running through her mind, he'd be so ashamed.

Jessica looked concerned, confused, and her eyes had started to well. "*Mommy.* He's crying." River mustered all her energy and pushed herself to a seated position.

"Don't cry," she said. She tried to sound reassuring, but the words came out hysterical, strained. Jessica began to cry, and a line of pain shot down River's back, like she was on the receiving end of an axe. She needed to leave before she broke in half.

She ran down the hall to the bathroom, turned on the shower, the water muffling the sound of Frankie's cries, and got in fully clothed. Unable to stand, she sat down and let the hot water rush over her. She rocked back and forth, muttering to herself how pathetic she was. She said the word "sick" over and over until it lost all meaning.

The rocking and the warm water eventually calmed her. Her thoughts slowed, and the allover pain began to fade. She got out of the shower, took off her soaked clothes, wiped the fog from the mirror, and looked at herself. Dark circles ringed her eyes, and her skin was mottled with red. She told herself it was exhaustion, hormones, that everything would settle. And this woman in the mirror, it wasn't her.

The first thing River noticed when she left the bathroom was the silence. Wrapped in a towel, she walked to the nursery. Jessica sat on the ground next to Frankie's carrier, holding a stuffed dinosaur up in the air, making it dance. Frankie smiled as he watched the toy move, his legs bouncing up and down in joy. When Jessica saw River, she held the dinosaur out, like she wanted River to take over. River shook her head, said, "You're doing great."

For the rest of the day, River avoided the touch of her children. Jessica enjoyed playing Mommy and took her job seriously. She sang to Frankie, fed him his bottle, and put his socks on. All River had to do was change his diaper and put him to bed.

Once both kids were tucked in for the night, River felt like a survivor and congratulated herself by eating a pint of cookies and cream ice cream at the kitchen counter. When she got in bed, she told herself all she needed was a good night's rest, believing things would be better in the morning.

That wasn't the case.

The next morning, as she rolled out of bed and put her feet on the floor, it felt like her bones were rebelling against her. The day's itinerary filled her with dread. But she forced herself through her routine, her motherly duties. By the time the kids were down for their afternoon nap, she was exhausted, ready to lie down. Before crawling into her unmade bed, River looked out her bedroom window. The snow had stopped falling a few hours before, and a line of animal prints trailed from the back of the house toward the woods, the tracks too small to be a deer but too big for a rabbit. A raccoon, perhaps?

The last thing River remembers is wondering how big a raccoon's feet were. She doesn't remember walking down the hallway, waking Jessica and Frankie from their naps. Or how Jessica's eyes remained heavy with sleep as she asked where they were going. She doesn't remember carrying Frankie down the stairs, leading Jessica by the hand, as the three of them made their way to the garage, the car. She doesn't remember Jessica asking if they were going to Grandpa's house or putting Frankie in his car seat. She doesn't remember turning on the car, locking the doors, or going back inside. She can't recall the police or the ambulance ride or the peppering of questions to which the only answers she could find were "I don't know" and "I love them." The next thing River remembers is waking in the hospital the morning after, handcuffed to the bed, her bones screaming. Before she talked to the nurses or the police or the lawyers she knew that something inside her had broken. And the damage, she could feel it, was beyond repair.

Growing up, Fit had a general idea of what took place in the garage on that winter day when she was three. Her memory contained a few frozen fragments—broken glass, Frankie's cries, the metronomic click of the car's engine. The story hung over her like a myth. To the people of Juniper Hills, she was the girl who almost died at her mother's hand. Saved by the mailman in the nick of time.

"It wasn't your mother," Dubs had told her from the get-go. "It was an illness. She got very, very sick. She loves you, you know that." And for a while, Fit believed him. She had no reason not to. Whenever she thought of her mom, she pictured her lying in a big bed, stuffy nose, tissues strewn about, and doctors bustling in and out.

Then one day, when Fit was about six or seven, she was over at Diamond's place and Diamond's mom—Mrs. M. to Fit—brought home a bundle of bathrobes from the casino. "They're practically brand new," Mrs. M. said, plopping them on the carpet. "And they were just going to get rid of them." Fit reached out and ran her hand over the plush fabric. "Nice, huh?" Mrs. M. continued. "Thought you girls could have a fashion show."

The robes were adult-sized; the excess fabric trailed behind them like trains as Fit and Diamond treated the breezeway like their own personal catwalk. Mrs. M. cheered them on and pretended to be a fashion photographer with her digital camera.

She snapped away, the flash going off every few seconds, and Fit couldn't help but wonder: If her own mom loved her so much, why wasn't she here? Why wasn't she standing next to Mrs. M., hands cupped around her mouth cheering Fit on? The illusion of her mother's love that Dubs had built in her mind began to crumble.

As Fit got older, she had even more questions. If prison was for bad people, why was her mom there? Why weren't Fit and Frankie allowed to see her? And in third grade, when a boy got suspended for punching another boy on the playground, the teacher sat the whole class down after recess and said, "It's not right to hurt people. Understand?" Fit nodded, because, yes, she understood.

Slowly, her curiosity turned to anger. And each time a classmate's mom brought cupcakes to school or Fit and Frankie got teased on the school bus for what had happened to them, the resentment inside her grew, the moments piling on top of one another, slowly constructing a wall. With each passing birthday and Christmas another layer was added, pushing out the sadness and longing. Until, eventually, there was a burning tower of fury in her, and it left no room for Dubs's excuses.

Per the judge's ruling, Fit and Frankie weren't allowed to visit River in prison until they were eleven. Fit knew that Dubs expected her to go, but her eleventh birthday loomed ominously on the horizon. And as the day crept closer and closer Dubs kept asking if she was excited to see her mom. Fit would shrug her shoulders and say, "I dunno," unable to explain the smoldering in her chest.

"There's nothing to be scared of," Dubs would respond, patting her on the shoulder. "The visiting area's real nice."

Despite Fit's lack of enthusiasm, Dubs put both of their names on the visitor's list for the second Sunday after her eleventh birthday. When the day finally came, Fit woke up in a panic and shoved her dresser in front of her bedroom door. Dubs knocked and called, "You awake?" When she didn't answer he said, "Coming in" and tried to open the door, but it only cracked an inch. "The heck?" he muttered, trying again.

"I'm not going," Fit said.

Dubs managed to push the dresser forward a few inches, opening the door just enough to pop his head in. "What are you talking about?"

Fit repeated herself, yelling this time. "I'm not going!"

"It's perfectly normal to be nervous," Dubs said. It wasn't fear or nerves, though, that kept her from wanting to go, but rather a question that had been stuck in her mind for months by then. "What would have happened?" she asked Dubs. "What if we weren't saved?"

Dubs looked like he'd been punched in the gut. Fit had always known that she and Frankie were lucky to be alive, but the words had no real meaning behind them. Lucky? Alive? It wasn't until that moment—Fit gripping her blanket, Dubs looking like he'd seen a ghost—that she actually *felt* it. A cool finger drawn across the bottom of her foot. And by the way Dubs looked at her, she could tell he felt it too.

"I hate her!" Fit yelled. She ran over to her bookshelf and started throwing books at the door, the first one missing Dubs's face by a few inches. His head disappeared from the opening but Fit kept going. Each time a book left her hand, crashing against the wall with a satisfying smack, Fit felt a small release, like steam escaping from the lid of a pot. And when there were no more books to throw, she sat on the floor, out of breath, feeling better and worse all at the same time. She hadn't wanted to make Dubs sad, but she took some comfort from the sorrow in his face. She wasn't the only one who hurt.

Her tantrums worsened after that. Something as small as Dubs asking her to clean her dishes could throw her into a screaming tailspin. She started mouthing off to teachers, bus drivers, anyone in a position of authority, which eventually landed her in the middle school counselor's office.

The counselor had obviously been filled in on the situation, one of his first questions being, "When you think of your mother, what's the first word that comes to your mind?"

"Nothing," Fit said. "I don't have one."

The counselor jotted something down on his notepad. "What makes you say that?"

"Because it's the truth," Fit said. The less she spoke about her mother the better. She already had enough fuel for a lifetime of hate. And Fit pretty much stuck by that, never speaking or thinking about River more than she had to.

Then during her freshman year of high school, an article popped up on her newsfeed: a woman had been convicted of killing her two-year-old son. He'd been drowned in the bathtub. Fit stared at the headline for a few moments before clicking on the story. At the top of the page was a picture of the woman, her face caught mid-sob, a line of spit dripping from her mouth. Fit read the first few sentences of the story before slamming her laptop shut.

She tried to forget about the article, but she couldn't shake the image of the mother, how her mouth was open so wide her face looked broken. And the next day, when the picture still wouldn't leave her, Fit did something she'd always stopped herself from doing: she Googled "River Underwood." There were pages and pages of articles that covered everything from the trial to the verdict to the sentencing. She read about how the defense claimed River had been in a fugue state caused by postpartum psychosis, how she had no control over her actions.

"She should be in a hospital," the defense was quoted as saying. "Not prison." Fit also read arguments from the prosecution, how they claimed that most women with postpartum psychosis don't try to kill their children. But what had sealed River's fate, Fit learned, was the initial police report. River had admitted to having "bad" visions for weeks. *It was planned*, read one pull quote.

Most of the articles contained few details about the actual day, as if the reporters themselves were horrified. After a little more digging, Fit found one in a small newspaper called *The Sun Times*. It was written just a few weeks after the incident. "Details Come Out in Mommy Attempted Murder Case," the headline read. The article spelled out River's actions, stating, "Underwood strapped the 8-month-old in his car seat and buckled the 3-year-old into her booster seat." Fit could hear the click of the buckle, feel the belt around her waist. She read on: "Then Underwood locked the car doors." A shiver went down Fit's spine. If any sliver of forgiveness had found purchase in her body, it left her at that very moment. As if buckling them in wasn't bad enough.

Fit saved the link to *The Sun Times* article. She would return to it sometimes late at night. She thought that if she cycled through the words enough times, she'd grow numb. But that wasn't the case. Each reading burned as bad as the last. River had locked the fucking doors, for Christ's sake.

With only one day left until River's arrival, dread grew like weeds in Fit's chest. And the fact that Frankie and Dubs were excited—no, *ecstatic*—didn't help. She could practically hear the buzz of their anticipation filling the apartment. Thank god Diamond had invited her to Riley's. Fit hated Diamond's boyfriend, but anything was better than listening to Dubs putz around the apartment for the rest of the night.

Fit tried to escape out the front door unnoticed, but just as she'd laid her hand on the doorknob, Dubs called out, "Hold up!"

She turned around. Dubs stood in the middle of the living room, a rag sticking out of one of the pockets of his fishing vest. Frankie was in front of the TV, organizing their haphazard collection of DVDs.

"What?" Fit said. "Diamond's outside."

"I thought we could do a movie night tonight," Dubs said. "Just the three of us."

Movie nights used to be their Friday evening ritual. They took turns picking what they watched. Dubs always chose a spaghetti Western, Frankie liked the obscure indies, and Fit normally went with an eighties rom-com. That was until Fit had ruined it the year before. She'd bailed on a movie night, using the excuse that she had to work on a school project with Pistols, when really, she and Diamond had been invited to a party thrown by a senior. The party ended up getting busted by the cops, and Fit, drunk on keg beer, had to call Dubs to come pick her up. Dubs hadn't said anything as she crawled into the front seat. He remained silent until she let out a small hiccup. "If you puke you're cleaning it," he'd said, not taking his eyes off the road. When they'd gotten home, Dubs stormed to his room without a word, and over the next few days he spent most of his time in the parking lot, tinkering with his truck. The following Friday he came out of his bedroom wearing his janitor's uniform, said, "I've picked up some extra shifts," and that was the end of movie nights.

Now, it was like none of that had ever happened, and Dubs looked excited.

"What do you say?" he said. "You can pick."

Frankie held up a DVD of *Sleepless in Seattle.* "We can watch your favorite."

She felt her resolve weakening. The idea of staying home, sinking into the couch, and splitting a box of Swedish Fish sounded nice, like old times. But, no. Frankie and Dubs had forgiven River, shown their true colors.

"Got plans," she said, and rushed out the door before she could cave.

Pistols drove a VW Beetle. He'd bought the clunker off his mom a few years ago and had enlisted the help of Dubs in fixing the old car up. A few weeks after Dubs had finished making the sucker purr like a kitten again, Pistols installed a muffler that made the engine rumble so loud that his car could be heard approaching from a quarter mile away. "He ruined a perfectly fine vehicle," Dubs had griped when he found out about the modification. Fit agreed, but she couldn't let Dubs know that. "It's rad," she'd shot back in response.

"Frankie didn't want to come?" Pistols asked.

The question tugged at the tangle of weeds in Fit's chest. "Nah, he's busy."

Pistols shrugged and started the car. Fit let the roar of the engine envelop her.

Diamond and Riley had been dating for three years. He was twenty-one and a member of the Mohegan tribe that owned Twin Suns. He worked at the casino "doing numbers." Fit wasn't sure what that meant, but whatever his job was, he had enough money to buy a house on a wooded street a few minutes from the reservation. A decent buffer of trees surrounded his house, so he could throw large, loud parties with no worries of a neighbor calling the cops.

From the first time Fit met Riley, she knew he wasn't good enough for Diamond. He was one of those people who always seemed to be looking over his shoulder, and it was obvious he only cared about himself. At parties he ditched Diamond for his friends, and when he and Diamond had plans he'd always show up late or never at all. Diamond shrugged those instances off, making excuses like "he's real bad with time" or "must've gotten caught up with work." Whenever that happened Fit wanted to scream, "Girl, you never take crap from anyone!"

Fit leaned her forehead on the car window and closed her eyes. The vibrations filled her head, seeming to block out all other thoughts. After a few minutes the car came to a stop and the roar of the engine diminished by about half. Fit opened her eyes and saw they were at a red light. Pistols looked over his shoulder at her and asked, "You good?" Earlier that month Diamond had told her that she'd overheard Pistols singing one of Fit's songs to himself. "He's crushing on you," Diamond had declared. And now Fit was on the lookout to see if that were the case, hoping it wasn't. Studying his face, she thought back to her old crushes: the rush she got in her chest when Liam Carson stood behind her in the middle school chorus, or how she found herself staring at Jenny Harper's legs in freshman Spanish and had a hard time concentrating when they were partnered up to conjugate verbs. Even when she and Jackson had first started messaging, Fit would grow giddy when she saw those three dots appear that meant he was typing. But none of those things happened when she looked at Pistols. She only saw him as a friend.

"I'm fine," she said, and Pistols turned back around.

Fit looked over at Diamond, who was putting on lip gloss in the mirror. Their eyes met in the reflection, briefly, and Fit looked away, kicking at a crumpled-up plastic bag on the floor by her feet, pretending the flutter in her chest was only nerves.

The light turned green and the sound of the engine filled the car. Fit pressed her hand on the glass, the vibrations starting at her palm and reaching outward until her fingertips buzzed.

Riley wasn't home when they got to his house. Diamond called him and said, "Hey, we're here," with a furrowed brow. Fit wondered if this was the time it would all become too much, that Diamond would finally see what a deadbeat Riley really was. But Fit got her answer when Diamond's face softened to a smile, giving a loving roll of her eyes. "See ya soon," Diamond said before hanging up.

"He's at Home Depot, that idiot," Diamond said, her words carrying a singsong bounce that irritated Fit. "He'll be back in twenty."

They waited in the backyard where Riley had a trampoline, a fire pit, and a picnic table. Beer bottles dotted the grass, remnants of the many late-night parties. They sat at the picnic table, playing Go Fish to pass the time.

Forty-five minutes later, Riley walked into the backyard carrying two full shopping bags. Diamond jumped up, wrapped her arms around his neck, and kissed him on the cheek.

"I had the best idea," he said, barely acknowledging Diamond's affection. His voice was animated and Fit wondered if he'd been drinking. "So, I was watching TV earlier," he continued, "and—I don't know—the thought just *came* to me." Riley dropped the bags on the ground and began to rifle through their contents. He pulled out a can of paint and held it up for them all to see like he was a model on the Home Shopping Network. "DayGlo! I want to make my house glow like the mother fucking moon."

Fit scoffed. "The moon?" She looked at Diamond, hoping that her best friend would *finally* see what a dumbass Riley was. But, with infatuation practically pouring out of her eyes, Diamond took the can of paint from Riley and said, "Love it!"

Riley emptied the bags out onto the lawn. He'd bought multiple cans of paint, brushes, and rollers. The works. He rubbed his hands together and said, "Let's get to it."

Riley decided they'd only concentrate on the back of the house that day. "I want to see it at night before I fully commit," he said. "Even though I know it's going to look fucking rad." He got a ladder from his basement, Pistols pulled the picnic table over to the side of the house, and they all got to work.

The green paint didn't look all that different from the current color of the house. Fit asked, "You sure you got the right stuff?"

"It's broad daylight, ya asshole," Riley called down from the top of the ladder. "Just wait until the sun goes down."

Fit tried to remain angry, but the work was fun, and she

was actually looking forward to seeing what the house looked like at night. They made decent progress, and after about an hour Fit's arms grew tired. She took a break, grabbed a beer from the fridge in Riley's basement, and sat on the edge of the trampoline. From farther away she could tell the difference between the DayGlo and the original paint.

She watched as Riley climbed down the ladder and started working next to Diamond on the bottom third of the house. Diamond kissed him on the cheek, then dabbed him on the forehead with her paint brush. Riley laughed. "Oh, you think you're funny?" He tried to get her back, but Diamond ducked and darted around the house. Riley followed. Fit heard Diamond's cries of laughter coming from the front yard, and jealousy stirred in her stomach.

She got up and walked over to the picnic table where Pistols stood, still hard at work on the side of the house. She sat down next to him and tugged at his jeans to get his attention. "Missed a spot," she said, pointing to a patch of unpainted siding. "There and there and there."

"It's a work in progress," he said, sitting down next to her. There was a spot of paint on the wood between them. She dabbed at it with her finger, then wiped the paint on the top of Pistols's hand. "There," she said, "beautiful." As they both laughed she leaned her head on his shoulder, a move she'd seen Diamond do a hundred times with Riley. Pistols put his arm around her. It weighed heavily on her shoulders, but she fought the impulse to shrug it off.

Diamond and Riley came shrieking back around the house. Riley scooped Diamond up in his arms, spun her around, and with the air of a great performance, Diamond leaned her head back and cackled into the sky. It hurt how much Fit wanted to swap places with Riley, be the one making Diamond laugh, making her happy. Diamond would never return those feelings and Fit knew that. Ignoring the urge to run up and push Riley out of the way, Fit convinced herself that it wasn't Diamond she was attracted to but rather the affection, the joy, the fanfare of it all.

Fit downed the rest of her beer and offered to grab refills for everyone. Pistols said he could help her grab the drinks.

"Nah," Fit said. "I'm good."

They were all a few drinks deep by the time they finished painting the side of the house. Dusk had begun creep into the sky.

"Let's go inside," Riley said. "Forget we ever painted this. So when we come out later, it'll be like—like the house is on *fire.*"

Fit snorted, her face warm and fuzzy from beer, "Exactly want we want. A house in flames." No one seemed to notice her sarcasm.

They moved to the living room, where Riley rolled a blunt like an expert. After they'd all taken a hit, Diamond said to Fit, "Looks like you lucked out."

The weed had slowed Fit's mind. "Huh?"

"Frankie's been posting snaps of himself cleaning all day."

Fit pulled out her phone and watched Frankie's Snapchat story: there he was scrubbing the floors, washing a window, beaming like he'd won the lottery. "Ugh!" Fit cried out and slammed her phone into the couch.

When they were young Frankie worshipped Fit. He followed her around wherever she went, sat as close as he could to her on the couch, and begged her to let him tag along whenever she went over to Diamond's. He'd even get upset when she wouldn't sit next to him on the bus. "You've got a little shadow there," Dubs used to tease. And even though Fit would sometimes pretend to be annoyed, her younger brother's insistence on being close to her was a comfort.

Fit knew that Frankie believed Dubs's stories, that their mother was sick, but there was a small part of Fit that had hoped when Frankie turned eleven, he'd stay home. He'd side with her.

But on the third Sunday after his birthday, Frankie came out of his room dressed in a button down and sweater and Fit knew she'd lost. "Have fun in jail," she snarked as he and Dubs headed out. After the door closed, the lock clicking into place, she picked up a pillow from the couch and threw it on the floor. Her side throbbed like something was being torn off her, sliced from her ribs.

And Fit felt that familiar cut of betrayal as she replayed Frankie's story. "They're acting like Camila Cabello is coming to visit or something," she said. "Are they forgetting where River's been the past million years?"

"Some of the best people I know have been locked up," Riley said.

"That's a *real* shocker coming from you," Fit said dryly.

Riley scratched his chin and took a pull from the blunt. "Prison doesn't mean shit. You know? One of my good buddies got sent away a few months ago. And it's not like I think any less of him."

Fit huffed a piece of hair out of her face. She knew no matter how much she tried to explain what she felt, no one would ever understand. If the articles were true, and River had no memory of what she had done, then Fit, and Fit alone, had seen the truth. Not even Frankie could understand what a burden that was to live with.

"Glad to hear you're keeping good company," she said.

Riley shrugged off the insult and handed the blunt to Pistols, who asked, "What'd he do?"

"Got busted for drugs," Riley said. "Him and a friend used to post up in the casino parking garage and deal from there." Riley leaned back into the couch and put his hands behind his head, looking as calm as if he were at the beach. "But they sold to an undercover cop. They had some pretty heavy shit on them, too, so that was that."

"I don't remember hearing any of this," Fit said. There had been other drug busts in town, and it usually only took a few hours for all of Juniper Hills to know the details.

"That's because management kept it hush-hush," Riley said. "There's been this big push to clean up the casino's image. Make the place more 'family friendly.'" Riley removed his hands from behind his head to make air quotes around the last two words. "They're cracking down on shit and making sure it doesn't end up in the papers." He nodded his head in Fit's direction. "I hear your good friend Marcus is leading the charge."

Fit thought back to how she'd been in Marcus's office more times in the past year than she had been in her whole life. She'd assumed it was because her stunts had become more intense, but now she wondered if the uptick was due to the casino's desire to become a squeaky-clean destination for families.

Without looking up from her phone, Diamond asked, "How many years did you say AJ got again?"

"Two," Riley said. "But he had a couple of priors. I think the other guy got off with community service or something like that."

"Damn," Pistols said. Riley leaned forward, took the blunt back, and said, "Yup."

He'd just finished exhaling when the doorbell rang.

Fit asked, "You having a party?"

Riley handed her the weed, a dumbass grin on his face. "You know how I do."

Within two hours, the house was full of people Fit barely knew. She went into the kitchen, the counter acting as a make-shift bar, and made herself another drink. She leaned against the wall and took a sip. The burn traveled in a smooth line down her throat. She closed her eyes for a few moments and took in the sounds of the party: the music, the chatter, the low hum of disobedience. When she pushed her way back to the living room, the spot where she'd left Diamond was now empty. She scanned the room, looking for her best friend, but every face she saw was a stranger. For some reason, her mind went to Frankie and Dubs. She pictured them sitting in front of the TV, laughing at whatever old movie Dubs had picked out, and she realized there would be no more movie nights with just the three of them. The mix of anger and nostalgia confused her, and her forehead and lower back broke out in sweat. The sounds of the party overwhelmed her. She had to get out of that house. As she pushed through the crowd, everyone's faces started to warp, like she was underwater. Like she was drowning.

Outside, the air had cooled and felt downright icy against her damp skin. She closed her eyes and took a deep breath. After a few minutes, she opened one eye, then the other, and feasted her vision on the side of the house. It was immediately clear that Riley had been wrong; the house wasn't in flames, it was electric. The proof was in the pulse, the current Fit felt just by looking at it. The brightness coupled with the crisp air brought a certain clarity to her mind. She became aware of the earth she stood on, the sky overhead, the glowing house in front of her, and she felt both large and small at the same time. And the word *Why?* rang through her head with such force it was as if the house was demanding answers: Why was she in the backyard? Why wasn't she at home with her family? Why did River, after all this goddamn time, have to come back into her life? And why was she the only one who was scared?

When Fit was a kid, she liked to tell people that she and Frankie were aliens left on Dubs's doorstep. She had repeated the story so many times that some part of her actually believed it. She knew she wasn't ready to give up the gag, and in a last-ditch effort she held her hands out to the house like she was warming them by a fire, trying her hardest to harness the power of the glow, tuck it away for when she needed it the most, for when she felt herself becoming human again.

For most of the trial, River felt like a spectator. It was as if those twenty-four hours that were gone from her memory had created two of her, giving her the ability to leave her body, fly high above the courtroom, and watch herself be accused of attempted murder. And when her lawyer, a balding man whose suits were always made of crisp fabric, argued that River was the victim here too, how she needed to be placed in a facility, she wanted to call out, "That's bull!" Even though River couldn't remember what she'd done, she knew she'd returned from the darkness a monster. She deserved to be punished.

There was a moment toward the end of the proceedings where the prosecutor, a tall woman with a smooth voice, looked over her shoulder, pointed a bony finger at River, and said, "Many mothers suffer from postpartum psychosis. But that doesn't turn them into murderers. There was a kernel of forethought, of malice, behind Mrs. Underwood's actions." At that, River imagined a small burnt and blistered popcorn kernel lodged deep in her mind. As the prosecutor continued to speak, her words falling away to a high-pitched hum, River placed her hand on the side of her head. She could feel the angry pulsing. She wanted to stop everyone, call the judge and jury over, and have them feel the warm skin right above her ear. Because once that happened, once they felt the evil in her, the trial would be over. Case closed. That's why when the verdict came back guilty on all counts of everything, River wasn't surprised. The jurors must have seen the malice in her, festering like an open wound.

River was initially placed in the hospital ward of Odell's Women's Penitentiary, where they prescribed her medication that made it feel like she was walking through mud and forced her to go to group therapy twice a day.

Dubs visited her as soon as he could, two weeks after the trial ended. "We can appeal," he'd said, looking uncomfortable sitting across from her at the gray-speckled table in the visiting area. "The lawyers think you've got a good chance."

"How are you going to afford that?" River asked. He'd already drained his retirement fund, sold his house—River's childhood home—to pay for the lawyers.

"That's for me to worry about," Dubs said.

River looked down at her lap, studied the dusty tan fabric of her uniform. "We'll lose again."

"But you don't *belong* here, Riv," Dubs pleaded. "I heard they'll try and move you out of the hospital wing as soon as possible. And you know where you'll go after that?" River knew, but she was too tired to answer, to even think about it. Dubs shook his head, his nostrils flaring. "Maximum security? It's ridiculous."

She wanted to lean her head toward him, tell him that if he listened real close he'd hear that evil beat coming from her brain, the sound of blood pumping through the kernel, contaminating the rest of her. "Save your money," she said. "Think about college. They'll need to go to college."

Dubs looked at her like she was asking him to take her off life support. "We'll figure out a way."

"It's what I want," River said, raising her voice. "*Please!*"

Dubs looked around like the guards were going to swoop in and tie her up, then let out a defeated sigh. "Okay, then."

They said their goodbyes, and as River was led out of the visiting room, her nine- to sixteen-year sentence stretched before her like a dark and hazy hallway.

For the first few years, River seesawed between numbness and despair. She'd float through the days and weeks not feeling anything, when out of nowhere the reality of everything she'd done would hit her, like it was hiding behind a corner, waiting for her to walk by. The guilt and the unbelievability of it all would buoy up and bring her to her knees.

But as time went on, River found it easier to escape those thoughts. She gave herself fully over to the movements of maximum security: being in her cell for the five checks a day, heading to the cafeteria for designated mealtimes. She didn't even have to think about how long she showered for. Seven minutes, no more or less. Eventually, River was able to stop thinking about most things. The guilt, the shame, how sometimes she missed her children so much she envisioned herself tearing down the walls of her cell with her bare hands, running through the woods in the direction of Juniper Hills, leaping over tree branches and rocks with the grace of a deer, and not stopping until she was able to brush her fingers against her babies' cheeks.

By the time River was moved to minimum security, weaned off the medications that made her feet itch and her hands swell, she had gotten so good at not thinking that it was as if she'd become a shell of herself, sleepwalking through the years, waking only occasionally when the kernel of malice dislodged itself, rose to the surface, and reminded her of the monster she was.

After thirteen and a half years in the women's penitentiary, River was released to a halfway house. She'd heard horror stories of such facilities, some people saying they'd rather stay in prison, but the house she was placed in wasn't that bad. She shared a room with two other women, the bathroom door locked, and visitors could stay for longer than half an hour.

Dubs and Frankie came to visit the first weekend she was there. Dubs poked around her room, flipping light switches, locking and unlocking the window, and once he'd made a full round he said, "Hey, not too shabby."

Frankie, who was about as tall as her now, sat down on the edge of her bed. "We got you a present," he said, reaching into his pocket.

Surprised, River asked, "For me?" The closest thing she'd gotten to a present over the past thirteen years was Dubs putting a little extra money in her commissary account around Christmas. "You didn't have to get me anything."

Frankie said, "Don't worry. We checked to make sure you could have this." He pulled out a silver rectangle a little smaller than the size of her hand. She knew it was a phone, having seen them on TV, but she'd never actually held one like this before. She ran her fingers around the smooth edges, was surprised by how light it was. "You can text me," Frankie said. "And Dubs. I put our numbers in there."

For a moment, River was happy. But soon the happiness turned to shame. She didn't deserve this, or him.

She looked over the phone, not knowing how to turn it on. The last cell phone she'd had was the boxy kind that flipped open. "I don't even know where to start."

"Here," Frankie said, taking the phone from her. "If Dubs can figure it out, I'm sure you can." He taught her how to text, how to make calls, and how to look up the weather. The ease with which he tapped and swiped impressed her. "You can watch videos too," he said. Frankie started to peck at the screen and when he was done he handed the phone to River and said, "Press the triangle to play."

River tapped on the screen when suddenly Jessica's face popped up. River froze. Her daughter looked different from all the school pictures Dubs had shown her. Jess looked like a young adult. She wore pink lipstick and heavy eyeliner, and chunks of her hair were wrapped in tinfoil. It looked like she was in a bedroom, the light casting part of her face in shadow. Jessica then began to sing, sort of, and the words pushed heavy on River's chest. She hadn't heard Jessica's voice in so long. It was deeper and steadier than she remembered, but somehow it sounded the same. When the video ended Frankie asked, "What'd ya think?"

River didn't know what to say. At some point while the video played she'd wrapped her hand around the headboard of the bed. She tried to let go but couldn't—her hand a claw stuck in the wood. She cleared her throat. "Was that tinfoil?"

After Frankie and Dubs left, River replayed the video until the phone battery died. She watched it again the next day and the day after that. Eventually, she found Jessica's other videos and realized her daughter was going by a different name. "Fit," River sometimes said aloud if her roommates weren't there.

As River grew more comfortable with her phone and navigating the internet, she discovered Fit's Twitter, Facebook, and Instagram. Over the course of the next two months, she was a silent observer of her daughter's online stardom, as fansites like "Fit's Freaks" and "HellYeahFittedSheet" popped up. River never let her phone out of her sight. It was the most valuable thing she owned—a glimpse into her daughter's life.

On River's last night in the halfway house, she couldn't

sleep, unable to stop worrying about the next day. She'd be released at 9:00 am, take a half-hour bus ride down the coast of Connecticut, and then a taxi to her father's apartment. Dubs had begged her to let him pick her up, but she insisted on making the trip herself. "I need to do this for myself." But as she tried to fall asleep she thought about navigating the bus station alone. How would she know if she got on the right bus? What if she missed her stop?

Halfway house rules stated that there was no technology allowed after the 11:00 pm curfew. But River didn't care. She had one night left and a clean record. She pulled the covers up over her head and looked at Jessica's Facebook pictures. Dubs had never come right out and said that Jessica hated her, but River had figured that out on her own. When Jessica wouldn't come to the phone, he'd used phrases like, "She'll come around" or "She just needs time." And when Jessica turned eleven and didn't come to visit, Dubs had said, "It's scary in here, you know, for a kid. That's all." But sometimes, when River would call Dubs collect, the person on the other end wouldn't accept the charges, wouldn't even say "no." There'd just be a *click* and River knew who the culprit was. She couldn't blame Jessica, and really it was Frankie and Dubs that River couldn't quite make sense of. She'd tricked them, somehow, into believing she was worth their time.

As River cycled through her daughter's profile pictures, photos she'd seen countless times before, she thought about what she was going to say to Jessica when she first saw her. "You've grown." "You're funny." A simple, "Hi, there." But nothing seemed right. River moved to Instagram, where Jessica had just posted a picture of herself. In the photo, Jessica looked off to the side, her hair covering half her face. Behind her was an intense, bright green backdrop.

**we light up the night**, the caption read.

River fell asleep an hour later, the warm phone cradled in her hand.

The next morning, Fit woke to the clanking of metal tools coming from the kitchen. Her head hurt, her mouth tasted like an apple left out in the sun, and she would have killed for a glass of water. The night before, she'd spent about half an hour in Riley's backyard, calming herself down, after which she'd gone back into the party and continued drinking until things became dark and unfocused.

She tried to fall back asleep despite the noise. But when an extra loud crash and Dubs's cry of "Shoot!" came echoing into her room, she gave up.

She grabbed her phone—8:14—and tried not to think about why Dubs was putzing in the kitchen. can you bring me some agua im dying, she texted Frankie.

As she waited for Frankie to respond or show up to her room with a glass of water, she checked her notifications. She'd gotten close to five hundred throughout the night. When she first started gaining notoriety the amount of likes and hearts she received filled her with bliss. Ten turned into a hundred turned into a thousand, and as the numbers grew so did her happiness. She'd read the name of each person, study their face, and sometimes she'd even creep on their profile, seeing where they were from or clicking through their pictures. But after a while the attention became expected, and the numbers stopped having as much effect on her. The real satisfaction, she'd found, came from the scroll. At any given time, she could scan through her notifications with the flick of a finger and count on the fact that there'd always be more, that the screen would keep refreshing with a list of people who had showed at least a second of interest in her.

Fit opened Instagram. As she read through the comments, she relaxed into the scroll and a sense of ease washed over her. She forgot about the pain in her head, the snap of sour in her stomach, and even her thirst dissipated for a bit.

After a while, she realized the noises in the kitchen had stopped. She put her phone down on her chest and listened to the silence. The break from her screen allowed her thirst and headache to sneak back in. She sat up slowly, but even the slight change in position intensified the pain behind her eyes. She needed water.

She found Dubs sitting at the kitchen table, his head in his hands. Tools were scattered about the counters, and the sink faucet, resembling a mini-crowbar, lay on the table in front of where he sat. Fit stood for a moment and watched him, a pang of guilt poking at her gut.

"Tired?" she finally said.

Dubs looked up, a bit startled. He rubbed his face, took his glasses from his front pocket, and said, "Resting my eyes. Think I need a new prescription."

"Did the sink break?"

Dubs picked up the faucet. "It's been leaking for a while," he said. "Finally found some time for it." He held the piece of metal close to his face and inspected the end where it should have been connected to the sink. "The last thread is worn down pretty bad." He held the faucet out to Fit. "See?"

She stepped forward. On the bottom of the faucet were five raised lines, like the ridges on a screw. She squinted, trying to see what Dubs was talking about, but there was no discernible difference. At least that Fit could tell.

"Hmm," she hummed, keeping her mouth closed, afraid her breath still smelled like beer, whiskey, and some smoke thrown in for good measure.

"Exactly," Dubs said. "If I can make it tight enough, though, things should be okay." He got up and began to look through his toolbox.

Fit swallowed and said, "I'm thirsty."

Dubs pointed down the hallway. "Bathroom."

Fit grabbed a cup from the cabinet, an old jelly jar with a worn picture of Mickey Mouse on the front, and went to the bathroom. She drank down a glass of water, the coolness washing away the gritty feeling in her throat, the tacky taste on her tongue. She gargled with mouthwash, refilled the cup, and went to see Frankie. His room was at the end of the hallway; technically it was a storage space, but since it had a window the landlord looked the other way when they'd started using it as a bedroom. The space was dark and cramped, but Frankie lovingly called it his "lair."

The door was open. Frankie was working on some sort of art project at his desk, hunched over, and his back faced the door.

Fit asked, "So this is why you're ignoring me?"

Frankie jumped a little at her words, and he quickly shoved something into the top drawer. He turned around and said, "Hey. What's up?" He flashed a weak smile and looked uncomfortable. Fit knew he was hiding something from her, his actions always so easy to read.

"What're you working on?" she asked.

"Nothing," he said. "Just messing around."

She nodded her head, stepped closer to his desk and saw

the surface was covered with pieces of cut-up paper, glue, and scissors. "Collaging?"

Frankie had recently gotten into making collages out of whatever material he could find: newspapers, old pieces of clothing, plastic bags. One day, he cut up a sponge and on the back of a paper bag created a sun rising over a field. "Do you know how expensive sponges are?" Dubs had asked when he first saw the picture. But later that night Dubs hung the paper bag on the fridge where it stayed for three weeks, until the glue started to give out and parts of the sun began to fall off.

"No," Frankie said. He stood up and straightened out the supplies sitting on his desk. Frankie loved showing Fit his work and his refusal to share further piqued her interest. She needed to see what he was hiding, so she thought of a way to distract him.

"I'm filming tonight," she said, flopping down on his bed. She'd been working on lyrics about a show featuring a down-on-his-luck accountant who finds out he has a child. "I'm thinking of being Ned," she said, referring to one of the show's smaller yet hilarious characters. She pulled up a picture of Ned and held her phone out to Frankie. He sat down on the edge of the bed, and as he looked at her screen a loud bang came from the kitchen. "What's going on out there?" he asked.

"The sink was 'leaking,'" she said, her use of air quotes on the last word making them chuckle.

They spitballed video ideas for a few minutes, Fit waiting for the perfect time to pounce and see what he was hiding in that top drawer.

"So, I'll part my hair in the middle," she said, "slick it back. What else?"

Frankie took a closer look at the picture of Ned. "I could make you a tie," he said. Fit used this moment of distraction to make her move. She wasn't fast enough, though, and she only got the desk drawer open an inch before Frankie swooped in and slammed it shut. She tried to push him out of the way, and he pushed back. Fit faked pain, yelping, "Ow, ow, ow," and when Frankie let up a little, she threw all her body weight into him. He stumbled backward, and she yanked open the drawer. Lying on top was a black piece of paper with white strips glued in the middle of the page that spelled out "WELCOME HOME."

At first Fit was taken aback by how simple and beautiful the collage was. Frankie's art was normally loud and colorful, but this piece was subtle, delicate. She picked up the sheet of paper, ran her pointer finger over the words. The white strips composing each letter appeared to be old receipts.

"I don't even know if I'm going to give it to her," Frankie said. "It's stupid."

Fit wanted to tell him that it wasn't stupid, that it was the *opposite* of stupid. She could tell he'd spent his time carefully placing each white slice, and she wanted him to be proud of his creation. He deserved to be proud.

Fit put the collage back in the drawer. "This isn't her home," she said and left his room.

"But she'll be here at noon," Dubs said when Fit asked if she could borrow the car.

"God, *I know*," she said. "I'll be back in an hour."

Dubs looked wary. "Promise?"

"Promise."

She drove with the windows down and the music loud, her hangover all but gone. A song she liked came on the radio, and she picked her phone up off the passenger seat. The coast was clear up ahead, no cars or pedestrians, so she opened Snapchat and began to film herself singing along. She kept one eye on the road and the other on how she looked in the screen. She noticed a car approaching and quickly stopped filming. One time, Dubs had caught her texting and driving as she pulled into the parking lot; she hadn't been allowed to drive for a week, and he'd warned her that if he—or any of his "eyes in town"—saw her on her phone while driving, she'd lose the car. "For good." So she waited until the car passed to post the video.

Fit was on her way to the post office to check her mailbox, which Dubs helped her open after her fans begged her for an address to send mail. Fit's freaks liked to send her gifts, chocolates (which she never ate), drawings, and a surprising number of figurines made of tinfoil. She hung the fan art on the walls of her room, put the gifts on her windowsill, and everything that didn't fit went in a box underneath her bed.

It had been a week since she'd checked her mailbox, and it was filled to the brim. Sandwiched between a postcard and a small white envelope were three package notices. Her heart sank. She peeked around the corner and saw Mr. Gibson, the very mailman who had saved her and Frankie, standing behind the counter. Mr. Gibson had been delivering the mail when he heard their cries coming from the garage. *I could see the car running from the side window,* he was quoted as saying in one of the articles Fit had come across. *And I knew something was wrong.* When no one answered the doorbell, he'd used a rabbit figurine by the front step to break the glass and climb through. From what Fit could tell, he'd been lauded as a local hero.

There were a few people in line and she thought about ducking out, having Dubs get the packages next time he checked the mail. She hated the way Mr. Gibson looked at her, like she was an injured duckling flailing on the side of the road. But she wanted her gifts and the tangible adoration that accompanied each one. Before getting in line, she put in her earbuds and pulled up her favorite song, blocking sound from the outside world.

When it was Fit's turn, she stepped up to the counter and handed Mr. Gibson the slips. He said something to her. She smiled and nodded, assuming it was small talk, but his face looked a little confused, and he spoke to her again. She took her earbuds out.

"I need a signature on this one," he said, holding up one of the slips. She signed the paper and Mr. Gibson shuffled off to the back room. He looked so much older in comparison to the photo printed alongside the newspaper articles Fit had dug up. His hair had thinned and his skin sagged under his eyes and around his cheekbones. He'd retired from his mail route a few years before—"Too hard on the knees," he'd said to Dubs one day—and became the man behind the counter at the post office. He came back holding three boxes. Fit looked at the floor as he placed them on the counter. "This one's heavy," he said, tapping the largest of the bunch. "Need help carrying it to your car?"

"Nope."

Fit picked up the packages. Mr. Gibson tipped his head, said, "Take care," and there it was, the very look she was trying to avoid: one of pity, like she was three years old again, still trapped in her booster seat. It was a look that confirmed all Fit's fears; as long as she remained in Juniper Hills, that's all she'd ever be to people—the girl whose mother tried to kill her.

She hefted the packages onto the passenger seat of the truck and checked the time. Almost eleven. She wasn't ready to go home so she drove around aimlessly until she found her way to the Dunkin' Donuts drive-through. She ordered two chocolate donuts and a strawberry Coolatta then parked in the corner of the lot.

As she ate, Frankie texted her **where'd you go?!** She pictured Dubs and Frankie worried about where she was, whether she was going to be back on time. Good, she thought. Let them sweat. Instead of responding she checked the replies to the snap she posted. It was a mixed bag, as always: **you look grt!!1!; suck a dick; lololol**. Fit loved each message, even the gross and mean ones, and responded to them all: **thx!!; no YOU suck a dick; lolol**. One fan had sent her a selfie with the words **fave song** written on the bottom. The girl resembled Fit: curly brown hair, oval face, light eyes. She stood in a nice kitchen with large windows that let in pale yellow sunlight. The room looked like the set of a cooking show. Fit wanted to bake something in the oven, sit down at the island and drink a cup of coffee. She hated the taste of coffee, but everyone always looked so content when they sipped from a mug in the morning. The time on the picture ran out. Fit didn't feel like writing the girl a reply.

After skimming through her notifications, she grabbed the stack of letters she received. The first one she opened contained a pencil drawing of her from one of her videos, the artist having framed Fit's face in a computer screen. Her fan art ran the gamut from world class to laughably bad. Frankie loved pretending to be an art critic. He'd pick up a drawing and in his best imitation of sophistication he'd say, "I really like how they captured your misshapen face here," or "You're so evolved that your eyes point in two different directions." No matter the quality, Fit kept every drawing and liked looking at them when she couldn't sleep.

Her phone buzzed. WHERE R U - DUBS. Fit couldn't tell

if Dubs was angry or just a little annoyed because he always texted in all caps. It was now 11:24. She knew she should head back soon. But when she pictured Dubs and Frankie sitting in the living room, dumb smiles plastered on their faces as they eagerly awaited River's arrival, she couldn't do it.

you up? she texted Diamond, who normally slept well past noon and was probably still at Riley's. When Fit and Pistols told Diamond they were leaving the night before, Diamond, drunk, said, "Laaame," but then gave them both long and loving hugs.

Fit's phone buzzed again, and her heart jumped a little thinking it was Diamond.

dubs is freaking, Frankie had written. he wants you home. Fit had half a tank of gas and twenty-three dollars in cash. She could make it to the beach, she thought, or Boston. But she knew she'd had have to return eventually. finnnnneeee, she responded before starting the truck.

Fit was back at the Meadow Lane Apartments by 11:49. As she sat in the idling truck, finishing off the last few sips of her Coolatta, a taxi pulled into the parking lot. The Yellow Cab parked in front of the building, and a short woman with tiny bird-like shoulders got out. The woman turned around and Fit froze. It felt like a chain had suddenly snapped itself around her arms and legs. River looked different than her mugshot— shorter hair, thinner body—but unmistakably her.

"Shit, shit, shit," Fit said through clenched teeth, the sickly sweet taste of her drink climbing back up her throat.

River slung a small blue duffle bag over her shoulder and shut the taxi door. She kept her head down as she climbed the stairs. Fit marveled at how frail and slight River looked, and she imagined pushing her over, sending her toppling to the ground. It wouldn't be that hard, she reasoned, a small flick of her finger would probably do the trick. River turned around and looked at the parking lot. Fit tried to slide down the seat, hide from River's gaze, but her legs and arms were locked. She felt exposed, out in the open for this tiny witch with the blue duffle bag to see. After a moment, River turned back around and finished climbing the stairs. When she rounded the corner and was out of sight, the invisible chain around Fit's body broke. She punched the steering wheel, the horn letting out a sharp beep, then put her head in her hands and squeezed her eyes shut. Yellow pinpricks filled the back of her eyelids.

Fit's phone buzzed once, twice, three times, but she didn't move. Whoever it was, she had nothing to say to them.

Fit opened the front door an inch, trying to be as quiet as possible. She was greeted by the sound of laughter. She then heard Dubs say, "Your coffee. Black, right?"

"Yes. Thank you," River said, her voice deeper, stronger than her size and overall appearance of frailty would indicate. Fit's phone, tucked in her pocket, buzzed, and the voices in the living room hushed. "Fit?" she heard Dubs call. "That you?"

*Well, fuck,* Fit thought, and she reluctantly pushed through the door. Dubs had taken his normal seat in the recliner by the window, Frankie was cross-legged on the floor, and River sat on the couch, perched on the edge of the cushion, looking uncomfortable and stiff.

"Hi, Jessica," River said, taking a sip of her coffee.

"I go by Fit," she said coolly even though she was shaking inside.

"Okay," River said. "Fit."

"Thanks for joining us," Dubs said. She could tell by his tone that he was upset with her but didn't want to make a scene. "Take a seat." He gestured toward the couch. Fit didn't want to be that close to River, so she grabbed a chair from the kitchen table and pulled it into the living room.

To an outsider, the scene would have looked normal, routine even—Dubs and River making small talk, Frankie looking on adoringly. Fit felt like she'd gone out to pick up the mail and had returned to some freaky, domestic alternate universe.

Fit looked at her phone. The buzz that had gotten her caught was a text from Diamond. Barely. What's up?

rivers here. Fit watched her phone, waiting for a response from Diamond, but nothing came. She'd probably fallen back asleep. Fit sent another message. this is the worst.

Dubs kept trying to get Fit to talk, and she deflected each of his conversational advances with a shrug. "Fit," he said, not giving up, "your mother has a pretty cool job."

"Yeah," Frankie said with palpable glee. "She eats snacks all day."

His intimate knowledge of River's life made Fit angry. "They don't care about having a criminal on staff?" she snapped, sick of River being treated like a hero returned from battle.

"Fit!" Dubs said, his voice sharp and staccato. "Enough."

"Sorry," Fit mumbled.

River stared intently at her coffee cup. "No. They don't."

Frankie asked, "How are you going to get there?"

"Bus," River said. "Eighty-nine line stops about a half-mile down the road, takes me right there."

"Well, days I'm not working," Dubs said, "I can give you a ride, sure. Or Fit."

Fit protested. "Says who?"

"Says the person who owns the car," Dubs said.

"Why can't she drive herself?"

"I don't have a license," River said, her voice low as if ashamed. Fit saw her opening, a sign of weakness, and went for it, asking, "How long has it been since you've driven?"

"Come on," Dubs said, leaning forward. "Quit it." But Fit couldn't. She stared at River and asked the question again. "How long has it been?"

River took a sip of her coffee, her knuckles white, then spoke slowly. "Well. It's been about fourteen years."

Fit leaned back in her chair, satisfied. "Huh? How about that."

"I'll have my license soon," Frankie said. "I can give you rides then."

"It's really okay," River said, her words a bit quicker. "I took the bus part of the way here."

Dubs shook his head, "Nonsense. If there is someone here who can drive you, whether it be myself or Fit," Dubs made a dramatic pause, looked Fit straight in the eye, "we'll do it."

"What am I? A taxi service?" Anger rose like floodwaters in her chest. "I didn't agree to any of this shit."

"Fine. Then you'll lose driving privileges."

"Fuck you," Fit said.

Frankie looked horrified. "Fit, *stop.* You're ruining it." His pleas only making her want to yell louder.

"Dude, you can't ruin what's already shit."

"Jessica," River said timidly, the single word pushing Fit over the edge.

"I don't see any fucking Jessica here!" she screamed.

Dubs rose to his feet, Frankie looked like he was about to cry, and River stared intently into her coffee cup. Fit relished in their unhappiness, that they finally felt like she did, but she wanted—no, *needed*—to push it one step further.

Fit looked around. Within reach, sitting on the end table, was a ceramic bowl that Frankie had made in art class in elementary school. Dubs liked using it for spare change. As Fit grabbed the bowl and lifted it above her head, she felt like she was of two different minds. One side rationalized that she was only picking the bowl up for effect, using it as a scare tactic. But the other, more sinister side of her just wanted to let loose and smash the piece of clay on the ground as hard as she could.

The bowl was heavy, smooth on the sides and rough on the bottom, and it felt dangerous in her hands.

"Really?" Frankie said, sounding tired. For an instant, Fit wanted to put the bowl down, wanted to stop inflicting pain. But then she looked at River, still sitting on the couch, and Fit noticed the "Welcome Home" collage on River's lap. From her vantage point, Fit could see that Frankie had added a gray border to the letters, giving them depth and dimension. Her whole mind now screamed *throw it throw it throw it.*

The crack of the bowl filled the entire room, followed by the sound of change spilling out on the floor. The pieces scattered everywhere, and before the nickels and dimes stopped rolling, triumph and regret swept through Fit's body.

The apartment was silent. Frankie bent down and grabbed a small triangular piece of the bowl. He held it in the palm of his hand and studied it. Fit felt sick to her stomach. She wanted to reach out and hug Frankie, beg for his forgiveness, but instead she looked at River and said, "Look what you've done."

Fit ran to her room. On her pillow sat a tinfoil tie. She picked it up, the trinket light in her hands, then hooked the tie onto the front of her shirt. Using her camera as a mirror, she looked at herself. The tie looked real. Shiny, but real.

Fit ignored Dubs's knock on her door, remained silent when he asked if she wanted to join them for lunch. "We'll be at Rosie's if you change your mind," he called out and a minute later she heard the three of them leave.

Shortly after, Diamond texted, Headed back from Ri's. Need me to call with a fake emergency???

nah, ill meet you outside, Fit responded. i gotta get out of here

Riley's car pulled in soon after Fit got to the bottom of the stairs. She pretended to be doing something on her phone as Diamond gave him a kiss goodbye and nodded her head cordially as he drove away. Diamond then sat next to Fit on the bottom step and asked, "That bad?"

Fit rolled her eyes. "I'll tell you later."

They walked to the convenience store a few blocks away. Davey, the owner, sat on a stood behind the counter and said, "Here comes trouble," as they walked in.

"Oh shut up, Davey," Diamond said, drawing out his name like there was a string of "e's" after the "y." "You know you missed us."

Fit and Diamond weaved their way through the aisles, not looking for anything in particular. Fit slid open one of the freezer doors, the cool air puffing out like a cloud. She stood there for a few moments, letting the vapor fall over her, until Davey called out, "I don't own the electric company too!"

Normally, Fit would have flashed a big smile, maybe teased him back, but she was too drained. She slid the door shut—"my bad"—and went and found Diamond in the canned food aisle.

"So, where'd the fam go for lunch?" Diamond asked.

"Rosie's," Fit said.

"Nice first meal out," Diamond responded sarcastically.

"Who cares?" Fit picked up a jar of maraschino cherries. "Maybe they'll have such a nice time they'll just forget about me."

Diamond put her hand on Fit's shoulder. "You good?" A cool line pulsed down the side of Fit's body.

"Yeah," Fit said, putting the cherries down and taking a step away. "I don't really want to talk about it."

"I feel that," Diamond said. She pulled her phone out of her back pocket and pointed it at Fit. "Okay, I got a scenario for you." As much as Fit wasn't in the mood to goof around, the instant she sensed Diamond was recording she perked up, straightened out her shoulders, and moved her head a little to the side because sometimes her nose looked gross straight on.

"Now," Diamond continued. "Pretend you've got ten hungry kids at home to feed." To an outsider, this may have sounded odd. But to Fit, this was normal. It was their thing. Diamond liked to point her camera at Fit without warning and spit out some random story line and Fit knew that was her cue to act out the first thing that came to her mind. Sometimes Diamond's setups were simple—"Imagine you just found a hot dog on the ground"—while others were more complex, like when Fit had to pretend that she'd just held up a bank in 1940s Chicago. Fit often wondered if Diamond spent her free time thinking of weird-ass situations. The clips never lasted more than thirty seconds, often ending in laughter, and Diamond would post them to her own Instagram with the hashtag #FittedSheetExclusives.

So, when Diamond told Fit to pretend like she had a hoard of hungry kids to feed at home, Fit acted without even thinking. She pulled the bottom of her shirt out, reached her arm around a couple stacks of tuna fish cans, and pulled them off the shelf. Most of the cans landed in the sling she'd created with the fabric of her shirt, only a few escapees falling to the floor. Behind the camera, Diamond grinned and said, "That's a lot of tuna."

"My babies need protein," Fit said in a breathy Southern accent.

Diamond raised an eyebrow. "Why is that?"

"They gotta get strong. The gotta win those baseball championships," Fit responded, pronouncing it "champ-EE-on-ships."

Diamond took a deep breath, and Fit could tell her best friend was about to crack. "I didn't know your kids played baseball."

"Coached 'em myself."

Diamond picked up a jar of marshmallow fluff from the shelf next to her. "Can we get a demonstration?"

"Sure can," Fit said.

Diamond tossed the jar in the air. "Catch."

Fit knew that what she was about to do was going to make a mess, would probably get them in trouble, but she didn't hesitate. The footage was going to be too good. She let go of the bottom of her shirt, releasing the tuna, and reached up with both hands. The cans hit the floor, and she caught the jar. She held the marshmallow fluff up over her head and yelled, "Touchdown!"

Diamond lost it, bending at the waist, practically wheezing she was laughing so hard. Fit started to crack up, too, and standing there in the convenience store, cans of tuna still spinning at her feet, Fit almost forgot why she was there in the first place.

"What the hell's going on back there?" Davey yelled from the front.

"Shit!" Diamond said, trying to catch her breath. "Hurry."

They both scrambled to the ground and started to pick up the cans. "I thought you would catch it in your shirt," Diamond said. "But that—that was gold."

"What can I say? I commit."

They'd managed to get about half of the cans back on the shelf before Davey appeared at the end of the aisle, arms crossed.

"I slipped," Fit said. "And the tuna caught my fall." Diamond snorted under her breath. Fit chewed at her cheeks to keep a straight face.

"Are you guys going to buy anything?" Davey asked. "Or did you only come here to break all my stuff?"

Fit grabbed a can of spray cheese off the shelf. "We're getting snacks. As soon as we clean this mess up." She grinned. Davey shook his head and walked away.

When the cans had been returned and placed into neat little stacks, Fit and Diamond snagged a bag of tortilla chips and headed to the counter.

"Am I going to go back there and a find a disaster zone?" Davey asked while ringing them up.

"What do you think we are?" Diamond said, feigning offense. "Neanderthals?"

"Need a bag?"

"Nope," Diamond said. "But can I get a pack of Parliament Lights while you're at it?"

He fetched the cigarettes from the back wall. "Anything else?"

"You're not going to card me?" Diamond had turned eighteen a few months before and loved flashing her ID any chance she got.

"Seen it," Davey said.

They left the store, calling "Bye, Davey!" over their shoulders, and walked to a playground by the apartment complex. Two boys played on the field, kicking a soccer ball back and forth. Scanning the jungle gym and swing set, Fit and Diamond chose the platform at the top of the slide to park themselves. Fit opened the chips and sprayed some cheese into the bag. She watched as the taller boy, who was in control of the ball, fake left and swoop past his friend.

"I was real shitty to Frankie today," she said, popping a chip in her mouth.

Diamond asked, "What'd you do?"

"You know that bowl he made in fourth grade? The one Dubs keeps by the front door?"

Diamond nodded.

"I broke it," Fit said. In the house her violence had felt like a triumph, but now all she felt was embarrassment, guilt.

"Damnnn," Diamond said. "That's harsh."

"I know," Fit groaned. She covered her face with her hands and leaned on Diamond's shoulder. "But they were all acting so—so happy."

"You surprised?

"No," Fit said. On the subject of her mother, she'd been outnumbered by Frankie and Dubs for as long as she could remember. "But seeing it happening. It's different."

Diamond licked the cheese off her fingers. "Frankie will get over it. He always does."

It was true—Frankie rarely stayed mad at her for too long—but Diamond hadn't seen the way he'd fallen to his knees, hovered his hands over the shards like he was magically trying to undo the damage she'd done.

"I guess," Fit said.

They continued to eat and watch the boys play. After a while they moved to the swings. As they pumped their legs, Diamond pointed at the road in front of them and said, "Blue Honda."

"Roulette," Fit said. "For sure." The road they faced funneled into the casino. Since they were kids, they would sit and watch the cars go by and guess the game of the gambler.

"White van thing," Fit said.

"Dice," Diamond answered.

They continued to swing as high as they could, shouting cars and answers at each other through the rushing air. Red SUV? Blackjack. Purple Audi? *Sex and the City* slot machine. And the green fancy car that Fit said was a Porsche, but Diamond was adamant was a Corvette? "High roller," Fit said. "Definitely heading to the poker tables."

They tired of the game and swinging, and as the sun began to set Diamond smacked the pack of cigarettes against her hand, unwrapped the plastic, and held out the open box to Fit.

"Nah," Fit said.

Her phone buzzed. R U COMING HOME SOON? - DUBS

Fit stared at the message. She imagined River sitting in the middle of the couch, Frankie and Dubs on either side, all of them grinning because she hadn't been there when they returned.

im at church 🙏

She knew the response would get under his skin. A religious man, Dubs used to drag them to church every week, but when Fit got to high school she refused to go, throwing a tantrum at the mere mention of a prayer.

NOT FUNNY

Diamond asked, "Trouble on the home front?"

"Nothing out of the ordinary," Fit said, holding out her hand. "Give me one?"

Diamond took the lit cig from her mouth and handed it over. There was a shiny Chapstick mark on the filter. Fit took a drag, held the smoke in her lungs, and tilted her head up to the sky as she exhaled.

A school bus drove by, probably transportation for some summer camp. "What do you think their vice is?" Fit cracked.

"They're probably showing them the slots," Diamond said. "Giving them an in-person example of who not to become." There was a heaviness in Diamond's voice. Fit wanted to reach out and hug her, kiss her on the forehead. She probably would have if the thought hadn't reminded her of the cool line that shot down her body earlier that day. If she hadn't spent the last few weeks convincing herself she didn't have a crush on Diamond. That she *couldn't*. Diamond was the one person who never expected Fit to be nicer or quieter or to forgive something that shouldn't be forgiven. And Fit couldn't risk losing her best friend.

She took a picture of Diamond, the last glimpse of sun fading behind her. "Dang," Fit said, showing Diamond the shot. "You look like a celebrity."

"Shut up," Diamond said, smiling and casually pumping her legs again. "But send that to me."

Night lazily fell over the park, the air cooled, and the mosquitos came out in full force. Diamond slapped her arm. "Fuckers." She scratched at the place she'd been bitten, a small bump already forming. "Let's bounce before we get eaten alive. Wanna sleep over?"

Fit wanted to, she really, really did, but she said, "I've got to face Dubs at some point."

When Fit got home, she hung out on the walkway balcony that overlooked the parking lot. She leaned on the railing, watching the cars go by. For as long as she could remember she always felt out of place, wrong for the town, but the apartment had been her one spot of refuge. It was small and run-down, but it was the only home she knew.

During the spare months Fit's father hadn't been deployed, he'd stayed in a dusty, shared duplex on the base. Fit and Frankie would visit him occasionally, or he'd take them out for burgers and fries, but the Meadow Lane complex was where they always returned. When Fit was in third grade, her father got stationed in San Diego and gave full custody over to Dubs. She remembered the way her dad fiddled with the pepper shaker as he told them the news, and how afterward Dubs had cleared his throat and said, "Don't worry. Nothing's going to change." And nothing did, really. Their father always sent them each a Christmas card, with a twenty or fifty tucked inside, and called them on their birthdays if he wasn't deployed, but other than that, Fit, Frankie, and Dubs went through life as their own little unit. Sometimes Fit used the size of the apartment as ammo against Dubs when they fought, but the reality was that the thought of lying on the living room floor, watching TV with Frankie as Dubs snored in his recliner, had always brought Fit great comfort. Now, that comfort was gone—replaced with a complicated mess of emotions she had no idea how to process.

Fit went inside, closing the door quietly behind her. A light was on in the living room and she saw Dubs sitting on the couch. He was in his pajamas, a pillow and blanket next to him, reading a magazine. He flipped the page. "Nice of you to show up," he said, nonplussed.

"You're up past your bedtime." She grabbed a seltzer from the fridge. Cracking the top open, she leaned against the kitchen doorframe and nodded her head at the couch. "What's this about?"

"I figured your mother would enjoy sleeping in a double bed."

Fit didn't like the image of Dubs spending the night on the lumpy couch. "First day here and she's already messing shit up."

He slammed shut his magazine. "You," he said, pointing a finger at Fit, "need to quit it with the attitude."

Fit took a sip of her seltzer, the bubbles tingling her nose. "Sorry," she said, neither telling the truth or lying. She waited for Dubs to respond, expecting him to speak the words she'd heard him say so many times before: unfair, bad system, sick. The words Frankie bought hook, line, and sinker. They were the cause of so many tantrums and fights, and when Dubs would list them off like groceries he needed to pick up on his way home from work, Fit couldn't help but want to break something—like *really* break something. But Dubs remained quiet as he flipped the magazine back open, licked his thumb, and turned the page. He thumbed through a few more pages before asking dryly, "How was 'church'?"

Fit smirked. "Jesusy."

Dubs nodded his head, then served her attitude right back. "The steeple must've burned down or something. You smell like an ashtray." The banter felt familiar, safe.

"That Father Kevin," Fit said, "he just can't kick the habit. You know he lit up right during the Lord's Prayer?"

Dubs smiled, and for a moment Fit thought maybe he'd forgiven her for the display she'd put on earlier that day. But soon his face settled back into seriousness and he said, "You owe Frank an apology."

Fit knew it was true but didn't want to admit it. She took another sip, swishing the fizzing liquid around her mouth.

"You hear?" Dubs said.

"Yes, jeez. Get off my case." She clanked the seltzer down on the counter. "I'm going right now."

The light was still on in Frankie's room. She knocked softly. "What?" Frankie answered, and Fit went in. Newspaper scraps were scattered on the floor, and Frankie sat in the middle of the mess, gluing pieces of paper to a shoebox.

Fit sat down on the floor next to him, picked up three slips of paper, and began to braid them. "How was Rosie's?"

Frankie shrugged. "Dubs made us order brownie sundaes, even though Mom and I were stuffed."

She imagined them at the twenty-four-hour diner, cozy in a booth, and wondered what they had talked about. Fit smushed the pieces of paper in her hand into a ball. "Was it weird?"

Frankie grabbed another chunk of newspaper, glued it to the box, then smoothed down the edges with a finger. He was ignoring her. She waved a hand in front of his face. "Earth to Frank-o."

He looked up at her and snapped, "What?"

"Jesus."

"Fit, I'm serious. What do you want?"

Fit fought the urge to snap back. "I wanted to see if you were okay. After—what went down earlier."

"What went down?"

"Yeah," Fit said. "When I—hulked out."

Frankie shook his head. "You couldn't even be nice to Mom for one day?"

She hated hearing him say the word *mom*, each utterance a small stick to her side. "It still weirds me out, okay? She makes me uncomfortable," she said angrily, because it was the truth.

Frankie looked at her. "It doesn't have to," he said, both frustration and compassion woven into his voice. She could have told him right then how sometimes she woke up in the middle of the night terrified, thinking that he'd disappeared. And how when that happened, she'd tip-toe to his room, crack the door less than an inch, and listen for his breathing. Maybe then he'd understand why she was being so mean.

"How do you do it?" she asked.

He moved some papers around. "Do what?"

How could he see past what River had done? How, after all the teasing and living in thrift store clothing his whole life, was he able to forgive her? He'd been defenseless. Eight months old. If it had been Fit in that booth, sitting across from River, she would have chucked the salt shaker right into the wall.

Fit picked up a few more pieces of paper and answered, "Turn this garbage into art?" She smashed all the scraps in her hand into one homogenous ball and flicked it at Frankie. It landed smack dab in the middle of his forehead. He grinned begrudgingly, a signal that even if he sulked around for a few more days he'd forgive her eventually and move on like he always did.

"Sorry about the bowl," she said. "I'm serious."

He shrugged. "It was ugly anyways."

As Fit walked down the hallway to her room, she paused for a moment outside Dubs's door and listened. There wasn't anything to hear.

Rosie's Diner hadn't changed much. The surrounding trees had filled out and the letters on the sign out front were a darker shade of blue, but other than that the place looked the same as when River and her high school friends used to pack the place on weekend nights. The restaurant was fairly empty, which River was thankful for, as her nerves were still raw from the shattering of the bowl. She'd tried to tell her father that staying in was fine, but Dubs waved her off, insisting she needed a "proper meal."

The eight-page menu was overwhelming, and when the waitress came to take their orders, River just pointed at the first item she saw: an egg sandwich.

The waitress then asked, "White or wheat?" River didn't know. When she'd first gotten to the halfway house a decision as simple as wearing a green or red polo shirt proved difficult. She'd gotten better in her few months there, but now, fully out in the wild, the inability to decide overtook her once more. "You pick," she finally told the waitress.

After they received their drinks, Dubs said, "You know, Fit isn't normally like that."

Frankie laughed. "Yeah, *okay.*"

"All right, she has a bit of a temper," Dubs conceded. "But once you give her some space, she's fine."

River took a sip of her soda, a shock of sweet overwhelming her senses. Originally, she had wanted to move into a small studio apartment near the halfway house, which she could afford if she worked enough. But when she told her father of the plan, he wouldn't hear of it. "That's ridiculous," he'd said. "You'll stay with us until you get on your feet." She tried insisting she'd be better off on her own, to which Dubs argued, "It'd be good for the kids to have you around." For a few weeks, River had let herself fall into Dubs's optimistic trap. But after Jessica's display that afternoon, she couldn't fool herself any longer. She'd lost her daughter a long time ago.

When their food came, River unwrapped her bundle of silverware, the metal feeling heavy in her hand. She put the fork down, the utensil clicking against the top of the table. Her sandwich was already cut in half, but she used her knife—a real, metal knife—to cut her sandwich into quarters.

In Odell's Women's Penitentiary, River had worked as a taster for a giant food corporation. It was the first program of the kind in any prison around the country, her fellow inmates were told, like they should consider themselves lucky. River was paid $2.19 an hour to start, with a ten cent raise every six months.

"Snacks make people happy," Gina, the woman who ran the program, always liked to say. "And you're a part of that." River knew Gina was full of crap but she couldn't help but wonder if Jessica or Frankie ever ate any of the products she tested. If they could sense that it was River who made their lollypop the right sweetness, ensured their chips were crisp.

The training for the job had been intense. Gina first taught the women how to break down the flavor profiles of a food and properly rate aspects like bitterness, saltiness, and sweetness.

She then instructed them how to look beyond those flavors and identify the structural components like chew and palpability.

One day River had been struggling to move beyond the incredible sourness of a sugar candy, when Gina told her, "Close your eyes. Imagine that sourness as a big circle of color." River did as she was told and visualized a neon yellow orb. Gina continued, "Now what I want you to do is shrink that circle down. Make it smaller, smaller, smaller, until it's barely visible. Like a spec of sand." The small yellow dot floated in River's mind, and she noticed the sour taste in her mouth had diminished as well. She opened her eyes, shocked.

"It worked," she said in surprise.

Gina smiled smugly and said, "Atta girl."

River got so good at this visualization technique that she started doing it at mealtimes. She'd shrink the flavor of the dog-food looking meatloaf or dry mashed potatoes down so small that sometimes she forgot what she was eating. Without meaning to she moved onto smells. The apple shampoo she bought at the commissary was a pale yellow, her toothpaste a bright white, and the collective smell of the women that surrounded her was a deep purple circle. When Frankie would visit, she'd picture his scent as a mint green bubble, blow it up as large as she could, and carry the large green circle around in her brain for the rest of the day.

The work of a taster was unpleasant, hard on the mouth. There was once a three week stretch where River only tested salt and vinegar chips, and by the end of the second week an open sore had formed on the tip of her tongue. It was a job that no one wanted to do if they didn't have to, so her skills were highly sought after. With the help of a job and life skills counselor who came to the halfway house once a week, she'd found a job at the Carolina Snack Co., and her job starting just two days after her return to Juniper Hills.

On the morning of her first day of work, River sat at the kitchen table with Dubs, drinking a cup of coffee.

"You'd think they'd give you some time to settle in," he said, one hand wrapped around his mug, the other tapping nervously on the table.

"What can you do?" River said, but part of her was looking forward to getting back to work, something familiar. Being back left River on edge. Jessica had barely acknowledged her, shooting her the occasional cutting glare, and Frankie and Dubs seemed to be overcompensating, bombarding her with questions like if she was okay or wanted some orange juice or wanted to watch *Jeopardy!* The night before, Dubs had said, "We could dial up a movie," and River had no idea what that meant, so she just nodded and said, "Sure. Dial it up." River had a hard time paying attention to the movie Dubs had chosen. She had felt like a spy, an intruder, like this was all a dream and any minute she'd wake up back in prison, staring at the cinder block ceiling.

Dubs looked down at his watch, sighed, and said, "We should get going."

As River got her jacket from the hallway closet, she ran her hands over her daughter's wool peacoat, pressed the sleeve up to her nose and inhaled. Orange. A large orange circle, like a sun, popped into her mind.

The drive took about twenty minutes, Dubs listening to sports talk radio the entire way there. "Building 2A," he said, pulling up in front of a squat gray building. "Here you are."

"Thanks, Dad," she said, feeling like a kid again being dropped off at school. "Appreciate it."

The inside of the Carolina Snack Co. reminded River of

the women's penitentiary: sterile walls and fluorescent lights that washed everything out. River was shown to a room at the end of a hallway. There were three long tables with a computer in front of each chair. The computers were much nicer than those she was used to working on. She marveled at how thin the monitors were and the modern-looking keyboards. She picked up the cordless mouse and turned it over in her hand.

"Is it out of batteries?" a young man, who was pulling out the chair next to her, asked. She jumped at the question.

"Sorry," he said. "Didn't mean to sneak up on you." He put his bag on the floor and his helmet on the table next to the computer.

"It's fine," River said, bracing herself for small talk. But the young man just said, "Cool" and then paid her no more attention.

The room filled up with workers. The supervisor was an older gentleman. He walked into the room carrying a large box, placed it on the front table, and said, "Come get your kits."

The group was testing the meltability and bitterness of clear sugar pellets that day. They looked like translucent Tic Tacs and each one was packaged in its own miniature Ziploc bag. The company used the same software River was trained on, so she was able to get right to work. In between each pellet, she cleansed her palate by eating half a saltine cracker and gargling with soda water. She'd then wait sixty seconds, giving her taste buds a chance to recalibrate. River became so engrossed in the process that she startled a bit when the supervisor announced it was time for a break.

The break room was just down the hallway. There were circular tables with folding chairs and a couple vending machines. The bitterness had ruined River's appetite, but she bought a ginger ale with quarters and sat at a table in the corner.

An older woman with a thin ponytail came and sat down a few seats away from River. She was eating from a small bag of pretzels.

"I hate the days we've just got to let things *dissolve*," the woman said. River smiled politely and the woman continued. "I need something with some crunch, ya know? Something I can really sink my teeth into." She popped a few more pretzels in her mouth, then said, "You're new."

"First day," River said, readying herself to lie. She had a batch of lines ready to go if this woman's questions got too personal. *I'm from Vermont. I've been a stay at home mom. I found this job on the internet.* But the only other question the woman asked was if River wanted a pretzel. River politely declined.

The rest of the day flew by, River entranced by the work. On the car ride home, she ran her tongue along the front of her teeth. They were fuzzy, a hint of bitterness still hung in her mouth. When they got to a stoplight she looked at the group of people in the car in the next lane. She studied their profiles, the way they held themselves. They could be anyone, she thought. *She* could be anyone.

When River got home she immediately went to the bathroom to brush her teeth. At Odell's, sometimes she had to wait hours with the lingering funk of whatever she had been tasting coating her tongue and mouth. River brushed and flossed, rinsed with mouthwash, and then, even though the fuzz was gone from her teeth, she brushed again.

Fit stewed in her bedroom as she tried to ignore the happy voices of Frankie and River coming from the living room. She'd spent the last week avoiding the apartment at all costs, spending most of her time at Diamond's or the casino. But Diamond was at Riley's, Dubs had the car, and it was too hot to walk anywhere. Fit had even considered texting Pistols, but she didn't want him to get the wrong impression.

She texted Frankie: **wanna help me film?** She hadn't posted a video in over a week, and her fans were antsy.

**Yea,** he responded. **In a bit.**

**omg nevermind . . . dont even bother**

She fastened the tinfoil tie that Frankie had made to the front of her shirt and began filming. Halfway through the first take, laughter erupted in the living room. Anger wormed inside her chest, and she opened her door and shouted, "I'm filming here! Quiet on set!"

Frankie yelled back, "Sorry your majesty." Fit swore she could hear them both snickering, and she slammed her door shut.

Frankie and River remained quiet afterward but Fit kept imagining the two of them whispering to each other on the couch, giggling like they were partners in crime. Fit finished filming, did a little editing, then posted the video to her channel. **new videoooo!** she wrote to her fans. **come hang w me in the comments ya freaks!!**

**Is it just me or does Fit look angry?** one of the first commenters wrote. Fit watched the video again. Her words didn't seem as upbeat as usual, lacking their normal punch. And in her outro, where she usually told her fans how much she loved them and blew them kisses, she'd only said, "See ya next time, freaks."

Fit wasn't surprised her fans had figured out something was up. They noticed when she got a haircut, even if it was just a trim, and they had a weird ability to tell if she was tired or hungry. Once, Diamond guest-starred in one of her videos and the comments were all about how great Fit's smile looked and they wondered if she'd drunk a bunch of coffee that morning. **1:46** ♡, one person had written. Fit went to the one minute and forty-six second mark of the video. It was the moment where she and Diamond attempted to high-five but failed miserably, missing each other's hands by a few inches.

Within ten minutes of her newest video being posted, a thread had started of people agreeing that Fit looked angry, forming theories as to why. Then, someone wrote: **THis might explain it??** Followed by a link. The link brought Fit to a discussion post on a website dedicated to YouTube personalities. Fit had only been a category on the site for a month and was ecstatic when she found out she'd been added.

She read the title of the discussion post, created four hours before: "THE MUMMY RETURNS." Fit's heart sank. "Shit." She thought about closing the window, forgetting what she'd seen. But the pull was too strong. She needed to see what people were saying.

**I have a friend that lives in her town and apparently her mom is living with her now.**

**So??**

**Lololo someones behind the times**

After this, one of the comments linked to a blurb in the "Police Log" section of a small, Southeastern Connecticut newspaper. The article, which was only a few paragraphs long, was posted a few months before. It summarized what River Underwood had done, and how she was being released into a halfway house. Fit didn't wonder how her fans knew it was her mom: she'd learned that the collective power of a fanbase was unstoppable, their ability to dig up buried information almost magical.

Fit continued to scroll through the discussion, stopping at a video someone had found on Obscure Media Reddit. The clip, which had 490 views on YouTube, was of a news anchor, looking serious. The quality of the video suggested it had been recorded by someone watching it on TV. On the top of the screen was the headline "MOTHER CONVICTED." The news anchor spoke: "River Underwood was found guilty today on two counts of first-degree attempted murder." The video then cut to River, wearing a gray prison jumpsuit, handcuffed, being led by two guards through a swarm of reporters. In all the research Fit had done, she'd never come across this video. She pressed pause: River looked straight ahead, her face blank and washed out by a bright light shining at her from somewhere off camera.

Fit wanted to hurl her computer across the room. She knew one day her fans would find out her past, but the unearthing of these details still hurt. The internet was *her* space. Her last fucking space where she didn't have a mom. Where she was Fitted Sheet, not Jessica Underwood, the girl who should be dead.

That night, Dubs ordered pizza and made them eat dinner together at the kitchen table. Fit tried to get out of it, but Dubs threatened to take her car privileges away for a week if she didn't join them. Fit, still seething from her discovery earlier that day, didn't speak. Dubs prodded her with questions, which she answered with a nod or a shrug. Everything River did annoyed Fit. The way she took a bite of her pizza and looked at her hands while she chewed, or how she laughed at Dubs when he made a stupid and unfunny joke.

"What are you guys up to tomorrow?" Dubs asked.

"Heading to the pool," Frankie said.

"Supposed to be hot tomorrow," Dubs said, wiping the pizza grease off his hands with a napkin. "You should take your mother, huh?"

Fit winced at Dubs's suggestion. "Pistols won't have room in his car."

"Take the truck. I'm not working tomorrow." Dubs smiled, his cheeks like cherry tomatoes. Fit was thinking about how to get out of this bind when River said, "It's really okay. I don't have a bathing suit."

"You can borrow one of Fit's," Dubs said. "She has a bunch from when she was on the swim team last year. Before she quit." Who did Dubs think he was? Loaning out her bathing suits like they were library books. "Those things cost me an arm and a leg," Dubs added.

"You made me join," Fit said. "I told you I was going to hate it. And guess what? I fucking did!"

"Then I guess they should be given to someone who will *appreciate* them," Dubs said. "And what have I said about watching your language?"

"Whatever." Fit got up from the table and stormed to her room. She yanked open the top drawer of her dresser and grabbed all her swim team bathing suits. They hadn't been used in over a year, but they were *hers*. Was no part of her life safe from River? Fuming, she returned to the kitchen and threw them on the floor. "An assortment to choose from, my lady."

River looked scared, and for a second the image of her in the gray prison jumpsuit entered Fit's mind. Suddenly, Fit felt childish, petty.

"What has gotten into you?" Dubs asked.

"Sorry," Fit said. "A *fucking* assortment to choose from."

The casino hotel's outdoor pool was open June through August, and weekday access was a perk for casino employees and their families. Over the years, Dubs brought Fit and Frankie to the pool every chance he got. It's where he taught them how to swim and make the biggest splash possible with a cannonball. Fit and Frankie liked to pretend they were guests of the hotel, making up their backstories as they splashed. Some days, they were visiting from California, their family living right next to Disneyland, other days, they'd lay on thick Southern accents and pretend they were from Alabama. They never came from the same place twice.

River had borrowed a shirt and a pair of basketball shorts

from Frankie. The clothes hung on her small frame, and from a distance, Fit thought River could pass as a teenager.

The three of them arrived before Pistols and Diamond. They snagged five chairs in the shade.

"I know Dubs made you come, but see," Frankie said, sweeping his arm toward the water. "It's not too shabby."

Fit used to think the hotel pool was one of the classiest places in the world, with its teal and silver bottom, and the three lion head fountains that spit water into the deep end. But the older Fit got, the tackier the place seemed.

"Dubs is stubborn," River said. "I get it."

"Oh, we know," Frankie said, laying his towel over his chair. "Right, Fit?"

She could have pulled a litany of examples from her memory but Fit wanted no part in Frankie and River's small talk and ignored the question.

River sat down on her chair and put on a baseball cap she'd had in her bag. Fit recognized it as Frankie's.

"He taught me how to drive on his old truck, stick shift," River said. "One of the first times he took me out for a lesson, we were in the parking lot of the school. I had managed to get the car going a couple of times without stalling when he says, 'I think we're ready for the open road!' I tried to tell him I wasn't, that I wanted to stay in the parking lot, but he wouldn't hear of it." River laughed, so did Frankie. Fit found herself wanting to smile, remembering how Dubs acted the same way when she had her learner's permit. But she fought the grin, furrowing her brow into a scowl.

Frankie, gazing at River like she was a movie star, asked, "How'd you do?"

"I was okay for a little, but then I stopped at a red light on Route 2. I was nervous and rushing. The car would jerk forward a few inches before stalling again. People behind us were honking, and I wanted to switch places with Dubs. But he said everyone could just hold their horses. Eventually, I—"

"Fancy meeting you here!" Diamond said, seeming to appear out of nowhere. Fit had gotten so wrapped up in picturing River stalled in the middle of the road that she hadn't noticed her friends arrive. "Oh, hey," Fit said. She'd been nervous about Diamond and Pistols meeting River, but Diamond didn't seem phased, asking politely, "Is this your mom?"

"Yep," Frankie said, making the introductions. They all shook hands. Diamond and River exchanged pleasantries, and then Pistols blurted out, "I have an aunt who was in prison for selling pot." Fit chuckled to herself. Diamond slapped Pistols's shoulder before turning to River and apologizing. "He's a freaking idiot."

River seemed not to mind, asking Pistols, "Where was she?"

Pistols thought about it for a second. "Somewhere close to Rhode Island?"

"Riverdale?"

"That's it!"

"I heard they have the best food in New England," River said.

Fit didn't like what was going on. She wanted to slap the smiles off everyone's faces. "What's there? Some sort of prison cooking channel?" Fit shot at River.

River blushed and tried to smile. Fit relished in the discomfort she'd created. After they got settled into their chairs Diamond asked if anyone wanted to play chicken.

"Totally," Fit said.

Frankie made no move for the pool. He was always her partner for chicken. "You coming?"

"In a minute."

"We can't play without you."

"I said I'd be there in a second. I want to hear the end of the story."

Fit threw her shirt on her chair, and it landed there in a rumpled, angry ball. She ran to the pool and cannonballed into the water. She blew out all the air from her lungs, letting herself sink to the bottom. When she hit the tiled floor, she opened her eyes—groups of legs treaded water, bubbles rising around the paddling feet. She listened to the muffled sounds from the surface. Someone jumped in beside her, their wake a rush of swirling water making it impossible to know who it was. Fit imagined it was Frankie, ditching their mom and following her into the pool. Her lungs screamed for air, and she surfaced with a gasp. She rubbed her eyes to clear her vision and saw Pistols treading water next to her. Frankie was still with River, now sitting on the edge of her chair, nodding along to her story.

Frankie joined them in a little while, but no one mentioned a game of chicken. As the afternoon progressed, the sun arcing over the water, Fit did her best to pretend it was a summer day unlike any other. But she kept catching herself looking over at River, who remained in her chair, reading. When Fit realized that she was staring, she'd dunk herself underwater, holding her breath until it hurt.

By the time the sun was hidden behind the casino, they were all pooped, and more than on board with Frankie's suggestion of food court ice cream. River and Frankie led the way, followed by Diamond and Pistols. Fit pulled up the rear, keeping her distance. As they walked through the sliding glass doors, Fit found herself watching the way Diamond moved, how her feet ever so slightly turned inward, her arms swaying softly back and forth. A drop of water snaked its way down Diamond's shoulder and Fit had the urge to trace the drop's path with her finger. She blushed and put her head down, studying the red and yellow zigzag pattern of the carpet underfoot.

They ate their ice cream in the lobby, sitting on the benches across from the aquarium. Fit looked for Maggie, the casino's new octopus, but she was nowhere to be found.

"Everyone's seen her but me," Fit complained.

"Patience, young one," Diamond said, licking her ice cream cone. "Your day will come."

River sat on the end of the bench next to Frankie. "When did they do this?" She pointed her spoon at the tank.

"A while ago," Frankie said. "When I was seven, maybe. How old were you, Fit?"

"I don't know," Fit said, even though she had vivid memories of the aquarium being installed right after her twelfth birthday. "A hundred."

"Dubs hated the casinos when they were first built," River said, ignoring Fit's quip. "He'd always get mad if he found out I was here. But it's become much more—" River paused. "More commercial, I suppose, since the last time I was here."

River sighed and looked down at her ice cream. Fit found herself wondering what it was like in prison, if it was really as bad as it seemed on TV, and, if so, how River had survived. Fit took a bite of her waffle cone. *She deserved it*, she reminded herself as she chewed.

They ate in silence for a minute, until Pistols asked, "Do you know what cell phones are?"

"She wasn't in a fucking cave!" Diamond said, hitting him again.

Pistols shrugged sheepishly and said, "I was just wondering."

River chuckled. "I know what cell phones are. But car phones are still a thing, right?"

They were all silent, until River smiled and said, "Just kidding."

Everyone laughed except Fit. This wasn't how it was supposed to be. Her friends were supposed to hate River, not treat her like some stand-up comedian.

"This is good ice cream," River said. "Real vanilla."

When River finished, she got up and threw the container away, then went to the bathroom. Fit walked up to the aquarium, inspecting it closer, trying to catch a glimpse of the octopus before they went home. After that proved futile, she checked her phone. She had a new email from someone named Reggie Jack, a name she'd never seen before. The subject line read **Talent Agent**.

**Hi, Fitted Sheet!**

**I'm Reggie, Dillon Rain's assistant. Dillon is a talent agent here in New York City. He saw your videos and would love to set up a Skype interview to talk. Let me know if you have any questions. I look forward to hearing from you.**

**Best,**

**Reggie**

As Fit read the email, the casino, her friends, and even River fell away. She read it twice to ensure she hadn't gotten it wrong. "Oh. My. God." She turned to the casino crew, still lined up on the bench. "Oh my god. Oh my god. Oh my god!"

Diamond asked, "What's going on? Is everything okay?" Fit didn't know how to respond so she walked over and handed Diamond her phone.

"Holy shit!" Diamond said after reading the email. "You're going to be *famous*!"

"Let me see," Pistols said, taking the phone from Diamond. Frankie stood on his tiptoes and read the message over Pistols's shoulder.

Fit's heart pounded. "But how do I know if he's legit?" She couldn't believe it. This could be spam. "He could be some crazy person trying to lure me to his car with candy."

"I'll Google him," Diamond said, and, after finding what she was looking for, began to read out loud: "Dillon Rain, senior associate at WeCord Entertainment, has over twenty years blah, blah, blah. He's for real!"

Diamond continued to scroll and said, "Oh, damn."

"What?" Fit asked. "What 'Oh, damn'?!"

"He's the one who discovered Shadin Hane!" Fit screamed. Shadin was YouTube's darling boy turned pop sensation. On his channel he sang and played piano, and his videos regularly got more than twenty million views. His songs were constantly on the radio and he was selling out stadium concerts. Fit hugged Diamond and they both jumped up and down.

"Fit's gonna be famous. Fit's gonna be famous," Diamond sang, clapping her hands.

Fit joined in, singing, "I'm gonna be famous. I'm gonna be famous." She began dancing to the rhythm of the words, and when she turned around she saw River watching them, smiling.

River asked, "What's going on here?"

"Fit's going to be a star," Pistols said.

River looked surprised. "Really?"

"What?" Fit said snidely. "Is that so hard to believe?"

"No," River said. "I'm just wondering what brought this about." Pistols spoke up before Fit could respond. "She got an email from a freaking agent!" Then he looked to Fit and asked, "What are you going to say?"

Diamond slapped his shoulder. "Obviously she's going to say yes, stupid."

"Well, I know that," Pistols shot back. "But *how* are you going to say it?"

Fit asked, "What do you mean?"

"I think you should play it cool." He crossed his arms, attempting to look laid back. "Act like you've got lots of other meetings, but you *suppose* you could fit him in."

"Nuh uh," Diamond said. "You should sound professional. This is business after all."

Fit had no idea how to come across as professional. She looked at Frankie. "What do you think?"

He rubbed the back of his head. "Well—"

"Shouldn't you run all this by your grandfather first?" River said, taking a few steps forward. "See what he thinks?"

Fit glared at River. "And let him ruin this for me with his worrying? No way."

She looked back to Frankie. He crossed his arms and gazed down at the ground. "Well?" she said, growing impatient. "What should I do?"

He shrugged. "How about you just say yes?"

"Okay, okay." Fit took a deep breath and began to type. **Hi Reggie! Of course! I would love to talk to Dillon over Skype. From, Fit**

She read the message aloud to the casino crew and they all nodded their heads approvingly.

"All right," she said, pressing send. "Off it goes." Diamond clapped, Pistols let out a small *whoop*, and it even looked like River was fighting a smile. Exhilarated, Fit had the urge to sprint across the gambling floor, shout at the top of her lungs that she'd hit it big, that she was one step closer to getting out and leaving all this behind.

As the group got ready to head out, Fit walked up to the aquarium and knocked.

"See," she said. "I don't need you, Miss Maggie!"

In the glass, she saw Frankie's reflection. He looked worried, but by the time she turned around, he was gone, following River toward the exit. Fit told herself it must have been a trick of the glass.

The cars rushed by as River walked home from the bus stop, the sound somehow overwhelming yet calming at the same time. Her mouth tasted like rotten citrus. At work she'd tested thirty lemon-flavored flakes, their taste so potent not even a bag of sour cream and onion potato chips could erase the tang from her tongue.

When River turned the corner into the complex's parking lot, she noticed a woman sitting at the bottom of the stairs leading up to the apartments. Her legs were outstretched, and she was smoking a cigarette.

River kept her eyes on the ground as she approached, and when she got close to the stairs, the woman said, "Hi, there."

River looked up, nodded politely, and said, "Hello." She kept on walking, but the woman asked, "You're Jessica's mom, right?"

River froze. She'd been dreading this moment, someone in town recognizing her, ridiculing her for what she'd done. She remained silent.

"Deb Moriarty," the woman said, standing up. "Diamond's mom." They shook hands, and River could see the resemblance.

"I met her at the pool. Nice kid."

Deb took a drag, was quiet for a moment, then said, "Thanks." River still wasn't totally sure what this woman wanted, so she nodded and made a move toward the bottom step, but Deb asked, "How's it going up there?" She gestured her hand up the stairs, flicking the ash off her cigarette. Compared to Dubs's constant pitying questions over the past week, Deb's words sounded genuine. River felt a little more at ease.

"It's fine," she said.

"Yeah?" Deb's skeptical tone struck at something within River's chest, and suddenly she got the urge to tell Deb the truth—that the stay still felt temporary. That she had no idea how to act around her family.

"It's a little cramped," River said. "But we're making it work."

Deb nodded, wiping her forehead with the back of her hand. "Supposed to be this hot all week."

"Really?"

"Yep."

"My dad refuses to buy an air conditioner," River said. "He set up a bunch of fans. But they don't do much."

Deb laughed, a broad, warm noise that River found inviting. "I've heard all about it from Jessica. I've got an A/C in my room. Sometimes, when it's blistering out, she and Diamond camp out on my floor."

River pictured her daughter sleeping next to this woman's bed. She wanted to ask if Fit snored or talked in her sleep. If she still kicked off her covers in the middle of the night. Jealousy filled River's throat. She swallowed, the taste of rotten lemon suddenly overwhelming her. Pointing at the pack of cigarettes on the front step, she asked, "Can I have one?"

"Be my guest."

River hadn't smoked in years, but the first inhale was sweet and thick, so pungent it masked the putrid taste of lemon. The smoke formed a light pink circle in her mind. They stood there for a few moments, smoking in silence, until Fit's voice came from the top of the stairs. River looked up and saw Fit and Diamond approaching.

"Where are you two off to?" Deb asked, her voice now carrying an air of motherhood.

"Out," Diamond said.

"Be back by eleven."

Fit stopped a few steps above River, and they made eye contact. The thought flashed through River's mind that Fit was waiting to be told what time she should be home. Instead, Fit pointed at the cigarette smoldering in River's hand, and said, "Dubs fucking hates that shit."

"Hey!" Deb said. "Cut that out."

"Sorry, Mrs. M.," Fit said, walking down the rest of the stairs. Embarrassed, River let the half-finished cigarette fall to the ground and crushed it with her heel.

Drained from work and lightheaded from the cigarette, River went inside and asked Dubs if she could take a nap. "You don't have to ask," he answered.

River lay in bed but couldn't fall asleep. She shoved her face into one of the pillows and tried to distinguish the smell. Laundry detergent? No. It hadn't been washed since she moved in. The smell, she realized, was her own. An off-white circle with undefined edges formed in her mind. Instead of napping, she studied the waifish shape for an hour.

Later that night, River and Dubs ate Chinese takeout alone in front of the TV. They watched a show about a group of detectives trying to solve the murder of an art dealer. River tried to pay attention, but she kept thinking about her small run-in with Deb and Fit, waves of embarrassment and jealousy hitting her all over again. It was during a commercial break that Dubs brought up the idea of therapy.

"Therapy?" River said. "For me?"

"I want to make sure that you have a support system."

River figured he'd been reading the packet of literature the halfway house had sent her home with. *Support system.* Those weren't his words.

"I'm fine, Dad," she said. "Promise." He tilted his head down and looked at her over the rim of his square glasses. His eyebrows crinkled upward, accentuating the wrinkles in his forehead. It was the same look he always gave her on his twice-a-month visits, when he'd eventually ask, "You feeling okay? Are you getting the care you need?" And River had known what those questions really meant: *Have they fixed you yet? Have they exorcised the part that's not my daughter?*

"Think about it?" Dubs said. "I know you had your women's group. And that was important, I think."

River looked at him, wondered how crushed he would be if he found out there was no such group. She felt guilty about having lied to him while she was in prison, but there were only so many times she could say "I'm fine. I don't need help," before she finally broke and told him, "I joined a support group. For moms." It hadn't been a *total* fabrication. River belonged to a crocheting group, and some of the women had children. The crocheters used plastic hooks, which had to be counted before and after every class, and they were taught three patterns: a doily, a scarf, and a small stuffed bear. They weren't allowed to use black yarn—which River had learned from one of the women was because of gang-related reasons—so every bear ended up with blue or green eyes. River had become friendly with some of the women, but for the most part she kept to herself, letting her mind get lost in the loop and pull of the yarn.

"Sure," River said, adding another lie to the pile. "I'll think about it." She took a bite of her chicken. It was spicy, and magenta bursts swam up the side of her vision.

When the show about the detectives ended, Dubs asked, "What do you want to watch?" River had no idea what programs were on television. There'd been one TV in the common room of the halfway house, but she never felt like joining in the fight for the remote.

Before prison, River never would have described herself as a pushover. She loved outwitting an opponent in an argument, Dubs always joking that she should be a lawyer. And Seth, her high school sweetheart turned husband, always called her "Miss Particular," claiming that around her he could never get away with being an idiot. But somewhere along the line River had lost that spark. She hadn't even been able to muster a fistful of despair when, three years into her sentence, a lawyer showed up at the prison with divorce papers and a custody agreement that made Dubs legal guardian of the children. She'd signed it without a fuss, thinking, *This is what I get.*

Dubs held the remote out to River. She declined. "You pick."

"C'mon, you've got to want to watch something."

River didn't, but to appease Dubs she asked, "Do they still play reruns of *I Love Lucy?*"

"Let's see." Dubs held the remote to his mouth and said, "I-Love-Lucy," annunciating the words as if he were talking to someone hard of hearing.

When he'd done this a few nights earlier, River was perplexed until Dubs's command had pulled up a list of shows on the screen.

*I Love Lucy* wasn't on. "I can record it," Dubs said.

River shook her head. "What we're watching is fine." She fought sleep through another episode. The actors all talked too fast and everything seemed incredibly fake. When it was over she stood up from the couch and said, "Can I go to bed?"

"You can sleep whenever you wanna, kid," Dubs said. *Kid.* River knew Dubs meant it as a term of endearment, but the word cut her at the knees, made her feel foolish.

As she tried to fall asleep, River couldn't stop thinking about the look of disgust on Fit's face as she'd walked down the stairs. A look that proved that Fit could see what Dubs and Frankie couldn't, that burnt-to-a-crisp kernel. River replayed the scene again, but this time she imagined herself stopping Fit from leaving the last step and saying, "Show me where it is, Jessica. I'll dig it out with my bare hands if I have to."

Fit sat on the floor of Diamond's bedroom, holding Diamond's pet rabbit, Dolores, in her lap. Fit had just Skyped with Dillon, and as she ran her hand over Dolores's soft fur, she attempted to process the details of the meeting.

Reggie had responded to Fit's email almost immediately, setting up a time for a Skype meeting the next day. Fit barely had time to get nervous. Dillon had been nice yet direct, and the conversation only lasted a few minutes. From what she could see in her screen, he was wearing a suit jacket and tie, his hair a shock of dark, and the edges of his goatee were so precise it looked like they'd been drawn on with a Sharpie.

"Sooo," Diamond said. "How'd it go?"

"He wants me to go to New York," Fit said, still stunned. That had been the main purpose of the call—Dillon inviting her to come meet with him in the WeCord offices in New York City. Fit had excitedly accepted, but it wasn't until she spoke the words to Diamond that the notion fully sunk in. "Holy shit. He wants me to go to New York!"

"Damn. Hide me in your backpack!"

"I wish," Fit said. She had actually asked if Diamond could come along, not as her friend, but as her chaperone. At the very end of the call Dillon had confirmed Fit was seventeen, and said, "Since you're a minor, you'll need an adult to accompany you." To which Fit responded, "My best friend is eighteen.

Does that count?" Dillon said no, that the adult needed to be a relative or guardian.

Diamond continued to pry. She wanted to hear everything, and Fit had to think. The call had gone by so quickly.

"Oh!" Fit said. "He said I should make more videos."

"About what?"

"Whatever I want," Fit said, practically repeating Dillon's words. "He called the internet a 'hungry beast.' And I've got to feed it."

At this, Diamond burst into laughter. "He said that?"

"Swear to god," Fit said.

Diamond got up and swooped Dolores from Fit's lap. "Are you a hungry beast?" Diamond asked her rabbit, then, to Fit, "Now get up and sit on my bed."

Fit did as she was told. Diamond plopped Dolores back into Fit's lap, then stood in the middle of the room and aimed her phone at Fit. "Ask Dolores a question."

Fit laughed. "C'mon."

"Just do it. Any question."

Fit looked at Dolores. The rabbit's nose twitched, and her eyes looked like two black marbles. "What's your favorite food?"

Diamond spoke in a cartoonish voice. "My human let me try a Dorito last week." Fit bit her lip to keep a straight face; Diamond sounded ridiculous. "Best thing I've ever eaten."

"Oh yeah? What kind of Dorito?"

"Cool Ranch. I fucking love Cool Ranch."

Fit tapped Dolores lightly on the top of the head. "I didn't know rabbits swore so much."

"Learned it from my human."

Fit looked at Diamond, and Diamond mouthed, "Keep going."

"Do you like your human?"

"Girl! She's the baddest bitch."

Fit sighed, smiled. "Yeah. I guess she's all right."

"Hey! Wanna dance?"

Fit stood up and held Dolores like a baby that needed to be burped. "I thought you'd never ask." Humming a song she imagined people would waltz to, Fit began to spin around in slow circles.

"You're a good dancer," Diamond said.

Fit closed her eyes. Dolores's whiskers tickled her ear as she continued to sway. "So are you."

Fit knew that if this were a cheesy rom-com now would be the moment where she'd stick out her hand and ask Diamond to dance. Instead, she held Dolores up over her head and said, "You can fly!"

When they were done filming, Diamond flopped down in the bean bag chair in the corner of her room, and asked, "So, did Dillon say what's going to happen in this meeting?"

"Not really," Fit responded. Much of what Dillon had said sounded like code—marketability, target audience, conversions—and she'd had a hard time keeping up with it all. "He said we'll discuss next steps."

"Next steps?" Diamond said. "What the heck does that mean?"

"I dunno," Fit said. She hadn't gotten the chance to think about that yet. Was he going to sign her on right away? Have a brand deal waiting for her? This was an unknown world to her, the business side of things, and she began to feel the enormity of the situation. "Maybe I'll show up and he'll just give me a million dollars."

Diamond smiled and rolled her eyes. "Well, right."

"I just hope Dubs doesn't make things too embarrassing."

"Imagine him in New York?" Diamond said, picking at a string hanging off the worn bean bag chair.

"That's going to be something, huh?" Fit said, doing her best impression of her grandpa, and they both started to crack up.

When Fit got home from Diamond's, Frankie, River, and Dubs were playing a card game at the kitchen table. Frankie asked, "Want me to deal you in?" Fit hadn't told him about her Skype call with Dillon yet. She was excited to share the news with him, and on her short walk back to the apartment she'd thought about what she would tell Frankie first: how Dillon said Fit's got that weird humor that's all the rage right now or how he'd practically *begged* her to come to New York. But when River chimed in, saying, "We just started," Fit stalked off to her room without a word.

The next day, the temperatures reached into the nineties. its hot af in this apartment, Fit texted to the casino crew. arcade?

In the coolness of the arcade, Fit was tracking a squirrel on *Fred Trucker's Hunting Adventure*—a POV shooter game she had gotten quite good at over the years—when Diamond came up and started watching. "Ten bucks you miss," Diamond said.

"You're on." The squirrel sat on the tree branch and flicked its tail back and forth. Fit trained the gun on it, her finger on the trigger. The gray animal jumped from the branch. She took the shot, missed. GAME OVER flashed on the screen. Fit put the red plastic gun back in its holder.

"That would've been cool," Diamond said.

Fit and Diamond met up with Pistols and Frankie, who

were playing *Dance Dance Revolution*. Frankie had a real knack for the game, jumping flawlessly from arrow to arrow. Pistols, who always fell short of Frankie's score, looked clumsy in comparison.

Diamond taunted her cousin. "You're a half second off." She did a drum roll on the side of the game. "Better catch up!"

"Shut up," Pistols said between moves.

Diamond leaned on the side of the machine. "So, what did Dubs say about New York?"

"Haven't gotten a chance to ask yet," Fit said. It was a half-truth. She hadn't wanted to ask him during the card game the night before, but when she saw him that morning, she chickened out. Dubs never quite understood what Fit did online. He told her her videos were cute but always brushed it aside when Fit told him it could be her career.

"New York?" Frankie said, jumping to cross his legs. The moves on the screen flashed green, indicating he'd gotten the points.

Diamond raised her eyebrows. "Didn't know it was a secret."

"It's not," Fit said. Her words came out loud, compensating for the fact that when she'd gone into her room the night before and listened to the sounds of the happy card game, she felt devious, even happy that she had a secret.

"What don't I know?" Frankie's feet sped up. Pistols was breathing heavy, doing his best to keep up.

"Mr. Agent Man wants Fit to go to New York," Diamond said. Frankie stopped playing, the moves he missed lighting up red.

"When did this happen?"

"Just yesterday," Fit said. "We Skyped."

Frankie asked, "Can I go?"

"Nah," Diamond said. "She already asked if I could go, and Dillon shut that shit down."

Frankie looked at Fit like he'd been tricked. Behind him, his score continued to fall. Fit pointed at the screen. "You're losing."

The game ended, and Pistols bent over, huffing. "Dude. I won. Can't believe I actually beat you."

Frankie jumped off the game. "Good for you." He headed toward the exit. It was the Fourth of July weekend. The casino had a huge fireworks display every year, one of the biggest in the area. As a result, the arcade was packed, and Fit lost sight of Frankie before he reached the door.

As a child, River's favorite holiday was Fourth of July. Her family hosted a huge block party every year. The whole neighborhood came, and each year the celebration seemed to grow larger and larger. Her dad was in charge of the grill, and her mom, with potato salad in one hand and coleslaw in the other, would weave between guests, making everyone feel like they were her favorite visitor. And when the sun went down, Dubs put on a fireworks show that rivaled that of the professionals. He prepared for weeks, taking several trips to New Hampshire where he could buy fireworks that weren't legal in Connecticut. He'd return with a trunk full of brightly colored cylinders with names like "The Sky King" and "Cloud Splitter" written on the side. River always asked if she could go with him, and the answer was always no. "I don't want you in the car with those bad boys," he would say. The restriction made it all the more exciting for River, each burst in the sky another act of defiance.

She thought about all this as she sat on the curb outside the apartment complex, her knees pulled into her chest. Earlier that day, Dubs had grilled for the family and a few neighbors. And now that the sun had set, River watched her father hand out sparklers to her kids and their friends. She was happy to be celebrating the holiday away from the stark walls of the prison, but the small display made her sad. The firework shows Dubs used to put on made all the dogs within a mile radius lose their minds.

Frankie walked up to her, held out an unlit sparkler. "Want one?"

She shook her head. "Maybe in a bit."

Frankie lit both sparklers and held one in each hand.

"Spin, Frankie!" Fit called out to him from across the parking lot. She was pointing her phone in his direction. "Spin."

River was fascinated by Fit's need to document everything, and she wondered if Fit went back and looked at everything she recorded. Or, if knowing the moment was there, saved on her phone, was enough.

Frankie followed Fit's orders and spun. The trailing light of the two sparklers encircled him, growing brighter and moving faster as he went. There was no way a phone could capture the overwhelming beauty of Frankie in that moment. River wanted to snatch the phone away from her daughter and say, "You're missing it!" The sooty smell of the sparkler hit her nose, and black and yellow specks began to form in her mind. *Not now*, she thought, pushing the colors away.

The neighborhood kids returned home after all the sparklers were used, and Dubs set up a few beach chairs in the open-air hallway outside the apartment.

"Not the best view," he said gesturing toward the road. "But it's too stuffy to go back inside." A few booms erupted in the distance.

"There goes the casino," Frankie said.

"We can't see them from here," Dubs added, "But we'll get the smoke soon enough."

River went in to use the bathroom. The air in the apartment was damp and noticeably warmer than outside. After washing her hands, she noticed a speck of dirt on her cheek. She wiped it away, but when the spot smudged, trailing a dark line across her skin, she realized it was ash. The soot had worked its way into the lines of her fingertips. She licked the tip of one of her fingers, trying to discern the taste.

Dubs and Fit were arguing when she went back outside.

"I don't have any time off," her father said, shaking his head. "Remember? Got my bunion removed. That sucked up all my leave."

Fit curled her lip. "Gross."

River sat down next to Frankie. It had only been a week, but she felt like they were already growing closer. Frankie would sit in the living room, working on his art, while River read a magazine or flipped through the endless channels on TV. One day, she landed on a show about two young men who were searching for ghosts. "I used to think my room was haunted," Frankie had said. "Almost every night I'd hide under the covers, terrified." He continued with his story, explaining to River how the second he heard a noise, any noise, he ran into Fit's room and crawled into her bed. When they grew too tall and too old for the same bed, Frankie would sleep on the floor. "Wow," River muttered when he told her this, when all she really wanted to say was, "That's the most beautiful thing I've ever heard."

River wondered what Fit and Dubs were arguing about. She looked to Frankie for answers.

"You know that email that Fit got? From the agent." Frankie kept his voice down, like he was a zookeeper talking about an animal stalking its prey. "He wants to meet with her next week, but she needs a chaperone. But Dubs over here claims he can't get time off on an account of his bum foot."

Frankie's hushed voice apparently wasn't quiet enough and Dubs said, "It was a *bunion*." Dubs tapped his foot on the ground. "Good as new."

"And a chaperone?" Fit joined in. "What is this—third grade? I need an adult. For *legal* reasons. Or some shit."

Fit and Dubs began bickering again. Frankie jumped into the argument, and the three of them fell into a pattern of fighting that could only develop from years of knowing someone. Like a choreographed dance. This is what it must have been like for her children growing up, River thought, Dubs having created a place for Fit and Frankie to be themselves. The faint scent of burnt paper could be detected in the air, and River fought to keep a gray circle at bay. She wanted to fade into the background, watch her family as they had been when she wasn't there. But then, she had an idea, and before she could chicken out, she said, "I'm an adult."

The three of them looked at her. "I'm an adult," she repeated, louder this time. The casino fireworks had stopped, and a car revved off in the distance.

Dubs clasped his hands together. "Welp. That is true."

Frankie said, "Yeah, Fit. It's a way you could go."

River couldn't help but feel a little proud of her suggestion. Fit looked down at her phone, the glow lighting her face. She flicked at the screen with her thumb, and said, "No fucking way."

The words took a few seconds for River to register, her newly formed hopes of traveling with her daughter dashed in three words. She took a deep breath, smelling the traces of the lingering fireworks residue, stretched the gray circle as wide as it could go, and disappeared into it.

"You asked for it, so here it is!" Fit said into the camera. "A day in my life."

Fit had polled her fans on what type of video they wanted her to film, and the suggestions poured in. They wanted to see more raps, how-to's, and one fan even wrote that she should record a duet with her mom. **f you!** Fit responded. But she was surprised to see a large volume of requests come in for "a day in the life vlog." Fit had seen lots of YouTubers do this sort of video, but she never thought her regular life was exciting enough to keep people interested. Other YouTube stars always tried to downplay how cool their life was, attempting to make themselves look unglamorous as they ran errands in their nice cars, played with their beautiful dogs, or went to meet with the editors of their books. In comparison, Fit had nothing.

It was the morning after the Fourth of July weekend, and Diamond's mom was driving Fit to the casino.

"Say 'hello,'" Fit said, pointing the camera at Mrs. M., who waved, then flicked the ash of her cigarette out of the window. Mrs. M. was a housekeeper at the casino's hotel and would often bring Diamond and Fit along on the busy days, like during a big concert or a holiday weekend. It paid minimum wage, but the tips were good, and sometimes Fit walked away from a shift with over a hundred dollars in cash. Diamond was supposed to come too, but that morning she'd woken up "sick."

In reality, Fit knew Diamond was playing hooky so she could play paintball with Riley and a group of his friends.

In the employee locker room, Fit changed into her uniform. The black button-down shirt was two sizes too large. The casino's logo sat over the chest pocket: red and yellow circles with the words "TWIN SUNS" embroidered below. The black pants were always too tight at the waist but baggy everywhere else. She filmed a quick shot of herself in the full-length mirror. "Don't I look fancy?"

Recording herself walk down the hallway, she pushed the cart to her first room. "Let's see what trash heap awaits us," she said, opening the door. The mess wasn't too bad. The sheets were rumpled on the bed, wet towels covered the bathroom floor, and a few pieces of junk were in the garbage bin. But other than that, it was tame compared to some of the damage she'd seen before. There was a twenty on the stand by the bed. She snapped herself waving the money in front of her face.

She attempted to film as much as possible as she cleaned, but soon realized how difficult it was doing everything one-handed. How did other YouTubers make vlogging look so easy? Instead, she opted for an after shot. "Spick-and-span," she said, scanning the room that was now in check-in condition.

As she got ready to leave the room she looked into the camera and said, "Okay, now we're going to play a fun game. It's called 'let's be a ghost.'"

When Fit wore the housekeeping uniform it was like she became invisible, like people didn't acknowledge that she was a real human being. She put the phone in her breast pocket, with the camera sticking out, still recording.

Two people were walking down the hall in her direction. The first was an older man in a suit, holding a newspaper and a cup of coffee. When he got closer, Fit said, "Morning." He kept his eyes forward, not looking at her, and gave the slightest nod of his head.

Doing her best impression of a sportscaster, she said, "And we're off to a good start."

The next person approaching was a young woman holding a bucket of ice and wearing a plush bathrobe provided by the hotel.

Fit smiled real wide and said, "Howdy." The woman looked straight ahead and popped an ice cube in her mouth.

"And there we have it folks," Fit said, tilting her head down to make sure the microphone was picking up her words. "Two for two."

As much as she despised the guests of the hotel, she always got the urge to explain herself to them. "This is temporary!" she wanted to shout after the woman with the bucket. "I'm more than this!"

Fit went about the rest of the rooms on the floor, cleaning them as fast as she could. Most of the guests left decent tips, and in one room she filmed herself lip-synching along to Adele's "Hello."

The room at the end of the hallway had two full-sized beds and a small sitting area. It wasn't quite a suite—those were found on the uppermost floors—but it was a little bigger than a normal hotel room. It smelled like cigarette smoke, and there was a cup on the bedside table with a few cigarette butts floating in it, the water stained a yellowish brown. The whole floor was non-smoking, and hotel protocol required Fit to call the front desk so a $250 "cigarette smoke cleaning fee" could be added to the guests's bill. She planned to do that after she cleaned.

When she walked around the side of the bed closest to the window, she screamed. There was a puddle of puke on the carpet. The smell of smoke must have masked the odor of the vomit. As she looked at the light-yellow oval, her stomach turned and her orange juice crept up her throat. She ran to the bathroom and threw up in the toilet. She sat on the cool floor of the bathroom for a minute, and when she stood up and looked in the mirror, she saw her face had lost all its color save for her bloodshot eyes.

Fit called the front desk. "We've got a puker."

"Guess they had a fun weekend, huh?" the woman on the phone said. "I'll send a wet vac up."

Fit rested in the sitting area, but she swore she could still smell the puke, so she moved into the hallway and waited there.

"I don't understand people," Fit said to her camera. "Why would you ralph and leave it there? It's a hotel!" A little bit of color had returned to her face. "It's not like you're going to have to clean it up yourself. So don't leave it in the room for housekeeping to almost fucking step—"

A sharp voice cut her off: "No phones while you're on the clock." The hotel's general manager, Winona, was approaching, pushing the vacuum in front of her. It was weird seeing Winona out on the floor. She barely left her office. None of the staff liked her and Winona made it obvious the feeling was mutual.

"Didn't know you made house calls," Fit said, her video still rolling.

"We're slammed." Winona held her hand out. "Now give me your phone."

"Sorry. I'll put it away."

"You wanna get written up?" Winona raised her eyebrows. She had a round face and a dark ponytail that looked so tight Fit wondered if it gave her a headache.

"Po-po's here. Gotta go." Fit turned off the video and handed her phone to Winona. Fit wanted to call her a bitch, but she held her tongue. As much as she hated the job, she needed the money.

Winona left the vacuum next to Fit. "You can come see me after your shift."

Fit cleaned up the vomit. The vacuum made a gross slurping noise, and she had to stop twice to gag. Then she finished up the rest of the room as fast as she could, giving the bathroom a quick wipe down and throwing the sheets on the bed, not even caring if the linens were smoothed out or if the corners were crisp. Right when she was about to leave, she remembered she was supposed to call the front desk and let them know about the smoking violation.

"Fuck that," she said to the empty room.

The vacuum was too large to haul around for the rest of the shift, so she left it outside of the room, figuring someone from facilities would stumble upon it and return it to the right place.

As she walked down the hall, heading for the elevator, she reached in her pocket to check her phone, panicking when she remembered it was gone. Out of habit, Fit kept checking for her phone over the course of her shift and a sting of loneliness hit her each time. She tried not to think about it, but she couldn't shake the ache of isolation. It clung to her as she moved from dirty room to dirty room, and at moments the feeling grew so strong it flared up into anger. Anger at Winona for being a big, old bitch, anger at Diamond for ditching her, anger at herself for getting her phone taken away in the first place. Fit turned the TV on in each room to distract herself from the feeling that part of her was missing. Without her phone she didn't have her fans, and without her fans she was no one.

As she wiped down the counters and vacuumed the carpet, she drafted mean tweets in her head that she planned to post after she got her phone back: **tfw ur bitch of a manager takes**

**your phone for three hours; think she's jealous because i have a life; WINONA THE BITCHIEST BITCH OF THE WEST.** And she couldn't wait for her fans' reactions. For them to like and retweet and to ask her **what's wrong?!?**

Fit marched into Winona's office as soon as her shift was done. Winona's phone, which was sitting face up on her desk, buzzed, the screen lighting up to show she received a text message.

"I thought phones were forbidden on the clock," Fit said.

Winona glared at Fit. "I'm management." She pulled Fit's phone from her desk drawer. At the sight of the purple, glittery case, Fit's shoulders relaxed. She snatched the phone from Winona's hand and started to check what she missed.

After changing, Fit waited in the lobby for Mrs. M. Their shift ended at the same time, but Mrs. M. was a shift manager and often got caught up doing paperwork. Fit bounced around from her Snapchat to her Twitter to her Facebook and back to Snapchat, a circuit of media Fit was happy to have back. She was so engrossed in her screen she didn't hear Mrs. M. approach.

"She's busy today."

Fit looked up. "Huh?" Mrs. M. pointed at the aquarium. Maggie, the octopus, was climbing up the side of the glass, legs fully outstretched, her body looking like a large purple asterisk. Maggie had probably been there the entire time Fit had been waiting. Fit walked up to the glass and stretched her arms out. Maggie's legs stretched farther. "Damn."

Mrs. M. asked, "Impressive, right?"

Fit nodded. She took a picture of Maggie, in all her glory, and sent it to the casino crew: **finally!**

Fit edited her vlog that night. She'd filmed some in the car after her shift, explaining why she'd gotten her phone taken away. She also filmed a little bit when she got home as the whole family watched TV. She made sure to keep River out of the frame.

Using some of the fan art she'd hung on her walls as the backdrop, she recorded the outro from her bed. "Like I said, you turds asked for this. So if it sucks, it sucks. Don't come crying to me." She blew a kiss to the camera. "Love you guys!"

The part where Winona confiscated her phone fell in the middle of the vlog. Fit had decided to blur out the faces of the two patrons she had walked past in the hallway, but she left Winona's face visible. She doubted Winona would ever see the video, but also Fit just didn't care. Let Winona get mad. She paused at different moments of the footage, seeing where it would be best to jump cut to herself shouting, "Bitch really took my phone!" in the front seat of Diamond's mom's car. Fit liked making cuts abrupt or disjointed, thinking it added to the comedic effect. She stopped on a frame where Winona held her hand out; Fit zoomed in on her face. Winona's lips curled slightly and what Fit had interpreted at the time as snarl was actually a smirk. In that frozen moment, Winona was enjoying playing the villain. She enjoyed being in control, holding the tiny amount of power she held over Fit's head. And the powerlessness that Fit had felt when she'd watched Winona trot off with her phone returned, amplified. "Screw that," Fit said, getting up from her bed.

When River had first suggested she could accompany Fit to New York, Fit reacted out of instinct, spitting the words before even entertaining the possibility. But now as she thought about how she didn't want to be bossed around by lowlifes like

Winona for the rest of her life, her stubbornness loosened, gave way.

Dubs was gone, working the night shift, and River slept in his bed. Fit opened the door to Dubs's room as quietly as she could. She stood in the doorway for a second, scared. Pushing through her fear, she began to walk forward. When Fit was only a step or two from the bed, River sat straight up, so fast it was like she'd been pulled by a string, her arms swinging out in front of her. To add to the frightening display, her half open eyes seemed to gaze at something far off in the distance. Fit was out of River's reach, but she still jumped back.

River's eyes focused, her face filling with shock. "Oh my god. Are you okay?"

Fit's heart thumped in her throat, but she played it cool. "Light sleeper?"

River ran her hand over her face. "I suppose."

"That's some spidey-sense shit." Standing there, Fit wanted her mother to say something horrible, to give Fit a reason to turn around and hightail it out of there. But River sat in front of her, silent, tiny, and frail like a baby bird. Fit had a hard time mustering the energy for hate.

"Are you still willing to go?"

"Go?"

"New York."

River nodded. "Oh. Yeah. Of course."

"Cool," Fit said, and left the room before River could say anything else.

On the Skype call, Dillon had told Fit to email his assistant with Dubs's full name for the train ticket, so when Fit got back to her room she started an email to Reggie: **My grandpa can't come, but**—Fit paused. She cringed at using the word "mom," but would it be weird if she'd called River "River" in the email?

She ran through the different options in her mind and then wrote, **but the name for the ticket will be River Underwood [mother].**

After she sent the email, she finished editing her vlog, no longer getting pissed off when she looked at Winona's face, and posted the video before she went to bed, the title coming to her in a flash: **F\*CK YOU WINONA (she stole my phone!!).**

River had a hard time falling asleep after Fit had woken her up. She'd stared at the ceiling most of the night wondering, *Did that really happen?* The next morning she sat at the kitchen table, bleary-eyed and groggy, and told Dubs the news. A small flicker of surprise crossed his face. He put his coffee down, cleared his throat, and said, "Huh, isn't that something."

"I guess," River said.

Dubs got up from the table, rinsed his cup in the sink, and said, "It'll be good for you. The both of you." He put his mug in the drying rack, and on his way out of the kitchen he leaned down and kissed River on the top of the head. "Sorry I can't bring you to work today," he said. "But we can talk more about the trip tonight." He smiled. "I told you she just needed some time."

Dubs hummed a tune to himself as he grabbed his truck keys and headed out the door. River should be excited, she told herself. But when she thought about the trip, all she could feel was a cold sense of dread at the bottom of her stomach.

The dread subsided when she got to work, and for most of the day the only thing that mattered was the saltiness of potato flakes as they dissolved on the tip of her tongue. But at the end of the day when she got off the bus and started walking back to the apartment, the pressure of Dubs's optimism returned. So when she saw Deb, Diamond's mom, unloading grocery bags from the trunk of her car, River offered to help.

"If you wanna," Deb said, handing River a bag.

Deb's apartment had the same layout as Dubs's, except her kitchen was open and a small counter separated the eating area from the living room. After they'd brought up the last load of groceries, the counter now full of bags, Deb said, "Want a glass of wine? Lemonade?" River's parole officer, who had only checked in once so far, said River should steer clear of getting "rip-roaring drunk" but the occasional drink was fine.

"I'll have some wine, sure," River said, trying to think of the last drink she'd had. Deb poured them both a glass of white wine, crisp and tart.

River sat at the counter, and Deb started to put the groceries away. "I heard you're going to New York," Deb said, putting a box of cereal on top of the fridge. River took another sip of her wine, its taste evoking the color of an unripened pear. She did her best to smile and said, "Word travels fast."

"The girls were over here earlier trying on outfits. Made a mess."

River chuckled. "It's a big opportunity."

"For you too," Deb said. And the anxiety that River had been trying to ignore bubbled up. Did everyone think this trip was going to be some magical fix? That Fit was suddenly going to forgive her? "You're getting a free trip to New York," Deb went on, grabbing a bunch of bananas.

River's neck eased. "Right." She turned and looked at the living room. "So, Jess spent a lot of time here growing up?"

Deb paused, put her hands on the counter, and said, "Yep. And Frankie. When the girls let him tag along." Deb surveyed the living room, like she was remembering something. River scanned the rug and the couch, trying to see what Deb was seeing, but all that stood before her was an empty room. Maybe it was the half glass of wine, the sleepy feeling in her eyes, but River said, "I've been gone a long time."

"That you were," Deb said casually, as if River had told her she had been caught in the rain. Deb pushed herself away from the counter, returning her focus to the unpacked groceries. "But not anymore."

When River was done, she thanked Deb for the wine, and headed out. All she'd eaten all day were potato flakes, so her mind was fuzzy and tepid as she walked down the breezeway. She thought about how quickly Dubs's face had shifted that morning from astonishment to hope, and if River were being honest, the small, shimmering thought of *What if?* had been bugging her all day. It was a strange feeling for River, as she'd stopped thinking about hope a long time ago, tamping it down with the rest of the hurt. The moment was fleeting, though, and as she rounded the final corner to the apartment, she listened to the dark whispering inside her: *Don't be stupid.*

Fit was up before her alarm. She'd barely gotten any sleep, running the details of her visit to New York over and over in her mind. Her meeting with Dillon was scheduled for noon and Reggie had purchased Fit and River early morning train tickets that got them to Penn Station at 10:36. A town car would pick them up.

A CAR! Diamond texted after Fit told her about the plan. WHO ARE YOU? It felt weird to Fit too. Almost like it wasn't really happening. She responded, im fitted sheet baby.

Fit had planned out her outfit the night before: a blue acid-wash crop top, high-waisted jeans, pink Converse, and a black fitted baseball cap with #LIT embroidered on the front, which Diamond had let her borrow. She got dressed and did her makeup, redoing her winged eyeliner three times until it was even on both sides. She put her hat on, inspected herself in the mirror, and thought she looked good, like someone who deserved to meet with a talent agent.

Dubs was at the kitchen table reading a section of the newspaper. River sat across from him, doing a crossword puzzle, dressed in khakis and a pea green polo shirt. It was a variation of the same outfit River had worn since she got back—khakis and a polo—but, for some reason, Fit had figured River would switch it up for their trip to New York. "You're wearing that?"

River looked down at her shirt, then back at Fit. "Me?"

"We're going to New York City." Fit paused for emphasis

between the last few words, like the beats of silence would explain to River that the outfit wasn't going to fly.

"I think you both look nice," Dubs said.

"She's going to stick out like a freaking sore thumb."

Dubs bristled. "Language."

"Freaking is not a swear." Then she added "Jesus" for good measure, the widening of his eyes—a signal for *stop right now*—somehow calming her nerves.

River said, "It's not like I'm the one they want to meet."

Fit knew that, but she was terrified of showing up to the meeting and reeking of small town, and Dillon would think she'd tricked him into thinking she was cooler than she was. Or worse, he'd sniff out their history.

Fit whined, "But it's about the whole *vibe.*"

"I have a purple shirt," River offered, "If you think that'd be better?"

Fit groaned and sighed, then stomped back to her room. She looked through her closet for something for River to wear, something that said, "I'm a normal mom" and "I love making casseroles!" Most of Fit's clothes were thrifted, her and Diamond often raiding Goodwill racks. She finally decided on a black, flowy T-shirt with a lace detail at the shoulders, and a light gray jean jacket. "Here," she said, putting the clothes on the kitchen table.

After River went into Dubs's room to get changed, Dubs looked at Fit, obviously annoyed. "Was all that really necessary?"

Fit crossed her arms. "Extremely."

The top was a bit long on River, but other than that it fit nicely. She held the jacket in her hand. "It's too hot for this right now."

Fit wanted to tell River she looked good, normal even. But

she hurled those thoughts to the side, pointed at River's white clunky sneakers, and said, "Too bad you've got such tiny feet."

As they were about to leave, Fit knocked on Frankie's door because he'd mentioned wanting to drive with them to the train station. There was no answer, and she figured he was still asleep. He'd been hanging out with Pistols the night before, and she'd heard him come in late. She knocked again. Nothing. As she marched away she grumbled, "See if I thank you in my acceptance speech."

They got to the train station early.

"You don't have to stay," Fit said to Dubs as the three of them waited on the platform. He looked at his watch.

"I've got time."

Fit knew he had to be at work in half an hour and would be cutting it close, but she was grateful to not be left alone with River.

The train platform was next to the Long Island Sound. A slow line of people filed onto a large ferry docked in the water, seagulls swooped overhead, and three boys performed skateboard tricks on the pier. Fit had been to New London many times, walking through downtown and along the water, but she'd never stepped foot on the train platform, ready to go somewhere. Everything looked different somehow. Like the air was fuzzy with rain or static. The noise of the seagulls annoyed her, the ferry looked decrepit, and every time one of the boys missed a trick Fit just wanted to yell, "Land one already!"

The approaching train sounded its horn. Everyone on the platform was dressed in a suit or carrying a briefcase, looking nonplussed, like they were waiting in line at the grocery store. Fit did her best to mimic their expressions.

She hugged Dubs, and he said, quietly, "Be nice."

Fit grinned. "When am I not?" He kissed her on the forehead and she wished he was coming with them.

Fit and River found two seats next to each other. Fit looked out the window, trying to find Dubs on the platform, but he must have left already. River was quiet as they pulled away from the station. Fit's stomach buzzed with excitement. She thought about texting Frankie or Diamond, but they'd both be asleep, so she distracted herself with Snapchat. She filmed the houses going by, took pictures of the seats, and when the conductor came by to punch their tickets, she took a snap of him, circled his hat, and wrote, *sexy*.

Almost immediately her fans wanted to know where she was going. Dillon had made it clear the meeting was informational only, requesting she not make any public announcements. "I can't promise anything," he'd explained. But Fit had to tell her fans something. "Hey freaks!" she said into her camera. "I know you all want to know what I'm up to. As soon as I'm allowed to say anything, I promise you'll be the first know." She pretended to kiss the camera.

River chuckled.

"What?"

"Nothing," River said, still smiling.

"Then why did you laugh?"

"That was cute," River said. *Cute*. From River's mouth, the word felt like an insult, and Fit went on the defensive. "I had to give them *something*."

River asked, "What's it like—having fans?"

"It's like being popular," she said. "Like really, really popular. And you're never alone or bored, which is pretty cool." Her heart swelled with love for her freaks. "They check in on me, like if I don't post for a day, they go crazy. Which was weird at first, but now I love it." Fit had the urge to tell River about how before she started making videos she'd turn to YouTube when she got lonely or bored. Her favorite YouTubers were like old friends, comforting faces. Now that she was on the other side, it was that same feeling, but times a thousand. Then Fit thought about the discussion post, how River had weaseled her way into this corner of her life too. "There's no privacy, though," Fit said. "They dig up everything."

River asked, "Really?" They made eye contact, and Fit could tell there was a mutual understanding about what she meant by "everything."

"Yep." Fit paused for moment, then said, "But I'm not sure how much Dillon knows. About me—what happened." River looked down and Fit already felt guilt grabbing hold of her for what she was about to say. "So, let's not bring it up, okay?"

River pulled a book out of her purse, flipped to a dog-eared page. "Of course."

The driver, an older man with a salt and pepper mustache, picked them up in front of Penn Station. He got out and opened the back door. The seats were black leather and a partition separated the front and back seats. As Fit climbed in, she felt like she was in a music video. When the driver got behind the wheel, he rolled down the partition.

"I'm Al. Let me know if the temperature's all right. And help yourself to some drinks." On the side, there was a small bar filled with soda, lemonade, and sparkling water. Fit grabbed a Diet Coke.

River hadn't spoken much since Fit had asked her not to bring up their history, and Fit couldn't tell if River was upset or if she was just being quiet. "Want a drink?" she asked nicely, overcompensating because River could not get mad at her. That's not how their arrangement was supposed to work.

As they drove, Fit looked up at the soaring buildings. "Woah, how tall is that thing," she said after they passed a particularly large skyscraper. She'd seen the city in movies, but none of them fully captured the magnitude of the looming architecture. The driver laughed.

"Ever been to the Big Apple before?"

In middle school, Fit's chorus had been invited to participate in a competition in New York. The trip cost three hundred dollars, and Dubs had agreed to pay. But right before the payment was due, he'd been sideswiped on the highway, and that was that. She'd told her friends in choir that Dubs had tickets for a Red Sox game that weekend.

"Never got around to it," Fit told the driver.

He then directed his question to River, "First time for both of you?"

"No," River said. "I used to come in for concerts. Take the commuter rail from New Haven."

Fit had a hard time picturing River at a concert, only able to see her for who she was now: a woman who went out in public in khakis and dorky white sneakers. She fought the intrigue of wanting to know what concerts River had attended, who she went with, and how old she'd been, by reminding herself that it was ultimately River's fault that she couldn't go on that chorus trip.

Changing the subject, Fit asked, "Ever driven anyone famous?"

"I'm afraid that's confidential," Al said, winking at her through the rearview mirror. Fit rested her hand on the leather seat and wondered who else had been in that car.

"Well, when I become famous, you can tell everyone that you drove around Fitted Sheet."

"I'll be sure to remember the name."

Fit continued to watch out the window, amazed at the amount of people on the street. The only time she'd seen that many people together, walking in a group yet all ignoring each other, was at the casino. But these city people were all headed to places more important than slot machines or blackjack tables.

When the town car pulled up to a stoplight, Al asked, "What time is your meeting?"

"Noon," Fit said. "It's a lunch meeting."

"Want me to take the long way? Swing you by the New York Public Library?"

Fit asked, "We won't be late?"

"I'll have you there by eleven-thirty," Al said, turning on his blinker. "I promise."

Fit was posting a selfie of herself in the backseat when Al stopped the car and said, "Here she is. Over sixty-thousand square feet." Fit leaned her forehead against the glass, craning her neck. "I can't see the whole thing. Can I get out?"

"Here," Al said, pressing a button on the steering wheel that opened the sunroof. "Pop your head out."

Fit stood up, her head and shoulders sticking out of the car, and looked out. The New York Public Library resembled an ancient Grecian building and must have been at least ten times bigger than her apartment building. She called down to Al. "Will I look like a dumb tourist if I take a picture?"

"This is New York. No one cares what you're doing."

Fit looked at the people as they passed by; none of them seemed phased by her sticking out of the sunroof. She felt like she could scream at the top of her lungs and no one would care. She snapped a picture of the building and then took a selfie with it in the background.

Fit sat back down. Al looked over his shoulder. "What do you think?"

"She's a beauty, all right."

He asked River, "Want a look?"

"No," she said. "Thank you."

Al closed the sunroof. "All right then. We'll be there in ten minutes." As they drove away, Fit looked at the pictures she'd just taken, trying to find the one that made the library look the biggest, the most impressive. The one that would make people jealous.

The elevator doors opened on the twenty-fifth floor and Fit sensed it immediately: she was somewhere unlike any other place she'd been before. And stepping into the lobby of WeCord Entertainment she thought, *This is where I need to be.*

The receptionist with incredibly white teeth told Fit and River to take a seat and that Dillon's assistant, Reggie, would be right with them. The lobby looked futuristic. Everything was black, sleek, and modern, and the people who buzzed in and out could have walked straight off the set of a perfume commercial. Fit fidgeted with her hat, looked at her pink converse and then at River. They did not belong.

All week, she'd been bragging to her friends and Frankie about how she was going to be famous. But now that the time had finally arrived for her to meet Dillon, she was nervous. What if he didn't like her or had decided to move in another direction? In a panic, she pictured him ending the meeting early, telling her he'd be in touch and never following through.

After ten minutes, Reggie came into the lobby. She wore all black and the right side of her head was shaved.

"Nice to finally meet you," she said, shaking Fit's hand. Her black platform sandals clopped as she led Fit and River down the hallway, past offices and meeting rooms. The walls were mostly glass, some frosted, others showing clear through to crisp, high-end workspaces. Fit fought the urge to film everything, not wanting to give herself away as an amateur.

Dillon's office was at the end of the hallway in the corner. He sat behind an enormous dark wooden desk and was looking at something on his computer, which had a screen bigger than the new TV Dubs came home with the year before.

Reggie knocked on the opened door and said, "Fitted Sheet is here to see you."

Dillon looked up. "Ah. Miss Fitted Sheet." He got up from his chair, buttoning his suit jacket. He was shorter than Fit had expected—only a few inches taller than her—and was impeccably dressed in a dark blue suit and light brown shoes.

After their introductions, he gestured toward the couches. "Please. Have a seat." Dillon's office was twice the size of the other offices they'd walked by. There were two white couches in the middle, a large TV screen on one of the walls, and behind Dillon's desk, which was sparsely decorated save for a giraffe figurine, was a bookshelf filled with awards. But the real showstopper was the view, his floor-to-ceiling windows overlooking the city.

Fit and River sat down on the couch, and Dillon sat across from them. He picked up an iPad that was lying on the table between the two couches and asked Fit, "What's your favorite color?"

"Mine?" Fit was thrown by the question, and Dillon's expressionless face gave away no clues as to what he was getting at.

"Yes," he said. "Yours."

"Purple." After Dillon made a few taps on the iPad screen, the glass wall of his office, which looked out at the hallway, turned a frosty-purple.

"Holy shit," Fit said.

"Right?" Dillon said. "It cost a fortune, but I love it." He tapped the screen again and the wall changed to green. Tap. Yellow. He handed the iPad to Fit. "Give it a go."

Different colored buttons covered the screen. Fit pressed blue, then red, then orange—the wall changing accordingly. At the bottom of the screen there was a button that had a spiral on it. Her fingers buzzing, she tapped it and the walls pulsed with different colors. She wished Diamond were there. Dillon's wall made Riley's DayGlo look like child's play. After watching a few cycles of the wall going from green to orange to blue, Fit asked, "Can I take a video?"

"Be my guest," Dillon said.

After Fit had sent a video to the casino crew and posted it so her fans could see it, she set the wall back to purple and returned the iPad to Dillon. He crossed his legs, leaned back a little, and asked, "Want to know how I found you?"

"How?"

"I went to dinner at my brother's place a few weeks ago. He and his family live upstate. When I got there, my niece was sitting on the couch, doing something on her phone. You see, she's thirteen, so unless I'm introducing her to someone famous, I'm useless." He looked at River. "I'm sure you know what I'm talking about."

"Sure," River said unconvincingly, but Dillon didn't seem to notice her lack of conviction and continued with his story. "I walk over to Teagan, my niece, and I see that she's wearing this large silver cuff around her arm." Dillon wrapped his hand around his bicep, demonstrating where the cuff was. "At first I thought it was solid metal, but when I got a closer look at it, I realized it was tinfoil."

Fit smiled. "That's awesome!" She loved when her fans sent her pictures of their own tinfoil creations.

"I hold out her arm," Dillon said, "and I say, 'Now, Teagan.

I know both your parents work for nonprofits, but I'm sure they could afford something a little nicer.' Teagan didn't find this funny. She rolled her eyes and then showed me one of your videos. You're good," he said and paused for a moment. Fit started to say thanks, but Dillon, his voice now livelier than before, kept on speaking. "It used to be that everyone was after the 'X' factor. You needed to shine on screen so people would invite you into their homes. But now people are watching you in bed, on their phones, inches from their faces. Nowadays, you need to have what I like to call the BFF factor." Dillon swept his arm in front of him like the letters B-F-F were written out in the air. "You're in their Twitter, their Snapchat, their Instagram—along with their *literal* best friends. And Fit, my dear, I think you've got it."

Fit's heart raced. "Really?"

"Absolutely." Dillon began to tap on his iPad again. "And once you're their BFF, they'll follow you anywhere. Even here," he said, and with one more poke of the screen the TV on the wall turned on, displaying Fit's YouTube channel. It was weird seeing her face so large. She asked, "You mean TV?"

"Yes, TV," Dillon said. "But also so much more." His words took on a life of their own as he explained something called a sales funnel, and how YouTubers navigated this new "media landscape." Dillon let out a sharp laugh. "But I'm getting ahead of myself. First thing's first—we've got to get you to half a million subscribers."

"We do?"

"That's when I can officially take you on as a client."

A bubble burst in Fit's chest, her hope crashing as quickly as Dillon had built it up. It had taken Fit eight months to get a quarter million subscribers. She couldn't bear to wait another eight months and dreaded having to return home empty handed. Her despair must have been apparent on her face because Dillon said, "Don't worry. I'm going to help you get to half a million as quickly as possible. You just won't be on the books."

His words made her feel a little better. "Okay?"

"I'll prove it. How many followers do you have now?" Dillon scrolled down until the number of subscribers showed on the screen. "Two-hundred, fifty-thousand and eighty-seven. Now. Do you know Shadin Hane?"

"Of course," Fit said, thinking of the video she'd watched the night before, in which Shadin played the ukulele and sang a song about Michigan. He was on tour at the moment and wrote an individual song for each stop.

"Well, he's an old friend," Dillon said. Fit knew that was an understatement, that Dillon was the reason Shadin was touring at all. And *god* she wanted that life. "I asked him if he could do me a favor today."

Fit sat on the edge of her seat, watching as Dillon took out his phone and texted someone. She had no idea what he was getting at, but she was captivated nonetheless.

Dillon said, "He's got the day off so hopefully—" His phone chimed. "Look at that. It's already done."

"What?" Fit said, sounding more desperate than she'd intended. "What's done?"

Dillon raised his eyebrows, ran a finger along his pristine goatee. "Check your notifications."

Fit opened Twitter and saw that @ShadinHane had tweeted: **OMG. Have y'all seen @FittedSheet? I'm obsessed xx.** The tweet included a link to one of her videos.

"Holy. Crap." Fit was in shock. "Shadin's huge!"

"That tweet should give you a good bump. Now, that's the sort of stuff I can help you with. If you're willing to commit."

Fit refreshed her notifications. In just one minute, Shadin's tweet was liked and retweeted over two hundred times. "Totally," Fit said. "One hundred percent. I'm in."

"Great." His voice was back to neutral. "I saw you've been posting a few more times a week. Which is wonderful. But, if you really want to go for it, you should post every day."

"Every day?" Fit felt like it had been a stretch just bumping it up to two or three videos a week.

"Minimum five a week."

"And that will work?"

"You get new followers every video, right?" Dillon was correct. There was always an uptick of subscribers on days she posted videos. "More content. More followers. It's a game. You've just gotta be willing to play."

Fit was quiet for a moment. Could she really make a video every day?

"Think about Shadin," Dillon said. "He's on tour. He tries to post every day. He's got ten million subscribers. And you know what else he has?"

Fit desperately wanted to know what Shadin had. "No?"

"A house in Los Angeles, an apartment in New York City. And he just bought a huge plot of land outside Tennessee. How does that sound?"

It sounded like everything she'd ever dreamed of. But before she could tell him this, River, who had been quiet up until that point, spoke up. "What about school?"

Fit whipped her head around, gave River the evil eye, and said under her breath, "What about it?"

"You're going to be a senior," River responded, then spoke directly to Dillon. "She's going to have homework. College applications."

Fit wanted to ask River who she thought she was, acting

so *parental* suddenly. But that would have blown their cover. She said, "It's summer."

"It won't be summer forever, Fit. School starts in six weeks."

Fit knew there were other YouTubers Dillon could have called. All he had to do was wait a few weeks, and another viral sensation was bound to pop up. But Dillon didn't seem bothered by what River was saying. He asked, "What do you do?"

"She's a teacher," Fit blurted out before River had a chance to answer.

"No wonder you're so worried about your daughter's education," Dillon said. "What grade?"

River beat Fit to the punch. "Sixth," she said. Fit was shocked at the ease with which River lied.

Dillon laughed. "You must have the patience of a saint." Then he leaned forward, looking intently at River and said, "I'm not going to lie. If Fit's career goes the way I think it can, she won't need college."

"That's what I've been saying!" Fit yelled, but neither of the adults paid her any attention.

"But what if this thing doesn't work out?" River sounded worried. "What is she going to fall back on?"

"College will always be there. Fit goes a year late and becomes an accountant."

Fit imagined herself behind a desk in some tan, boring office and cringed. River sounded like Dubs, obsessing over school. Fit had never been interested in college. School wasn't her thing. She knew Dubs had been saving for her and Frankie to go to the state university a few towns over. She also knew that Frankie was dead set on going to a fancy art school in Rhode Island that cost $46,000 a year. If she didn't go to college, Dubs could take the money he'd been saving for her and spend it on Frankie. Hell. If she became rich enough, she could cover the cost herself.

"Gross," Fit said. "No way in hell am I going to be an accountant. I'll live stream my whole day if I have to."

Dillon laughed.

"I don't know," River continued. "It sounds too good to be true."

"Here," Dillon said, picking up his iPad. "Let's see if I can prove I mean business."

Fit's YouTube account was still on the TV screen, showing the same subscriber count as before: 250,087. A refresh of the page revealed a new number: 260,589. Dillon grinned. "Ten thousand new subscribers a minute. Not too bad, huh?"

Fit blinked in awe. "Holy crap."

"That's nothing." Dillon waved his hand at the TV screen like he was batting away a fly. "There's so much more I can do for you."

Fit had full faith in Dillon. She believed he could make her famous and didn't care what River or Dubs or anyone else thought. This was the path she needed to be on and Dillon was leading the way.

Reggie knocked on the door. "Food's here."

"Come on in!" Dillon said. And in walked a delivery man carrying two large bags. "I hope you like sushi," Dillon said. "Because we got a ton."

The only time Fit had sushi was when the kitchen messed up a room service order, the cooks giving it to the cleaning staff to share. "I love it," Fit said. The delivery bags were filled to the brim; it must have cost a fortune.

River excused herself to use the restroom, and a few seconds after she left, Fit said, "I should probably wash my hands too."

She caught up to River right outside the bathroom door and hissed, "What the hell was that about?"

"What?" River asked.

"That shit about school." A woman came out of the bathroom. Fit smiled and waited until she was out of earshot. "You think you can come here and suddenly pretend to be my mother? Frankie and Dubs might buy your excuses, worship the couch cushion you sit on, but I don't." She knew if Dubs were here, he'd be pissed, his face the color of a tomato, but she couldn't stop herself. "You're here because you're my only option."

"You think that's what I came here expecting?" River said. "You've made your feelings very clear, Jess. But Dubs asked me to look out for you. All that these people see when they look at you is dollar signs. I'm not going to let them take advantage of you. Got it?"

Mrs. M. had spoken to Fit like that a hundred times before, Dubs, too, but on River, the tone was jarring, unexpected, and stunned Fit into silence. River turned around, her ponytail flicking back and forth as she pushed open the bathroom door.

The delivery person was just leaving Dillon's office when Fit returned. All the plastic covers were off the trays, and the sushi sat in beautifully colored uniform rows.

"Please," Dillon said. "Dig in."

"Sorry about her," Fit said, as she took a picture of the spread.

"Your mom?" Dillon said casually as he popped a piece of fish in his mouth.

"Yeah. She's normally not so . . . annoying."

Dillon waved the comment away. "Trust me. That was nothing. I've dealt with much worse."

"And just because she's asking lots of questions doesn't mean I'm not committed."

"Oh. I'm *glad* she's being a little skeptical."

Fit started to load up her plate. "Really?"

Dillon sat down on the couch. "It's the stage parents that I worry about. The ones who are willing to sell a lock of their child's hair for a buck." Dillon crossed his legs. "Your mom, she's just being a normal parent. Not everyone is so lucky."

Fit looked over the sushi. She took a piece from the platter labeled "California Roll" and popped it in her mouth. As she chewed she thought about what Dillon said. *Lucky.* She wanted to laugh. No one had ever called her lucky. To Dillon, she and River must have looked like any other mother and daughter. River, it seems, had actually helped Fit's case.

River came back in, her hair now wrapped in a bun, and Fit felt a pinprick of guilt, like someone was poking a pencil between her ribs. She picked up a plate from the table and held it out to River. "Try the California roll. Shit's dope."

From the moment River stepped into Dillon's office there was something about him that made her uneasy. Maybe it was the pretentious way he adjusted the cuffs on both shirt sleeves before standing up or how his cologne was so strong that when they shook hands all she could see were ice blue dots. Whatever the reason, he left her on edge. She tried to tell herself that she was overwhelmed—the train, the car, the buzz of people as they zipped through the lobby—it had all been a lot to take in. But as Dillon talked about Fit like she was a commodity, dollar signs practically spilling out of his eyes, River felt something inside her move and it was impossible for her to keep quiet. The conviction with which she spoke about school and college was surprising even to herself. And when Fit followed her out into the hallway, River rode that high of confidence to fend off her daughter's insults.

But that energy waned as she washed her hands and thought about going back into Dillon's office. She wanted to retreat, wait out the rest of the meeting in the confines of the ladies' room, but she'd made a promise to Dubs. She had to keep an eye out for Fit. Her only consoling thought as she headed out of the bathroom was that Fit's opinion of her was so low—*her only option*—that she wasn't sure how much more damage she could do. But her worries were unneeded. When she got back to the office the food was set up and there wasn't another peep of business talk.

Once they'd finished lunch, Dillon telling Fit he'd be in touch and River that it was great to meet her—which she highly doubted—there were still a few hours until they had to catch their train back to New London. Al was waiting out front for them and offered to show them a few more places around the city. Fit jumped at the chance, saying, "Hell yeah." Even though River was exhausted, raw from the day, she couldn't help but chuckle. She could agree with Dillon on one thing—Fit had charisma, even when she was swearing, and River wasn't surprised that people on the internet were drawn to her daughter. She'd wanted to tell Fit this on the train, but she hadn't thought her words would carry much weight.

As they drove, River took in the city. She hadn't been to New York in over twenty years, when she and Seth, barely in their twenties, would go to loud concerts in dark, dirty music halls. She tried to remember what she looked like back then, but she could only conjure a hazy picture. The person she used to be was as unfamiliar to her as the hordes of city-dwellers coursing along the sidewalk in their corporate attire.

One of the places Al took them was to Battery Park to see the Statue of Liberty. "Breeze feels nice," he said, smiling, as the three of them walked through the park. When they got to the water's edge, Fit leaned up against the railing, started taking pictures, and River stood next to her. Lady Liberty looked so small across the New York Harbor. River had gone on a tour once of the statue when she was in high school, and what she remembered most was the overwhelming magnitude of the green woman.

"She's better up close," River said.

"I wouldn't know," Fit said. River waited for the insult, the angry barb, but Fit turned back to her phone and continued to take pictures.

River didn't need an insult to know that it was her fault that Fit had never seen the Statue of Liberty, had never even been to the city. All because River had been too embarrassed to call Dubs when Frankie was a baby, when things had started to feel off. She'd known there was something wrong when she stopped showering, had the overwhelming desire to shave her head because brushing her hair seemed too exhausting. And when that first spark of evil entered her brain, telling her how much easier things would be if her children were just gone, she could have picked up the phone and told Dubs, "Hey, I'm having trouble staying afloat over here." If she'd had done that, Fit and Frankie would have grown up in a house, no matter how small, with a backyard where they would have enjoyed family cookouts, set up a Slip 'N Slide when the days got really scorching. Once a year, she and Seth would have splurged and taken the kids into the city to see a Broadway show or the Rockefeller Christmas tree lit up in all its glory. And on one of those trips, River was certain, they would have taken a ferry to the Statue of Liberty, climbed up into that big crown, and taken in the expansive and humbling view. River hadn't picked up the phone, though, instead letting things spiral out of control. So now Fit was left looking at the Statue of Liberty from a half mile away, where the beacon of hope looked no bigger than a plastic figurine.

Al walked over to the them and said, "Look at that view! Let me get a picture of the two of you."

River had started to say "no thanks" when Fit held her phone out to Al and said, "Sure."

Fit slid in close to River; their arms touched.

"Put your hand on your hip," Fit said, putting her own hand on her right hip, so her elbow stuck out to the side. "You'll look better that way." River could detect no underlying snark in Fit's words, so she followed her daughter's instructions, ignoring the awkwardness of the pose.

Al took a few pictures, saying "how great" as he snapped away. When he was done, Fit looked through the shots. "Cool," she said and held out the phone for River to see one. Their smiles looked bright and genuine. River wanted to ask Fit to send her the picture, but she didn't want to push her luck.

For the rest of the trip, River wouldn't go as far as to say that Fit was nice to her, but she wasn't outwardly mean either. She wondered if this was a small step forward for the two of them, or if it was all in her head and things would be back to normal the next morning.

Al dropped them off at Penn Station right on time, and they found two seats next to each other. As the train pulled away, River checked her phone and saw she had a text from Dubs: HOW'D IT GO? If Dubs had texted her in the middle of the meeting, or even right after, she would have told Dubs about the feeling she got from Dillon. How she could practically smell his need for money. But River felt good about the day, the best she'd felt in a while, and she didn't want to ruin that. She would let Dubs in on her concerns when the time was right. When she could properly explain how she felt, while ensuring Fit didn't fly off the handle.

Went well, she texted Dubs back. On the train now.

When Al offered to take a picture of Fit and River in front of the Statue of Liberty, Fit's gut response was to say "Fuck no." But she caught herself before the words slid out. What if Al reported back to Dillon that Fit and River acted strange? That something was off about them? This was for her future, she told herself. And she kept repeating it like a mantra until Al dropped them back off at Penn Station.

"I'll be sure to remember the name," Al said as he dropped them off. "Fitted Sheet. Hard to forget."

Fit didn't want to leave Al's car, the city. Ever since she'd stepped foot in New York earlier that day, she'd felt different, like she was where she belonged. As the train pulled away from the station, Fit wanted to flag the conductor, tell him there'd been a mistake and she needed to go back.

Dubs picked them up in New London, still in his uniform, his eyes heavy from a long day's work.

"How was it?" he asked, hugging them both.

"Amazing," Fit said.

Jumping into the truck, Fit took the middle seat and River sat next to the door.

"Did you have a nice time?" he asked, directing his question to River. Fit didn't know how River was going to respond. The two of them had been quiet on the train home, but the silence had been different: it wasn't filled with its typical nasty charge. At least that's how it felt to Fit.

"Yeah. Sure," River said.

"Good good," Dubs said. He pulled away from the curb, smiling. And maybe it was because the highs and the lows of the day had exposed Fit's dreams like a live wire, but his smile nearly broke her heart.

When they returned to Meadow Lane—Dubs easing into the parking spot and letting out a small groan as he climbed out of the truck—the apartment complex looked smaller than it had that morning. The dim lights in the windows cast a pitiful glow out into the night. It was as if they had returned not to Juniper Hills but to the set of a cliché movie about a town that had seen better days.

Even if that was the case, there was one redeeming factor about being home: Fit couldn't wait to tell Frankie about her trip. She'd been texting with Diamond the whole train ride home, but she wanted to tell someone in person. She wanted to see Frankie's reaction when she told him about the rush of the people, the awards all lined up behind Dillon's desk, and how the entire city seemed to vibrate with an energy that Fit wanted to get back. But when she yelled "Yo, Franco!" once they got inside, Dubs told her he was over at Pistols's.

"He headed over there with a two-liter of Mountain Dew." Dubs sunk into his chair and kicked off his shoes. "A few hours ago."

"Gross," Fit said, flopping down on the couch.

"I'm sure they're still awake. If you head over there, just bring a key." Dubs closed his eyes. "I'll be with the sheep pretty soon."

"Nah," Fit said. "I'm good."

River sat on the couch next to Fit and the three watched TV. As a commercial came on for a knife that could cut through a metal can, Fit, for the second time that day, felt like the life she was living wasn't real. How could the same person that was eating sushi in a swanky office building in New York City a few hours earlier now be sitting on a Goodwill couch in a town where people hung around in the parking lot of Dunkin' Donuts for fun?

After a little while, River got up and said, "I'm tuckered out. And I've got to work tomorrow. Good night."

"Mhm," Dubs said, his eyes closed.

"Night," Fit said.

River washed up, then closed the door to Dubs's room, after which Dubs said, "Knew it."

"Knew what?"

Dubs opened one eye and looked at Fit, his head still lolled back like he was asleep. "That you'd come around."

"I am *not* coming around."

Dubs closed his eyes, chuckled. "Okay."

"Whatever." She got up from the couch. "See you tomorrow."

Fit couldn't sleep that night, thoughts of New York City running through her head. How the city smelled, felt, sounded. As she lay in bed, listening to the traffic outside, she Googled "new york city apartments." She scrolled through the listings, looking at all sorts of apartments, when she came across a beautiful two-bedroom condo. It was on the top floor of a building with windows that had a beautiful view of the city. She took a virtual tour of the space, moving from room to room, imagining herself sitting at the kitchen table, lounging on the couch, even spreading herself out on the crisp cream-colored carpet. As she looked at the apartment, something in her bloomed. She wanted that apartment. For as long as she could remember, she had wanted to "get out" but she'd never chosen an actual destination. Now she had one.

The apartment was $5,000 a month, an incomprehensible amount of money to Fit. But she thought of what Dillon had said about Shadin. He had a house in LA, land in Tennessee, and an apartment in New York City. All things that Dillon said she could have if she followed his advice. So she got started that night. She edited the videos that she'd taken on her phone into a vlog. The hours she spent editing flew by, and by the time 2:00 am rolled around she was ready to film her outro.

"I love you all so much. And I can't wait to make things happen. I'm determined and ready, so you all better watch out! Fitted Sheet is coming for ya."

Fit sat across from Diamond at a table by the casino pool, the midday sun hanging high and hot. Diamond unbuttoned the top of her casino uniform. "Fuck, I'm sweaty."

She'd been cleaning rooms all day, and the casino crew was meeting up with her on her break. Somehow, the same boxy uniform that made Fit feel like the frumpiest frump that ever lived made Diamond look cool.

Pistols and Frankie were inside the casino grabbing snacks from the vending machine.

"Shadin shared another one of my videos last night," Fit said.

Diamond nodded and said "I saw" without looking up from her phone. It had been two weeks since Fit had gone to New York City and met with Dillon, and she'd posted a new video every day for thirteen days straight. Thinking of ideas had been easier than she thought it was going to be, effortless almost. They'd come to her at all times of the day, and she kept a running list of them on her phone. She'd been making the videos in such rapid fire that sometimes she even forgot to wear tinfoil. People noticed, for sure, but they didn't seem mad. Her subscriber count was now over 300,000 and she obsessively checked the number every hour.

Fit could tell Diamond was in a bad mood by the way she slouched down in her chair and hiked her shoulders, but it was good to see her friend. She hadn't seen much of Diamond since she got back from New York. Diamond had been working and spending time with Riley, and most of Fit's time had gone to making videos and interacting with her fans.

"I wish you could play hooky for the rest of the day," Fit said. "We could lay by the pool and drink spiked Diet Cokes."

Diamond leaned her head down on the table. Fit wanted to reach out, stroke the back of her neck. "I wish," Diamond groaned.

Fit asked, "Gross rooms today?"

"Same old shit." Diamond ran her finger across her upper lip and wiped the sweat on her pants. Fit wished she knew how to lift Diamond from this funk.

"What if I pretend an asteroid is hurtling toward Earth?" she said. "And I'm like getting pissed because I'm rushing to do my liquid liner and keep messing up?"

"That's a good one," Diamond said, but made no movement to film or participate in their usual antics. Fit felt powerless as she watched Diamond, hunched over, continuing to type. She wanted to yell at Riley for being too thick to see Diamond's hurt, at Tufts for being so damn cheap, and at the casino for trapping Diamond for another year. Fit imagined Diamond coming home every day, like Dubs, tired and smelling of cleaning products. The unfairness of it all was devastating.

Out of this vision came an idea. Diamond could move to New York with her. Fit had saved the link to the top-floor condo in Manhattan and looked at it every night. She'd also been using Google Maps to scope out the neighborhood, picturing herself walking down to the local coffee shop where she'd grab an iced tea and a chocolate croissant. She liked to imagine herself sitting on a bench, watching people go by as she ate. But now, she was picturing Diamond with her, and she couldn't believe she hadn't thought of it before. Fit would pay the rent, so Diamond could work and save money.

The plan had almost fully unraveled in Fit's mind when Frankie and Pistols entered the pool area, carrying their food. They walked side by side and Fit noticed that Frankie was almost as tall as Pistols. It was weird. Frankie had always been visibly younger than the three of them, but now he looked like he could be their age.

Fit, somewhat flabbergasted, nodded her head in Frankie and Pistols's direction and asked, "Since when did those two bozos become best friends?" She'd barely seen Frankie since her meeting with Dillon. He kept saying he'd help her film, but when she was ready to shoot, he'd always be hanging out with Pistols.

Diamond looked up from her phone. "Pistols probably thinks he's got a better chance with you if he's nice to your brother. Idiot."

Fit then tried to imagine Pistols as the one in New York with her, walking through the park, having a picnic. But it wasn't right.

Frankie and Pistols plopped their food on the table. Frankie's burger was almost as big as his head, piled high with cheese, bacon, and avocado.

"Jesus," Fit said. "I thought you were going to the vending machines. Did you blow your whole allowance on that?"

Frankie took a large bite, looking like he was attempting to fit the whole thing in his mouth at once. "Worth it," he said as he chewed. He and Pistols both laughed at the gross display. Fit grew annoyed with them both. She wanted them to leave so she could tell Diamond about her newly formed plan in private, watch the burden of the casino lift from Diamond's shoulders.

"Well, I've got to get back to work," Diamond said.

"Have fun," Frankie said. Diamond flipped him off, and Pistols and Frankie broke into laughter again. They looked like children. Fit kicked Frankie underneath the table.

"The hell?!" he said. Fit wanted to tell him that he was better than this. He'd never acted like a gross teenager before, so why start now?

"You're an idiot," she told him. He shrugged it off and continued to eat.

Fit watched Diamond's back as she walked toward the casino, to the door that would take her to the hallways where all the cleaning carts were kept. Where Diamond would become just another employee, trying to make a buck.

A few days later, Fit woke up to a text from Dillon: Helen Ortega's going to tag you in a challenge this morning. Helen was another one of Dillon's clients. She got her start doing funny makeup tutorials. Fit wasn't a huge fan of challenges, thinking they were kind of dumb, but that didn't matter. If Dillon thought it was a good idea, she'd do it.

An hour after Dillon texted Fit, Helen posted a video of her doing the ghost pepper hot sauce challenge. Fit had seen a few other YouTubers participate in the challenge. The goal was simple: see how many pieces of hot-sauce-covered food you could eat before calling it quits. Helen, a vegetarian, chose fried cauliflower and was able to eat four pieces before tapping out. At the end of the video, her nose red and eyes puffy, Helen tagged three YouTubers that she wanted to see do the challenge. One of them being Fit.

ghost pepper?! i dont know, Fit texted Dillon after she watched the video. thats the hottest pepper in the world dillon!

Your choice, Dillon said. It will be good for you. I can overnight supplies. LMK.

Fit looked through the comments on Helen's video and came across one that said, **no way Fitted Sheet could do it. Talks a big talk but she seems like kind of a baby.**

There was a thread of comments underneath, agreeing. Fit was tempted to log into her fake YouTube account, the one where no one knew it was her, and tell this person they were an asshole. Instead she shared Helen's video and said, **ur on!** 🔥

Dillon overnighted the hot sauce. Fit brought Frankie and Pistols along with her to the grocery store, where she bought a bag of frozen chicken wings.

"What do you think it tastes like?" she asked as they drove home. "Do you think it's as bad as everyone says it is?"

"You couldn't pay me enough to find out," Frankie said.

Fit nudged his shoulder jokingly. "You don't want to give it a try?"

"No way," Frankie said.

"How about you, Pistols?" she asked. He thought about it for a second.

"Yeah. I'd try it."

An idea popped into her mind. Rumors ran wild on YouTube. Fit had seen it happen so many times. Pistols was cute and had a quiet, almost mysterious demeanor to him. She could totally see her fans shipping the two of them, while wishing they could date him themselves.

"Want to be in the video?" Fit asked. "We can race or something."

"I don't know," Pistols said. He had a deck of cards in his hands. He looked down at them and shuffled.

"Pleeaasse," she said.

Pistols smiled, continued shuffling. "Fine, sure."

As soon as they got back to the apartment, Fit opened the box, cutting through the tape with a kitchen knife. Two bottles of ghost pepper hot sauce were carefully cushioned in crumpled up newspaper. On the label was a skull and crossbones, fire coming out of the skull's mouth and the word "Beware" written below.

Fit opened one of the bottles, smelled the sauce, and a tightness immediately hit her throat. She began to cough.

"Holy shit," she said through the coughing. She handed the bottle to Pistols and he held it up to his nose for a second before recoiling.

"Damn," he said. "You sure about this?"

No, Fit wasn't sure about it. She'd stayed up the night before watching other ghost pepper challenge videos, and every person looked miserable afterward: their faces red, their noses running. One YouTuber had to leave the filming to throw up. But the views on each were outrageous. Pain worked. Fit didn't understand why, but if it was what the people wanted, then she'd do it.

"What?" she responded. "You're scared?"

"Nope," Pistols said. "Just seeing if you were." He held the bottle out for Frankie to smell.

"No way," he said. "I'm not an idiot."

Frankie heated up the frozen chicken wings in the oven as Fit set up the shot, having Pistols sit in every chair as she tried to find the best angle. One that would make the cramped, beat-up kitchen look quaint.

She set milk and bread on the table, having read that both could help calm the heat. "You think that's going to do anything?" Frankie asked.

"Shut up," Fit said, even though he was right. The other YouTubers had tried milk and bread and even crackers, and none of it seemed to work.

After Frankie got the wings out of the oven and put them in a bowl, the three of them crowded around the steaming chicken. An almost somber, serious tone took over.

"Want to do the honors?" Frankie asked, holding out the bottle of sauce to Fit. She took the bottle and poured the thick angry liquid over the wings. Frankie stirred, the heat of the chicken acting almost as a diffuser, kicking the spice into Fit's face. Her eyes watered. Pistols took a step back and said, "Shit."

Frankie used tongs to plate up the wings: five for Pistols, five for Fit. The rules were easy: the person who finished first, or ate the most in five minutes, won. Fit and Pistols took their seats and Frankie got ready to film. He'd been out the last few videos she'd filmed and even though she very much dreaded what was about to happen, she was happy to see his face behind the camera.

"Whenever you idiots are ready," he said.

Fit took a deep breath and started her intro.

"Hello freaks!" In all the videos she'd filmed since she met with Dillon, she'd tried to act more like she was talking to a best friend. "I've decided to do something very, very dumb. And I'm joined by my good friend Pistols." She reached out and put her hand on his shoulder. A gesture she wouldn't naturally make. A gesture that made Pistols look at her and offer her a slightly crooked smile, before he averted his gaze and looked down at his hands. Even though Fit wasn't interested in Pistols, she thought a little flirting was harmless. It wasn't like she was telling him she liked him.

Fit explained the rules and when she was done, said, "All right Frankie. Count us down."

Frankie held up three fingers. "Three, two, one."

Fit's plan was to take big bites and swallow as soon as possible so the sauce wasn't in her mouth for too long. The first few chews weren't so bad; she tasted something tangy but didn't feel the slam of the heat. She wondered if the other YouTubers had exaggerated their pain. But then, like a crack of lightning, the heat kicked in and Fit had to fight the urge to spit out the smoldering chunk of chicken. The entire lower hemisphere of her face burned and tingled. She forced herself to chew through the pain, then swallowed.

"Fuuuuck," she said as the pain made a very clear path down her throat and chest. She looked over at Pistols. His eyes were watering, and his face had turned bright red. He was almost done with the first wing.

"How are you doing that?" she said, the pain getting worse as she spoke.

Pistols ripped the last piece of meat off his first wing, grimacing like it was the hardest thing he'd ever done, and then placed the naked bone on his plate.

"Oh my god!" he screamed. "That's fucking hot!"

"No shit," Frankie said, smirking behind the camera.

Pistols started on his second wing.

"I'm in trouble," Fit said, waving a hand at her mouth. Fit took another bite and powered through the pain, which was so intense she couldn't taste the chicken, or even the sauce for that matter. By the time she was on her second wing, her mouth was both numb and in excruciating pain at the same time. Her nose was running, and she probably had snot all over her face, but she didn't care.

Fit kept an eye on Pistols as they both continued to eat. At times, even though she was in so much pain, she'd have to stop and laugh at the look on his face. "We're the biggest idiots," she said at one point.

By the time Fit got to her third wing, Pistols was on his fifth, and the pain had spread from Fit's core out to her arms and legs. Her mind also felt hazy, like the heat from the sauce was somehow cooking her brain.

"I feel drunk," she said. "I think this sauce is spiked." Then Fit started laughing. She didn't know why exactly, but she couldn't stop.

"I literally can't comprehend what you're saying," Pistols said, then he started giggling too. Fit had no idea how loud they were or how long they were laughing. It was like they were suspended there, powerless to stop. But somehow, the laughter made the pain easier to handle.

"One minute left," Frankie said, pulling Fit somewhat out of her delirium. She took a sip of milk, which did not decrease the heat in any way.

Pistols groaned as he took another bite. Fit knew he must really like her if he was willing to go through that much pain for her. If the effects of the ghost pepper weren't so all encompassing, she might have felt bad for using him. But the only thought that fought its way past the pain was that she needed a good thumbnail for the video, an image that would really catch people's attention. For the last thirty seconds she pretended to cry while she ate. Really, really cry. A girl sobbing with a chicken wing. Who could resist that?

Pistols finished his fifth wing just as Frankie called time. Fit had eaten four. She shoved a piece of bread in her mouth, and Pistols chugged a whole glass of milk.

"Shit," Pistols said after he'd emptied his glass. He breathed in and out like he was having contractions. "When's it going to go away?"

Fit had only done research about how bad the pain would be, not how long it lasted. But at the moment, she couldn't imagine it lasting any shorter than forever.

"I don't know," she said, her mouth still full of bread, her cheeks pushed out like a chipmunk's. Fit then looked at the camera and spoke with her mouth full. "Well, there you have it! The worst fucking video in the history of the world." Even though she knew it wasn't. She had a feel for what her fans liked, what the internet craved, and she'd manipulate the different aspects of the video to satisfy that craving. She tagged three other YouTubers to do the challenge, just as Helen had tagged her, and said, "But if you're smart you won't do it" before signing off.

The pain remained half an hour later. Fit lay on her back on the kitchen floor. It felt like the ghost pepper was digging its way deeper, seeping into her muscles and bones. Pistols, who was still at the table, was dealing a game of cards between him and Frankie when River got home. She came into the kitchen, stopped abruptly, and looked at Fit. "Everything all right?"

"Yeah," Fit groaned.

River poured herself a glass of water, then turned around and leaned against the sink. "Good day of filming?" she asked, nodding at the camera. Fit didn't answer.

"It was horrible," Pistols said.

"These idiots ate hot sauce with ghost peppers in it," Frankie said.

River laughed, looking over at the bowl of chicken wings. "This it?" She then dipped her finger into the bowl and tasted the sauce. Her expression didn't change, like she'd just eaten lukewarm chicken noodle soup.

"That's not too bad," she said.

Fit sat up. "Well, try eating a whole wing."

"Oh. I don't think it'd be that hard." River smiled and winked at Frankie and Fit grew irritated. Fit hated to admit it, but ever since New York, something had changed between her and River. Nothing big. They were by no means close, but Fit had stopped being mean for no reason. She could pass River in the hallway without wanting to rip the wallpaper off the wall. Just a few weeks before, River's wink may have thrown Fit into a tantrum. But now she was merely annoyed.

"I doubt you'd get through one," Fit said.

"I bet I could eat two," River said, wiggling her eyebrows a little. "Without flinching."

Fit asked, "Wanna bet?"

"Sure," River said. "How about if I win, I get to sleep in one of your rooms for a week. So Dubs can get off the couch."

"Fine," Fit said. "If you eat two—without flinching—you can have Frankie's room."

"Hey!" Frankie yelled.

"Don't worry," Fit said to him. "It's impossible."

Frankie sighed. "Fine. And what do we get if you lose?"

"*When* she loses," Fit butted in. But River didn't seem bothered or shaken by this, and she answered as if she hadn't even heard Fit.

"I'll show you the tattoo I got in prison," River said. Frankie and Pistols both gasped, but Fit wasn't buying it.

"Yeah, right. I call bullshit."

"I guess we'll just have to find out," River said. "Shall we get started?"

"Yeah," Fit said, getting up from the floor. "I want to see this."

Frankie served up a few chicken wings on a plate and set it in front of the other empty chair at the table. River sat down, picked up one of the chicken wings, and studied it for a little while. Just as Fit was wondering if she was going to back out, River dug in. She ripped away a chunk from the meaty part of the wing and chewed. And chewed. And chewed. Fit waited for a reaction, but nothing happened. River almost looked like she was enjoying it. Fit waited for the pain to hit and River's face to change, but River showed no signs of slowing down. It was as if she were eating a saltine cracker.

Meanwhile, Frankie and Pistols were losing their shit. They gasped, cheered, banged on the table, and the energy in the room grew thick with excitement. Fit tried her hardest to not get caught up by Frankie's and Pistols's emotions, but she couldn't resist. The pull was too strong, and she was still in a slight haze from the hot sauce she'd ingested. She looked at River, amazed.

River finished the second wing as easily as she had finished the first. Frankie started chanting, "One more! One more!" and Fit and Pistols joined in.

Frankie was filming the scene on his phone, the thought of which hadn't even crossed Fit's mind. She was entranced, wanting to be nowhere else but watching her mom eat ghost pepper sauce like it was nothing. Fit didn't realize how wrapped up in the moment she'd gotten, until Dubs, who'd gone to run errands after they'd gotten back from the post office, opened the door to the apartment and said, "Jeez Louise! I could hear the bunch of you down the hallway." The four of them grew silent for a moment, then Frankie began to giggle, and the laughter spread until they were all in an uproar. Fit let herself be swept up by the happy hysteria.

When Dubs got to the kitchen doorway, it looked like he was prepared to scold them, tell them to quiet down, but he looked from Fit to River, and said, "Hmm. Carry on."

Their laughter trailed off as he walked away from the kitchen.

"All right," River said. "Did I hold up my side of the bet?"

"I can't believe it," Pistols said.

"That was so cool," Frankie added.

Fit was impressed, as well. It had been almost an hour since she'd eaten the wings, and her mouth and stomach still burned, her muscles achy from the severity of the pepper. She wanted to know how River had done it. Did she have no taste buds? Did everything she ate just taste like dust?

"I'd say Frankie better get used to sleeping on the couch,"

Fit said. She got up from the table, grabbed the camera from the tripod, and said, "This goes live tomorrow. I've got to start editing."

Just as she was closing her bedroom door, she heard Frankie say something, unable to make out the words, but it was followed by a burst of laughter. Hidden under the pain of the hot sauce coursing through her veins was a pang of loneliness. She was missing out on something. She wanted to go sit back down at the table, feel the weightlessness that comes with losing time while laughing and amazed. But she went in her room and closed the door behind her. Once she started editing the footage, she turned the volume up to block outside noise.

A few hours later, when she was zooming in on a long strand of snot coming out of her nose, something she knew her fans would find funny, she got a text from Diamond.

Your mom BEASTED those chicken wings!

omg i know! did Frankie tell you?

Saw it on FB

Perplexed, Fit went to Frankie's Facebook page. Thirty minutes before, he'd posted the video he'd taken of River eating the last chicken wing: **my mom ate ghost peppers and didn't even flinch.**

The video had already been shared sixteen times and liked by fifty-two people. Fit watched the thirty-second clip. In it, River was eating her last wing and Fit could hear herself laughing in the background. She sounded wild and out of control.

"Frankie!" she yelled as she stormed down the hallway. His door was open. He and Pistols were playing a video game on an old PS4 that Pistols had given Frankie as a hand-me-down a few months prior.

"What the hell?" she said.

"What's up your butt?" Frankie said, not taking his eyes off the screen.

"The video you just posted." Frankie and Pistols ignored Fit, so she stepped in front of the TV.

"The fuck?!" Frankie said, pausing the game.

"I can't believe you did this!" Fit started to play the video, held it up so Frankie could see. Their voices sounded far off and tinny.

Frankie looked unmoved. "Did what?"

"My video's going up tomorrow."

"Yeah. We heard." He rolled his eyes.

"No one's going to care about my video if yours goes viral."

Pistols, who was sitting on the floor, spoke up. "Hey, Fit, I'm the one who told Frankie to post it. So if you're going to be mad at anyone, be mad at me."

"That's not the point. He knew what he was doing."

Frankie raised his eyebrows. "What are you? Scared my video's going to beat yours?" His voice was thick with attitude. He never used to speak like this. Not until recently.

"I'm the one with the following, remember? I don't see an agent calling you up over your art pieces."

Fit regretted the words the moment they left her mouth. She wanted to apologize, tell Frankie that the framing was always better in the videos he helped shoot, and the artwork he created out of scraps astounded her.

"Get out of the way," he said, his voice angry and sharp.

"Not until you take it down," Fit said.

"C'mon, Fit," Pistols said. "You know Frankie could post the same video as you and you'd still get a million more views."

"I said that's not the point!" Pistols shrank backward, his shoulders hunched forward. Fit wasn't totally sure of the point, but she was *pissed* and wasn't budging until Frankie deleted the video.

Frankie smirked and said, "How about this. I take it down. Then post it at the same exact time as you."

Fit lunged at him, grabbing for his phone, which was on the bed next to him. He tried to push her away, but Fit got a hand around his wrist, digging her fingernails into his skin. She continued to reach with her other hand, but he was able to keep her away. They continued to struggle—Fit digging deeper into Frankie's wrist with her nails, Frankie creating a human shield between him and his phone—until Fit felt hands on her shoulders. Someone pulled her off Frankie. Fit thought it was Pistols, and she was ready to lay into him. But when she turned around, she saw it was River who had separated them.

They were quiet for a moment. River looked serious, concerned. "What's going on here?"

"Frankie posted a video of you eating the hot sauce. He needs to take it down."

"I don't need to do anything! Fit's just being a bitch."

Fit flipped him off.

"Hey, hey. That's enough," River said. "Can I see the video?"

Fit played the video. She was expecting River to side with Frankie; they *were* best friends, after all. So Fit was surprised when River sighed and said, "How about we take it down, Frankie?"

"See!" Fit said. "You can't just go posting videos without people's consent!"

"Fine, whatever," Frankie said. His lips were pursed tight, and when River handed him back his phone, he snatched it away forcefully. "You all fucking suck." When he was done deleting the video, he said, "Fine. Done. Happy?"

"Yep!" Fit turned triumphantly on her heels and walked

quickly out of his room. She'd won. She should have been happy. But if she were being honest with herself, to her brother, even to Pistols who had retreated to the corner of Frankie's room, she'd have to say she felt like shit.

After Fit left the room, Frankie picked up his controller and said to Pistols, "Come on. Let's finish." Frankie's cheeks were red, and his lips trembled. River wanted to explain her decision. She didn't care if there was a video of herself on the internet. In fact, it had made her happy that Frankie wanted to share something she'd done. But Fit no longer left the room when River entered, she no longer shot her dirty looks when they crossed paths, and when River ate the chicken wings, Fit seemed happy. Happy! River couldn't risk undoing all those small victories, so she'd taken Fit's side.

"Forget about the bet," River said. "We'll keep business as usual. Me in Dubs's room. You in here."

"Whatever," Frankie said. "I won't be home tonight anyway so you should sleep in my bed."

River scolded herself as she left his room. She should have stopped at one wing. That would have been enough to impress them. But she'd gotten cocky, careless, and it had come back to bite her.

That night, after Frankie headed out with Pistols and Dubs left for work, River went into Frankie's room and began to change the sheets. All his belongings were meticulously kept, his room baring a distinctive white and blue color scheme. It was a far cry from Fit's room, which was loud and bright with pictures and posters plastered on almost every surface.

Frankie treated his walls like an art gallery of his own work.

He rotated the pieces out every month, he had explained to River when she first moved in. There was a note card thumbtacked below each art piece that had the name of the work along with a description.

When River was done changing the sheets, she sat on the bed and looked at the creations on display. He must've changed them recently, as River didn't recognize any of them. One was a red plastic cup covered in googly eyes that was called *The Lookout*. The next was a picture of a peacock crafted entirely out of Band-Aids (not used, Frankie was sure to point out in the description). And over the foot of his bed was Frankie's interpretation of *The March of Progress*, the famous work of art that showed a caveman slowly evolving into a modern-day human. Frankie's drawing mimicked the picture, but instead of a caveman evolving into modern man, Frankie's showed Yoshi, a small green turtle-like creature from one of his video games, into Luigi, a human character from the same game who had a mustache and a green hat. River had never been artistically or musically inclined, and the creativity coming from both her children baffled and elated her.

As she tried to sleep, she kept picturing Frankie's hurt, Fit's hatred, and was haunted by her own hubris. The images of the fight remained with her at work the next day too. She kept having to spit out the ice chips she was tasting, unable to concentrate on the flavors. After the fifth time, River let out an audible sigh, and Lorrie, the woman sitting next to her asked, "What's got you?" Lorrie was the woman with the long, stringy ponytail that had offered River pretzels on her first day—they'd become somewhat friendly. Lorrie was the type of person who seemed to be able to talk to anyone about anything, and she'd plop herself down next to River while they were on break or at the beginning of their shift. At first, River was put off by

Lorrie, wary of her seeming insistence on becoming friends. But River grew to enjoy Lorrie's company and the funny commentary she made under her breath. She also appreciated that Lorrie never asked questions, never wanted to hear anything more than what River was willing to say. That's why when River answered Lorrie's question with a quiet "nothing" Lorrie didn't push any further.

"Well, if you run out of ice chips," Lorrie said, "let me know. The less I have to eat the better."

At the end of the day, as River was packing her stuff, Lorrie invited her to grab a drink. She had posed the question before, and River was about to give the same answer she always gave—a polite "thanks, but no thanks"—until she remembered the situation at home. She hadn't seen Fit since she was tearing her off Frankie, and Frankie had barely acknowledged River when he left the apartment with Pistols. The embarrassment came surging back, and she could practically taste the heat of the pepper climbing up her throat.

"Sure," River said. "Why not."

Lorrie clapped her hands together. "I knew I'd wear you down!"

They went to Legends, a bar in the shopping plaza next to their office building. River did her best to act normal as they entered the small dark bar, as if relaxing with a coworker after their shift was an everyday occurrence for her.

Framed stills from 1980s movies decorated the walls. They claimed a booth in the back corner, where a picture from *Pretty in Pink* hung on the wall next to them. When the waitress came around, Lorrie ordered a gin and tonic with two limes, holding up two fingers as she repeated the number, and River got a ginger ale. When their drinks came, Lorrie held her glass up in the air and said, "Cheers to cleansing our palates."

As they sat at the table making small talk, River's mind couldn't sit still. One moment she'd be caught up in the inconsequential conversation, and the next she'd feel like a third person, watching herself and Lorrie chitchat across the booth. After Lorrie had finished her second gin and tonic, the server brought the check. River looked up the time of the next bus on her phone—twenty minutes—and was reminded of the uncertainty she was returning to.

"There you go again with that sighing," Lorrie said, taking the final sip of her drink. "What's eating you?"

River hadn't even realized she'd sighed. She picked at the damp napkin in front of her and said, "Pretty sure my daughter hates me."

Lorrie let out a half-amused laugh. "I think that means you're doing it right."

"I don't know," River said. "I never thought a teenager could make me feel so—so dumb."

"They're pretty good for that," Lorrie said. "When my girls were in high school, my husband and I had a jar. We'd add a couple bucks to it anytime they said they hated us. Once it got full, we'd use the money to go out on a date. For a while there we were heading to the Olive Garden every other week."

"Sometimes it really gets to me," River said. "I don't know. My dad thinks I should go to therapy."

Lorrie squinted her eyes, unconvinced. "For getting in a fight with your daughter?"

River shook her head. "I struggled a bit . . . postpartum." The words came out before she realized what she was saying, but after she spoke she felt a subtle relief, like a bubble popping in the air, quiet, unceremonious.

"I didn't realize you had a young one at home," Lorrie said.

River stirred the ice in her drink with her chewed up straw.

"It was a little while ago. But I still haven't gotten quite back on track."

And Lorrie, who never seemed to take anything too seriously, looked River right in the eyes and said, "I'm sorry. That must've been hard."

River's instinct was to brush off what Lorrie said, tap on the side of her head and argue, *If you saw what was in here, you wouldn't be acting all nice. You'd be disgusted.* But River thought about the past fourteen years of her life, how they somehow added up to a negative number, and said, "Yeah. Thanks."

"Who needs a track anyway," Lorrie said, back to speaking like her not-so-serious self. "Sounds kinda boring."

River pulled out a few bucks from her wallet. "I suppose." She would have given anything for boring.

On the bus ride home, River kept thinking about what she'd said to Lorrie. She hadn't realized she'd been holding onto Dubs's suggestion of therapy until she'd spoken the words out loud. On top of the group therapy she'd participated in in the hospital ward, she'd also met with a psychologist a couple times a week during those early years. There had been two doctors who switched days, and she couldn't remember what either of them looked like or what they said. All she could conjure up was a blurry face and a low buzz. Not that it mattered. Therapy was for people who could somehow be saved.

The house was empty when River got back. Dubs was working second shift, and there was a note on the fridge from Frankie saying that he was with Pistols and Fit was hanging out with Diamond. Frankie seemed to sleep over Pistols's every other night. She wondered if he normally spent that much time out of the house, or if it was something she'd done.

Sitting on the couch, she ate a small dinner of chips and hummus as the sun set outside. Compared to the chatter-filled air of the bar, the quietness of the apartment was soothing, and she sat in silence for a while, clearing her mind. After it got dark, River decided to go to bed. As she got up from the couch, she was struck by the thought that she was going to bed in a completely empty apartment. She was spooked yet excited.

Frankie's note also directed for River to take his bed that evening. In his room, River tried to read but couldn't concentrate on the words. Instead, she found herself studying Frankie's drawing of the morphing video game characters. She imagined a similar drawing but with different versions of herself: as a child, a teenager, and as an adult, both before and after prison. In her drawing, though, there'd be an empty space that started right after Frankie was born that spanned until she woke up in the hospital. She had no memory of that person and what she had done. How could she ask for forgiveness for something she didn't even remember?

When she got up to turn off the light, she took a closer look at the drawing and then read the index card underneath.

### THE MARCH OF LUIGI

*In this pen and paper drawing, we see the steps that it takes to get from lovable Yoshi to scheming Luigi. It's unbeknownst to the millions of people who have played the Mario video games that there is an evolutionary link between the two characters. "No way!" they say. "They look nothing alike!" people cry. But to the naysayers I ask this: If an alien were to land on Earth, would it realize that a newborn and a ninety-eight-year-old were of the same species? Perhaps. But also, perhaps not.*

All week, the air had been heavy and humid, and even though Fit hated Riley she'd been happy when Diamond sent the group a text asking, Riley's? He's got central air.

They chilled in the living room. Diamond sat next to Riley on the couch, her foot placed delicately on top of his, and Frankie and Pistols were on the floor playing a game of blackjack. Fit was spread out in the large armchair, filming snaps and telling her fans to watch the video she'd posted that morning.

They'd been lounging a few hours when Riley grabbed his wooden stash box from the coffee table. He began to roll a joint, a meticulous process Fit had seen him do countless times. When he was done he lit it and took a hit. He then passed it to Diamond, who took a drag and held it out to Frankie.

"No way," Fit said.

Frankie ignored her, taking the joint.

"Hey, Frankie. You're not smoking."

"Oh yeah?" he said, annoyed. Their fight over the video was just a week old, and they'd dealt with their argument like they always did—by ignoring each other until they were over it. Even though Frankie had begun talking to her again, Fit could tell he was still harboring something against her.

"I'll tell Dubs," Fit said.

"Bullshit."

"You're fifteen. You can hang with us, but you can't smoke."

"It's not like I haven't done it before."

Furious, Fit looked at Pistols. "Is that what you two have been doing?"

"What does it matter to you?" Frankie said. "Soon you won't have to worry about me."

"What's that supposed to mean?"

"When you're off being famous."

The words deflated Fit's anger and guilt took over. In Fit's escape plan to New York City (which she still hadn't mentioned to Diamond), Frankie was left at home. Not because she didn't want him around, but because she wanted to give him a normal life. He'd always been a good kid, the one in the bunch that was going to go to college, get a solid, respectable job as an art teacher or running his own gallery. But now Riley and Pistols were ruining that.

"Fine," Fit said. "Become a fuck-up." Frankie took a hit, holding the joint easily. He didn't cough as he exhaled. It was obvious he'd done this before.

"Welcome to the Fuck-ups Club, kid," Riley said. "It's more fun over here."

Everyone but Fit started laughing. When it was her turn to smoke she said, "Can't. I'm doing my collab tomorrow. My voice has got to be in tip-top shape."

Dillon had set up a collaboration video between Fit and one of his other clients, Ty Skyview. "Ty Skyview?!" Fit had repeated in disbelief after Dillon had informed her of the plan over the phone. Ty had been on YouTube for ten years. He'd risen to internet fame by playing the character Mr. Bubbles, a weird, older man who spoke with a nasally voice and was always petting a stuffed cat. Ty then created a separate channel where he made videos as himself. He also had another vlog channel where he documented his day-to-day life. In total, he had more than ten million followers, and each of his videos, even if it was just him trying out different lipsticks, got millions of views. "Well, *excuse* me," Riley said after Fit passed on the blunt. He took another hit and blew the smoke in Fit's direction. "There. A little contact high for ya."

"Very funny," Fit said, flipping him the bird as the rest of the group laughed. "I know you guys are just jealous."

The next day, as Fit picked out what she was going to wear, she started to freak out. In his videos, Ty was always perfectly styled. There were Tumblrs and fan channels dedicated to his clothes and makeup, and he seemed to pull off even the most outlandish outfits with ease. Fit pulled on a sleeveless Teenage Mutant Ninja Turtles T-shirt she'd found at Goodwill and tucked it into high-waisted, sailor-esq shorts. She wanted Frankie's advice on whether she looked dumb or not, but he wasn't in his room. She went into the living room. Dubs was sitting at the table eating pistachios and River was sitting on the couch, checking her phone.

"Frankie gone?"

Dubs cracked the shell off a nut, nodded his head. "He's with Pistols."

He must have left when Fit was in the shower.

"Of course," Fit said, rolling her eyes. She thought about telling Dubs what Frankie had been up to the day before, but then she'd be dragging herself into the mud too.

"You look nice," River said.

"You think?" Fit said. "For a three-dollar shirt, it's not bad."

"*Teenage Mutant Ninja Turtles* used to be one of my favorite shows," River said.

"Well, thanks," Fit said heading back to her room. She changed her shoes three times before deciding on a pair of Doc Martens that Diamond had given her as a hand-me-down. They were a half-size too big, so Fit had to wear extra-thick socks to fill in the excess space.

Fit headed out in Dubs's truck. It was hot and she drove with the windows down, deciding that showing up with wind-blown hair was better than rocking pit stains.

Ty lived forty-five minutes away in Rhode Island. He was one of Dillon's few clients who lived on the East Coast. When Fit pulled onto Ty's street, the first thing she noticed was how all the houses looked the same: two stories, four front-facing windows, and a stone pathway leading from the road to the front door. Each house was a different pastel color like eggs in an Easter basket. The neighborhood was tame and neutral, the exact opposite of Ty.

Ty's house was a pale-yellow version of every other house on the street except for the "For Sale" sign with a SOLD sticker staked into the front lawn. A silver BMW and a lavender moped were parked in the driveway.

Ty answered the door wearing a long silk robe, his chin-length hair bright teal. He'd documented the process of dying his hair the week before in one of his vlogs, but it looked more vibrant in person, making his dark eyes pop.

He had a small camera in his hand and pointed it at Fit as he opened the door. She instinctively shifted her face a little to the right, her better side, and ran her hand through her hair to give it a little more volume.

"Miss Fit!" Ty said, holding his arms out for a hug, the fabric of his sleeves hanging down like red curtains. "Come in, come in" he said after letting go.

The house was cold; Fit could hear the quiet hum of the air conditioner. The entryway was spacious, crisp, and void of almost all color, a jarring contrast to the painter's palette that was Ty.

"You find the place okay?" he asked, pushing his hair behind his ears, revealing long, dangling earrings.

"We go to Misquamicut a lot," Fit said, referring to the state beach not too far from Ty's house. She wasn't sure why she told him that. It was a lie. They hadn't been to the beach in years and only visited as an occasional treat when she was a kid.

"Wonderful, wonderful." Ty put the side of his face next to Fit's, holding the small square camera out in front of him. "Look who's here!" he said. "Fitted Sheet! We're filming a collab today and I'm so damn excited." Fit waved at the camera.

"I'll post this tonight," Ty said to Fit. "Get people excited about our videos. Come on. I'll give you the tour."

He led her down the hallway to a large open room. Half was the kitchen, with its marble counters and shiny stainless steel appliances. A long glass table covered in boxes sat at the far end of the room. Like the entryway, the kitchen was simple, with few flourishes. The room seemed elegant and fancy.

"Don't mind the mess," Ty said, flicking his hand toward the boxes. "The movers will be here in a week and I've barely started packing."

Ty spoke quickly, his words animated. He held the camera out to film himself, scanned the boxes, and put the camera on Fit.

He asked, "Want a seltzer?"

"Sure."

Ty grabbed a bottle from the fridge and two wine glasses from the cabinet. "I've packed most of my glassware," he said. "Except, you know, the essentials."

The stem of the glass felt delicate in her hands.

She asked, "Where are you moving?"

Ty groaned. "LA."

"Duuude, that's awesome."

Ty raised one eyebrow, a move she'd seen him do many times in his videos. An expression his fans loved to turn into gifs or memes. "Ever been?"

"No."

"It's horrible." He took a sip of his seltzer, then spoke to the camera as if it were another person. "Horrible, I tell you!" He then waved his hand and said, "But enough of my bad mood. Let me show you the rest of the house."

At first Fit thought it was a little weird that he insisted on showing her every part of the house. But she supposed if she had a big house she would want to show it off too.

"This was my childhood home," Ty said as he led Fit up to the second floor. "I bought it from my parents when they retired. Now they live in a condo on the beach in South Carolina."

It clicked for Fit then, why Ty lived in a suburban and boring area.

There were four rooms on the top floor. Ty's robe billowed behind him like a cape as he walked down the hallway, explaining what each room used to be and what he had turned it into. His brother's old room was now an office, their mother's craft area was now Ty's craft area, and he'd converted his childhood bedroom into a walk-in closet, which looked straight out of a movie: racks of clothing hung on the walls, and a tower of cubes stood in the middle, full of shoes and accessories. Fit wanted to shove her face in the clothes, run the fabric through her fingers. But everything was kept so pristine she felt like she was in a museum and nothing should be touched.

"Ugh," he said. "I can't even think about packing all this up yet." With a swoop of his robe, he left the room. Fit followed.

On a small table in the hallway, Fit noticed three purple jagged stones, each standing about half a foot tall.

"Woah," Fit said, lightly touching the top of one. "What are these?"

"Amethyst points," Ty said. "They're supposed to bring strength."

"They're very witchy," Fit said.

"You should get one. They're only like three hundred dollars a stone. I've got a gem guy, if you want." Ty spoke as casually as if he were discussing buying a shirt or a bag of Twizzlers. Of course, that number seemed insignificant to him. His YouTube videos alone, each racking up millions of views, must have brought in tons of ad money, not to mention his books, merch, and brand deals. He'd turned himself into a mini-empire. She looked at the amethyst and wondered if that's what it was like to be rich, you got to throw a bunch of money away on rocks. "Yeah," she said. "I might take you up on that."

Ty's bedroom was at the end of the hallway. "I almost kept my old room," he said. "The thought of taking my parents' room freaked me out. But it's *way* bigger."

The walls of his room were pale teal, like a muted version of his hair, and a painting of a bonsai tree hung above his headboard. Fit walked over to a set of shelves that were full of awards. On the top shelf was an award shaped like a teardrop inscribed with "Tyler Coates: Activist of the Year. 2011."

"That's my GLADD award," Ty said. "Still the best after-party I've ever been to in my life."

Fit thought about Ty's famous coming out video. He was one of the first YouTubers to post a video talking about their sexuality, and it had gotten him national attention.

"We're almost done," he said. As they walked back down the stairs, Fit couldn't help but wonder what the tour of her apartment would be like. She pictured herself saying, "This is the couch where my grandfather sleeps. And here, in the kitchen, is the dishwasher that overflows at least once a month." She'd show off Frankie's closet-sized space and her own colorful mess of a bedroom, before sweeping her arm toward Dubs's door, doing her best impression of Ty. "And this," she'd say like she was talking to a live audience, "you don't want to miss this, folks. This room has been taken over by River. That's right. The woman who tried to kill me sleeps a hop, skip, and a jump away from my bed."

Ty led Fit out onto the porch, which overlooked his perfectly square backyard. A fence ran along the edge, separating Ty's property from his neighbor's identical house and lawn. An underground pool took up the right corner of the backyard: noodles and inner tubes floated along the top of the water. "We used to have a crappy above ground pool, with a lumpy bottom and weak sides," Ty said. He made a clicking sound with his cheek. "I'm going to miss this place."

"Why are you moving then?"

"Work. I should have moved a few years ago. I spend half my G-D life there. But I got a development deal with Lionsgate, so I finally gave in."

Fit didn't know what a development deal was, but she knew Lionsgate made movies. Real movies that got played in theaters. "I'd kill to move to LA," she said.

"I'd let you take my place if I could."

Fit imagined herself in one of Ty's colorful outfits, standing on the balcony of an LA penthouse. "Oh, c'mon. It can't be that bad." She knew that a lot of the big YouTubers lived in LA. They complained about the traffic, but other than that, they all seemed to love the location.

"Trust me. Everyone there is obsessed with how they look, how other people look, how famous you are, and how much you're willing to spend on a smoothie made from sunflowers and dirt."

Fit laughed. "But you always look fab."

"Aw, baby girl. You're too sweet." He leaned on the railing and looked out at the lawn. "We have one last stop on the tour. My pride and joy. My studio."

Ty's finished basement resembled a professional TV studio. There were three different sets, all with their own group of filming equipment: cameras, light boxes, microphones. Fit had seen all these sets in Ty's videos and had assumed they were in different parts of his house.

"Damn," she said.

"It's taken me years to get it just how I want it. And now I've got to pack the whole damn thing up. Which one do you want to film on?"

Fit scanned her options. One set had a rustic wooden table, the section of wall behind it painted yellow. The next held two director's chairs and a small tree in the background. And the final set, tucked in the corner, had a plush loveseat with shelves on the wall behind it full of candles, books, and other trinkets.

Fit went and sat in one of the director's chairs. She liked the way it felt, high and powerful. She looked down at the plant, saw the dirt and a dying leaf. "Damn, real plants and all," she said, gently touching one of the leaves.

"Yep," Ty said. "It's really easy to tell when plants are fake."

In the back corner of the basement sat a vanity, light bulbs surrounding the mirror. It looked like something out of one of the old movies Dubs liked to watch.

"This is where I put my face on," Ty said, flicking a switch that turned on the light bulbs.

Fit looked at herself in the mirror. Her eyes seemed sunken in, her hair frizzy, and her face was red and blotchy. "Oh my god. Do I really look like that?" She'd put makeup on that morning, but she could barely tell.

"These mimic camera lights. No one looks good without their face painted. Don't worry. I can help." Ty slid open the drawers of the vanity, which were filled with different types of makeup: foundation, eyeshadow, mascara.

"Use whatever you want," Ty said. "I have plenty of clean brushes." Fit loved watching makeup tutorials on YouTube, but her small stash of drugstore cosmetics wasn't even able to replicate half of what the beauty gurus did.

"I wouldn't know where to start."

"Oh girl. I got you."

Ty took some before shots of Fit with his camera. He then pushed her hair back with a bandana and wiped her face down with a makeup remover cloth. As Ty methodically worked, it was obvious he knew what he was doing, and for the first time all day his face held a serious look. He wanted the reveal to be a surprise, even to Fit, so he had her face away from the mirror.

He grabbed a stick of bronzer from the bottom drawer, and Fit asked, "That's not too dark?"

"Trust me. Your cheekbones are going to be able to cut glass once I'm done with you."

Fit didn't question him again.

The last step was lipstick. After Ty applied the light pink shade, he took a step back and looked at her. "My job here is done."

Fit looked at herself in the mirror. All her features were more defined, exaggerated even, and she looked like a better version of herself.

"No fucking way," she said, getting up close to the mirror, inspecting this new face.

"It might look a little over the top," Ty said. "But once

you get on camera, you'll still look like Miss Fit. Just with a little extra pop."

"I love it," Fit said. "I want to look like this all the time."

As Ty did his own makeup, Fit checked her Twitter feed. Before meeting up, they'd decided to do a Q&A video. That morning, she and Ty tweeted to their followers that they were doing a video with the other person and everyone should send their questions. There were a ton of responses. Fit scrolled through, screenshotting the ones she wanted to ask Ty. Most of the replies were funny, genuine, and thoughtful. But mixed in, of course, was hate. Fit got a lot of heckling, but it was nothing in comparison to what she was seeing. Homophobic slurs, people telling Ty he should go die. Fit looked over at Ty, thought about how sweet he was, how gently he'd blended her eye shadow into the crease under her eyebrow.

"Ugh, I hate people."

Ty started applying his mascara. "What's going on in the trash heap of the world today?"

"Trolls just being trolls."

Ty laughed. "What else is new?"

He applied cherry lipstick, smacked his lips, and asked, "How do I look?" His eyes looked like two gems against a backdrop of flawless skin, and if Fit's cheekbones could cut glass, then Ty's could cut diamonds.

"Beautiful."

"Oh, you're just saying that," he said with a wink.

He told her to sit down in one of the director's chairs, and he got behind the camera. He turned on two large lights pointed directly at Fit's face, and she had to squint her eyes against the brightness.

"Jesus Christ."

"You'll get used to it."

The lights made everything behind the camera impossible to see. Ty had disappeared along with the rest of the basement.

"I'm literally blind," Fit said.

"Just pretend that all your fans are behind the camera."

"Yeah, right."

"True. True. You know how loud they'd be?"

Fit had seen videos of Ty's fans reacting to him when he was at a signing or on a panel at one of the major YouTube conferences. Ty always looked shocked to hear the wave of screams that erupted when the audience first got sight of him. Even though he was from the league of veteran YouTubers, the ones who had been around almost as long as YouTube itself, Ty's reaction was always one of surprise. Fit could hear Ty shuffling behind the camera, and she wondered if his reaction was genuine in all those videos. If really, after all these years, he was still in awe of his celebrity.

Fit asked, "How loud would my fans be?"

"Your ears would be ringing for days," Ty said, only a voice behind the camera.

Fit imagined herself walking out on stage, people screaming for her. She got goosebumps.

"Alrighty," Ty said, coming out of the darkness and sitting next to her. "We're recording."

They filmed Ty's video fist. Fit had an assortment of questions she'd picked out. They ranged from mundane, like advice on how to ask out a boy over text, to ridiculous. "If you could ride on the back of any animal," Fit read, "what would it be?"

"Vulture," Ty answered quickly. "Easy. I'm obsessed with them."

Ty took the questions seriously, often pausing for a moment to truly think them over. Ever since Fit had stepped foot in Ty's house, she'd been able to feel his presence—strong and cool. But once he sat down in the chair next to Fit, the camera rolling, there was something different about him. A little extra magnetism pulling her to him. She had a hard time keeping her eyes off his face, and when he was weighing the pros and cons of the question "Would you rather have no knees or no elbows?" speaking to the camera like it was an old friend, Fit finally understood what Dillon meant by the BFF factor. She couldn't quite put it into words, but Ty had it. She knew why he was one of the greats.

Fit had become so wrapped up in the filming, consumed by Ty's energy, that she was surprised when he said, "Well, that's a wrap! Be sure to subscribe to my channel and Fitted Sheet's."

Ty got up and turned the lights off. "Not so bad, huh?"

"You were great."

"Oh stop," he said. "You're gonna make a girl blush."

Ty said the lights needed a few minutes to cool off, and when he ran upstairs to use the restroom, Fit checked her Snapchat. She'd been posting to her story throughout the day and sending personal snaps to the casino crew. Her fans were going crazy. **Tell TY I LOVE HIM!** She could tell that the casino crew had watched all her snaps, and none of them had sent anything back in response. But Diamond had posted a few snaps on her own story: Riley driving, the dashboard of his car with the road outstretched in front of them, a video of the wind blowing in Diamond's face.

Ty came back downstairs. "You all right?"

"Yeah. Yeah." Fit said. "Just reading some hate comments."

"Girl," Ty said. "You have *got* to learn to ignore that shit. Otherwise it'll drive you crazy."

"I know," Fit said, trying to push the image of Diamond away.

Ty asked, "You ready to film?"

"Hell. Yes." Ty turned the lights back on and settled into his seat.

"You're running this one," he said. "Whenever you're ready."

Fit tried to absorbed Ty's energy, that quality that was more than just camera presence. She sat up a little straighter, smiled, took a deep breath, and was ready to make a kick-ass video.

Ty picked out great questions for Fit and kept saying how he had a hard time choosing from the onslaught of queries. As Fit rattled off her answers, something in her chest swelled: her fans actually wanted to know more about her. They didn't think this video was just some dumb gimmick for views.

"Ohhh, this is a good one," Ty said after he'd scrolled for a little while. "How did you get your name?"

Fit let out a little laugh. She was expecting this question. She'd been asked it many times before and had been planning on doing a full video with Diamond as a guest star to tell the Fitted Sheet origin story. It was hard to explain in 280 characters. Even in this Q&A video, she wasn't sure she'd be able to do the vignette justice.

"It was an ex-boyfriend," Fit said, thinking back to Jackson, wondering what she'd even seen in him. Fit knew that Ty liked to keep the content he appeared in relatively clean, so she gave the PG version. "He was really annoying, so I started ignoring his texts toward the end. He got *so* mad. And when we broke up he called me an unmanageable mess. Like a fitted sheet."

"Rude!" Ty said. "What'd you say to that?"

She thought about Diamond, how the two of them had laughed their butts off about the text, but Fit wanted to give the fans a little more drama. "I chased him out of my place," she said. "I threw one of my shoes at him and said, 'I don't want to be freaking folded!'"

"Dang," Ty said. "You told him!" They high fived.

Ty hummed as he picked out the next question. Fit felt high from the adrenaline, Ty's presence, and she craved to keep going.

"Okay. Okay. This is a good one." Ty pushed his hair behind his ears. "@downcomfy95 asked 'What's it been like living with your mom?'"

The energy that Fit had been zooming on took a nosedive. "What?"

"Your mom. What's—" and before Ty could finish, Fit said, "Nope. Next question."

Ty looked puzzled.

Fit gripped the canvas bottom of the chair. "I don't talk about that."

"But your fans want to know. There are so many questions having to do with your mom."

"Next-fucking-question," she said, angry with both Ty and her fans.

"See for yourself." Ty held his phone out to Fit. She could feel the tears coming, and she didn't want Ty to see her cry. "Want me to call Dillon?" she asked nastily. "Tell him I'm canceling this whole fucking thing?"

Ty looked surprised. "He's the one who told me to bring up your mom in the video."

"He said what?"

"I thought you knew."

Fit felt like an idiot, like she'd been tricked. "I can't." She jumped out of the chair, almost knocking it over, and ran up the basement stairs. She couldn't breathe. She had to get out of the house. She ran through Ty's kitchen, past the dumb boxes, and out onto his porch. She gripped the railing and tried to make sense of what had just happened.

Ty knew. That wasn't surprising. And it wasn't a revelation that her fans knew. But Dillon? Had he known the whole time?

Had he just been humoring Fit and River as he went along with their lies? Or had he done the digging after they'd left, suspecting something was off about their mother-daughter act?

Fit screamed, the noise coming from somewhere deep in her stomach.

After a few minutes, Ty came out. He leaned against the railing and lit a cigarette.

"I know you're not old enough, but . . ." he said, holding out the pack to her. Fit took one, the first inhale taking the edge off.

They didn't speak, the noise of a lawnmower a few houses down filling the silence. Fit wanted to cuss him out, wanted to call him on his bullshit, but she was hoping he would speak first.

Ty put his cigarette out in a planter filled with butts. "It's horrible for the skin, but what can you do?"

Fit exhaled, looked him straight in the eye, and gave him the dirtiest look she could.

"Listen," he said. "I thought you knew."

"Well, I didn't."

"You're going to have to talk about it someday."

"Says who?" Fit put her cigarette out with the bottom of her shoe.

"Let's just say you're missing out on a real opportunity if you don't. You're the girl who lived, for Christ's sake!"

"What's that supposed to mean?"

Ty turned around and leaned his back against the railing. "Dillon might be intense, but he's good at what he does. He just has this ability to make people famous."

Even though Fit was still full of rage, she couldn't help but watch Ty's every move. The sleeves of his robe swayed in the slight breeze.

"You'd be famous without him," she said.

"I'm not so sure," Ty said. "A whole bunch of us YouTubers owe him our careers. He thinks about what each of his clients has to offer. It was his idea for me to make the coming out video. You know how much exposure I got off that thing? I was on regular TV for weeks."

"So you're saying this one video is going to make me famous? Bullshit."

"You know how many wannabe actors in Hollywood would kill for your story? People can't resist a heartwarming tale of a family coming back together."

"That's so *not* the case. I hate her," Fit snapped even though Ty's logic was beginning to make sense. "I never talk about it."

"People change," Ty said. They were quiet. Fit thought about how she used to visit survivor forums, comforted by the fact that she wasn't alone. But she never participated, the thought of sharing her story turning her stomach. "What if I *can't* talk about it?"

Ty looked at her, his face soft and sympathetic. "You're a YouTuber now," he said. "You know what that means?"

"What?"

"You're not just the actor. You're a writer and director."

Fit looked back out at the lawn. Was she willing to lay her family drama on the line for more views? She thought about how nice Ty's house was, and how she was still so far away from half a million subscribers. She'd been making videos every day, but at the rate her fan base was growing, it would still be a few months until Dillon could sign her. And now, Ty was presenting her with an idea that could probably cut that time in half.

"Fine," she said. "I hope you're fucking right."

It wasn't easy. Not at first. Ty asked her the question again, doing a masterful job of pretending like it was the first time he had uttered those words, and Fit had to fight the instinct to tell him to shove it. Instead, she thought about what Ty had said. How she was the director of her own life.

"You know, Ty," she said. "It hasn't been that bad."

"No?"

"Better than I'd anticipated, actually."

"Do you want to give a little explanation? For those folks who might not know exactly what @downcomfy95 is referring to?"

No, Fit didn't. Muscle memory made her want to throw in a "fuck you" or a "I don't have a mother" but she was an actress now. And behind the camera was an audience full of her fans, waiting to be impressed.

"My mom became very sick after she had my little brother, Frankie. And she tried to hurt us."

"She locked you in the garage, right? With the car running?" A flash of glass: Frankie's red cheeks. Fit looked at Ty. Had he done this research on his own or had Dillon fed it to him?

"Yes," Fit said. "With the car running. But we were rescued." She turned back to the camera. "She claims no memory of this, but she still went to prison. She's out now—and living with us."

"And what's that been like for you?" Ty asked. His face showed genuine concern, but she couldn't tell if he was acting or truly worried.

Fit took a moment. She may have looked like she was trying to work up the courage to reveal a truth she'd never spoken of before. But in her mind she was weighing her options: What would her fans want to hear? What would make them talk? Because, if she were being honest, the truth was too boring. The past few weeks had been fine. River worked a lot. Fit ignored her sometimes. Other days they sat on the couch together and watched TV. It wasn't as horrible as she thought it was going to be, nor was it anything to write home about. A lukewarm story at most. But nothing lukewarm went viral.

"We're becoming a family again," Fit said. "She is my mom, after all."

One of the first things Fit did after she found out that Ty lived in Rhode Island was look up how far his house was from the fancy art school that Frankie wanted to go to. When she saw that the campus was only a half hour from Ty's, she'd decided that after her collab with Ty she'd go to the college's bookstore, surprise Frankie with a T-shirt.

She left Ty's house in a faint state of shock, and as she drove down the highway, letting the GPS on her phone guide her toward campus, she tried to process what had just happened. When Fit had agreed to talk about River, she'd been thinking about the views, the thumbnail, the shocking title. It wasn't until she started speaking the strange and unfamiliar words about River that Fit thought, *What's this going to unleash?*

Toward the end of the video, Ty had asked, "Postpartum depression. That's pretty common, right?" He'd looked at her like she was a fountain of knowledge, but the truth was she didn't know much. She wracked her brain for anything she could offer him.

"She had postpartum psychosis, so it's a bit more rare," Fit responded. She'd heard Dubs use the term, and there had been bits and pieces about the illness scattered throughout the articles she'd found. "There's some statistic like one in one hundred moms get it," she said. "Or maybe it's five hundred?" A tickle of embarrassment had snuck up her throat after she'd said this, but she pushed it away with the rest of her doubts.

Fit was lost in these thoughts when her phone's GPS spoke up, notifying her that the exit for Providence was coming up in a mile. She got into the right-hand lane, double checking over her shoulder to make sure her blind spot was clear, and tried to stop thinking about the video. What's done was done.

She found the campus easily enough, parked, and Googled a campus map that would lead her to the bookstore. After she figured out where she was going, she opened a new browser and typed "postp" into the search bar. Fifth in the list of autofill suggestions—right after "postpartum depression screening"— was "postpartum psychosis." Fit stared at the words, the cursor blinking on and off a few times like a metronome, before she closed the browser and hopped out of the truck.

At the bookstore, she picked out a classic gray T-shirt with the school's crest on the front. There were flashier designs, but they felt a bit tacky. Frankie had better taste than that.

Fit paid and then took her time walking back to the truck. The campus was quiet, as it was summer break, and Fit snapped pictures of the red brick buildings and the uniform trees that lined the walkways. She walked past a gray stone building, with columns and arches, and saw a group of three students sitting on the steps. One of them was lying down, her arm over her eyes to block out the sun, and the other two were reading. They looked so collegiate, unbothered and cool, in their ripped jeans and grungy T-shirts. Fit could imagine her brother sitting right beside them, talking about exams, parties, or whatever college kids talk about. She took a picture of the building, making sure to get the students in the frame too.

When Fit got home, Frankie was in his room, watching YouTube videos on how to make slime. "How was it?" he asked.

"Dude's loaded," she said. "You'd love his studio." She tossed the T-shirt, still in the plastic bag, on his bed. "I got you a present."

"Is this some of Ty's merch?" he asked, sitting up and grabbing the bag.

Fit laughed. "You'll see."

Frankie pulled the T-shirt out, inspected the front. "No shit!" he said. "Where'd you get this?"

"Where do you think I got it, dummy? Ty lives close to campus."

Frankie quickly changed into the new shirt, his curls getting pushed into his face as he pulled it over his head. "What do you think?" He stood there, beaming, arms out, and Fit thought about the video. He was part of this too. She should warn him.

"Looks cool," she said, holding her phone up to take a picture. "You should go show Dubs."

Dillon texted Fit the next day.

**Ty said it went great.**

She was still mad at Dillon for going behind her back, so she responded with a clipped, **yeah.**

**Can't wait to see it. Ty is hard to impress.**

She wanted to ask him how long he'd known, but Fit knew how easily she could snap and didn't want to risk that happening. If someone as famous as Ty still needed Dillon's help, then so did she.

**good it was fun**

The night before the video was scheduled to come out, Fit and Diamond were sitting on the bottom of the apartment stairs. Riley was supposed to pick Diamond up, and he was half an hour late. Fit was keeping her company.

The summer had been dry and hot, the grass around the bottom stair patchy with brown spots. Fit pulled a piece of dead grass out of the ground. She and Diamond hadn't seen each other since before the collab with Ty.

Diamond asked, "You mean he has an entire closet full of silk clothes?"

"Maybe half the closet. But Di, this place was amazing."

"Sounds like it. So, you did a Q&A?"

"Yep." Fit threw the dead lump of grass out onto the sidewalk. "He asked about River."

"No shit. Did you castrate him?"

"No. Imagine the views though?" They both laughed. "I answered. I talked about her."

"Damn," Diamond said, dragging out the word a little. "Does Frankie know?"

That morning, Fit had heard both River and Frankie out in the kitchen while she watched YouTube videos in her room. She tried to make herself leave her bedroom, warn them about what was coming, but she couldn't bring herself to get out of bed.

"Is that a no?" Diamond kicked a little bit of dust toward Fit, leaving a mark in the dirt. "Do they know?"

Fit plucked another hunk of dead grass out of the ground, a whole mess of dusty roots coming with it. "Not yet. But I'll tell them."

Diamond sighed, like she knew Fit wasn't telling the truth. "It's going to be a whole lot worse if they see it on their own."

"They'll understand." Fit didn't even believe the words as they came out. "I just need to get to half a million," she said, trying to justify herself.

Diamond rolled her eyes playfully. "So you can get signed. Yeah, I *know*."

"Make fun all you want," Fit teased back, "but let's see if you're still laughing when I get us a swanky apartment in New York City."

As soon as the words slipped out of Fit's mouth, she wished she could take them back. She hadn't mentioned her New York City plan to Diamond yet, wanting the moment to be perfect.

Fit waited for Diamond's response, terrified. The cars along Route 12 let off a slow buzz. The sun felt hot at Fit's back, intensifying her regret. But then Diamond laughed, the noise tearing a happy hole in the summer sky.

"All right, miss big shot. When you get us that apartment

I'll stop calling you on your bullshit." Diamond smiled as she spoke, her words tilting upward. "But until then? You're still my favorite idiot. Got it?"

Fit wanted to reach out and kiss Diamond, her plan suddenly more tangible than ever. Fit smiled, looked back down at the dirt, and traced her finger through the scuff mark Diamond had left with her shoe.

"Got it."

Riley showed up forty-five minutes later. Fit felt a small pang of jealousy when Diamond climbed into his car, but she wasn't angry. Even if Diamond hadn't realized how serious Fit was about New York, something inside of her had made her say yes.

Fit's computer wouldn't have been able to handle the files from Ty's camera, so he edited the video for her. When he was done, he sent her a link where she could download the file. All set.

She put the cursor over the link and hesitated. She thought about how the video would affect River, Frankie, and even Dubs. But then her mind went to Diamond and the city.

She uploaded the video to her channel, scheduled it for 8:00 the next morning, and turned off her computer, so there was no temptation to delete it.

She distracted herself on Instagram. A YouTuber she followed took a selfie of herself with a ribbon in her hair, and Fit thought it looked cute. Frankie was hanging out at Pistols's, like he had every night that week, so she texted him: got any ribbon?

After ten minutes with no response, she grew impatient and went into his room. There wasn't any ribbon in his art supplies bin. She opened the top right drawer of his desk where he sometimes kept supplies and rifled through the contents. She paused when she saw a small bundle of money tucked into the corner. Fit picked up the stack of bills up and flipped through it. It was mainly twenties and fifties, and she estimated it was at least five hundred dollars. Where *the hell* had Frankie gotten all this money from? She thought about texting him but instead decided to wait: some things are better done in person. She put the money back, closed the drawer, and returned to her room.

no why? Frankie responded a few minutes later.

nevermind, she wrote back.

The next morning, Fit woke up to a text from Ty: Told you so!

For a moment, she didn't know what he was talking about, her mind still heavy with sleep. But then it hit her. The video. It was live. Had been for two hours.

She went to her channel. The video, which she'd titled **"TALKING ABOUT THE TIME I WAS ALMOST KILLED (COLLAB W/TY SKYVIEW)"** had almost 65,000 views, and her subscriber count had increased by 4,000.

HOLY SHIT!!!!! she texted Ty. I HAVENT EVEN SHARED IT WITH MY FREAKS YET

She scrolled through the comments. There were haters ragging on her and River, but those remarks didn't bother her. She'd grown accustomed to a certain level of vitriol thrown her way. But what did surprise her was the overwhelming amount of love. People were thanking her for talking about her experience, for trusting them with this information. **You're an inspiration to us all!** one of the top comments said. **We ♡ you Fit, we ♡ you so much**, read another.

Fit scrolled through the comments for an hour, amazed, becoming so absorbed it was if she was no longer in her bed, but rather swimming in a sea of positive words and heart emojis.

There was a loud knock on the door, and Fit jumped. "Jesus! What?"

Frankie came into her room and stood there, fists clenched, his mouth looking like he'd just sucked on a Lemonhead.

"What got into you?" she said, feigning ignorance.

"Are you serious?" he said. "You're going to make a video about our family, about mom, and not warn us!"

"Didn't know I needed permission to talk about my own life," she said.

Frankie's lips pressed together even tighter. He looked like he wanted to hit something. It must have been a shock for him—to see the title, watch the video. The elation Fit had been swimming in just moments before soured.

He asked, "Does Mom know?"

"I don't know," Fit said, shrugging her shoulders as if he were asking her what the temperature was outside. "You think she subscribes to my channel?"

"You're such a bitch! Anything for a little bit of fame, huh?" Frankie's top lip started to tremble. His voice wavered.

"It's more my story than yours anyway," she said.

"What does that mean?"

Fit wanted to tell him it was because she remembered. She could still see his beet-red, baby face. His open mouth. Hear his scream.

"I'm inspiring people!" she said. "My fans think I'm brave." She held up the computer toward him for proof.

"Bullshit!" Frankie said. "You're only thinking of yourself. You've been like this ever since you got back from New York. News flash. You're not famous. Not by a long shot."

"You're just jealous that *I'm* going to make something of myself and you're going to be stuck here, making art out of tin cans for the rest of your life." As the words came out, Fit knew how terrible they were. She tried to stop herself, but just as with the bowl, her insults came crashing down.

"Fuck you," he yelled as he left her room. It wasn't until Frankie slammed his own bedroom door, that Fit remembered about the money. That she still needed to ask him about it. Later, she thought. After he'd calmed down.

Dillon called a few hours later. "The numbers are looking fab-u-lous!" Fit hadn't spoken to him since her clipped text messages, since feeling blindsided by him, but those thoughts were now far from her mind.

"Damn straight," she said.

"This video's got legs." Fit wasn't sure exactly what he meant, but she could tell by his voice that he was happy "Listen," he went on. "I've got to run to another meeting, but I've lined up something pretty exciting for you. LiveWire wants to feature you in a video."

"No shit," Fit said. LiveWire was a huge online media site, their videos always getting millions of views.

"Believe it. They want to come to your place and everything."

"My place?"

"Yeah. People love a small-town vibe. They want to focus on the whole mother-daughter thing."

Fit's stomach dropped. "You mean River?"

"Who else would I mean?"

"No way." Her words came out harsher than she expected. "I mean—she's very private. I'm not sure she'd be up for it."

The line went quiet. Had he hung up on her? Was he mad at what she said?

"Do you want to reach half a mil?"

"I do, but—"

"Then convince her," Dillon interrupted. "I've got to go. I'll email you the deets."

Fit laid back on her bed, contemplating what to do. River would never go for it, neither would Dubs. But this opportunity was too amazing to pass up. It was LiveWire for Christ's sake. LiveWire! She couldn't sit idle and watch it flit by. If this was the response the internet gave her after a mere mention of River, imagine the splash a video of the two of them, side by side, would create. Fit sat back up, determined, and began to form a plan.

River placed a small sliver of chocolate on her tongue, and as it began to dissolve she separated out the flavor profile. She'd been tasked with rating the salt level of various chocolate samples. But just as she had isolated the saltiness, a small yellow circle, her mind wandered to that morning. To Fit. To the video.

The bit of the chocolate had completely melted away by the time she got her mind back on track, the flavors dulled so there was nothing left for her to work with. She grew frustrated with herself but remained silent; she didn't want Lorrie to pry the truth out of her like with the chicken wing incident. This was different, so different River still couldn't comprehend what had happened that morning.

She'd been sitting at the kitchen table, drinking coffee, when Fit came out of her bedroom, holding her computer.

"Can I show you something?" Fit had asked.

"Sure."

River remained quiet as Fit typed on the keyboard. Fit hadn't necessarily been chummy with River since the chicken wing debacle, but the lingering tension had diffused.

Fit finished typing and asked, "Promise not to be mad?"

"Mad at what?"

Fit turned the computer toward River. On the screen was a video. River read the title and thought she was going to be sick.

"It came out yesterday," Fit said, looking at the screen. "And I thought you should see it."

When the video was done, River sat there in silence.

"Are you mad?" Fit's voice sounded earnest. "I should have told you earlier. I just didn't know how."

River gripped her mug, unsure of how she felt, and all she had been able to say was, "I have to catch the bus."

River messed up the chocolate testing three more times before the group was given their break. She went into the bathroom and watched the video again on her phone. It was less jarring this time. And in place of the shock, something else started to creep in: a notion that maybe she hadn't truly ruined everything on that day fourteen years ago.

River noticed that there were twice as many comments as there had been that morning. She began to scroll through them. There were people telling Fit how brave she was, thanking her for her story. River read the comments, holding her breath for the hateful ones about her. To her surprise a different theme began to emerge. Among the love thrown her daughter's way, there was also compassion for River. People saying their mom had struggled after having them too. **Lexapro literally saved me after I had my youngest**, one comment read. River thought back to the train ride to New York, how Fit had said that having fans felt like never being alone. River hadn't been able to wrap her brain around it then. How could someone you'd never meet make you feel less lonely? But as River hid in the bathroom stall, scrolling, she started to understand.

You meant what you said? she texted Fit before going back to work. In the video.

Fit responded immediately: yes ♡

Later that night, Fit heard River turn the TV on out in the living room. They were the only two in the apartment so Fit took the opportunity to execute the next step of her plan. She set an alarm on her phone to go off in five minutes, then went into the kitchen. After filling a glass with water, she leaned on the wall next to the kitchen and asked River, "Your taste buds do good today?"

River chuckled. "Relatively speaking. You have a good day?"

Fit shrugged. "Did a little of this, a little of that. The usual."

River's face had turned ghost-white while watching the Q&A that morning. Fit was certain she'd ruined her chances at getting River on board with the LiveWire video. However, a small opening of hope appeared when River had texted her from work, and Fit was determined to squeeze through that opening if it was last thing she did.

"I'm sorry about the video," she said. "That was pretty shitty of me. Not giving you any warning."

River took a deep breath, nodded. "I suppose."

"I wasn't sure how you'd react." Fit made her voice a little softer. "I was scared."

Fit looked down at the floor, but she could tell River was looking at her.

"Honestly?" River said. "I'm happy that you're talking about it. That you're opening up. I thought—"

Fit's alarm went off.

"Sorry," she said, pulling her phone from her back pocket. She looked at the screen. "It's Dillon. I should take it."

"Sure, sure," River said.

Fit turned off the alarm, held the phone up to her ear, and took a step back into the kitchen. She faced away from River.

"Hey," she said, then paused for a moment. "Good, good. What's up?" She glanced over her shoulder, saw River watching her. *Perfect.*

"I don't know," Fit said, imagining Dillon asking her about the LiveWire video again. "I know it would be good exposure, but I'm not sure it's the best idea. I don't even know if she'd be willing."

Pause.

"Yeah. She's here. We were just talking, actually."

Fit let out a big, exaggerated sigh. "Fineee. But I'm not making any promises. I'll let you know."

Fit pretended to hang up. She sat down on the couch, a cushion away from River. "Sorry about that. Dillon just being Dillon, you know?"

"What did he want?"

"It's dumb."

"C'mon, tell me."

Fit felt her plan working. She bit her cheek to keep from smiling. "Some reporters want to come here and interview me for a video."

"That's great," River said.

"Yeah. I thought so at first. But there's a catch. They want to do a mother-daughter piece. They want to interview the both of us."

"Oh."

"Right? I told Dillon no. That you've been dragged into

this enough. But he keeps hounding me. Saying it could be great for my career. You know how he is."

River seemed to mull over this information. "They'd come here?"

"I guess they want the real 'small-town vibe.'"

"Hmm," River said. Fit could feel that River was interested, that she was getting close. She needed one last push.

Fit looked at her phone. "It's fine. I'll tell him you're not up to it." She began to compose a fake text message to Dillon.

"It's only an interview?" River said.

Fit stopped typing, looked up at River. "Yeah."

"And it'd be good for your career?"

"Stupid good."

River nodded and took a deep breath.

*Come on*, Fit thought. *Just say yes.*

"I could do it."

"Really?" Fit said, excited. She leaned forward and wrapped her arms around River, squeezing tight. "Thank you, thank you, thank you."

When she let go, River looked shocked, then said, "Of course. I mean, how bad could it be?"

Her words sounded honest, and Fit couldn't help but remember how panicked River's face had become while watching the Q&A. How once the video had finished River looked at Fit in horror, her eyes wide and anxious, almost as if she were drowning. But this time was different, Fit reasoned with herself. River knew what she was getting into.

"Right?" Fit said. "It's going to be great. I should call Dillon back." She got up from the couch, pushing the image of a frightened River from her mind, and as she made her way back to her room she felt an unfamiliar feeling of power come over her.

its on!! she texted Dillon.

Perfect, he responded almost immediately.

Dubs was a harder sell.

"They're coming here?" he said, flabbergasted. Fit had woken up early the next morning to catch him after his shift, hoping he'd be too tired to argue.

"And your mother agreed to this?" he said, River having just left for work.

"She practically insisted."

Dubs ran a hand over the top of his head. "No. I'm putting my foot down."

"Dubs, C'mon!"

"Your mother's only been out for what, two months now?"

"I tried to tell her the same thing," Fit said. "I originally told Dillon, no. But when River found out, she said she wanted to do it. I swear."

"Oh, come on," Dubs said. He sat in his reclining chair, still in his wrinkled uniform. "You know she'd do anything to get in your good graces."

Fit was growing impatient. She had the urge to storm out, yell that he was ruining her life. But she stopped herself, knowing that wasn't how she would get her way. She shrugged her shoulders and looked at the ground.

"I don't know. I thought this is what you wanted." She tried to sound embarrassed, humble. "For us to be close or whatever."

Dubs gave up with a sigh. "It better be scheduled for a day I'm here. Got it?"

"Got it." Fit walked over and kissed Dubs on the forehead.

He smelled like bleach. For a second, Fit wondered if what she had done was wrong.

"Guess we better get this place cleaned up, huh?" Dubs said, chuckling to himself.

"I guess so."

The LiveWire crew was scheduled to come on Friday.

"As in two days away?" Dubs said, exasperated.

"It was Friday or Monday," Fit said. "And I know you work on Mondays."

"Well," Dubs said, looking around the apartment. "We've got some work to do."

The next two days were a blur. Everyone except Frankie pitched in. Even Diamond came over at one point to help Fit organize her room.

Dubs brought home some heavy-duty cleaner from the casino—"to really get the gunk out"—and on Thursday he took the kitchen table outside to give it a good polish.

"You don't have to do this," Fit had said as she helped him carry the table down the apartment stairs.

"It's been on my to-do list for a while."

When Fit went back inside, Frankie was making a peanut butter and jelly sandwich in the kitchen.

"Thanks for all your help," she said sarcastically. He grimaced as he screwed the top of the peanut butter jar back on. They hadn't exchanged more than a few words since their fight. Fit leaned up against the counter. "You should put some new art in the living room. If you want."

Frankie took a bite of his sandwich.

"Nah," he said, and then left the kitchen, leaving his dirty knife on the counter.

"Slob!" she yelled after him.

Later that night, after Fit had finally decided on the outfit she was going to wear, she went out into the living room and saw that Frankie had replaced all his art on the walls with new work.

Dillon insisted on being present during the filming. He showed up at 11:00 am, just like he said he would. Dressed in skinny jeans, a linen top, and wayfarer sunglasses perched on top of his head, he looked out of place in the apartment, too cool for such a rundown dump. But, if he did feel out of place, he didn't let on. He looked just as comfortable standing in the living room as he had in his top floor corner office.

He and Dubs shook hands.

"Great to finally see where Fit does her work," Dillon said. Dubs was still holding a rag in his hand, having brought in the dry and newly polished table just moments before Dillon arrived. "We do what we can," Dubs said.

"And you," Dillon said, turning his attention to Frankie, who had emerged from his room to linger in the hallway with crossed arms. "You must be the artist." Dillon walked over and shook Frankie's hand. "Fit speaks very highly of you."

"It's just tinfoil," Frankie said, acting unmoved, but Fit could tell by the slight flush in his cheeks he was flattered.

Once they all took a seat, Dillon said to River, "I'm so glad you agreed to do this." He looked like he was about to say something else, but, afraid he'd somehow give away that he hadn't been on the phone call, Fit cut in. "When are they getting here?"

Dillon checked the time. "They said they were an hour away about forty-five minutes ago. They're sending a reporter and a camera person. That's a big deal. Normally, they just send out one person. Make 'em sweat, you know. But not for you guys," he said, directing his words to both River and Fit. "They must think they're onto something."

"Well, duh," Fit said, putting her arm around River's shoulders. Dubs and River both laughed, but out of the corner of her eye, Fit could see Frankie shake his head then walk back down the hallway to his room.

Fit excused herself and returned to her room. She had to finish her makeup, hoping to recreate the look Ty had given her. She didn't have all the products that he had used, but he had sent her home with a contouring stick and highlighter. She left the door open, keeping half an ear on the conversation out in the living room. As she applied the contour under her cheekbones, trying to make her features really pop, she saw Frankie appear in her mirror's reflection. He leaned against her doorframe and shoved his hands in his pockets.

"Creep," she said, continuing to do her makeup.

"I know what you're doing," he said.

"Oh yeah? You're a fan of contouring?"

"Acting all buddy-buddy with mom like that."

She turned around and looked at Frankie. "Is that illegal or something?"

"I know it's all clickbait," he said, the words sharp and biting. "That's all she is to you."

He spoke loud enough that Fit was worried that his voice would carry out into the living room. She got up, yanked him in her room, and shut the door. "That's bull," she said.

"I know you, Fit." Frankie's face was turning red and splotchy, exactly like Dubs's did when he got angry. "I was here for all of it, remember? Every fight. Every swear. You know how shitty it was growing up with you?"

"Well, I think I had a pretty good reason to be mad, Frankie," she shot back.

"Mom was sick," Frankie said. "I *know* you still don't get it. Now you're spouting off this crap to Ty about wanting to be a family? About forgiveness? I was the one that went to visit her every month, Fit. *Me.*"

Fit had always known that Frankie was a better person than her and held onto the fact that since he admired her, was always by her side, there had to be some good within her too. Frankie shook his head, like he was getting water out of his hair and said, "Tell me that you forgive her. Say the words and I'll leave you alone."

Fit didn't know how she felt. She tried to appease him, to tell him she was doing this for him, too, but the words refused to come out.

Frankie curled his lip in disgust. "If only your fans could see the real you. They'd hate you." He turned around to leave, and as he reached for the door handle Fit said, "Well, I know what you've been up to!"

He stopped and looked over his shoulder. "Me?"

"Yeah. You and Pistols."

Frankie looked worried, then anger took over his sweet face. "Stay out of my fucking business," he said before whipping the door open and leaving. His reaction confirmed that he was up to something, and Fit was determined to figure out just what that something was. But as she sat down to finish her makeup, she tried to clear her thoughts. She had a show to put on.

The two LiveWire employees arrived shortly thereafter. The woman who would be interviewing her, Adele ("Yes, like the singer" she'd said upon introducing herself) looked closer to River's age. She spoke and carried herself like the type of person who owned a room the second she walked in. She and Dillon obviously knew each other, Adele giving Dillon those fake cheek kisses Fit thought people only did in movies. Coming in after Adele, camera equipment slung over both shoulders, was Dalphene. She didn't look that much older than Fit. She was tall with broad shoulders and had long dark hair that was pink at the tips, and Fit thought she was cute.

Adele introduced Dalphene as an intern. "She's at NYU film school." Dalphene smiled sheepishly, waving at everyone.

"Hey," Fit said, maybe a little too loudly.

Adele got right to work, scoping out the apartment for the best place to film. "I've been watching your videos all morning," Adele said as she poked her head into the kitchen. "You're funny."

She finally decided on the corner of the living room, right next to the window, after Dalphene commented on the natural light. They moved Dubs's reclining chair out of the way, and dragged over the kitchen table, shiny with its new polish.

"See," Dubs said to Fit, as he helped Dillon move the table. "Good thing I shined this puppy up."

Dalphene set up the filming equipment as Adele explained the plan for the video. "We'll do an interview and an activity."

River, sounding nervous, asked, "Activity?"

"A few hours ago, LiveWire asked our followers what sort of objects y'all should make out of tinfoil." Adele had been carrying a small canvas bag over her shoulder. She opened it and pulled out a roll of tinfoil. "We'll pick a few at random. You'll have a minute to do your best, and the one that looks the best wins. But obviously, winning isn't really the point."

"Frankie would be the real winner," River joked. The mention of Frankie stabbed a little at Fit. But she pushed it away.

"You never know," Fit said, then looked at Adele. "Sounds fun."

Dolphins, castles, Saturn and its rings: people had sent in a whole slew of requests. Fit read through the responses as Dalphene got her mic'd up.

"This person says I should make a big ol' dick," Fit said, looking up from the screen of her phone.

"Jessica!" Dubs called from the kitchen, where he and Dillon had retreated to stay out of everyone's way.

"What? I'm just reading what people have sent." And at this, Fit saw Dalphene, who had been so serious up until this point, crack a smile. Fit smiled too.

"Save it for the camera," Adele said. "It's part of your charm. That pretty face and the dirty mouth."

"See, Dubs," Fit called back to the kitchen. "It's part of my charm."

Dubs came to the edge of the living room. "I don't know about that."

"Don't worry," Adele said to Dubs. "We'll make sure both your girls come across great."

"All right." Dubs turned his attention to River, who had

been mic'd already and was sitting in a chair behind the table. "But you don't have to answer anything you don't want to."

"I'll be fine," River said, then she looked at Fit and winked. Fit winked back. Dalphene finished clipping the microphone on Fit's shirt and said, "You're all set."

Fit took a seat next to River. Dalphene looked through the camera and then turned on the big light that she'd set up. It was so bright it made the whole apartment disappear. All Fit could see was the camera, the table, which shimmered under the lights, and River.

River held her hand up to shield her eyes.

"You'll get used to it," Fit said, trying to sound as sage as Ty had.

Adele's voice came from the darkness. "Ready?"

"Yep," Fit said, then turned to River. "You?" River put her hand down, nodded.

The first object they had to make was a daffodil. Adele counted off "three, two, one, create!" and Fit and River both got to work. About halfway through, Fit realized hers looked nothing like a flower. "I'm going for something a little bit more–uh–interpretive," she said.

"At least yours resembles a flower," River said. "Mine looks like a UFO." River held up her saucer-shaped tinfoil, looked at Fit, and shrugged meekly. They were quiet for a moment, and then, as if planned, they both burst out laughing. As their laughter filled the room, Fit thought about how good it was going to sound on camera. People were going to love it.

The rest of the filming went great. Adele's questions were mainly softballs. How was Fit dealing with the recognition? "Pretty well, I think. I'm keeping my focus on making good content." Did River have a favorite video of Fit's? "The one with the crown. I can't remember the TV show."

Every couple of questions or so, Adele would task them with something else to make out of tinfoil. They shaped their favorite foods: an ice cream cone for Fit and a cupcake for River.

"I guess a sweet tooth runs in the family," Adele said from behind the camera.

They'd just finished making a chihuahua and were laughing about how disproportionate Fit's was, when Adele said, "River. Are you aware of what is being written about you online?"

The air left Fit's lungs, deflating her laughter.

"I've read the comments, yes," River said. "On a few of the videos."

"What about this one, from user JackHAt298: **That woman shouldn't be allowed within a hundred feet of her children. Or anyone's children.**"

River's smile was gone, her face slack. Fit knew the drama Adele was trying to stir up would be good for views, but she still had the urge to reach out and slap the woman, hiss, *You're ruining our good time.*

A few beats of silence passed. "River?" Adele prodded from behind the camera. "What would you say to Jackhat 298 if they were here right now?"

River shifted in her seat and Fit couldn't take it anymore. "Mr. Jackhat can shove his opinion up his ass."

"So you like having your mom here?" Adele asked.

"Yeah," Fit said, defensively. "So what if I do?"

"What's it been like since River moved in?"

The air in the room seemed to still. In Fit's mind, it became clear that this was the moment the video had been leading up to. The answer to Adele's question was obvious.

"You know," Fit said, "growing up I used to pretend I didn't have a mom. I think it made things easier to handle. But now I know that was dumb. Childish." Fit smiled at River, then looked directly back at the camera. "Of course I've got a mom. And she happens to be really terrible at making things out of tinfoil."

When they were done with the video, Dalphene turned off the lights, the rest of the apartment becoming visible again. Dillon and Dubs were standing in the back of the living room. A twinge of guilt hit Fit's stomach when she saw Dubs so happy, hope practically spilling out of his ears.

"Bravo!" Dillon said.

Fit asked, "It was good?"

"So good," Adele said matter of factly. "Now. Dalphene is going to shoot some B-roll. And then we'll be out of your hair."

Fit showed Dalphene to her room.

"Wow," Dalphene said. "It's bright."

Fit grew embarrassed, her room suddenly feeling childish. "Yeah. Most of this stuff is kinda dumb."

Dalphene hoisted the camera onto her shoulder. "No. It's cute." She looked through the viewfinder and slowly panned the whole space. Fit took a step back so she wouldn't be in the shot.

"Now pretend like you're doing something," Dalphene said.

"Doing something?"

"Yeah. It's supposed to look like you're getting interviewed. Even though we won't use what you say."

"Okay." Fit stood there for a moment, unsure of what to do.

Dalphene must have sensed Fit's unease. "Tell me about some of the pictures." She pointed at the wall of fan drawings.

"That's fanart," Fit said. "I keep some of my favorites on the wall."

Dalphene continued to film as she asked, "Do a lot of fans make you stuff?"

"Tons." Fit pulled her box of fan memorabilia out from underneath her bed and showed Dalphene the stacks of paper. Looking at the pictures made her think of Frankie, of what he'd accused her of doing.

"You all right?" Dalphene asked.

Fit held up a particularly bad drawing to the camera, smiling earnestly. "Has a certain charm, doesn't it?"

After Dalphene had gotten a few close-ups of the art on the walls, the desk, and the books on the bookshelf, she popped her head outside the door and looked down the hallway.

"Good, they're still talking," she said and placed the camera on Fit's bed. "Adele would kill me if she knew I was going to ask you this." Dalphene took her phone out of her back pocket. Fit's heart started to race. She was excited, a little scared, thinking Dalphene was going to ask for her number.

"Can I take a picture with you? My roommates and I love your videos. They're all super jealous I'm here."

"Oh my god, sure," Fit said.

Dalphene put her face next to Fit's, held her phone out in front of her, and they both smiled. Excitement surged through Fit's body. Not because they were so close that Dalphene's long hair tickled Fit's arm, but because Dalphene was a fan. A real, live fan.

Dalphene took a few pictures, then put her phone away. "Any other ideas for B-roll?"

"We could go out to the parking lot?" Fit said, not wanting their time together to end. "The sign to the building is like a hundred years old."

Dalphene was filming the "Meadow Lane Apartments" sign, with its faded flowers and chipped paint, when Dillon came down the stairs, talking on his phone. He walked over to the them.

"Hold on a sec," he said to whoever he was on the phone with, then leaned over to Fit. "Great job in there. Couldn't have scripted it better myself."

"Think people will like it?"

"For sure. Trust me on this one. I've got to get back to New York, but this launches the middle of next week. So get ready."

"'Kay."

"Thanks, Dalphene," he said, then walked back toward his car, a shiny Mercedes Fit had watched him drive into the parking lot a few hours before.

"Didn't know he even knew my name," Dalphene said.

"He's a lot."

"Adele wouldn't shut up about him on the way here. Says he's one of the best."

Dillon got into the driver side of his vehicle, its engine turning over.

"I'll be right back," Fit said to Dalphene, who had now started filming the front of the building. Fit jogged over to Dillon's car and knocked on the tinted window. He rolled it down.

"What's up?" he said, his phone still to his ear.

"Did you know about my mom before we came to New York?" The question had been growing in Fit ever since she'd filmed with Ty.

Dillon paused. His sunglasses shielded his eyes, so she couldn't read his expression, but his nose crinkled for a second. He then asked, "Does it matter?"

Fit thought about the interview she'd just done. Getting out of this place, this town, seemed more real to her than ever.

"No," she said. "I guess not."

Later that night, Fit left her room to grab a glass of water. She thought everyone was asleep, but there was a light on in the living room. Peeking into the living room, Fit found Dubs sitting in his recliner. The TV was on, but the volume was so low the show was barely audible.

"Past your bedtime," Fit said. Days that Dubs didn't work the graveyard shift he was normally asleep by nine.

"Couldn't sleep."

"Couch finally get to you?"

"No," he said, sighing. "When it does, you'll know. I'll be requisitioning your bed."

"No way, old man." Fit sat down on the couch, all the furniture back in its proper place.

Dubs was watching an old black and white TV show that Fit didn't know the name of. "How do you know what's going on?" Fit asked. "You can't even hear it."

"Rerun," he said. "I've seen this one plenty of times." A man was walking across the lawn. "He's about to fall." And in a few steps, the man fell, unconvincingly, into the grass.

Fit and Dubs both laughed.

"You know," Dubs said, still looking at the screen. "I thought I'd messed up."

Thinking he was talking about his television prediction, Fit said, "Nah, you called it."

"Insisting your mother live here. I thought I'd made a mistake."

"Oh."

"But after today, I feel a bit better. I suppose. Like we're heading in the right direction."

Fit thought about the fight she'd had with Frankie, how ashamed he'd looked when she couldn't answer his question about forgiveness. Why couldn't she have told him the truth? That talking to River had gotten easier? That when she saw River's face the urge to throw things wasn't as strong?

"Do you think I'm a bad kid?" she asked Dubs. "For breaking stuff all the time?"

"You haven't broken anything in at least three weeks," Dubs teased. "That's gotta be a new record."

Fit didn't have anything to say to Dubs's normal ribbing. He crinkled his forehead and asked, "Everything okay?"

"Those lights were really bright," she said. "Gave me a headache."

"Take an aspirin. Lie down."

"I will," Fit said. "Soon." They continued to watch TV in silence, and after a few minutes, Dubs said, "Watch. He's going to fall again." And sure enough, Dubs was right.

Sitting in bed that night, unable to shake Frankie's words, Fit looked up "postpartum psychosis" on YouTube. She was shocked by how many videos her search yielded. There were informational vlogs, news reports, documentaries—all with titles like *Dealing with postpartum depression and psychosis* or *POSTPARTUM PSYCHOSIS MADE ME HALLUCINATE*. She scrolled and scrolled, the videos never ending, before finally stopping and clicking on one at random. It was called *My Story: Postpartum Psychosis and Help.*

The woman in the video looked to be in her mid-thirties.

She sat at a table in a poorly lit dining room. The image quality wasn't great, so Fit assumed the video had been filmed on a computer or phone. The woman's words were composed and measured as she began to explain how she had always wanted to be a mom, how excited she was to have children. She smiled as she spoke about how great those first three months were. "But after that," she said, "I felt like I couldn't go on." The woman closed her eyes and took a deep breath.

"The worst of it was—" The woman paused, and, as if she'd been struck by something invisible, her face twisted in pain and she let out a sob. Fit paused the video, not wanting to watch the rest. She logged into her fake YouTube account, the one she used when she didn't want anyone to know it was her, and commented, **thanks for this.**

A few days after filming the LiveWire video, Fit checked her email and had a pay statement waiting for her from YouTube. She opened it, figuring it would be the normal hundred or two hundred dollars, so she couldn't quite believe it when she saw the number: $567.89. She checked her bank account to make sure it was correct, and sure enough, the money was there.

"Holy shit," Fit said. Dillon really did know what he was talking about. More videos, more views, more money. After doing a celebratory dance in front of her mirror, she got the itch to go shopping, see the money in action.

Frankie was still mad at her, so she slipped her shoes on and headed over to Diamond's. When she rounded the corner, the slap of her flip-flops echoing in the breezeway, she saw Pistols chilling outside his apartment. He was sitting down, back against the wall, shuffling a deck of cards. Music played from his phone, amplified by the coffee mug it was sitting in—a makeshift speaker.

A small hesitation crept into her stride. She hadn't seen Pistols since the chicken wing video went live. His presence in her video had created a frenzy in the comments, just like she'd hoped. Her fans asked **who is that, are they dating, is he single?!?** One fan commented, **find someone that looks at you the way pistols looks at fit at 3:13.** Pistols had texted her a few days after the video came out. Mannnn your fans really love seeing you in pain. And Fit had wondered if there was more beneath that text. If he'd read the comments too. If they'd given him hope, made him think that Fit was crushing on him right back. Fit had waited a few hours to respond, finally writing yah.

"Your new room?" Fit said to Pistols as she got closer.

"Mom's working the night shift tonight and said I was being too loud," Pistols said. "Not everyone can sleep through an explosion like Mr. Dubs."

"He'd have to, or his snoring would wake him up every night. Diamond around?"

"Just missed her," he said. Fit assumed that Diamond was off with Riley, but not wanting to ruin her good mood she didn't ask. Pistols shuffled again. "Wanna play?"

Fit thought about going back home. She could wait until Diamond was free or see if Frankie was still being pissy over their fight. But she couldn't ignore the number she'd seen in her bank account. "I have a better idea," she said, and showed Pistols the email she'd gotten. His eyes opened wide, impressed. "Damn, Fit. That's a nice chunk of change."

"Right? Let's go to Best Buy."

Pistols laughed. "You're wasting no time."

Pistols drove, and when they got to a stoplight, he rolled his window down and yelled, "She's going to be rich!" at the car in the lane next to them. The woman driver either ignored him or couldn't hear his voice over the grumble of the car. Fit laughed and called out too. "Better believe it!"

Fit wanted a vlogging camera. Her normal camera was too heavy to carry around, and her phone wasn't the greatest quality. She tested out every camera in Best Buy—even the ones she couldn't afford—by holding them out in front of her, pretending like she was filming a vlog. She eventually decided on a rose-gold Nikon. The camera was about as big as her palm, twice as thick as her cell phone, and for an extra thirty bucks she could add a mount that made it even easier to hold.

"This is the one," she said.

Pistols tapped at the price on the display—over three hundred dollars—and said, "You could probably find it used or for real cheap on Amazon."

"Don't care," Fit said. Everything she bought was used or on clearance. She wanted something brand new, full price. She'd earned it. They made their way to the checkout line, and when she paid, the feeling of sliding her card through the credit card machine was so satisfying she wanted to do it over and over again.

"You up for some fro-yo?" she said as they left the store. "My treat."

"Okay, Miss Money Bags," Pistols said.

There was a frozen yogurt shop across the plaza. They both took stacks of the small sample paper cups and taste-tested practically all the flavors, even though Fit always got cake batter.

"So, when does your big LiveWire interview come out?" Pistols asked as he piled scoops of M&M's on top of his pistachio fro-yo.

"In a couple days," Fit said. There had been a weird lull in the apartment ever since the filming. None of them had really talked about the video, but she could feel it lurking behind all their interactions. "I just want it to drop already."

When they finished piling on their toppings, Fit once again enjoyed the smooth slide of her card as she paid for the both of them. They sat at a table outside, shaded by a big umbrella. "Yo, thank you," Pistols said.

"You're the one that's telling people I'm going to be rich," she said. "'Member?"

As Pistols took his first bite, Fit thought about what Frankie had said—that everything she did was clickbait. Did Pistols think she'd used him in her video? He wanted to be a card dealer, so he, out of everybody, should understand that games have rules. And she'd only been following the cardinal rule of YouTube: do what you can to get views. She dug into her yogurt, telling herself that Frankie had only said those things to get under her skin. But when Pistols took a Snapchat video of the two of them, saying, "Miss Fancy over here treating me to dessert," she couldn't ignore the tight knot at the back of her throat.

The thirty second teaser LiveWire posted of the video looked like a professional movie trailer: it started with a few seconds of Fit standing in front of the apartment complex, then moved to Fit and River sitting next to each other, laughing. Adele's question could be heard in the background. "So, do you forgive your mother?" The clip ended with Fit staring directly at the camera, the screen going black before she could answer.

Fit used the video as an excuse to bug Frankie. He'd been standoffish ever since the shoot, ignoring her, or answering her questions with a grunt. She'd seen him sneak out a few more times, heading to Pistols's car in the middle of the night, and she was determined to make him talk.

She knocked on his door.

He called out sharply. "What?!"

She went in. There were art supplies on his desk—tissue paper and glue—that looked like they had been abandoned mid-project. He was sitting on the floor, leaning up against his bed, and shuffling a deck of cards. They purred in his hands.

"You're getting good," she said, telling the truth. "You might even be better than Pistols."

"Yah," he said, not taking his eyes off the cards.

She held her phone out to him. "Did you see this? Your art makes an appearance."

He took the phone from her and watched LiveWire's teaser. "Cool."

"Hopefully, all this is good for you too. You know, your art and stuff."

Frankie nodded his head, handed Fit her phone back, and resumed shuffling. They were both quiet, the sound of the cards folding on top of each other filling up the room. She wanted to explain that what she was doing, why he was mad, wasn't just for her. If she made enough money, she could send him to art school in Rhode Island, he could lounge on the stairs of a collegiate looking building without a care in the world.

"I should get working on my next vid," she said after a minute or so. "Do you have any tacks?" She knew where he kept them.

"Yeah," he said, gesturing to his desk. "In the middle one."

"Here?" Fit said, opening the top drawer, where she'd seen the stack of money before. As the drawer slid out, Frankie jumped to his feet, shouting, "No!" But it was too late. The drawer was open and Fit was looking down at the stack of clipped money. She picked it up; it felt bigger than before.

"What the hell is this?" she said.

He gripped his cards tightly in his right hand. "What does it look like?"

"It looks like a lot of money for someone with no job."

"Pistols and I have been doing landscaping work," he said. "Under the table." He sucked in his cheeks.

"In the middle of the night?"

"Yeah. In the middle of the night." Frankie ripped the money from Fit's hands, shoving it in his pocket. "Get out of my room."

"I'll figure it out eventually," Fit said as she left his room, fuming. If Frankie wouldn't tell her, she'd go to Pistols. She was determined to uncover what Frankie was keeping from her.

But the LiveWire video came out the next day and Fit suddenly had bigger things to deal with.

**Why did Fitted Sheet's mother try to kill her?**

**YouTube star Fitted Sheet talks about forgiveness, troubled past**

**If your mother tried to kill you, would you forgive her? Fitted Sheet tells her story**

The tweets that LiveWire put out with the story were all clickbait. Fit cringed as she read them, but she had to admit they worked. Within an hour the video had 30,000 views. After a couple hours it was at 50,000 and by the time Dillon called at noon, the number had crept to almost 200,000.

"Have you seen it?" Fit said, picking up the phone.

"How could I miss it?" he said. "You're everywhere. But that's actually not why I'm calling."

"Oh yeah?" Fit said, her words filled with confidence and pride. "What website wants to talk to me now? TMZ? E!?"

"Even better," he said. "I sent the video to one of my contacts at ClickCon. And they loved you."

"No shit," Fit said. ClickCon was an internet video and vlogging conference that took place every year in Los Angeles. She knew it was coming up soon because all the YouTubers she followed were posting about it.

"I explained that it would be dumb not to use this moment you're having. So I got you on a panel."

"Shut. Up. You're serious?" Fit's heart was pounding.

"Dead. You're slated to be on a panel called 'The Future

of YouTube.' I know it's last minute, but this will be huge for you. Plus, you've always wanted to go to LA, right?"

Dillon continued to explain the details but Fit had a hard time paying attention. She was going to be in a room full of fans. Her life was going to look like all the other YouTube stars who posted vlogs and pictures from the conference.

"If you can get yourself there," Dillon said, "the spot on the panel is yours. I'll cover your and River's registration."

"River?"

"Yeah. You need a guardian. Plus, she's kind of part of this now."

Fit knew the plane tickets and hotel rooms were going to be expensive, especially so last minute. But she didn't care. She was going to be on a panel. Nothing could stop her.

"I'm there. Can I tweet about it?"

Dillon laughed. "Tweet away."

Still on the phone with Dillon, Fit wrote and posted, **SEE YOU AT CLICKCON FREAKS**

The day the LiveWire video came out, River lost count of how many times she watched it. She played the clip when she first woke up, when she was on break at work, and that night as she lay in the middle of Dubs's bed. Fit had warned her to stay away from the comments, saying, "Trolls are going to be trolls." But River, growing curious, couldn't help herself.

The words people wrote stung, but in a sense, she felt she deserved the hate. One comment caught her eye: **She's lying. There's tons of ways to remember**. The person had included a link to an article about repressed memories. That article led to a string of others, and River soon realized there were endless resources on recovering hidden memories. Maybe, River thought, if she could remember what had happened, she could truly apologize for what she had done and finally, hopefully, move on.

Some of the articles River found suggested hypnosis, others aromatherapy, and some said medication was the best route. Then she came across a video by a man, Dr. Ron, who claimed to be an expert in dissociative amnesia. His voice was calming and soothing, and he instructed River to close her eyes, envision her mind like a big white room with a black door in the corner. River found it easy to follow Dr. Ron's instructions, even enjoyed turning her mind into an empty space. Dr. Ron then told River to populate this room with objects close to the memory she was trying to unearth. She imagined Frankie as a baby and Fit at three years old. "Put as much into the room as you can," Dr. Ron urged, and River added in a miniature submarine that swam in the space over her head. She placed a small replica of the house, garage and all, on the floor. The red Honda Civic was there too. As she placed these objects in the white room, she slowly approached the black door. "Behind that door," Dr. Ron said, "is the memory you're looking for." And River felt an odd sense of excitement and dread as the door got closer. "When you put your hands on the doorknob, I want you to rid the room of everything and make the room dark. As dark as the door." River swept all the objects from the room and turned off the lights. Dr. Ron then explained that on the count of three, River was to open the door, and there, if everything had been done right, the memory would be. "One, two, ready?" And when Dr. Ron said "three" River turned the doorknob and the door swung open, revealing another dark room, full of nothing.

Frustrated, River kept researching. She read about going back to the actual place where the incident happened. "Location often acts as a trigger," the article said. In her mind she could go back to the house, but maybe she needed to physically visit.

The next day after work, River went to the bar with Lorrie and a few other coworkers. River had been taking Lorrie up on her offer of visiting the bar after work a few times a week. Sometimes it would just be the two of them; other nights they managed to wrangle a few other workers who were eager to wash away the taste of the day with a drink.

River had been hoping to get Lorrie alone at some point in the evening, but the two people at the bar with them, a young couple River had never met before, remained steadfast in their seats. After Lorrie finished her second gin and tonic she got up to use the bathroom. River waited a few seconds and then excused herself from the table.

The bathroom was in the back of the bar. River stood outside the door, leaning against the wall, trying to look casual, but when Lorrie came out of the bathroom River stood up straight, quickly.

"Sorry," Lorrie said. "Didn't mean to scare you."

"You didn't," River said. "I actually wanted to ask you something."

"Okay."

"A favor."

Lorrie nodded her head for River to go on.

"Could you drive me somewhere tomorrow? After work?"

"Where?"

"Just a house," River said. "I'm not going in."

Lorrie raised her eyebrows questioningly. "You in trouble?"

"No, no!" River said, laughing nervously. She realized how outlandish her request must have sounded. "I'm thinking of moving. There's a room for rent that I'm interested in. I'd like to get a feel for the neighborhood. But the bus doesn't go there."

"Why not," Lorrie said. "Tomorrow it is." She winked at River and they went back to the table.

Fit knew one of the first things Dubs was going to ask about ClickCon was how much it was going to cost to attend. After she got off the phone with Dillon, she had immediately crunched numbers. Plane tickets, hotel, food, and transportation: the total came to about $1,500. After buying her new camera, she had $647 left in savings.

She had texted Diamond to see if Mrs. M. could get her some shifts at the hotel that week, adding, plssss this is important.

friday and saturday morning, Diamond had responded. mom says don't be late lol

That would be another $200 to $300. The rest could be put on Dubs's credit card. If her YouTube checks were all as much as the last one, she could pay him back in a few weeks. A month, tops.

Two days after Dillon had called with the news of the conference, Fit looked at herself in bathroom mirror and whispered, "You can do this."

Fit strolled into the living room and stood directly in front of the TV. "I have an announcement."

Frankie threw a piece of popcorn at her. "Get out of the way."

She glared at him. "Shut up." Then to everyone, she said, "I've got big news. I've been invited to ClickCon. And here's the plan."

Fit barely stopped to take a breath as she explained the call from Dillon, the conference, the money. "But most importantly," she said at the end of her monologue. "This could be my big break."

The room was quiet for a moment and then Dubs asked, "And your mother has to go?"

Fit nodded. "I'm only seventeen."

Dubs sighed. "I don't know." He rubbed his hand through the few sparse hairs on the top of his head. "How much is this escapade going to cost again?"

Before Fit could repeat the numbers and her plan, River spoke up. "I have some money saved."

Genuinely surprised, Fit said, "Really?"

"Yeah. It's not a lot, but it's something."

"I don't know," Dubs said. "Four days is a long time to be gone."

"It'll be like a family vacation," Fit said, trying to play to Dubs's sentimental side. "Some good bonding time."

Frankie rolled his eyes but Fit ignored him.

Dubs thought for a little bit, and she could tell he was struggling with his decision.

"Fine," he finally said. "You can go. But you pay off anything on my credit card before school starts. Got it?"

"Jesus Christ," Frankie said. "I can't believe you're falling for this bullshit."

"Hey, sir!" Dubs yelled at Frankie. "*What* has gotten into you lately?"

Before Frankie could answer, Fit butted in and asked, "Yeah, Frankie. Want to pitch in for the trip?" She wasn't going to let him ruin this for her. "You've got a little something saved up, right?"

"Fuck you," he said, getting up from the couch, bumping into her shoulder as he left.

"Jeez," Dubs said after Frankie slammed his door shut. "What's got him all riled up?"

Fit shrugged her shoulders. "No clue."

Fit busted her butt during her first shift at the hotel, finishing her assigned section early and then picking up a few extra rooms. She walked out with $165 in cash.

The next day, she was assigned the top floor. "No way!" Fit said, when Diamond's mom gave her the news. The top floor was all penthouses and suites and was normally reserved for the veteran housekeepers. It's where the big tips came from.

"Diamond told me what you were saving for," Mrs. M. said, checking something off on her clipboard.

"Oh my god. Thank you!"

Mrs. M. smirked. "Just don't get used to it."

Diamond tagged along that day and followed behind Fit as she pushed the cart to the first room. "I can't believe you're here on your day off," Fit said.

"I'm bored," Diamond said. She took a long sip of her iced tea. "Riley's working the lunch shift, so he should be out in a few hours."

Fit did her best to hide her disappointment and said, "Oh, cool," while knocking loudly on the first door.

The suites on the top floor were nothing like the hotel rooms Fit was used to cleaning. Some were as big as her apartment, having multiple rooms and king-sized beds. One of the penthouses even had a jacuzzi in the bathroom. The tips were bigger, too, one of the guests leaving her a hundred-dollar bill.

"Holy shit," Fit said, waving the money in front of her face.

"How's it smell?" Diamond said, poking fun.

"Like success."

Diamond laughed. "You're stupid." In some of the rooms, Diamond would lend a hand—helping Fit strip the bed or empty the garbage cans—but most of the time she would plop herself down on the couch, stretching out her long limbs like she owned the place.

In a room about halfway down the hallway, Fit opened the mini-fridge and found an unopened bottle of champagne.

"Ooh la la," she said, holding it up for Diamond to see. Champagne wasn't standard fridge inventory, so the guests must have ordered it or brought it in themselves. "Looks like these folks never got to celebrating."

"Damn," Diamond said, taking the cold bottle from Fit's hands. "This shit is expensive too."

Diamond began to unwrap the foil covering the cork.

"What are you doing?" Fit said, reaching out to take the bottle back, but Diamond was too quick and spun away from Fit's hands.

"Calm down," Diamond said, continuing to open the bottle. "They checked out, right?"

"Yeah."

"Then finders' keepers." The cork came out with a loud *pop*; Fit jumped at the noise. Diamond took a sip from the bottle, then handed it to Fit, who followed suit. The bubbles tickled the top of her mouth, and in that moment, Fit forgot that she was wearing the scratchy polyester housekeeping uniform, or that she'd been picking up dirty towels all day. She envisioned her and Diamond in a penthouse of their own, where it'd be champagne every day.

By the time they moved to the next room, they had almost drained the entire bottle. Fit's face was hot, her chest heavy with glee.

Diamond stood in front of the window and looked out. Fit stood next to her. They were on the side of the hotel that overlooked the Connecticut River. There was a factory on the opposite bank, a bridge a little bit upstream. Fit could see the cars crossing over the bridge, made miniature by the distance.

"It's actually kind of pretty, huh?" Diamond said.

Fit burst out laughing. "You *must be* drunk to think this shithole is pretty."

Diamond took a swig from the bottle then held it out to Fit. "Finish it off."

Fit complied, throwing the bottle away when she was done. As she began to clean the room, her moves felt slow yet fluid, like she was a duck gliding through water.

At one point, Diamond went into the bathroom, and Fit heard her say, "Holy shit!" Diamond came out, holding a long chunky necklace that sparkled under the lights.

"Woah," Fit said, walking over to Diamond, taking the necklace from her hands. Up close, she could see the design resembled leaves on a vine. It was heavy for its size.

Fit asked, "Are these diamonds?"

"Looks like it."

"I wonder if it's real."

"You think someone staying in a room like this would have costume jewelry?" Diamond said. "Of course it's real."

Fit ran her fingers over one of the leaves, which was made

of five small stones, then held the necklace up to Diamond. "Want to try it on?"

"You're not scared you're going to get in trouble?" Diamond teased.

"Shut up. Turn around."

Fit placed the necklace around Diamond's neck and clasped it shut.

Diamond spun around with a flourish. "How do I look?"

"Like a mother-fucking boss," Fit said. "Let me take your picture."

Diamond climbed up onto the king-sized bed and started jumping up and down. Fit snapped away, trying her hardest to capture Diamond suspended in mid-air. She took ten, twenty, thirty pictures—she lost track. A small part of her wished some- one would walk in and catch them, so she could point to Diamond and say, "Look. Look how happy I made her."

Then, in a great fall, Diamond crumpled to the bed in laughter; her legs and arms delicate, crooked lines tangled up in the blankets. Fit belly flopped on the bed next to her.

"Let me see the pictures," Diamond said.

"'Kay. Let me find a good one." Fit held the phone above her face and started to scroll through the camera roll. "Of course you look like a model in all of these."

"Lemme see," Diamond said, holding her hand out. But before Fit could toss it over to Diamond, the phone slipped from her hand, the corner hitting her in the forehead.

They both started cracking up, Fit unable to keep her eyes open, she was laughing so hard. She could feel Diamond's laughter through the mattress.

"Owww," Fit said, rolling to her side. She rested her fore- head on Diamond's shoulder.

After the laughter died down, Diamond said, "You know what's gross?"

"Hm?"

"These are probably sex sheets."

"Eww," Fit said. "That's nasty!"

Diamond then picked up a pillow, shoved it toward Fit, and said, "And this! This is a sex pillow!"

Fit squealed in disgust and delight, pushing the pillow back toward Diamond.

"What?" Diamond said. "You're afraid of a little sex juice?"

"Oh my god, you're so gross." Fit rolled over and got on her knees to gain leverage, she pushed forward. Their faces were so close together. Diamond's lips were right there. Fit couldn't help but think how easy it would be to kiss Diamond, and before she could stop herself she leaned forward a tad bit more, the pillow still between them, and pressed her lips to Diamond's.

Diamond pulled away.

Fit sat back on her heels. "Shit." She was filled with shame, embarrassment. "Shit. I'm sorry." Diamond pushed herself back, leaned against the headboard, and looked at Fit like she had two heads.

Fit tried her best to remain calm. "I'm drunk," she said, like it was no big deal. "I can't even, like, feel my face right now."

Diamond raised an eyebrow. "I always knew you were a lightweight, but damn." She let out a small laugh through her nose. Fit laughed, too, a little too hard to seem real. She wondered if Diamond had bought the excuse or was planning her escape.

Fit then said, "So, I guess I should change these nasty-ass sheets."

Diamond took off the necklace and helped Fit clean the rest of the room. They were both quiet, more serious. Instead of happy drunk, Fit now felt on edge, overanalyzing Diamond's every move. Her mind went back and forth between *I fucked up* and *everything is fine.*

They moved onto the next room. Diamond had spread out on the couch and was taking selfies when her phone rang. "Yeah, cool. I'll be right there," she said, then hung up. "Riley's off his shift. I'm going to head out."

Fit had just finished stripping the bed. "Have fun," she said. Her voice shook as she gazed at the bare mattress.

"Make that paper," Diamond said, and she was gone.

Fit's knees buckled, and she fell forward. She shoved her face into one of the pillows, screamed, and beat her fists against the naked bed.

She pulled herself together enough to finish her assigned rooms. She funneled her emotion into energy, slamming the trash bins against her cart, tearing the sheets from the beds, and punching the vacuum back and forth over the carpet.

As Fit was leaving the casino, $300 in hand, she received a Snapchat from Diamond. Fit didn't look at it right away, trying to ignore the notification, but on the drive home it nagged at her like a bug bite begging to be itched. After she pulled the truck into the parking lot of Meadow Lanes, she checked her phone again, and there was another snap from Diamond. She couldn't take it anymore.

The first snap was a video taken from a car's window, recording the side of the road as it whisked by. The second one was a selfie of Diamond and Riley: Diamond's arm lovingly draped over his shoulders, Riley kissing her cheek. Diamond smiled like she'd won the lottery. After the time ran out on the picture, Fit couldn't help but replay Diamond's face after she'd kissed her: shocked, disgusted, and recoiling in horror. Fit's eyes began to burn.

She rushed up the stairs, hoping no one was watching TV so she could make it to her bedroom uninterrupted. But when she opened the door of the apartment, River was sitting at the kitchen table, rubbing her forehead, a tall glass of water in front of her. River looked up and they made eye contact. Something in Fit snapped and broke, and she couldn't hold it in any longer. She started sobbing. River got up from the table, walked over, and, without a word, took Fit into her arms.

"She walked in and broke down," River said.

"Couldn't pay me a million bucks to be a teenager again," Lorrie said. It was after work the next day, and they were on their way to 11 Windward Lane, Lorrie driving them in her old off-white Subaru. The air freshener dangling from the rearview mirror smelled like licorice, sending white and black swirls into River's vision.

It hadn't been until Fit calmed down a little, her crying turning into a soft whimper, that River fully processed that Fit was letting herself be held. River led Fit to the couch, gently, handling her like a stray cat that had finally been lured out from underneath a porch, and any sudden movement would bring the claws out, send it running. For the rest of the day, they'd watched a marathon of a cooking show, occasionally chuckling at the way the host said "Yum-o."

Lorrie pulled onto Windward Lane. River had been giving her directions and was a bit shocked at how easily she remembered the way to her old house. For the most part, the street looked the way River remembered it, but there was something different, a slight shift that she couldn't pin down.

"Cute neighborhood," Lorrie said.

"It's the last house on the left." A bead of sweat dripped down River's side. "At the end of the cul-de-sac."

Lorrie pulled to side of the road and put the car in park. "Here we are. Lucky number eleven."

The house was yellow now, instead of blue, and the garage looked like it had been renovated. There were no windows, the doors were a different style, and the entire structure seemed bigger. River wondered if the new owners had torn the old garage down, had wanted to rid themselves of the building where that horrible woman had done that horrible thing.

As she stared at the house, River remembered the pain in her body after Frankie was born, the wings of razor blades that sprouted from her shoulder every time he cried. *Good,* she thought, *it's working.* But when she shifted her thoughts to that day, nothing came.

She unbuckled her seatbelt and opened the front door.

"I thought you were only looking?" Lorrie said as River got out of the car.

"I just need to be a little closer." River stepped onto the lawn. It was the same lawn where she and Seth would stretch out a blanket and lay with Jessica in between them, the same shrubs she pruned once a week, the same step where she and Jessica waved goodbye to Seth the day he left on tour. But these weren't the memories that River wanted or the ones she deserved. She deserved the worst, the images that had burrowed a hole deep in her brain and refused to come out. She knelt down, ran her hands through the grass, and closed her eyes. All she saw was green and brown specs.

River heard the front door of the house open. She looked up and saw a young woman, holding a small white dog, standing on the front steps.

The woman called out, "Can I help you?"

"Yes," River said. "You can." The woman could invite River in, let her stand at the sink, stare out at the backyard. But before

River could say any of this, Lorrie yelled from the driver seat through the open passenger side door, "We just had a big meal! Feeling a little car sick."

"Want some Tums?" the woman on the step asked. River stood up, brushed her hands on her pants. "No. Needed some air was all."

River got in the front seat and buckled up. Lorrie pulled away, waving at the young woman. The woman, dog still cradled in her arms, waved back.

As Lorrie headed away from Windward Lane, River leaned her head back and closed her eyes, exhausted from the defeat.

Neither of them spoke until Lorrie pulled up in front of the apartment complex.

"I appreciate it," River said.

Lorrie waved her hand, like she was batting at a fly. "Yep."

River got out of the car, and just as she was about to close the door, Lorrie called, "Hey, River!"

River bent down. "Yeah?"

"I don't think you need to go back there."

River nodded and shut the door.

It was rare for Fit and Diamond to go more than twenty-four hours without texting. But Fit hadn't heard from Diamond in almost two days. The dull ache of loneliness filled her, sucking all her motivation out of her. The trip to ClickCon was three days away and she had so much to do: pack, promote her panel, make a video. But she couldn't muster the energy to do any of those things, and instead had been watching music videos all day.

She was watching Rihanna's music video for the song "Bitch Better Have My Money," mesmerized at how Rihanna made kidnapping look cool, when the line, "Bitch better have my funnies" ran through Fit's head. Fit's mind then went on a ride, each thought tumbling onto the next, until she was reliving the memory of her and Frankie fighting over the funny pages, Dubs threatening to cancel the newspaper if they couldn't get ahold of themselves. For the first time in two days, Fit felt inspired to create.

It took her an hour to write the lyrics. Then she got into her outfit: a one-piece bathing suit from her short-lived swim team days, a pink shower cap, rain boots, and an inner tube made out of tinfoil. She grabbed the stack of newspapers sitting in the recycling bin under the kitchen sink and headed outside.

The kiddie pool was propped up against the side of the building. She dragged it to the strip of grass next to the parking lot and then filled it with sheets of crumpled newspaper.

After she set up her filming equipment, she took a selfie using the tripod, the pool in the background, and posted it.

**Newwwww videooooo**

She did three takes of the rap. The lyrics were easy enough to remember. Each verse was short and described the love life of a different comic strip character. The refrain was "Bitch better have my funnies, funnies, funnies" repeated twice.

During the first take, Fit stood relatively still, kicking the newspapers around a few times. On the second, she picked up handfuls of the paper and threw them up in the air. And the third time Fit performed the rap, she rolled around in the pool, rubbing the pages over her body like they were suds in a bubble bath. But there was something missing in each of these takes, that little rush in Fit's stomach that let her know she was onto something good.

She was setting up for her fourth take when Riley's car came careening into the parking lot.

"Fuck," she muttered to herself. "Fuck, fuck, fuck." She looked around for a place to hide. She thought about burying herself under the pile of newspapers or making a dash for the back of the apartment complex. But she figured those things would draw even more attention to herself. She decided to stand still, like a tree, and pray she wouldn't be spotted.

Her efforts failed. Riley noticed her right away. He walked over, squinting against the sun, looking angry. Fit panicked, worried that Diamond had told him about the kiss.

Then he broke into laughter. "Shit, girl. Looking fly."

"Shut up," Fit said, annoyed yet relieved. Riley was chewing on a toothpick. He took it out of his mouth and pointed it at Fit's feet. "And what's this one about?"

"I'm doing a parody. Of a Rihanna song."

"Okay, okay. I feel you."

Fit saw Diamond coming down the stairs. Diamond looked over at Fit and Riley and paused, her foot hovering above the next step for a split second. The hesitation in Diamond's stride was so slight, Fit wasn't sure if it was real or if she was being paranoid.

Diamond joined them, looking Fit up and down. "Cute."

"She's doing a parody," Riley said. "Of Rihanna."

"Cool," Diamond said. She then hit Riley's shoulder. "Ready?"

"Chyeah," Riley said. "Yo, Fit. You coming tonight?"

Fit didn't know what Riley was talking about, but she could tell by the way Diamond stiffened, averting her gaze, that she hadn't been invited on purpose.

"Nah," Fit said. "Gotta pack."

"Ah, right. You've got fancy stuff to do in LA. We'll be going all night if you get bored."

Fit watched the two of them walk to Riley's car. When they were halfway across the parking lot, Diamond reached out and intertwined her fingers with Riley's. And something in Fit switched. Diamond could grow old in this shitty town and waste the rest of her life with idiots like Riley for all she cared.

Riley peeled out of the parking lot, and when Fit smelled the burnt rubber she knew exactly what her video needed.

Fit finished editing the parody just before midnight, uploading it as soon as she was done. She couldn't wait for people to get to the end, to watch her pull a lighter out of her shower cap and light the newspapers on fire, the orange flames creeping waist high before the screen goes black.

The next two days went by in a flash. The packing, the pro-moting, the buzz of anticipation that hummed beneath Fit's fingertips: it all made her worries about Diamond's silence and Frankie's late-night disappearances fade away.

And before Fit knew it, she was landing in sunny Los Angeles.

"From out of town?" the Lyft driver asked as he pulled onto the highway. Fit had been snapping practically everything they passed since he'd picked her and River up at LAX.

"Connecticut," Fit answered as she filmed the five lanes of traffic.

"The Nutmeg State," he said. "You on vacation?"

There were so many ways Fit could answer. She was here to get famous, get rich. She was here so she could stand at the window of her New York City apartment, drinking the finest champagne money could buy.

River spoke up first. "A conference. She's on a panel."

The hotel for the conference was fully booked, so Fit and River had to rent an Airbnb about ten minutes from down-town. The street the house was on was lined with palm trees. The one-bedroom apartment, which took up the third floor of the small house, was homey. The bedroom had a full-sized bed, and the couch in the living room pulled out. Fit put her bag down next to the cream-colored couch, assuming that was where she'd be sleeping.

"You take the bed," River said.

"Really?"

"You've got a big day tomorrow." Fit wanted to tell River about the email Dillon had sent her the day before. **Make sure people see the two of you together.** She felt the pull to warn River, tell her tomorrow might be a big day for the both of them. She pointed at the blue anchor that adorned the living room wall.

"Looks like a Pier One threw up in here, huh?"

Registration started at 8:00 am. The conference hall was overwhelming. It resembled a large mall with its echoing atrium, zig-zagging escalators, and hoards of teenagers moving in packs. And for the first time since Dillon told her about the panel, Fit got nervous.

Dillon had registered Fit as *Talent*, which had a separate check-in line.

"Guess I'll be over here," Fit said to River, cheekily, over-compensating for the flutter of nerves. "In the *talent* section."

After Fit got her registration packet, which included her nametag strung on a lanyard—*FITTED SHEET: CREATOR*—she took out the conference map. She was looking for the room her panel was going to be in, when she heard someone call her name. She looked up. Two young girls with red hair approached her. The smaller one started waving, called her name again.

"Fit!"

By instinct, Fit tried to remember where she knew these girls from. School? The casino? Church on the rare occasion Dubs convinced her to attend? It wasn't until the smaller girl said, "I've been watching you since the beginning," that it clicked. They were fans. And Fit was no longer a daughter waiting for her mother. She was a celebrity.

The girls were obviously sisters, maybe two years apart. The younger, smaller one, who Fit assumed was around twelve, did most of the talking. The other sister, whose red hair was pulled into a bun on the top of her head, seemed shy and timid.

"We were just watching your newest video last night. Right, Chels?" The younger sister then patted the older on the back of her arm. The gesture was so sweet, familial, that it made Fit sad. She wished Frankie were there.

"Hey," Fit said. "Let's take a picture!"

Fit stood in the middle, her arms around their shoulders. The younger sister held her phone out in front of them and started snapping. The girl had taken a few pictures by the time River came over with her registration bag in hand and asked, "Want me to take it?"

Fit saw a flash of recognition cross the young girl's face.

"I'm good," the girl answered, then said to Fit, "We should go get in line."

Fit hugged both the girls and said, "Tag me in those." As she watched them walk away, Fit saw the older sister whisper something in the younger girl's ear. Then, in tandem, they looked back over their shoulders at Fit. No, they were looking at River. Was that contempt or disgust she saw in their eyes? Fit had the urge to yell across the room, *What are you looking at, huh?* But the crowd swelled, and the two girls were gone.

The conference center reminded Fit of the casino: loud, windowless, and full of people who wanted something. But what these people wanted wasn't money. They wanted her. She was recognized every few minutes, each time as exhilarating and surreal as the last. Most of her fans were teenage girls—a few boys and older women were thrown in the mix too. Fit was happy to stop and take pictures, smiling wide for the whole internet to see.

Fit and River had been walking around for an hour when a woman asking to take a selfie with Fit said, "You, too," and beckoned River to join in.

River, surprised, declined the invitation. "No. That's okay."

"Quit being a wiener," Fit said, pulling River into the picture. The image of them in the fan's phone showed how uncomfortable River looked. So Fit turned to her mother and kissed her on the cheek. River burst out laughing.

Each fan encounter bumped Fit's high. It was a more intense version of the feeling she got when reading comments or scrolling through her notifications. As she joked, smiled, and took pictures, she felt powerful, like each person was giving her a splash of their energy. By the time she and River had to head over to the room where her panel was being held, Fit felt like she could run a marathon, lift Dubs's old truck over her head, talk to every single person in the room for hours on end. If this was what being a celebrity was like, Fit thought, *sign me up.*

"The Future of YouTube" panel had three other YouTubers on it who had all become popular that year. There was Roy Simone, a teenage boy from England who covered pop songs, singing all the parts and using a mixing board to blend them together. Next, was Faith Hailsham, a young woman who hosted her own cooking show; the food she created just as beautiful and precise as her production quality. And the last

YouTuber was Comet, one that Fit was most familiar with out of the three. Comet had short bleached hair, always wore all black clothes, and gave off an air of otherworldliness. Their videos were odd, yet captivating. More performance art than traditional entertainment. Their most recent upload was them sitting at a desk, white sterile walls in the background, saying the word "leaf" over and over. When Fit watched the two-minute video it already had 750,000 views. No one knew Comet's real name, where they'd grown up, who they were beyond the person in the videos. And Comet's fandom was strong, spurred on by the mystery. There were a few times Fit had even found herself on a "Comet truther" forum, wondering what planet this person came from.

Roy, Faith, and Comet were already in the waiting room behind the stage by the time Fit arrived. Roy and Faith talked to each other in the middle of the room. Comet stood off to the side, their hands in their pockets; they looked smaller in real life.

Alyssa Kalley, a YouTuber turned talk show host, was the moderator of the panel. "Great," Alyssa said when Fit walked in. "We're all here."

Fit and River mingled with Roy and Faith, Comet never approaching them. After a few minutes a conference employee with a headset wrapped around her ears came into the room. "We go on in ten."

"I should probably find a seat," River said, hugging Fit. "You're going to do great." The embrace felt reassuring, calming. But Fit could tell she was being watched. She looked up and saw Comet staring in her direction.

Fit pulled away, embarrassed, and said, "Duh."

At 2:31, Alyssa walked on stage and the audience cheered wildly, the noise sending a shiver of excitement down Fit's spine. Fit and the rest of the panel members stood backstage, waiting for their cue.

"Out of all the panels at ClickCon," Fit heard Alyssa say to the audience, "this is the one to be at. In a few years they are going to be the stars selling out stadiums, acting in their own TV shows. And you're going to get to say 'I saw them when.'" Applause rose from the crowd again. Fit willed Alyssa to hurry up; she wanted to be out on that stage.

"Without further, ado," Alyssa went on, her voice louder now, "I introduce you to the future of YouTube!"

The four panelists walked on stage. The noise crashed over Fit like a wave, filling her ears and enveloping every part of her body. The room was full, holding at least five hundred people, all of whom were on their feet clapping and screaming. Fit began to blow kisses into the crowd, then waved with both hands. She spotted a few girls wearing their own tinfoil accessories. Fit pointed at them and mouthed, "I love it!"

When the cheering subsided, Alyssa spoke again. "Ready to get started?" The crowd gave one last wild cheer. Fit wanted to turn to Alyssa and say, *no, let them scream forever.*

A year ago, if someone had told River she'd be in Los Angeles, surrounded by teenagers and watching her daughter on stage, she would have told whoever they were to stop yanking her chain. But here she was, sitting in the second to last row of the auditorium, listening to the crowd lose their minds.

When the panel got underway, River took a video of Fit and texted it to Dubs and Frankie. Look at her go!

LOTS OF PEOPLE, Dubs responded.

She's a natural, River wrote back. And it was the truth. River was amazed at how comfortable Fit seemed on stage. Fit's words carried confidence, bravado, and she spoke about her experiences with YouTube with such eloquence. River thought she was going to burst with pride. Fit was the funniest too. At one point, the moderator asked the panelists where they saw themselves in five years. Roy and Faith answered first. Then the tall blonde one who wore all black and answered each question with a jarring lack of enthusiasm, said, "Still making my art."

It was Fit's turn. River was on the edge of her seat, waiting for her daughter to speak.

"Well," Fit said, leaning forward to talk into her microphone, "I'd like to support myself, my family. My aspirations aren't quite as high as saying the word leaf over and over, but to each their own." In response to Fit's answer, the crowd rippled with laughter. River wasn't sure what was so funny, but she joined in, letting herself be swept away by the power of Fit.

The panel flew by.

"I can't believe it's over!" Fit said once they were all backstage, the high of the live performance acting like that of a completely new drug. "Let's do it again!"

Alyssa laughed. "I'm sure there's some fans waiting for you outside. There's a back door too," she said, pointing over her shoulder. "If you'd rather slip out unnoticed." At that, Comet headed toward the back exit, their long black jacket giving them the illusion of gliding across the floor. Fit had felt them tense up, ever so slightly, when she made the joke about Comet's video. She wanted to make sure that Comet knew it was only a wisecrack, that she meant no ill will. But Comet disappeared out the door. Fit didn't have the time to chase after them. Her fans awaited.

There was a small crowd waiting for her outside. She walked right into the middle of the group of fans. She felt like a hot, beaming sun, the universe she built with her own two hands swirling around her.

Fit stayed for an hour, signing autographs, taking pictures, trying to learn as much as she could about each fan. Many wore their own tinfoil creations. Some had traveled hours, even days, to get to the conference. "Just to see you," one girl, no older than ten, said. By the time the last fan left, the first day of the conference was over.

"I've got something planned for tonight," River had said in the Lyft on the way back to the Airbnb. "I think you're going to like it." River insisted on keeping her plan a surprise and no matter how hard Fit begged, she wouldn't give an inch.

"I've got it! We're going to the Playboy Mansion," Fit called out back in the Airbnb as she reapplied her makeup in the bathroom mirror. The quietness of the apartment rung in her ears.

"Eww," River said. "As if Dubs would ever trust me with you again."

In the cab on the way to River's surprise, Fit checked Snapchat. There was a ClickCon story consisting of a public stream of pictures and videos from the first day. About halfway through the story there was a video from Fit's panel. Fit could hear the audience laughing, the caption reading, "When Fitted Sheet calls out Comet for being fake."

"Idiots," Fit said.

River asked, "Who's that?"

"This person thinks I dissed Comet on the panel."

"You did seem to poke a little fun."

"I meant it as a compliment," Fit said.

"Maybe you could send them a little text message," River said. "If you're worried."

"Nah," Fit said. "Comet can handle it."

Ten minutes later, the driver pulled up to the Beeker Aquarium. A marquee hung on the facade of the brick building. A NIGHT WITH THE FISHES.

"An aquarium?" Fit asked.

"Frankie helped me pick it out," River said. "I was trying to find something that wasn't touristy. Something a little cooler than the Walk of Fame. Frankie told me how much you love the aquarium at the casino."

Fit didn't know what to say. The idea was so thoughtful it stunned her into silence.

"You hate it," River said, the excitement gone from her voice.

"Oh my god, no!" Fit said. "I fucking love it."

River clapped her hands together. "Oh good. Let's go."

As they walked toward the entrance, Fit noticed the way River's steps bounced, the jaunty side to side swing of her ponytail. Fit had never seen River so cheerful, so relaxed.

The aquarium lobby was set up for a cocktail party. Circular tables with long tablecloths were placed throughout the room. There was a bar, food stations, a jazz trio in the corner.

"Damn," Fit said. "This is swanky as hell."

"Oh yeah. It's like a whole thing," River said, waving her hand in front of her. After presenting their tickets and getting their hands stamped, Fit grabbed them plates of food, not sure what half of the appetizers were, but picking up one or two of everything. River got them sodas from the bar and they posted up at a table on the edge of the room.

The look of the guests ran the gambit: some looked like they were ready for a night on the town, others could have just walked in off the street. Fit popped a square piece of white cheese in her mouth, taking it all in. After swallowing it down she asked River, "Want to play a game?"

"Sure."

"It's called 'Guess How Much They're Worth.' Frankie and I used to play it at the casino when we had to wait for Dubs. I'll go first." Fit scanned the room, saw an older man in cargo pants and a T-shirt standing at one of the tables of food, loading his plate with shrimp. Fit nodded her head in his direction. "Two point four million."

River looked over at the man. "Really? He's acting like he's never seen a shrimp before in his life."

"Those are the ones that'll fool ya," Fit said. "Give it a try."

River looked around the room, and then said under her breath, "The woman by the bar." Fit saw who River was referring to. The middle-aged woman wore a suit, her hair pulled back tightly. "She looks like a lawyer," River said. "I'd say half a million. But, she owns two houses."

"Oh, getting creative are we?"

River grinned. "And a Porsche!"

Aquarium tours left every ten minutes and guests were able to join whenever they wished. After Fit and River had their fill of food and people watching, they joined a tour. Their guide was a young man who wore a polo shirt with "Beeker Aquarium" stitched across the back. He led Fit and River and two other guests from room to room, describing each animal's physical characteristics, their natural habitats, and a few interesting facts here and there. Fit took pictures and videos as they went along.

They then entered a room full of octopi, all in separate tanks. The octopi were different sizes and colors, and in the corner of the room was a purple octopus that looked just like Maggie, the octopus at the casino, except bigger. The animal sat on a rock in the middle of the tank, its tentacles stretched out in front of it. Fit took a picture of the octopus and thought about sending it to the casino crew, telling them she'd found Maggie's twin. She decided against that, though, and posted the picture to her public story and captioned it, **A queen on her throne**.

The tour guide showed them sharks and starfish and eels.

Fit got to pet a stingray, the fleshy body warm to the touch. When she was done she turned to River and said, "Your turn."

"No way."

"Oh come on. It's not that bad."

"I can see it fine from here."

"Chicken," Fit said, then started clucking under her breath. River told her to stop, but Fit continued until finally River cracked, smiled, and sighed. "Fine. I'll do it."

River squealed with delight as she pet the stingray. And it was as if Fit could feel River's happiness, her adrenaline-filled joy.

"See," Fit said, after River took her hand out of the water. "Aren't you happy you did it?"

River winked. "Very."

The guide stopped in front of a set of double doors and faced the group. "This is the last stop on tonight's tour," he said, rubbing his hands together. "The grand finale, if you will."

River leaned over to Fit, whispered, "I read about this."

"This is our world renowned twilight room," the tour guide went on. "We ask that you keep your voices down while inside. There is plenty of seating, so feel free to stay as long as you wish."

It was dark beyond the double doors, and dim strips of lights on the floor guided the group down the small hallway. It was like entering a movie theater, but instead of seeing a screen, the wall was aglow with jellyfish, swooping and swimming through the black water. The sight stopped Fit in her tracks. It was beautiful.

"Told ya," River said quietly.

A few other guests were sitting in the stadium seating, their faces awash in the neon glow. Fit and River made their way to the top row. Save for the occasional whisper, the room was quiet, a silent respect hovering in the air.

In awe, Fit watched the jellyfish. There must have been thousands of them. She marveled at the way they danced through the water and wondered how they moved among each other without getting tangled.

Guests came and went quietly. After a few minutes, River leaned over and said, "I'll have to thank your brother."

Fit nodded. "We used to stand in front of the aquarium for hours. Sometimes, I thought if I stared too long, the glass would break. The cracks would start off small, like spiderwebs. But they'd spread quickly, getting bigger, like the way an earthquake tears through the earth. When the glass couldn't take it anymore, the water would come tumbling down on me. And I'd be washed away." Fit sat there, stunned at what she'd just said, having never uttered those words to even Frankie. "But I was a dumb kid."

"No, Fit," River said, reaching her hand out and grabbing Fit's. "No."

Fit was good at lying, even to herself. There had been countless nights during her childhood where she'd lain in bed and constructed a new life for herself, the images becoming so real she often fell asleep thinking she was an emperor in Rome, an heiress to a fortune, or an astronaut in the space station, orbiting the earth.

So, as she tried to fall asleep, curled up in an unfamiliar bed in LA, she began to doubt herself. She panicked. The fans, the cheering, the jellyfish: had it all been made up? She scrambled for her phone, opened Snapchat, and replayed her story. Everything she remembered, it was all there.

# 43

The next morning, River was exhausted. Happy, yes. But physically and mentally drained. She didn't know how Fit did it: the cheer, the smiles, the intense concentration on each fan. They'd been at the conference for an hour when River told Fit she was going to grab a cup of coffee, sit down for a little bit.

"I'll text you when I'm done," River said.

"Don't forget," Fit said. "Ty's panel is today."

River got a large black coffee and sat at a table in the corner of the food court. The coffee was cheap but strong. She guessed Columbian blend, dark roast.

River had always been a wallflower, never a performer, and she relaxed as she watched people order their food, bring it to a table, eat, laugh, talk with their friends. And almost everyone, at some point, checked their phones. Most of them looked at their phone for longer than they did anything else. Smartphones were something River had to get used to when she arrived in the halfway house. Of course, she knew what they were, but the idea of constant connection and communication was something she wasn't prepared for.

As she watched the conference attendees go by, all texting or taking pictures or watching a video on their phones, River imagined a web of light connecting all these devices. One of River's greatest fears was that she'd done permanent psychological damage to her children. And when Dubs would report time after time that Fit refused to open up, to talk about what happened to her, River was afraid her daughter would never be able to let anyone in. But River now knew that wasn't the case. Fit was connected to more people than River could ever have fathomed. She looked to the lights for proof.

Ty was on a panel called "The Legacies," featuring famous YouTubers who had been making videos for more than ten years. The event was taking place on the main stage, the biggest room in the conference center. Ty had texted Fit that morning: come see me before my panel!

The corridor behind the main stage was lined with dressing rooms. Fit had to give her name to a security guard, Ty having put her and River on a list.

They got to Ty's dressing room, his name written on the whiteboard next to the door. Fit knocked.

"Come in!" Ty yelled. He was sitting on a couch, cross-legged. His hair now a silvery gray.

"Miss Sheet!" he said, standing up, his silk shirt flowing elegantly around him as he walked over to give Fit a hug. He then shook River's hand. "You must be Momma Sheet."

The room was nice. There were two couches, leather chairs, a vanity in the corner bigger than the one in Ty's basement. Up against one of the walls was a table with drinks and snacks. They all took a seat.

"So this is how they treat a legacy, huh?" Fit said.

"Oh shut up," Ty said, swatting at her. "I *told* them it was a dumb name."

"It suits you."

"If you insist," Ty said, pretending modesty. "How's ClickCon treating you?"

Fit tried to find the word to best describe the last day and a half. Amazing, rad, so so so fucking cool, but nothing seemed to do it justice. "I'm in love," she finally said. "With all of it."

"Aw, you're still in the honeymoon phase," Ty said. "That's cute."

"Tell me you don't love this," Fit said, gesturing around the room. Ty remained uncharacteristically quiet for a moment, then said, "Yes. I do. But it's also a job."

"The best fucking job in the world," Fit said.

Ty laughed. "Okay, okay. I surrender."

A conference employee knocked on the door then popped their head in. "Fifteen," they said.

"Got it," Ty replied. "I'll be ready." He sighed. "You two should grab some seats. Don't want to end up stuck in the back."

He hugged them both goodbye, and just as Fit was about to walk out the door he said, "Oh! Fit. I'm having a party at my house tonight. A little offsite YouTuber get together." He then looked at River. "Of course, if that's all right with you. I promise I'll treat your precious cargo with the utmost care."

Fit caught herself looking at River for permission, something she'd never done before. She grew slightly irritated—she didn't need River's approval for anything—but a small part of her wanted River to say no. On the way back to the Airbnb from the aquarium, they'd made plans to go to the Walk of Fame that night, both thinking it would be hilarious to do something so touristy.

River asked Ty, "Do you live in a safe area?"

"Ha!" Ty said, theatrically. "My neighbors call the police if a flower is out of place."

"Then, yeah. Sure. I could use a night in."

"Great!" Ty said. "Fit, I'll text you my address."

As they walked back down the corridor, past the other

dressing rooms, Fit said, "Can we go to the Walk of Fame tomorrow?"

"Sounds good," River said.

The room of the main stage had to be three times bigger than the room Fit's panel was in, and it was almost full. Fit and River found seats in the second to last row.

When Ty and the rest of the Legacies walked on stage, the sound was immeasurable, everyone in the audience leaping to their feet. The crowd cheered for a solid five minutes, everyone holding their phones up, recording a glimpse, a fractured moment. Fit thought about what Ty had said, about her being in the honeymoon phase. And as she watched Ty wave to his fans, she thought, *yeah, right. There's no way anyone could get sick of this.*

Ty lived at the top of a hill.

"Nice places," the Lyft driver said as he led his car slowly up the winding road. To Fit, it seemed like the higher they climbed, the fancier the houses got. Each one was unique, had its own personality, a work of art someone had obviously spent a lot of time crafting. It was a far cry from Ty's old cookie cutter neighborhood.

"Here we are," the driver said, pulling off to the side of the road. Ty's house was partially blocked by trees. There were several cars parked in the driveway and on the street: BMWs, Audis, Bentleys. As Fit walked by a silver Jaguar at the bottom of the driveway, she ran her finger lightly across its smooth side.

Halfway up the driveway, Ty's house came into full view. It was perched on the side of the hill, reminding Fit of a bird. It looked steady yet ready for flight.

Fit climbed the front stairs. She could hear music, laughing, people having a good time. She took a deep breath, told herself, *you're really here,* then rang the doorbell. No one came to the door, so she let herself in. The music and chatter grew louder as she walked down the hallway and turned the corner into a large room with ceilings at least twenty feet high. The space was full of people. Large windows gave a view of the backyard, where Fit could see a pool, a patio, and more guests.

Ty was in the corner of the room, drink in hand, talking to two people Fit didn't recognize. She walked over to him.

"Miss Fit!" he exclaimed when he saw her. He'd changed his outfit from earlier that day and was now wearing a ripped tie-dyed shirt that showed more skin than it covered. He kissed her on both cheeks. "I wasn't sure you'd come!"

"You think I'm that lame?"

Ty leaned his head back and let out a cackle. Fit could smell the alcohol on his breath. "Never, my dear. Now. What did you think of my panel?"

"The best one of the whole conference," Fit said.

"Oh, stop," Ty said, but his voice indicated he meant the exact opposite. Fit hadn't said that to inflate his ego—she meant it. The size and sound of the crowd made the audience at Fit's panel seem puny in comparison.

"I'm serious," Fit said. "You were marvelous."

Ty put his arm around Fit's shoulder and led her to the other side of the room where the bar was. "Tell me, Miss Fit. What do you want to drink?"

Fit looked at the row of bottles lined along the bar and on the shelves behind it. At Riley's parties, Fit was so used to grabbing a bottle of whatever and mixing it with Sprite. "I'll have what you're having," Fit said. "It seems to be doing the job."

"You saying I'm a lush, Miss Fit?" he asked coyly. He went behind the bar and made her a drink, pouring alcohol from three different bottles, then adding a slice of lemon and a few ice cubes. "A whiskey sour," he said, handing her the glass. They clinked glasses, and Fit took a sip, ready for the acrid bite of whiskey. But the liquor went down smooth, warm. "Come on," Ty said. "I'll show you around."

YouTubers fell into many different categories. There were comedians, ASMR folks, gamers, beauty gurus, artists, musicians, and cooks. There were solo acts, duos, trios, and groups. And it seemed like every genre of YouTuber was represented at Ty's party. As Ty led Fit around his house and out to the backyard, he pointed out who each person was and what group they belonged to. The pool and patio area looked like it was straight out of a music video. People played beer pong and cornhole. Fit followed Ty to the edge of the lawn. It overlooked the city, a grid of twinkling lights under the gray, dusk sky.

"Los Angeles sucks, huh?" Fit said, nudging Ty's elbow with her own. He smiled, took a sip from his glass. "I *suppose* it's grown on me."

A group of people walked into the backyard. Before heading off to greet them, Ty said, "Enjoy yourself tonight, Fit. I'm over the moon you came."

Fit scanned the backyard. She recognized some of the people there, but she didn't actually know anyone. She wished the casino crew were there. But *no,* she said to herself, pushing the thought from her mind. She didn't need them.

She took a picture of the city, the slate sky, and captioned it, **Livin the life.**

Fit chugged the rest of her drink, walked up to a small circle of guests, and although she was nervous, she joined their conversation like she had known them forever. After that, the rest was easy. She moved from group to group effortlessly. She treated everyone like friends and associates. "I'm totally going to share one of your videos!" she said to a gamer named Phil. "We should one hundred percent do a collab," she insisted to a chef. And when she found herself in conversation with a tattoo artist based out of New York who had two million followers, she said, "When I turn eighteen, I'm coming to you." Fit had never put much thought into a tattoo, but she couldn't help imagining the amount of views a video called "MY FIRST TATTOO" would get. As she moved about the party, grabbing herself another drink, the smooth whiskey warmed her entire body and she felt invincible, like everything she said was aces.

Fit was sitting at a table, listening to Yalin Haney, a legacy YouTuber, talk about a stalker he once had, when Comet walked into the backyard. They were wearing all black, once again. Online, people were still talking about the joke that Fit had made about Comet, claiming that Fit had intentionally insulted them. That morning, Fit had replayed the video a few times, trying to see if Comet's face revealed how they felt about the joke. But for the whole twenty-second clip, Comet remained calm, unmoved.

Comet looked around the backyard, and it seemed like they

didn't know anyone at the party, either. Comet then glanced over at Fit. The two made eye contact. Embarrassed to have been caught staring, Fit looked away quickly.

"And it was chocolate!" Yalin said. Even though Fit had missed the ending of the story, she laughed the loudest at the table, slapping her thigh and throwing her head back. When the laughter died down, Fit looked over her shoulder, inconspicuously. Comet had moved and was now standing in a group by the beer pong table.

Fit kept tabs on where Comet was throughout the night, glancing at them for only a second at a time. She didn't want to get caught looking, but she wanted to get them alone. Fit was on her third, maybe fourth drink when she noticed Comet standing next to the pool by themselves. As Fit walked across the lawn, the grass felt a little unsteady under her feet.

Comet's back was to Fit.

She asked, "You going in?"

Comet turned around, looked at Fit, and took a sip of their drink, a clear cocktail with a lime floating on top. "Didn't bring a suit," they said.

"Me neither," Fit said. "Ty claimed I could borrow some of his clothes, but I'd feel bad. Pretty sure he only owns silk." Comet's expression remained cool and steely, unnerving Fit. She didn't like not being able to make someone laugh. She pressed on. "Is this your first ClickCon?"

"Yes."

"Are you enjoying it?"

Comet shrugged. "One supposes. You?"

"It's a little overwhelming. But awesome."

Comet nodded in agreement. "There's a lot of screaming."

Fit laughed, but Comet remained quiet. It hadn't been

a joke. Nobody could be this much of a robot, Fit reassured herself. There had to be a way to win Comet over.

"I really enjoy your videos," Fit said. "So does my brother. He's an artist. Makes all my props."

"Is he here?"

"No," Fit said, the question feeling like a pin prick in her stomach. "He's home. In Connecticut."

Comet took another sip of their drink. The sun had set since Fit arrived, and strands of Christmas tree lights hung over the pool.

Fit wasn't getting anywhere so she gave up her act. "Are you mad at me?" she asked, the words blunt and straightforward. "Pissed about the joke I made? People are, like, all on my ass because they think I dissed you or whatever."

Comet remained quiet. Fit's face got even hotter. She was about to turn away, head back to the table where she was having fun, when Comet said, "All right."

"All right? Soooo, you don't hate me?"

"No."

Relief spread through Fit. "Oh, thank god."

"Plus," Comet added. "I know you're just jealous."

Fit detected a hint of mischief in Comet's expression.

"Hold up," Fit said. "Was that a joke?"

"A mere observation." And there it was again, a flash of sarcasm that Fit knew so well.

"Admit it. You think you're funny." Comet looked at the ground. Fit grabbed their shoulder, gave it a playful jostle, and sang, "Comet thinks they're funny. Comet thinks they're funny."

Comet rocked back on their heels, and when they looked back up at Fit they were smiling. "I'll leave the jokes to you." Fit had done it, she'd gotten through. She was triumphant.

Just then, Ty came out of the house in swim shorts and no

top, carrying a tray of shot glasses. "Get your shots here!" he yelled like he was selling peanuts at a baseball game. "Everyone grab one!" He walked around the backyard, making sure everyone got a shot. Fit grabbed two, handing one to Comet. Once Ty's tray was empty, he climbed on top of the table, the party quieting down. He held his shot glass up to the sky and said, "Thank you all for coming tonight. I couldn't be happier. This one," he said, pausing to reach his glass a tad higher, "is for the fuckers who made fun of us in high school."

Ty downed his shot with his guests following suit. To Fit, it didn't taste like much and she only felt the warmth when it hit the back of her throat. Ty then jumped off the table, ran to the pool, and cannonballed into the water. Everyone at the party burst into applause.

It was as if Ty's cannonball had cracked the party open, let something loose. The music got faster, the voices louder, and the games became more intense. Fit felt the electricity of the party. She could tell Comet felt it too, their voice growing animated, the movements of their body looking more natural and less practiced.

At one point, Phil, the gamer, ended up on the roof, poised to jump into the water.

"Do it! Do it!" Fit started chanting, then the whole party, even Comet, joined in. "Do it! Do it!"

Phil leapt off the roof, screaming on the way down, and hit the water with a great splash. Fit clapped, jumped up and down, and wrapped her arms around Comet's waist.

A song came on the speakers that made everyone go, "Ohhh!" and people started dancing. Fit joined in, grabbing Comet by the hands. She insisted they dance with her. Fit ignored the way her vision blurred around the edges or how she felt like she might lose her balance if she closed her eyes for too long. She embraced the feeling of the night, the party, the sweaty bodies moving around her, and one thing became clear to her: she was no longer an actor or director or writer. She was Fitted Sheet.

She and Comet danced for one song, then another, and possibly another. Fit lost track of time.

"Let's take a break," Comet said at one point, taking Fit's

hand and leading her to the side of the lawn. They sat down on the grass and Fit leaned her head on their shoulder. She hadn't realized how hot she was until then, the night air cool on her skin.

"How much is true?" she asked.

"What's that?"

"Your videos. The way you act."

"Wanna see something?"

Fit hummed, "Mhm."

Comet scrolled through their phone. "Here," they said, holding their phone out to Fit. "Look."

It took a second for Fit's eyes to focus on the screen, on the picture of three normal looking teenagers. They all wore the same school uniform: cable knit sweaters and blue trousers. They were sitting on what looked like gymnasium bleachers, smiling, their arms around one another.

"Guess which one is me," Comet said.

Fit was shocked. "No fucking way." She zoomed in, searching face to face, and there Comet was, sitting in the middle. Their hair was long and dark, and they looked so much younger, but it was undeniably them.

"Holy shit."

Comet nodded. "I know. Six years of Catholic school. A lot of good that did me."

"You look like a completely different person."

"I *am* a completely different person."

Fit, thinking of how quickly her freaks had found out about her mother, asked, "How have your fans never dug this shit up?"

"Two years ago I paid some hacker to scrub the existence of my former self from the internet."

"It worked?"

"The guy was a pro. There's no trace of who I used to be."

"Woah," Fit said. "What's it like?"

"Freeing, I guess. Like I'm in control."

Fit closed her eyes. She could hear the party, the music, and beyond all that a slight breeze rustled through the tops of the trees.

"To answer your question," Comet said. "No. It's not all fake. It's art. And isn't that the realest thing?"

Excited by Comet's story, emboldened by the booze, Fit lifted her head and kissed Comet. Her body buzzed. Comet ran their hands along Fit's back. Fit leaned in, wanting more, wanting everything.

"Ow, ow!" Fit heard Ty yell. She pulled away from Comet and looked over to the pool. Ty and few other people were in the water, looking over in the direction of Fit and Comet. "Get it!" Ty yelled.

She and Comet both started laughing. Fit flipped Ty off, then rested her head on Comet's shoulder. Her head felt heavy, and when she closed her eyes her mind began to spin. She snapped her eyes open and took a deep breath.

Comet asked, "You good?"

"Yeah," Fit said. "Let's go swimming."

Fit went in the pool in her bra and underwear. Comet wouldn't get in. "Wimp!" she taunted.

Then she was sitting on the side of the pool. Laughing. Shivering. Comet wrapped a towel around her. There was a fire pit. Graham crackers. Fit sat in the grass, saying she should get home. Her mom. She'd be in trouble. *Soooo* much trouble.

"Momma's girl," Comet teased. "Momma's girl," the rest joined in.

"Nonononono," Fit said.

"Momma's girl, momma's girl."

"Wanna hear the truth about a fucking momma's girl?"

River woke up on the couch. Outside, the sky was gray. She checked the time on her phone: 5:38.

"Shoot," she said aloud. She'd tried to stay up the night before, waiting for Fit, but she'd been so tired she must have fallen asleep and slept the whole night through. Then it dawned on her. She would have woken up if Fit had come back. She got up to check, hoping Fit had somehow snuck in so quietly that River didn't hear. But Fit's bed was empty, her suitcase flung open just as she had left it.

She called Fit. No answer. She texted Fit, R u ok?! River paced the living room, going from wall to wall and then back again. This was all her fault. She never should have let Fit go to that party. She didn't even have Ty's address or phone number. She imagined the disappointment on Dubs's face when he realized that she had somehow tricked him into believing that she was responsible enough to be trusted, when he saw the real her. She stopped in the middle of the living room, pressed the heel of her hand into the side of her head and could feel her heavy pulse mocking her. *And you really thought you could be a mother?*

It was almost 9:00 am in Connecticut. Dubs would already be home from work, asleep. She'd give it an hour. If she didn't hear from Fit by seven, then she'd wake Dubs, suffer the consequences of her irresponsibility.

She called Fit once more. And again, no answer.

Fit opened her eyes. She saw her own hair, a blue silk pillow, the back of someone's head. Comet's head.

She rolled on her back, her head still swimming from the night before. This was Ty's guest room, she knew that much, but how or when she got there, she had no idea. She looked around for her phone, found it on the floor next to the bed: 6:10. She had four missed calls and three text messages, all from River. Please call me when you get this please! the last message read.

I'm okay!!! Sorry!!! I fell asleep here!!!

GOOD, River texted back immediately. Come back now.

Heading out.

Fit closed her eyes. She had no intention of leaving right away. She wanted to lie next to Comet for a little longer, drift back to sleep.

She was listening to Comet's slow breath when her phone buzzed. It was a text from Frankie.

Ur such a fucking bitch, he said. How about you stay in la forever

Fit had no idea what he was talking about. What the???!?!?!

Frankie then sent her a link to a video. She clicked on it.

The video was seventeen seconds long. It was filmed on a phone, at night. Fit's wet hair hung over her shoulders in ringlets. She was wrapped in a towel, sitting cross-legged on grass. A firepit flickered in the corner of the frame.

For the first few seconds, Fit giggled. Then Comet's voice came from behind the camera, saying, "I don't believe you."

"You calling me a liar?" Fit responded, her words slow, like her tongue was coated in maple syrup.

"So, you're saying you're not a momma's girl? I saw y'all hug."

"Pshhh. Wanna hear a secret?" Fit smirked, lifted her eyebrows.

"Tell me."

"It's all for show. An act. And it was *easy* too. So, so easy to get everyone to believe me." Fit began to sway back and forth. "*Oh River. Be my best friend. I love you. Blah. Blah. Blah.* Gag me with a shoelace.*"

Comet asked, "Why not tell the truth? It's not like people could blame you."

"Because everyone loves a good reunion story, right?" Fit then pushed herself off the ground and stumbled toward the camera, getting so close that her nose and eyes took up the whole screen. "Because I'm Fitted Sheet. And nobody gets in my way."

Fit then took a few, clumsy steps backward, crumpled to the ground, and stretched her arms out in the grass. She laughed at the sky. The screen went black.

At first, Fit couldn't move. She was in shock, unsure how to process what she'd just seen. What she had done. She had the urge to turn off her phone, pretend she hadn't seen the video, sleep for the rest of the day. She and Comet could spend the afternoon by the pool, eating chips and salsa. Then she reasoned with herself, maybe it wouldn't be that bad. Maybe people would think it was a prank.

She checked her notifications and quickly realized that would never be the case. She was screwed. Her shock turned to anger. She shoved Comet awake.

"What were you thinking?" she said. Comet rolled over toward Fit, opened one eye and scrunched their brow.

"'Bout what?"

"Posting that video! Of me. Saying that stupid shit."

Comet laughed, then rolled on their back. "Don't blame me. You were the one who said I should get it on camera."

"I was drunk. People are tearing me apart out there!" Fit held up her phone for added effect. "I look like an asshole."

"I thought it was kinda cute." Fit's first reaction was to smile. But then she thought about Frankie's message. What if he showed it to Dubs? Oh god, what if River had already seen it? "You need to take it down."

"And what if I don't?"

"Comet, this could ruin me. You know that."

"You know, Fit," Comet said, putting an arm behind their head. "The truth tends to come out when you're drunk. This might be the first video of yours that's truly honest."

"What do you know about being honest?" Fit's voice was louder. She sat up. "You're the one pretending you're this mythical creature who, like, farts rainbows. And doesn't have a family or friends and is one with their *art.*"

"I'm not pretending. I'm free of everything that I used to be."

The even tone with which Comet spoke made Fit even angrier. "Bullshit. If you really were free, you would have deleted that picture on your phone. You wouldn't have shown it to me." Comet clenched their jaw. "Part of you misses that old life. Whatever it was. Part of you wants that person back."

They both were silent. Fit stared at the empty blue wall

across from the bed. Comet finally spoke. "At least I don't use people."

"Take it down."

"You know that won't do much. It's already out there." Fit knew that was true. Chances were someone already had the video saved, replicated. But she had to do something.

"I don't care. Delete it."

After Comet deleted the video, Fit ordered a Lyft, gathered her things, and left Ty's house with a pit in her stomach.

On the drive back to the Airbnb, Fit tried to recall what had happened the night before. After her jump into Ty's pool, her memories only came in fragments. She could feel the towel around her shoulders, the grass under her head, and the need to impress Comet. She vaguely remembered wanting to be tough, unaffected, cool.

Halfway through the drive back, the pit in her stomach went from nerves to nausea, and a throbbing pain appeared behind her eyes. Looking at her phone, scrolling through the words of the people telling her she was a monster or hilarious or both, made it worse. Fit closed her eyes, leaned her head back, and tried not to think of anything.

River answered the door of the Airbnb looking angry. Fit panicked, thinking Frankie had texted River a link to the video too. But then River let out a sharp breath and said, "Oh my goodness! You had me so worried." She pulled Fit in for a hug, an embrace Fit knew she didn't deserve.

"I'm going to puke," Fit said, pulling away from River and running to the bathroom. She made it to the toilet just in time. After Fit was done throwing up, she lay on the bathroom floor, resting her cheek on the cold tile. Her stomach felt a little better, but her head still throbbed and she didn't have the energy or the will to get up.

"Everything okay?" River called softly from the other side of the door.

Fit groaned.

"I'm coming in, okay?"

Fit watched the door open, first seeing River's bare feet appear. "Oh, Jess." River kneeled on the ground and pushed Fit's hair out of her face. "What happened?"

Fit didn't have it in her to lie. "I drank too much last night. They were handing out shots." Just thinking about alcohol made Fit's stomach turn.

"Oof, yeah. I think I can still smell them."

Fit then started to cry. "I messed up. I really fucked up."

"I don't know a single person who hasn't regretted a night of drinking," River said. "It happens."

Fit continued to cry, the tears sliding over her face and onto the tile.

"C'mon," River said. "Let's get you off the floor." River helped Fit up and led her to the bed. She pulled the covers down and Fit crawled in. River tucked Fit in and turned the lights off. "Go to sleep," River said, leaning forward and kissing Fit on the forehead. "You'll feel better when you wake up." Fit desperately wanted to believe that was true.

A few hours later, Fit woke up and had to puke again. After she was positive there was nothing left in her body to get rid of, she went back into the bedroom, ready to retreat under the covers. River was setting a small bottle of ginger ale and a box of crackers on the bedside table.

"I ran to the convenience store," she said, opening the soda and holding it out to Fit. "It's warm. Should be gentle enough for you to handle."

Fit took a small sip, the sweetness a welcome taste. "Why are you being so nice to me?"

"You're not feeling well."

"Yeah. But it's a hangover. Shouldn't I be in trouble?"

River smiled. "Come here. Sit down." They both took a seat on the edge of the bed. "I once stayed out all night in high school. Came back with the worst hangover of my life," River said. "Dubs didn't say anything, but somehow he knew. He didn't ground me or anything like that. But he made me help him clean out the garage. All day. It was horrible."

Fit mustered enough energy for a smile. She could imagine Dubs doing that. She thought about showing River the video, apologizing before things got worse, but she couldn't bring herself to do it. She screwed the cap back on the ginger ale and said, "Thanks for this."

River stood up. "What time do you have to be at the conference?"

*Never*, Fit wanted to say, dreading having to see Comet, her fans, or anyone, really. "I have a meet and greet at one."

"You can grab a few more hours of shut eye, then. I'll wake you."

Fit fell into a deep sleep, and when she woke up next, River gently jostling her awake, she felt like a new person. The headache and shakiness were gone, and she felt a tiny bit hungry.

"We should leave in half an hour," River said.

Fit's phone had died while she was sleeping. She plugged it into the charger, and as she got ready, she couldn't help imagining how her fans were reacting. She envisioned her phone was full of storm clouds, all waiting to break open and flood everything.

Fit came out of the bathroom, hair and makeup done, and River held up a brown paper bag. "Got us donuts."

They sat on the couch, eating. When Fit was halfway through her chocolate donut, she heard her phone chime multiple times.

"I think that was you," River said.

"It can wait."

Fit didn't check her phone as they left the Airbnb or in the cab that River had called. And before they entered the conference center, Fit reached in her pocket, found the power button, and pressed it down. The action made Fit feel powerful, rebellious even, but her heart still raced as they walked through the sliding glass doors and into the lobby.

"You feeling okay?" River asked.

"My stomach's a little off," Fit lied. "I hope I don't get recognized. I might barf."

"I'll lead," River said. Fit kept her head down, pushed her hair in front of her face, and fell in behind River. She was terrified a fan was going to stop her, make her answer for the video. But with River's help Fit was able to make it to the exhibit hall, where her meet and greet was, unnoticed.

They turned down the row the WeCord entertainment booth was in, and Fit saw a crowd of people, huddled in a mass exactly where she was headed. She stopped in her tracks.

"Wow," River said. "People are eager to meet you."

"I'm, um, going to make sure my hair look doesn't look like crap," Fit said, her voice wavering. "I'll be right back." Fit ran to the bathroom in the corner of the exhibit hall. She went into the stall on the far end and slammed the door shut. She couldn't breathe. There was no way she could do the meet and greet. Nope. No fucking way. She'd tell River she was sick. They'd leave the conference, spend the rest of the day in the Airbnb watching bad TV. And tomorrow they'd fly home, away from this place.

Fit turned her phone on. She needed to email Dillon and tell him she was canceling the event. She had twenty-five unread emails. The top one was from Adele at LiveWire.

Subject: **Drunk Video**

**Hey Fit. Saw your video. Care to make an official comment? Story will go live at 3pm CST. Let me know.**

Without thinking, Fit threw her phone in the toilet. As it splashed and sunk to the bottom, Fit felt both regret and relief. She needed to escape.

River noticed that Fit's face looked pale as she hightailed it off to the bathroom. River worried, but she wanted to give her daughter space. And judging by the previous day, if anyone could pull themselves together to impress a group of people, it was Fit.

A young woman, mid-twenties, walked up beside River and said, "Excuse me?"

"Yes?"

"I'm from *Fame! News*. You're Fitted Sheet's mother, right?"

"I am," River said. "Fit should be out in just a minute."

"Actually, I was hoping to ask *you* a few questions."

"Me?"

"I'd like to get a comment from you about Fit's most recent video." River assumed the woman was talking about the video where Fit lit the plastic kiddie pool on fire. One of the neighbors had complained, and the day before they left for California Dubs made Fit re-soil and seed the patch of charred grass.

"I thought the fire was good for theatrical effect," River said. "But I wish it had been done in a more controlled environment."

"Oh," the woman said. "I was talking about the video from last night."

"Last night?"

"You haven't seen it?"

River wondered when Fit had found the time to post a video the night before. "No. I haven't."

The woman pulled up a video on her iPad. "It's quick," the woman said. "Just press play."

From across the room, Fit saw River speaking to someone, a woman. Fit didn't think much of it until the woman began showing something to River on an iPad. Fit's heart skipped a beat. This couldn't be good.

"Hey!" Fit yelled out, her voice echoing against the high ceilings. She rushed over to River's side. "What are you showing her?" Fit demanded of the unfamiliar woman. "What the fuck are you showing her?"

River's eyes widened, her mouth fell open. "Jessica!" she gasped. "What has gotten into you?"

Fit ignored River and pestered the woman again. "Showing her a little video, are you?"

The woman flashed a newscaster smile, extending her hand to Fit for a shake. "Tish. *Fame! News.*"

"I don't give a fuck who you're with, lady."

Tish straightened up a little, her smile gone. Speaking directly to Fit, she said, "Yes, I was showing your mother the video. I would like a comment from her. One from you, as well."

"You can kiss my ass." Fit's voice was loud. She could see that people were starting to take notice, turning to watch, but she couldn't stop herself. "How's that for a fucking comment?"

River grabbed Fit's arm. "Enough!"

Everyone that had been waiting for the meet and greet now had their phones out, pointing them in Fit's direction.

"Come on. Let's leave," Fit said to River.

"Not until you tell me what's going on. What is this video?"

"I will," Fit said, "Later."

River didn't say anything, didn't move. At that moment, Fit realized there was no joke or swear or any amount of yelling that was going to get her out of this one.

Fit turned to Tish. "Show her."

"You sure?"

The fake concern enraged Fit. "You're getting what you want! Just do it!"

"I'm not the enemy here, Fit."

"Yeah, fucking right," Fit yelled at the top of her lungs. "You love it. I bet you got off this morning just thinking about how juicy this little piece of gossip was." It seemed like everyone in the whole hall had stopped to watch Fit. She felt trapped, like an animal in a cage. She held up her middle fingers to Tish, then spun around to the meet and greet crowd. "Is this what you want?!"

Fit took off running. Out of the exhibit hall, across the conference floor, zigzagging between groups of conference goers, and finally out through the sliding glass doors.

She slowed after rounding the corner of the building, her breath sharp and shallow. She leaned against the wall and slid down to the ground. River soon followed, also out of breath. "What the heck happened in there?"

Fit shook her head. River kneeled making eye contact with her daughter. "Please?"

"You're going to hate me," Fit said. "For real this time."

"Try me."

Fit looked at her mother, took in the gentle concern of River's face, and wondered if she'd ever see such compassion again. "Can I see your phone?"

Fit pulled up the video on River's phone, pressed play, and

handed the phone back. When Fit heard her own voice, slow and drunk, coming across the speakers, her skin crawled. She put her hands over her ears, bent her head down to her knees, and started counting. When she got to twenty, she lifted her head.

River asked, "Is it true? Have you been using me?"

"At first. Yeah."

River got up, her hands on her hips, and started pacing the sidewalk.

"I'm sorry," Fit said, her eyes hot. "Please don't hate me."

River pursed her lips and shook her head. "No. You know what? This is my fault. I never should have let Dubs talk me into moving in. I *told* him it was a bad idea." River looked off into the distance. "But he knew how to bait me. How if you forgave me, somehow, everything would be better." River turned to Fit, tears in her eyes, her nose bright red. "And you knew it too! What an idiot you must have thought I was! How could I not have realized what was going on?"

"It wasn't all lies," Fit said, crying now. "I'm happy. Happy that you moved in."

River chewed at her bottom lip. "Oh yeah? And how am I supposed to believe anything you say?"

Fit didn't have an answer.

River walked away, back toward the entrance Fit had just escaped through, and when River was out of sight, Fit kicked the ground. Kicked it again. Kept kicking until she was out of breath, her lungs begging her to stop.

Fit sat on a bench outside, by the entrance of the conference center. She wore her sunglasses, kept her head down, and only had to turn down one person's request for a picture.

River had disappeared into the building an hour before, and Fit was beginning to worry that River had snuck out some side door, leaving Fit with no phone and no way to get home. But soon the glass doors opened, and River exited the conference center. She walked over to Fit, her face expressionless, and said, "Cab should be here any minute." They didn't speak on the car ride back to the Airbnb. When they got back to the apartment, River walked into the bedroom and said, "I'm taking the bed tonight," before shutting the door, only coming out a few hours later to ask if Fit wanted to order pizza. They ate quietly in front of the TV.

After they'd cleaned up, River said, "We leave early tomorrow. Don't stay up too late," and went back into the bedroom.

Physically, Fit was exhausted, but her mind kept cycling through the events of the day. She wished she had her phone. She hadn't gone back to get it, even though it was most likely ruined, and she felt like she was missing a limb. At that very moment, someone was probably commenting on her drunken video, calling her a **drunk raging bitch**, but she'd rather be distracting herself with those comments than reliving the moment she tore out River's heart, in turn breaking her own.

Fit found a show on Animal Planet about pugs. She turned

the volume down so it wouldn't wake River. The warm glow of the screen calmed her, and soon she was asleep.

Dubs picked them up at the airport. Fit had been nervous that Frankie had told him about the video, but his wide smile and warm embrace proved otherwise. On the ride back to Meadow Lane, Dubs peppered them with questions about LA and the conference. Fit anxiously waited for River to tell Dubs about the scene at the exhibit hall, what Fit had said on the recording. But River remained quiet on the ride back, answering Dubs's questions with a word or two.

By the time they got back to the apartment, it was past 11:00 at night. "Frankie home?" Fit asked.

"He's with Pistols."

*Of course*, Fit thought. "Well, I'm pooped. See ya losers tomorrow." Before Fit headed off to her room, Dubs gave her another hug and said, "Good to have you back, kid."

*No it's not*, Fit wanted to say. *If you only knew. If you only knew who I really am.*

Fit dropped her bags on the floor of her room and flopped down on the bed, the covers feeling comfortable, familiar, safe. She hated to admit it, but she had missed Meadow Lane, the apartment, Dubs.

She looked at the fan drawings on the wall and wondered if she was going to receive art or presents or letters ever again. She wondered if the people who had taken the time to draw for her and send physical pieces of mail had seen her Momma's Girl video and regretted wasting their time. If that were the case, she couldn't blame them.

Fit's laptop sat on her desk. She hadn't been on the internet in over twenty-four hours. While her fingers itched for the scroll, the hiatus had also been kind of nice. On the plane, she watched an entire movie, read a magazine, and stared at the clouds. But the feeling that a part of her life was missing never fully went away. She turned on her computer. The purr of it coming to life filled her with both dread and comfort.

The first thing she did was check her email. She needed to explain herself to Dillon. There were pages of unread messages. From the subject lines she could tell they were a mix of hate mail and requests to speak with her. She didn't find it odd that so many people had unearthed her email address. Her fandom knew how to dig.

Mixed with all these messages was an email from Dillon, titled: **Congratulations.** At the top of the email was a picture: a screenshot of the main page of her YouTube channel. Fit was confused, thinking Dillon might have copy and pasted the picture on accident, but then she saw the subscriber count. Half a million. Under the image, Dillon wrote: **I see you made quite the splash at ClickCon. The contract will be drawn up this week. Welcome to the team.**

Fit didn't know whether to laugh or cry. Ever since meeting with Dillon in his swanky corner office, she'd wanted nothing more than to hit half a million subscribers, be signed on as a client. But sitting in her room, staring at the number she'd been dreaming of, there wasn't an ounce of celebration in her.

**53**

Once the video finished playing, Fit's drunken monologue coming to an end, River took a deep breath, inhaling the hot, grimy Los Angeles air, and all she could see was copper. *This,* she thought staring into the metallic shimmer, *this is what hope does to you.*

She ran back into the convention center, rode the escalator up to the top floor, and made angry loops through the hallways. How could she have been so foolish, she asked herself, to think that she'd paid her dues? What had she even expected out of this trip? For Fit to welcome her back with open arms?

At one point, she stopped in front of an empty conference room and remembered the cheers of the crowd when her daughter stepped out on stage. Fit didn't need her, River knew that now, and the words *I should move out* marched across her mind like ticker tape. Over the course of that night and the plane ride the next day—where she and Fit sat next to each other like strangers—River's anger waned, morphing into a prickly sadness, but the thought of moving out wouldn't budge. By the time the plane touched down in Connecticut, her mind was made up. She needed her own place.

River had to work the day after she and Fit got back. She was exhausted but welcomed the escape from the apartment, unable to take her father's hopeful gaze as he bugged her for details about her and Fit's "little vacation." At work, barely paying attention to the palatability of the chewy cherry flavored candy she was testing, she planned out how to best tell Dubs she was moving out. It needed to be quick, she decided, like snapping a wishbone, leaving her no time to wimp out.

When she returned to Meadow Lane that afternoon, her mouth still tasting like the pink candy, Dubs was on his hands and knees weeding by the front shrubs. He sported his summer vest and a bucket hat. She kneeled next to him, and asked, "Doesn't the apartment pay for people to do this?"

"Sure," Dubs said. "Doesn't mean I can't help."

River pulled a weed out of the ground and added it to the pile Dubs had started.

"Make sure you get them at the root," he said. "Or else they'll come right on back." River yanked out another weed, which brought with it a hunk of roots and clotted dirt the size of a strawberry.

"There we go," Dubs said.

River looked at the small divot in the ground where the weed used to be, took a deep breath, and said, "I'm going to get my own place."

Dubs sat back on his heels. "Huh."

"Your apartment is cramped enough without me. You can't keep sleeping on the couch."

He took off his hat, used it to wipe the sweat from above his lip. "Did something happen out there?"

River thought about the reporter, the video. "Can I tell you something and you won't freak out?" she asked.

"Depends on what you've got to say."

"I've been watching these dumb videos. About trying to recover repressed memories."

Dubs looked at her like she'd told him his favorite fishing spot had run dry. "And what drove this?" he asked.

River shrugged. "I don't know."

"That," Dubs said, "I find hard to believe."

River looked at the ground, ran her fingers through the dirt. For so long she'd convinced herself that she'd returned from the darkness a ruined woman, an evil stain beating in the back of her brain. And frankly, she was exhausted.

"I wanted to understand why," she said. "Understand what happened to me." Dubs shook his head. He looked like he was going to say something, but River spoke first. "And don't say it wasn't my fault, Dad. That's not enough anymore."

"And why's that? Why isn't it enough?"

River didn't have any answer beyond, "Because it isn't."

"Sometimes things just happen," he said. "And they're not going to add up all nicely for you." He put his hat back on, leaned forward, and yanked out a scraggly tuft of grass.

"If you insist on leaving, I respect that," he said, adding the weed to the pile by his feet. "But you're the one breaking it to the kids."

He pulled a few more weeds, and River ran over his words in her mind. Maybe he was right, she thought. Maybe she was looking for an answer that wasn't there.

Dubs asked, "You hear me?"

"Yeah, Dad," she said. "I'll tell them." River dug her hand into the wet earth, the ground smelling like the color of a ripe blueberry.

Dubs picked up grinders, intent upon having a family lunch. It had been two days since Fit had gotten back from LA, and she still hadn't spoken to Frankie. He'd either been at Pistols's or locked in his room, refusing to answer her when she knocked. And now that they sat across from each other at the kitchen table, he refused to even look at her, keeping his eyes down as he picked at his turkey sub.

He looked tired and Fit knew why. The night before, as Fit was reading a thread of comments on Comet's most recent video, she heard Pistols's car start in the parking lot. She'd looked out her window just in time to see Frankie get into the passenger side. Pistols pulled out of the parking lot in a hurry and headed down Route 12. Fit had tried to stay awake and was planning to ambush Frankie when they got back, but she couldn't keep her eyes open, falling asleep with her laptop on her stomach.

Dubs shifted in his chair, cleared his throat. "Your mother has something she wants to say."

Fit looked over at River, who was rolling a piece of lettuce in between her forefinger and thumb. They hadn't spoken since LA, either.

"It's been great living here," River said. "But I'm going to be moving out. Getting my own place in a few weeks."

Fit's stomach sank.

"I'm staying in the area. I'll still be close."

"Why?" Frankie demanded. That whole summer, Frankie had looked so much older, but as he stared at River, eyes wide and pleading, Fit could still see remnants of that young boy who used to crawl in bed with her when he couldn't sleep.

"Dubs can't stay on the couch forever," River answered.

Frankie pointed at Fit. "This is because of you!"

"No, no," River said. "This is *my* decision."

"Bullshit. This is because of what you said, Fit. In that fucking video."

Everyone at the table then started yelling at once: Dubs warned Frankie to watch his language, River kept insisting that moving out would be best for everyone, and Frankie continued to berate Fit. "You're selfish and stupid and I hate you!" he screamed.

Fit was the only one who remained quiet, and as she watched this maelstrom before her, a great weight of shame fell upon her for having caused such destruction.

Finally, Dubs slammed his hands on the table and yelled, "Enough!" Frankie shot up and stormed off to his room.

Dubs looked from Fit to River, bewildered. "One of you better tell me what the heck is going on."

"It's nothing, Dad. Really," River said.

Dubs turned to Fit, raised his eyebrows. She looked down at her hands. "Yeah. I don't know."

Frankie left again that night. Fit was watching an old movie about Paris with Dubs and River when Frankie came out of his room, his backpack slung over his shoulder. "I'm getting out of here," he said. "Spending the night at Pistols's."

"Be back tomorrow," Dubs said.

Fit looked over her shoulder at her brother. "What're you guys up to tonight, huh?"

Frankie's eyes narrowed. He turned around and left the apartment.

Fit was prepared that night. She remained dressed, had her shoes on, and sat at her window, waiting for Frankie and Pistols to appear. She had a perfect view of Pistols's car, which was parked against the fence. She waited for half an hour and was about to give up when she saw Pistols and Frankie sauntering across the parking lot.

Dubs was working that night, and River was already asleep, so getting out of the apartment was a breeze. She ran down the hallway, the front stairs, and banged on the passenger side window just as the engine roared to life. Frankie jumped. After seeing it was Fit he rolled his window down.

"Jesus," he said. "You want to break the glass?" His face was hidden in the shadows of the car.

"Hey, Fit," Pistols called from the driver side. Fit gave him a slight nod, then said to Frankie, "Where are you going?"

"Go away," Frankie said. "And mind your own business."

"You're sneaking off every night. Hiding money. I know you're up to something."

"Leave me alone," he said, his voice serious. "Don't you have anything better to do? More people to shit talk?" He rolled up the window. Fit smacked the glass again, hard, but Frankie ignored her. She ran and stood behind the back of the car. "I'm not moving until you tell me what you're up to," she yelled over the engine.

Frankie got out, looking pissed, and opened the door to the back seat. "Get in."

"Where are we going?"

"We don't have time for this, Fit! Get. In."

Fit slid into the back seat and buckled up.

"And no filming any of this, okay?" Frankie said.

"My phone's broken," she snarked. "And I don't have my camera on me, dipshit."

Pistols, putting his car in drive, added, "Even though I know I make good videos." Fit couldn't make out his expression in the dark, his face a silhouette against the streetlight, and his tone of voice didn't give away whether he was joking or angry. Had he jumped ship like everyone else? Had he figured out that she'd used him in hopes that her fans would ship them, give them some dumb name like #Fistols or #Pit.

She'd been telling herself that it was a game, but now, thanks to Comet, she knew what it felt like to be on the other side. And she wasn't sure she wanted to play anymore.

She figured out where they were going pretty quickly. It was a route she could travel in her sleep, and it only led to one place.

When they got to a stop light, the car quieting down enough for her voice to be heard, she said, unimpressed, "We're going to the casino?"

"Ding, ding, ding," Frankie said, sarcastically. "We have a winner."

They parked in the garage connected to the hotel, took the elevator up to the twenty-fourth floor, the second highest. She followed them to a room at the end of the hallway. Pistols knocked three times fast, two times slow, three fast again.

The door opened and Riley stood there, drink in hand, grinning like an idiot.

"Hello, hello, my wonderful people!" he said. His face was sweaty. Fit could tell he was drunk, or at least getting there.

"Are you serious?" Fit said to Frankie under her breath. He ignored her.

Frankie and Pistols shook Riley's hand as they walked in. Fit entered last, and Riley pulled her in for a hug. He smelled like alcohol and soap.

"I'm so glad you could finally make it," he said. "See your little bro in action."

The room was a fancy suite, with a bedroom, a living room, and small kitchenette. The couches and chairs in the seating area had been moved against the walls to make room for two long card tables and the five fold-out chairs positioned at each one. A few other people were there; some of them Fit recognized from Riley's parties, others she'd never seen before in her life.

Frankie set his backpack on one of the tables, unzipped it, and pulled out four decks of cards, all still in their plastic packaging. He handed two decks to Pistols. He then took out two rectangular wooden boxes and placed one on the table in front of him. Pistols grabbed the other one. When Frankie opened his box, Fit saw that it held three rows of chips, the kind she'd seen so many times on the gambling floor. Suddenly, everything made sense.

Riley asked Fit if she was going to play. "Fifty dollar minimum," he said.

"Even if I had the money, I wouldn't waste it on poker."

"Blackjack," Riley corrected her. "Poker can get a little bit, I don't know, long." With that, Riley went off and started talking to a couple of guys sitting on one of the couches.

Fit went up to Frankie. "Have you lost your mind?"

"What?" he said, stacking the chips in front of him, each pile a different color.

"You're fucking gambling. In a casino. This is wrong on so many levels."

"Riley knows what he's doing."

"You're putting your faith in Riley?" Fit said, her voice creeping louder. She didn't know what she was angrier about: the fact that Frankie was taking part in Riley's dumb idea, or that she'd been kept in the dark. "The guy who got high and painted his house with DayGlo?"

"Keep it down."

"Oh, you can't tell me what to do," Fit said. Before she could go on, Frankie grabbed her by the arm and pulled her toward the door. His strength surprised her. When they got into the small foyer, Fit pulled her arm free. "How long has this shit been going on?"

Frankie shrugged. "A month."

"A month?! And I'm just finding out now?"

"I knew you'd freak out."

"Of course I'm going to freak out. This is illegal shit. There's a casino *downstairs*."

"Yeah, but up here, Riley's the house. And the house always wins." Frankie spoke directly, sounding almost clinical. "He pays well."

Fit wanted to wring Riley's neck. First he'd taken Diamond from her, and now Frankie. "This is the last night you're doing this. Hear me?"

"Or what?"

"I'll tell Dubs."

"Then I'll show him the video of you drunk."

They stared at each other, both unflinching. There was a series of knocks on the door: three short, two long, three short. Frankie unlocked the door and swung it open. Diamond stood in the hallway.

"Shit," Fit said. "Am I the only one who didn't know about this?"

"Nice to see you too," Diamond said, pushing past the both of them.

Frankie locked the door. "I've got to get back to work." Fit took a seat in a leather chair in the corner of the room arms crossed. She was mad as hell.

Fit had no phone to distract her, and she certainly didn't feel like making small talk with anyone, so all she could do was watch. Riley continued to take his duties as drunk master of ceremonies seriously, greeting each new guest with enthusiasm. Frankie meticulously stacked the chips in front of him, then made sure the chairs at his table were evenly spaced. People occasionally walked up to him, clapping him on the shoulder or shaking his hand. "Send some luck my way, okay?" one guy said to him. Everyone seemed familiar with each other. It became clear Fit was an outsider, watching a well-versed routine she'd been purposefully left out of.

After twenty minutes or so, Riley got up and stood between the two tables.

"Thank you for joining me," he said, "At Riley's casino!" People began to clap. Riley let the applause go on for a few moments before quieting the group. "Dealers are the bank." He waved his hands toward Frankie and Pistols, who both stood at attention. "Now, let's play!"

The seats at the tables filled up. People threw their money down and chips were handed out. Frankie unwrapped a new deck of playing cards, crumpling up the plastic and putting it in his pocket. On the table in front of him, he fanned out the cards, face up, in the shape of an arch. He counted them, making sure the deck was complete. When he was done, he swept the cards back together, shuffled them three times, and then the game got underway.

Even though Fit was pissed at Frankie, and felt betrayed, she couldn't help but be impressed. The way he handled the cards, dealing them out smoothly to each player, he looked like a professional. Like he belonged on the casino floor, not up here in this stupid hotel room. Fit hated that that was the case.

People periodically rotated in and out of the games. Riley made the rounds between players, making sure everyone had a drink, offering to grab a refill even if the player's cup was only half empty. At one point, Diamond got up and joined Pistols's table. When she was done, having lost all her chips in fifteen minutes, she got up from her seat and walked across the room. Fit trailed her out of the corner of her eye, trying to be inconspicuous, and watched as Diamond went into the bedroom, which had remained dark up until then.

A loud groan came from one of the tables. Fit looked over and saw Frankie pulling in a large pile of chips. A guy sitting at the end of the table had his face in his hands. He moaned again and said, "Shit." He lifted his head, looked at his lost chips now collected in a messy pile in front of Frankie, and said, "That's all my fucking money." Fit could tell by his slurred words and the glossy hue in his eyes that he'd had one drink too many.

Frankie started to sort the pile of chips by color.

"You think that's funny?" the guy said to Frankie. "Me losing half my rent is some sort of joke to you?"

"No," Frankie said calmly, stacking the red chips into two small towers.

"Then why'd you smirk?"

Frankie kept his eyes on his hands and said, "I didn't."

Fit leaned forward a little in her seat. She could tell this guy was looking for a fight.

"Yeah, you did," the guy said, his voice louder. Some of the other guests had turned to look at him. Riley had taken notice, too, and was walking toward Frankie's game.

The guy, face flushed, slammed his hands on the table, making the chips jump. He shot to his feet and yelled, "You fucking did it again!"

Fit sprung up from her seat and started to lunge toward the guy, wanting to give him a piece of her mind, but Riley swept in before Fit even took her first step.

"My man, my man," Riley said casually, putting his arm around the guy's shoulder. "What seems to be the problem?"

"This punk was laughing at me," the guy said.

Riley chuckled. "Frankie? I doubt it. He's one of my best." Riley then looked at Frankie. "What do you say, little man? Did you laugh?"

"No," Frankie said, shaking his head.

"See? Must have been a harmless miscommunication." Riley gave the guy a little jostle and asked, "Right?"

The question seemed to snap the belligerent player out of his anger. His eyes darted around the room; everyone was still staring at him. "I guess you're right," he said, sounding embarrassed. "It's just that I don't get paid until Friday. That was all I had."

"That's a shame," Riley said sympathetically. "But come Friday, you'll be good as new. Ready to win it all back."

The guy looked sheepishly at the floor as Riley led him away from the tables and toward one of the couches. After the guy sat down, Riley reached into his pocket and pulled out a small bag filled with a couple joint's worth of weed. "Here you go. On the house. This should get you through the week."

The guy took Riley's gift, his eyes a little brighter, and said, "Thanks, man."

Fit looked back over at Frankie, who had finished stacking up the chips and was now shuffling the deck of cards. He'd looked relaxed while he was being falsely accused, didn't even flinch when the guy pounded his fists on the table. A bit of pride swelled in her chest.

Instead of sitting back down, she walked over to the doorway of the bedroom. Diamond was sitting on the king-sized bed, leaning against the headboard, her legs crossed. She was on her phone. Fit cleared her throat and Diamond looked up. She acknowledged Fit with a half nod, and then looked back down.

Fit asked, "Can I come in?"

Diamond didn't say anything. The silence was awkward, heavy. Fit wasn't sure what to say and took a gamble on humor.

"It's not like I'm going to try and kiss you again." Diamond smiled a little. A glimmer of hope. "Nope," Fit went on. "You missed your chance."

Diamond let out a small laugh. "Oh my god, you're so dumb."

Fit walked in and sat on the edge of the bed, her back facing Diamond. "Sorry for being a bitch earlier," she said. "This all kind of took me by surprise."

"You're good," Diamond said.

A cheer came from the living room. "Frankie's pretty good, huh?"

"Better than Pistols."

"Who would have thought dorky little Frankie could look so cool." Fit picked at the comforter. "Have you been coming the whole time?"

"Yeah."

"Why didn't you tell me? At least about Frankie?"

"He begged me not to. Said he was going to tell you himself."

"Well. He didn't."

Diamond looked at Fit, raised her eyebrows, a look Fit knew meant she was missing something obvious.

"What?" Fit said, defensively.

"Are you really that surprised he didn't tell you?"

Fit thought about how mad he'd looked after the LiveWire video. "I guess not."

They were quiet for a few beats, the sound of laughter coming from the other room. "Oh, come on. Don't look so sad. *Momma's girl*." Diamond had a sly look on her face, and Fit couldn't help but smirk a little. Fit groaned and fell back on the bed. "Christ, what a nightmare."

"It wasn't that bad," Diamond said. Fit gave Diamond a stop-bullshitting-me look and Diamond said, "Okay, okay. It was a little bad. But look on the bright side. You got a whole Snapchat story about you. **Has Fitted Sheet been stretched too far?**"

Diamond started laughing. Fit joined in and soon she was laughing so hard she started to cough, the horror of ClickCon loosening its grip on her ever so slightly. "Thank god I threw my phone in the toilet and didn't have to see any of that shit. I blame Comet."

Diamond asked, "What were you doing hanging out with them anyways?"

Fit told her about the insult, the party, the shots. She shook her head, embarrassed, and said, "I can't believe I made out with them."

"You did what?!" Diamond said. "Lemme guess. Their lips tasted like moon dust."

"They wish," Fit said. "We got in a huge fight the next morning. I wanted them to delete the video and they kept insisting that the truth comes out when you're drunk, or whatever."

A cry of triumph came from the living room, followed by the sound of chips being dragged to the end of the table. "And now Frankie and River hate me. Dubs would too if he knew how to get on the internet."

"Was Comet right?" Diamond asked. "Were you telling the truth in that video?"

Fit got up from the bed and walked to the window, which looked out at the Connecticut River. The lamps in the room were dim, making it so Fit could see outside—the bridge, the water, the lights along the bank—and her own reflection. The two images blended.

"I wish I could be like Frankie," Fit said. "It would make things a lot easier. You know how much I've always hated River. But now that she's here, now that I can reach out and touch her—" Fit paused. She'd begun to see how Frankie could accept River for who she was, not what she'd done. But Fit couldn't put her realization into words. "Every fight I've ever had with Dubs or Frankie, there was a part of me that knew they'd be back. I knew there was nothing I could do that would make them leave me forever. But seeing River watch that stupid fucking video of me—I knew there was no coming back from that."

"You never know," Diamond said.

"She's moving out," Fit said. "Because of me."

Fit watched a trail of lights snake its way down the water. She knew there was a boat under those orbs, it was just too dark to see. Frankie had every right to be mad at her. All he'd ever wanted was a family, a mom, and she'd made a mess of everything.

When Fit and Diamond returned to the main room where the card games were being played, something about the atmosphere had changed. There were more people, the music was a bit louder, and a group of guests by the windows were passing around the tail end of a joint. The room was nonsmoking and Fit took a little pleasure in thinking about how Riley was going to get smacked with a smoke-cleaning fee the next day. Watching him hold court playing a drinking game with a bunch of people, Fit doubted he cared.

"Does it normally get this crowded?" she asked Diamond.

"Usually, yeah," Diamond said.

"Why doesn't Riley have the games at his house?"

"That's what *I* keep saying," Diamond said, sounding thankful that someone had finally agreed with her. "But he says the suite gives it a professional feel or whatever."

Riley called over to the two of them, "Come play Aces!"

"We'll start next round," Diamond answered. She then said to Fit, "I'll grab us some drinks."

Fit went over and joined the game. Two couches had been pushed around a coffee table, on which sat a pile of cards and a couple of beers. The rules of Aces were simple: each card had an action, and the players took turns drawing from the deck. The last person to perform the correct action, or do the wrong one, had to drink. It was their go-to game at parties.

Diamond sat down next to Fit and handed her a red cup. Fit took a drink. The alcohol was harsh on the back of her throat, especially in comparison to the smooth cocktail that Ty had made her. But something about the sharp, stinging taste made her feel at ease.

Fit got tipsy as the game went on, as, it seemed, did everyone else. At one point, a guy sitting on the couch across from her leaned forward for a card and dropped his beer on the floor. He and another player scrambled to pick up the bottle as the drink glugged out onto the carpet, but it kept escaping their hands. The scene looked like a comedy routine, and the surrounding crowd erupted in laughter. Fit couldn't help but join in. As she slapped her leg and tried to catch her breath, the feeling of betrayal that had stung her at the beginning of the night felt far away.

Two smaller games of Aces broke out, as some of the people wanted to play Quarters instead. Fit stayed with the card game and was shouting "Drink!" at a girl sitting next to her when there was a knock on the door. It wasn't the secret knock that everyone else had been using to gain entry, but a loud pounding.

The room hushed. People looked worried. Some glanced toward the door, while others looked to Riley. Frankie and Pistols both stopped dealing.

The knock came again. Someone turned off the music and the room became eerily quiet. Riley, now serious, got up and made his way toward the door. Fit's heart fluttered in her throat. She looked around the room and taking in what the casino security would see: underage drinking, weed, gambling. And there was Frankie, smack-dab in the middle of it all.

Riley looked through the peephole and let out a little laugh. He opened the door and Fit instantly recognized the uniform of a security guard. Her stomach dropped. She thought of Dubs, how angry he'd be at getting called to the security office once again. But then Fit noticed the security guard didn't look angry. He was smiling. He and Riley shook hands and gave each other a half hug.

Riley invited the guy in and asked, "We in trouble?"

"One of your neighbors called in a noise complaint," the security guard said. "*Those damn teenagers and their loud music,*" he added in a whiny, high-pitched voice. Laughter rippled across the room. Fit looked around and everyone seemed to have relaxed. "Marcus was going to come up at first," the guard continued, "but I told him it was probably nothing. That I'd check it out."

The thought of Marcus standing in the middle of the room sent a shiver down Fit's back, but the news didn't seem to phase Riley.

The security guard then said, "I'll just tell him it was a couple watching porn real loud or something."

Riley grinned. "We're good then?"

The guard nodded his head. "Keep the music down a little and you're fine. I'll offer to patrol the hotel for a minute."

"Thanks," Riley said, reaching into his pocket, pulling out what looked like a hundred dollar bill. He handed it over as they shook hands. "Appreciate it."

Riley escorted the guy out, then walked back into the middle of the games, his confidence returned. He looked toward the wall to the right and shouted, "Sorry, neighbors! We'll keep it down!" Everyone found this funny except Fit.

"What are you all looking at me for?" Riley said. "Let's get back to business."

The music came back on, people returned to their conversations, and Frankie and Pistols resumed dealing.

Fit, still uneasy, asked Diamond, "Has that happened before?"

"Once or twice," Diamond said casually. "Riley only hosts games on days where he knows someone working security. But he knows pretty much everyone."

Fit looked around the party, a small pit still in her stomach. Diamond must have noticed the apprehension on her face because she shook Fit's knee and said, "Relax. Riley knows what he's doing."

"Yeah?" Fit said.

"Yep," Diamond said. She then picked up Fit's empty cup and said, "Time for a refill."

Fit tried her best to trust Diamond and believe that Riley's connections were enough to keep them out of trouble. She continued to play Aces, continued to drink, and maybe it was the warmth of her buzz or the fact that the whole room had the vibe of one of Riley's old parties, but her anxieties began to lift.

Eventually, one of the blackjack games ended, leaving only Frankie's table open. The music got louder, the lights got lower, and Fit was certain that neighbors on all sides could hear the party. But the thought of another noise complaint or security knocking on the door didn't worry her. For the first time since ClickCon, she was having fun.

The final game wrapped at about three in the morning, the casino crew and Riley the last ones in the room. Riley counted out Frankie's and Pistols's cut.

"You should play next time," Riley said to Fit, his voice a little calmer now that everyone had left.

"Sure. With all the money I have."

"I thought you were famous." That word, *famous*, it felt like an insult.

"Doesn't mean I have money."

"Maybe your brother can spot you."

Frankie folded up his small stack of bills, put them in the front pocket of his backpack. "Yeah, right. I earned this."

Those left helped Riley carry the tables and chairs to his car. "Last one to the elevator is a loser!" Pistols yelled, and the five of them took off running, the clanking of the furniture ringing loudly down the hall. They all screamed, not caring who they woke.

Diamond headed off with Riley, and Pistols drove Fit and Frankie home.

"Are you going to rat me out to Dubs?" Frankie asked her as they headed up the stairs to the apartment. She paused midway up the steps, looked at Frankie, and said, "You know you could get in some serious trouble. Riley's little scheme is messed up on so many levels. What if it had been Marcus at the door?"

"Riley always gets a room with a safe," Frankie said. "If he'd looked out the peephole and seen someone he didn't know, he would've flashed the middle finger behind his back. That's the signal. Pistols and I would've gotten everything into our backpacks and into the safe." Fit was shocked at how mature Frankie sounded.

"And you trust Riley?" she asked.

He nodded. Fit's stomach churned with anxiety, but as Frankie pushed his curly hair out of his face she thought about how much she'd missed him. He'd been giving her the silent treatment since she'd gotten home from LA. If she tattled on him to Dubs, he'd probably never speak to her again.

"You can't keep this up during the school year," she said.

"Told Riley I could only do it this summer."

Fit looked at the sky over Frankie's head. It was almost 5:00 and the light gray of morning was creeping in at the horizon.

"Fine," she said. "Give me your old phone and we have a deal."

"You know the screen's cracked to shit."

"It's better than no phone at all."

"What happened to yours?"

"Threw it in a toilet."

He smiled, his nose crinkling. Fit wanted to pause the moment, keep Frankie young and sweet forever.

"Deal," he said.

Dillon sent Fit an update. **Contract should be there soon. Needs to be cleared by one more person.** He went on to explain how Fit would need to fill out a few forms in order to get her signing bonus: $5,000.

Fit stared at the number for a while. That was more money than Fit had ever seen at one time in her life. And Dillon had mentioned it so casually, burying the detail in the middle of the email.

This was what Fit had been working toward, what she'd been dreaming of. Why wasn't she happier?

**PS**, Dillon added at the end of the email. **The silence is building your allure right now, but you'll have to post something soon. Or else people will start to forget about you.**

Fit hadn't posted anything since ClickCon. Not a tweet or an insta or a snap. Even the thought of it exhausted her. She still lurked on social, reading what people said about her. The fuss about Comet's video and her explosion before her meet and greet had died down. Now people were speculating where she'd gone. **I heard she was in rehab**, one person wrote. Another comment read, **What if she never comes back?** If Fit were being honest, the thought of never returning to YouTube, of people forgetting about her, sounded kind of nice.

She opened the note on her computer where she kept a running list of video ideas. **Tinfoil umbrella; 7th heaven; Chapstick challenge but with ketchup?!?:** none of them excited her.

She closed her computer and went out into the living room. Dubs was sitting on the couch, putting his shoes on.

"You're up early," Fit said. He was working the graveyard shift that night.

"Couldn't sleep. I've got some work to do on the truck. No use in wasting precious time lying in bed." He pushed himself up from the couch, went in the kitchen, and got his toolbox from under the sink.

She asked, "Need some help?" He looked at her questioningly, then shrugged his shoulders. "Why not?"

The summer sun bared down on Fit's shoulders, and the parking lot reflected the heat. She and Dubs didn't speak much. Every few minutes he asked her to hold something or hand him a tool. She enjoyed it: the quiet concentration, the precision with which Dubs worked, even the rusty, sour smell of the truck's old engine. She was holding a plastic cap in one hand, shining a flashlight with the other, when the thought of the contract crept into her mind. "Dubs, I don't know what to do."

"Keep the light steady. I'm almost through."

"No. Dillon wants to represent me. I'm getting a contract."

Dubs turned the wrench a few times. "What's got you stumped?"

"I don't know."

Dubs took the plastic cap from Fit, popped it back where it belonged. He turned around, leaned on the front of the truck, and took a rag out of his front pocket. He began to wipe his hands methodically. "This have something to do with what happened in California?"

"River tell you?"

"No. I tried, believe me. But she's steadfast, I'll give her that. Kept insisting nothing happened."

Fit turned the flashlight over in her hands. "I screwed up."

"I deduced that much."

"Like. Beyond repair."

Dubs finished wiping his hands and shoved the rag back in his pocket. "No such thing." He turned toward Fit. "You just have to try a bit harder." He leaned forward. "And whatever the answer is, it probably won't be that fun."

Fit leaned her head on the side of the truck. "Dammit."

"Language," Dubs said. "Now. I need a light here."

True to his word, Dillon sent the contract two days later. **Take a look**, he wrote in the email. **Let me know if you have any questions.**

Fit scrolled to the bottom of the message, hovered her cursor over the icon of the attached contract, but couldn't bring herself to open it. Instead, she responded to Dillon and told him she'd look at it right away, adding a string of exclamation marks to overcompensate for her unease.

**Great**, he wrote back. **Got your next video scheduled?**

**yeah got something big planned**, she said, even though she had no desire to film, and immediately logged out of her email.

Over the next few days, she didn't tell anyone about the contract, but it was never far from her mind. She gave herself pep talks—telling herself that this was the freaking opportunity she'd been dreaming of—but every time she opened Dillon's email she thought of LA, of sitting outside the convention center, the sidewalk hot on her legs, watching as River's mouth fell open in disgust.

Fit had nothing. She'd been staring at the same empty Word doc for hours, trying to write, but every lyric she hummed, every joke that ran through her mind sounded stupid, childish, making her want to throw her computer across the room. Someone knocked on her door.

"Yeah?" she yelled, thankful for the distraction.

To her surprise, it was Frankie. He was holding a can of store brand soda, his backpack over one shoulder. Almost a week had passed since she'd found out where he'd been sneaking off to in the middle of the night, and although the air between them had grown softer, his one-word answers and hours spent alone in his room made it clear he hadn't fully forgiven her yet.

"I thought you were Dubs," she said. "He's been on me to do laundry all day."

"Same," he said, flicking the tab of the can, the sound tinny and flat. "I'm going to the casino." He looked over his shoulder before adding, "To shuffle."

She'd heard him sneak out a few times over the past week, always assuming he was heading out to deal, but this was the first time he'd let her know where he was going. He took a sip of soda and asked, "Got anything going on tonight?"

"Filming," she said.

He looked at her incredulously. "Finally posting something?"

She glanced down at the blank screen in front of her and said, "Trying to."

He nodded. "All right." And although Fit still believed Riley's private casino was his most idiotic idea to date, she couldn't help but crave an invite, hoping that's why Frankie had knocked on her door.

"Well," he said unceremoniously, "see ya."

Her cheeks burned. She began to type gibberish on the keyboard, trying to look busy, and mumbled, "'Kay, bye."

Frankie disappeared from her doorway; five minutes later Pistols's car revved to life out in the parking lot, setting off a small twinge of envy at the base of her skull. She looked at the Word document, the flashing cursor practically taunting her, and gave up. **Do you want to save?** a pop-up asked when she tried to close the file. She almost laughed. There was *nothing* to save.

For the next few hours, she zoned out on Netflix and YouTube, thoughts of her jealousy and writer's block slipping from her mind. She was reading a comment thread under Ty's latest video, absorbed in fan theories on what his new shoulder tattoo meant, when her phone buzzed. It was a text from Diamond: game got busted

Fit barely had time to panic before Diamond followed up with a flurry of messages, the words arriving in rapid fire.

security

F got away

i think

Fit read over the words twice, before responding, WHAT?!? is he okay? are you okay?!?!

Ya. Waiting for lyft

wheres frankie?!

Fit stared at the cracked screen. Three little dots appeared below her last message. Those three small circles, Diamond's answer, was all Fit cared about.

Took off running idk where

Fit got up and slipped on her sandals. From the living room she could see Dubs standing at the sink, his back facing her, washing a dish. He'd changed into his uniform. It was 11:36, and he'd be leaving for the casino any minute. Fit held her breath as she walked quietly to the door. She gingerly scooped the truck keys from their hook and left the apartment. She ran down the hallway, not worrying if Dubs heard the door shut behind her. There was no way he could catch up.

There were two ways to the get to the casino from Meadow Lane. The route the casino crew and Dubs always took was lined with gas stations and fast food chains. There were sidewalks and street lamps, and it was the way she figured Frankie would take if he were to walk home. She called him, but there was no answer. She propped up her phone in the cup holder, waiting for a message from Frankie, Diamond, even Riley.

She wanted to speed, find Frankie as fast as possible, but she forced herself to go slow, scanning the side of the road for any signs of her brother.

Her phone buzzed, jingling against a couple of spare coins. Her heart sprang, praying it was Frankie. "DUBS" popped up on the screen. She sent the call to voicemail. Not even a minute later, he texted her.

WHERE DID YOU GO JESSICA I HAVE TO WORK

Even though he always wrote in all caps, she suspected this time he was actually yelling. But she could deal with Dubs later. Her sole focus now was Frankie.

As she crept along at what felt like a snail's pace, she thought every tree, shadow, person on the sidewalk was her little brother. But they never were. Diamond texted Fit a few more times, wanting updates, but Fit couldn't take the time to answer and risk missing him. When she got to the casino, she drove around the parking garage, checked the entrances, and then parked in the bus drop-off area. Only one bus sat in the lot; the driver stood in front of his vehicle, smoking a cigarette.

The parking lot was down a small hill from the casino and adjacent hotel. Fit looked up at the looming buildings, their bright lights tearing apart the heavy night, and she had a sinking feeling that Frankie had been caught. Security could have nabbed him after he and Diamond parted ways. She pictured her brother sitting against the stark white walls of the security office, Marcus pacing in an angry circle behind his desk. If only Fit had told Dubs about the game, had done the right thing instead of being selfish, Frankie wouldn't be in this mess.

The bus driver dropped his cigarette on the ground, stamped it out with the heel of his boot, and Fit remembered what Riley had said, that the casino was trying to clean up its image. What if Marcus wanted to set an example with Riley's stupid game? What if the cops had gotten involved? She shook her head, trying to banish the thought from her mind. If Frankie had a record, he could kiss his fancy college goodbye. He'd never get to sit on the steps of the library, next to the kids who wore ripped jeans and tattered shirts that probably cost more than Dubs's truck. If any of those kids got arrested, their parents could bail them out, hire a good lawyer to make the charges go away. But for Fit and Frankie, that wasn't an option. The odds of having a normal life had been stacked against them ever since River walked into that garage fourteen years ago. College was going to be Frankie's way out, his winning hand, but that could all be ruined now. Fit wanted to run at the casino, rip it down piece by piece until it gave her Frankie back. She would sacrifice herself to the Twin Suns if that's what it took, give herself over to a lifetime of cleaning hotel rooms if the tradeoff was her little brother's safe return.

Another bus pulled into the lot and honked at Fit to get out of the way. She left the casino and headed back to the apartment, taking the other, less populated route.

Fit was about halfway home, gripping the steering wheel in worry, when she saw Frankie. He was walking in the grass on the right side of the road, backpack on, shoulders hunched forward. His curly hair caught the beams of the headlights, making it look like he was wearing a glow-in-the-dark helmet. Relief flooded Fit's body. She pulled the truck up beside Frankie, rolling down the passenger side window.

"Hey, there," she called. "Where ya headed?"

"Leave me alone," he said, keeping his gaze on the ground in front of him. The truck rolled along slowly.

"Come on, Frankie. Get in."

"I want to walk."

"You think I'm going to leave you out here to get snatched up by a coyote?"

He turned to her and shouted, "Just go away!" There was a cut underneath his right eye, blood dripping down his cheek. At the sight of the wound, Fit slammed her foot on the break, put the car in park, and ran out to him.

"Jesus, Frankie." She put her hands on his shoulders to keep him from walking any farther. "What the hell happened?"

"Nothing."

"You're walking on the side of the road with a gash on your face. That's not nothing. Who did this?"

"Security guard," he said, still not meeting Fit's gaze. "A couple of them broke up the game. I don't know how they found out. One took a swing at me, got me by the shirt." Fit looked down and noticed that the top of Frankie's collar was ripped.

"Was it Marcus?" Fit asked.

"No," he said. "It was two guys I've never seen before."

"Good," Fit said. "What about Riley's plan? With the safe?"

"One of the guys pushed his way in before we could hide everything." He shrugged his backpack off, unzipped it halfway to show Fit the contents: a mess of cards, money, and chips.

"What happened to everyone else?" Fit asked.

Frankie kicked at the ground. "Pistols and I ran in opposite directions. I don't know if he made it out. No freaking clue about the rest of them."

"I'm going to kill Riley," Fit said. And she meant it, her anger as hot as lava. It was okay for the rest of them to be fuck-ups, to run from security guards, but not Frankie. "And Pistols," she added. "*And* Diamond for not telling me earlier." She squeezed his shoulders. "I'm going to kill them for corrupting you."

"No one made me do this. I wanted to."

"I thought you were smarter than this," Fit said. "How could you let yourself get sucked into something so stupid?"

"Like you care."

Frankie tried to push past Fit, but she stopped him. "Of course I fucking care."

"All you've talked about since Dillon emailed you was how you can't wait to ditch this place. Leave everyone behind. Some of us will be stuck here, Fit. We can't all be YouTube stars." Frankie was yelling now. "I saw an opportunity, and I took it. I'm not your fucking sidekick anymore."

The cut on Frankie's cheek had opened up again, releasing fresh blood. And Fit wished it were her standing on the side of the road, bleeding. It *should* have been her. She was the bad kid. The one who was grounded half her life, got detention at least once a week, gave a rat's ass about consequences. If anyone had corrupted Frankie, it was her.

"That's not how it is," Fit said, taking his hands. "Frank, you've got to believe me."

He ripped away from her grip, tears in his eyes. "I knew from the beginning that all that shit with mom was fake. Thanks to Comet, now everyone knows you're a fucking liar."

Frankie was crying, his tears and blood mixing. He sat down on the curb, put his face in his hands. He released heavy sobs that jerked his shoulders up and down. Fit listened to his ragged breaths. She could tell he was on the verge of hyperventilating. Her phone went off again.

She sat down next to Frankie and began to rub his back. After a few minutes his breathing calmed, and his sobs grew softer, less violent.

"You know, I got a contract this week," Fit said, still rubbing his back. "To officially become a part of WeCord Entertainment."

Frankie lifted his head.

"But I don't think I'm going to sign it."

"Why not?"

"I'm not sure it's what I want." For so long, Fit was positive she wanted to be famous. She wanted the millions of fans screaming her name. But the internet had changed her, betrayed her. "That person in Comet's video, it's not who I want to be."

The crickets chirped in the woods, the sound carrying high into the vast velvet sky above. Fit's phone buzzed again.

"I took the truck without telling Dubs. He was supposed to be at work at midnight. He's probably had at least four heart attacks by now."

Frankie laughed meekly, wiped his nose on his sleeve, and

got up from the curb, and made his way toward the passenger side of the truck.

Dubs's yelling woke River up. She went out into the living room and saw her father pacing back and forth, his face bright red.

"What's going on?"

Dubs stopped and looked at her. "Your daughter just up and took my truck! Without asking. Knowing full well I'm supposed to work tonight."

"Where did she go?"

"Beats me. She's not picking up her phone." Dubs ran his hand over his forehead. "Maybe if you call her she'll answer."

River doubted it, but she tried anyway. The line rang five times before going to voicemail. Dubs called his work, told them he was having car troubles. "If she's not back in ten minutes," he said, after hanging up, "I'm going to have to take a taxi."

River felt sick to her stomach, wondering if this was all her fault, if she should have told Dubs about what happened at ClickCon. Dubs's pacing made her feel worse.

"I'll go see if Diamond is around. Or Pistols. They might know where she is."

She didn't wait for Dubs to respond and headed out the door. It had been hot that day and as she walked across the parking lot the air smelled like tar. Small dots that looked like rain sitting on asphalt popped into her mind. The light was on in Deb's apartment. She knocked softly, not wanting to wake anyone if they were sleeping. Deb answered the door in a robe and slippers.

"I'm sorry to get you out of bed," River said.

"Just watching some infomercials."

"I was wondering: Is Diamond here?"

Deb looked concerned. "She's with her boyfriend. Is everything okay?"

"Yes, yes," River said, feeling bad for alarming Deb. "Fit took my dad's truck. And she's not answering our calls."

Deb's face relaxed a bit. "I'll call Diamond. See what she knows."

"No need. I'm sure Fit will be back soon."

As River was making her way slowly up the stairs to their side of the apartment complex, she heard a car pull into the parking lot. It was Dubs's truck. River walked quickly over to the truck as Fit climbed out of the cab. "You had us scared half to death!" River yelled. Fit turned around. "Where were you?"

Before Fit could answer, Frankie came around the side of the truck. River was shocked by the sight of him. There was blood all over his cheek, dripping down to his chin. She ran up to him. One eye was puffy and swollen shut.

"My god," she whispered.

"I'm fine," he said.

"You are not fine." River turned to Fit and asked, "Is this why you left?"

Fit didn't answer. Instead, she took Frankie's arm and started walking him toward the apartment building. "Go wait by the trash cans," Fit said. "I'll come get you when Dubs is gone." Fit then shoved Frankie off in the direction of the grass.

"And you," Fit said to River. "Don't say anything to Dubs about Frankie. I've got this."

River followed Fit up the stairs. "You're going to pretend your brother isn't out there in the backyard, wounded?"

"It's just a cut."

"Fit. I'm serious. You need to tell Dubs what's going on." A few doors down from the apartment Fit stopped in her tracks. River followed suit.

"So am I," Fit said. "Now let me handle this." River was taken aback by how stern and authoritative Fit was. But the second Fit opened the door, it was like a switch had been flipped and all that seriousness flooded away.

"Yo! Dubs!" Fit yelled nonchalantly. "I'm home."

Dubs came out of the kitchen, his face so red it looked like he'd been out in the sun all day.

"You're home?" he said, angry, astonished.

"Yep. Catch." Fit tossed the keys to Dubs, who caught them in front of his chest.

"You're home?!" Dubs repeated, yelling this time, his voice unsteady. But Fit didn't seem to notice. "Where the heck were you?!"

"Diamond had a hankering for ice cream. I drove us to DQ." Fit walked over to the couch, bouncing with each step. She sat down, kicked her legs up, and pulled out her phone. "I would have called, but it's illegal to talk on the phone and drive. Safety first, right?"

Dubs looked at Fit. He opened his mouth to say something, but nothing came out. Fit could have easily told the truth, that something had happened to Frankie, but River could tell that no amount of yelling was going to crack her daughter. Even though River was mad at Fit for lying, perplexed even, a bit of pride swelled in her chest.

"You've really done it this time, Jess," Dubs said. "I'm late for work, but you can be rest assured you're not going to get away with this."

"'Kay," Fit said, not looking up from her phone.

After Dubs left for work River sat down in the reclining chair and stared at her daughter. Fit finally looked up. "What?"

"Why'd you do that?"

"Do what?"

"Cover for Frankie."

Fit shrugged her shoulders. "I owed him."

River scratched her head. "And I suppose you're not going to tell me what really happened?"

"Nope."

The living room window was open, and River could hear a car door slam. "You must've owed him big. That was quite the show." Fit continued to look at her phone, bouncing her foot up and down. River heard a car pull out of the parking lot.

"I think he's gone," River said. "If you want to go get Frankie."

Fit stood and started to walk toward the door. She stopped halfway and turned around.

"You don't have to move out," Fit said. "If you don't want to. I should be gone in a year."

River had looked at an apartment that morning. It was a studio, only one stop away on the bus. The kitchenette had a sink, a two-burner stove, and a mini-fridge. "No oven," the woman showing her the apartment had said, "but plenty of counter space for a toaster oven." Standing in the middle of the bedroom/living room, looking out the windows at a grocery store parking lot, River realized that it wasn't the video that had made her want to move out. The thought had been inside her well before Los Angeles. The video had just given her that extra push.

River studied her daughter. Fit was explosive and hard to handle, but she was herself. Ever since River had started apartment hunting, something had changed inside her. She'd been excited at the thought of figuring out who she really was underneath the layers of regret and shame.

"Yeah," River told Fit. "I do."

Frankie remained quiet when Fit went and told him the coast was clear. When they got back inside the apartment, River stood up, like she wanted to comfort him, but Frankie bolted for his room, his head down.

Fit grabbed the first aid kit from the bathroom and went into Frankie's room. He was lying on his bed, staring at the ceiling.

"You're going to ruin your pillowcase," she said.

"Good."

"C'mon. Let me clean you up."

Frankie sat up and swung his legs over the side of the bed. He kept his head down, hunched over like a wounded animal. Fit sat next to him and gently dabbed the cuts with a hydrogen peroxide-soaked cotton ball. He winced as the liquid touched his open skin.

"Baby," she teased him. "Now hold still." She slathered the cut in antibacterial cream, then covered it with a large square bandage. Once she was done, she looked down at his ripped shirt. There were scratch marks on his neck.

"Damn. It's like you got attacked by a werewolf."

"Don't miss anything," Frankie said. "I have no idea where that guy's hands have been."

As Fit soaked another cotton ball with hydrogen peroxide, she thought about what Frankie had said to her on the side of the road, how he thought she would abandon him one day.

"I never told you this," she said, dabbing at the angry and red wounds, "but when I picked up that T-shirt from your dream school, I walked around the campus a bit. I could *so* see you there."

Frankie rolled his eyes.

"I'm serious," she said. "I know it's expensive. But part of the reason I wanted Dillon to sign me so bad was so Dubs would get off my case about college. Then he could just put all his money toward your education. And, I don't know, if I got really big—like *Ty* big—I could just pay for it all."

"Yeah?" Frankie said.

"At least part of it."

Frankie inhaled deeply, and Fit could feel herself getting choked up. They remained silent as she continued to clean the gashes. When she finished applying the ointment she said, "There. No turning into a werewolf tonight."

"Thanks," Frankie said weakly. "So how mad was Dubs when you got back?"

"Thought the vein in his forehead was going to burst right open."

"Am I in big trouble?"

Fit shook her head. "Nope. Dubs still thinks you're at Pistols's." She sat next to him on the bed. "I, on the other hand, am grounded until I'm thirty."

"You didn't have to do that," Frankie said.

"Consider us even." Fit looked at the piece of art that hung on the wall over the foot of his bed. It was new, one she'd never seen before: he'd glued toothpicks in the shape of deer antlers to a piece of black cardboard.

Frankie asked, "Dillon really wants to sign you?"

"Yep," Fit said.

"And you're not sure you're going to accept?"

"I don't know."

Frankie looked at her skeptically.

"Don't look at me like that," she said. "This past week has been brutal."

"Why? Because people were mean to you on the internet?"

"No, Frankie. Because I was a fucking monster. That's who I am now. You said it yourself."

Frankie got up from his bed and opened his craft box. He pulled out a few rolls of tinfoil, tape, and a pair of scissors.

"Get up," he said.

"What are you doing?"

"Just do it. I've had this idea for a while."

Fit stood.

"Put your hands on your hips," he said. Fit followed his directions and he began to drape tinfoil over her shoulders. Frankie worked diligently and quickly. "What are you making?" she pestered.

"You'll see," he said.

It took Frankie half an hour to finish his creation, not allowing Fit to look in the mirror until he was done.

"Ready?" he said, after he'd added the final piece of tinfoil.

"Ready," she said.

The person in the mirror looked like Fit, moved like Fit, but she couldn't quite believe it was her. "Holy shit," she said. "Frankie, it's brilliant."

"Now," he said. "Tell me this isn't you."

Fitted Sheet broke her post-ClickCon internet silence with an Instagram picture.

In the post, she's standing in the middle of a parking lot, a tan building barely visible in the darkness behind her. She's wearing a full-length royal robe and a crown, both made of tinfoil, crafted so well they look real. In her right hand, she's holding a foil staff. The streetlight overhead illuminates her outfit, making her glow.

Her face is serious and her eyes bore straight into the camera. The caption is only two words: **miss me?**

# ACKNOWLEDGMENTS

Without the support of my family, friends, and teachers this book would not have been possible.

I must first thank my dear Pug Squad for their encouragement and thoughtful readings of this story in all its stages—I feel lucky to have found you all. Thank you to Simon for your critiques, keeping me accountable, and putting up with my deadlines.

Thank you to Jabari Asim for your guidance as I made the scary plunge into novel writing and attempted to turn a seed of an idea into a book. Thank you to Pablo Medina, Tim Parrish, Jerry Dunklee, Linda Simone, Mr. Zotos, and Mrs. Malavazos, who have all made an impact on my writing at some point in my life. And a special thank you to Robin Troy, who was the first teacher who made me believe I could be a fiction writer. Thank you to Ellen Duffer, Ladette Randolph, and everyone at *Ploughshares*.

I must also thank my friends who have stuck with me throughout the novel writing process, even when I sequestered myself to my apartment for weeks on end: Michelle, Kit, John, Kellee, Tori, Sarah, Sean, Maren, Jamie, Adam, and India. And thank you to Shannon—your excitement about my writing has meant more to me than you know.

Thank you to Kim Kohrs for taking the time to help me with fact-checking.

Huge thanks to my editor, Mari Kesselring, for believing in these characters and this story as much as I do. Your thoughtful and spot-on edits helped this book reach its full potential. And thank you to Caroline Larson for liking my #PitMad tweet and introducing me to the wonderful team at Flux Books.

Lastly, I must thank my family, who have always shown me nothing but love and support. To my sister, Abbey, for being a smart and ambitious role model, and my dad, Oliver, for setting me up on a typewriter when I was in elementary school and encouraging me to write. And thank you to my mom, Elaine, for being the best storyteller I know; this book is as much yours as it is mine.

# ABOUT THE AUTHOR

Erin Jones received her MFA in Creative Writing from Emerson College, where she is now affiliated faculty. She is the former head of marketing at *Ploughshares,* and her work has been published in *The James Franco Review*, *The Ploughshares Blog*, *Rock & Sling*, and other publications. She was a 2017 finalist for the Boston Public Library Writer-in-Residence fellowship and calls Boston home. *Tinfoil Crowns* is her first novel.